D1004089

STRAW BOSS

By the Author

FICTION
Strike the Bell Boldly
The General
The Bank
The Pedlocks
Man of Montmartre
Geisha
Lion at Morning
Beach House

NONFICTION
WAR CRIES ON HORSEBACK
TREASURY OF THE WORLD'S GREATEST PRINTS
SALUTE TO AMERICAN COOKING
THE REAL JAZZ, OLD AND NEW

PLAYS
HIGH BUTTON SHOES

STRAW BOSS

a novel

—— by ——

Stephen Longstreet

G. P. Putnam's Sons
New York

SBN: 399-12196-X

Library of Congress Cataloging in Publication Data

Longstreet, Stephen, 1907-
  Straw boss.

  I. Title.
PZ3.L8662Sv [PS3523.0486] 813'.5'4 78-5258

PRINTED IN THE UNITED SATES OF AMERICA

TO HARRY AND RENEE LONGSTREET

From a lifelong facination with the American labor scene I have drawn only the mood of the invented action of this novel. The people come from my imagination and do not attempt to picture any person living or dead. Nor have I used any actual union organizations; the DWU, the LBO, and the WNUSA exist only (on ink and paper) in these pages.

In the old days when the country was younger and a very rich man could say: "God gave me my money," when the workers had a grievance they would pick someone by chance, and the man with the shortest straw would be the appointed one to talk to those in charge of management. In time he could become the spokesman for the group, and was called "the straw boss." When the organizations of workers began to rise in power, he would often become a true boss with great powers for good or evil to the rank and file.

—LOUIS ADAMIC
(1899–1951)

A man's reach should exceed his grasp, or what's a heaven for?

—ROBERT BROWNING

BOOK ONE
MIKE'S WORLD

CHAPTER 1

The two railroad dicks at the Oakland freight yard dragged him out of the Sunshine Route box car No. 283B, at 6:10 in the morning, and into a dismal, drizzly, cold morning. He had been sleeping, curled up around his twine-tied bindle (what others called a bundle), really half asleep, half awake, as he had done all night, waking at intervals because of the cold. Hearing the *click click* of the wheels of the mile-long freight. It had been coming down the piny high places past Red Bluff to Yuba City, and there had been snow shifting in through the loose joints of the car.

He had shivered and slept, dreaming of the smell of the strong coffee with chicory his mother brewed and hearing the wail of the dawn whistles that called the workers to the tire plant, the truck foundry, the girls to the cigar factory, men to the canal scows and barges waiting to be unloaded. If his brother Moz (nobody at home called him Martin) hadn't wet the bed . . . it was creepy to lie and think, as a twelve year old, that the whistles announced the end of the world—the wild, stern, angry sound of the whistles proclaiming Doomsday . . . their *hoot hoot* also bringing up another day for his old man to go wrestling the carcasses of black tires into a final shape, building them up layer by layer in the chemical reek, working with the skin-destroying bonding goop merging with hot rubber.

If there was a pernickety and perverse winter, so cold the chickens' feet froze to their perches, there was usually a scarcity of coal, and he and Moz would go steal coke from the truck factory piles—also seek out crates and boxes for fire wood to wheel home on the remains of a baby carriage. If Moz hadn't wet the bed and the whistles were thinning out their calls, he could curl up for half an hour of funky sleep, then rising on Ma's continual calls, crawl into the garments he wore all winter, garments left on the floor, now lifted to dress for school, his homework undone. In that extra sleep he was smiling, feeling Miss Lambkins' high school teacher thighs—Milltown, New Jersey. What a fine set of knockers on Miss Lambkins, long stemmed legs, she asking the class of hunkies and swenskis, migrated southern white trash and a couple of black kids, "Did we all brush our teeth this morning like good boys and girls?" And that 'Talian bastard Tosgonno whispering, grabbing his jock, "Oh yes, Miss Lambkins, pulled my duff twice." He would kick his dago behind for that—for the rights to fantasy lovemaking with Miss Lambkins—seeing her walk down the hall, her magnificent ass active like two cats fighting in a bag, that belonged to him. He smiled at the images he dredged up and curled himself tighter into sleep.

The stocky yard dick (as Miss Lambkins repeated her question) shoved the cut-down ax handle into the ribs of the sleeping twelve year old Mikoloj Brandicki; he instantly became twenty-four-year-old Mike Brant, awake, the dream fragmenting as he woke to a mean scene in which he had another role.

"Get out of there you sonofabitch!"

"All right, all right. . . . " Like Uncle Waldo used to say—out of the snatch and into the cold.

The second yard dick grabbed Mike's worn parachute jumper's jacket as the first man seized both his legs and they bounced him brutally onto the sharp, oil-stained, gravel ballast. Bumps-a-daisy, he thought, bumps-a-daisy, you cocksuckers. Also, he rolled quickly to one side—the old army training—to avoid a whack of an ax handle across a shoulder, sprang to his feet in a motion that was almost one continual action, the bindle wrapped in a frayed raincoat hitched by a loop of rope still over the crock of one arm.

His reflexes had been fast, and he backed up, stood with his spine against a pile of redwood timbers. He had a fist raised, looking from side to side, noticing a gathering already of some vicious bastards at a cement-mixing machine watching the fun. From someplace a yard engine sounded—like potatoes boiling, he thought—and then there was the clutter of a metal container-section being raised onto a Santa Fe flat car.

(Funny, he thought, already sweating in the cold, how you pick up things that don't matter when the big thing that does matter is about to happen to you.) These two yard dicks with their cut-down ax handles were going to work him over. Mike flexed his arms, opened and shut his fists, braced himself to launch—if there was an opening—a quick head butt into a fat gut, dodging under the lifted hickory. Then, if he could get in a quick judo chop, army-training style, at the back of a burly neck . . . and if lucky—if, if, if—maybe a hard knee into a set of balls. Maybe then he could split to where there was a break in the high wire mesh fence by the big shiny cans marked DOW and DUPONT and some busted sacks showing red-leaded ends of steel forms.

It was a chance; he had to take it or get the clobbering.

He thought, so this is welcome to San Francisco, the wide blue Pacific. But no flags, no banner, just these two eager pricks and their ax handles going to work me over but good. Jesus, Mary and Joseph, for this I was a tourist two days in that freezing freight car . . . so these two company finks with that mean look of man beaters, who were, what in high school Miss Lambkins called sadists. . . .

Look at the old lust to bust heads in their eyes, and I'm sure as grief going to get it; oh boy, are the cocksuckers going to try. But they're past their prime, and, with their beer bellies and that twenty year flab, they'll back off. Hell, they must spend a lot of time lying to each other about their quiff hunting days and all the pussy they once scored; now their prostrates must be big as coconuts. What are they waiting for . . .

Maybe I can sweet-talk my way past them rather than take them on. Brace yourself, Mike, flex the old muscles. Like the phys-ed sergeant Wasserman used to say teaching killer games to the new soldiers: "All you have to do is reflex faster, move quicker than Flynn—see? and you have any sized sonofabitch off balance."

He wished Davey Wasserman were with him now, even with the one arm. Davey, he was a good man in a brannigan, bar room or camp, or backing you up on a body count mission in some gook village. . . .

All the time Mike had been thinking one of the yard dicks was staring at him, beating the heft of his club into the palm of an open hand, and holding back with a shake of his head the stocky man, who was breathing open-mouthed at the idea of whacking out this drifter.

"Come on, listen," Mike said, "I was only taking up space in a empty box car. I didn't steal any freight. Search me." All the time the old, dumb smile of a kid who had shit in his pants.

"I'm just a working stiff see, like yourself. Think of *you* being *me*."

The stocky yard dick gave a bronchial bark, then asked, "Where you steal the soldier jacket?"

"Got it for free in Korea. Came in a set with a M-16."

"No crap," said the taller dick—the one with the acne scars. "You was there?"

"Yeah I was there." The tall sonofabitch was wearing an American Legion button on his horsehide jacket. Maybe try a bit of the ol' bullshit here: "Didn't I see you in the KO bar in Seoul?"

"Naw, I got nicked at Inchon. I never had no Seoul twat."

The cement workers had lost interest in the scene and were pouring concrete again.

The stocky yard dick stuck his weapon into Mike's midriff. "What the fuck is this, you two—a soldiers' reunion?"

"Look, Mac, all I want," Mike said, "is to get the hell out of here. I got a job waiting in Monterey, yeah, in a cannery."

"Where you from?" asked the Legion man with a nod of reassurance.

"Been up in Seattle all fall working a dock crane, but there's a strike up there. The DWU is trying to organize the whole Northwest."

"Fuck off, fuck off," said the stocky yard dick waving his ax handle. "You're just lucky, soldier, we didn't break your fuckin' ass."

I bet, thought Mike, I bet you get your jollies that way.

"You feed lately?" asked the Legion man.

"I got enough for a stack of wheats and coffee."

The day was brightening in the west, the Bay Area's morning mist still hung low. "Here, take a buck," said the Legion man. "Don't let Charley here bother you none. He's got an ulcer from ass-kissing the company. He's got a pension coming in six months."

"Thanks." Mike nodded, took the dollar. The stocky man turned away, "Fucking commies, both of you."

* * *

A heavy yard engine—an old reconditioned Baldwin—
was passing, pulling two private cars lettered in gold:
L. A. Rams Football Team. Mike quickly made his way
around the last car, moving on packed cinders, the bay
shiny beyond in the odor of decaying cargos. Yellow fer-
tilizer spilled from a row of paper bags being moved
indifferently by six blacks loading it onto a Mack.

Mike sweated, breathing hard, mouth open; I could of
taken 'em both, could of taken them . . . the old fart
with an ulcer and a thin ex-soldier looking a bit creaky
like he had lost some of his marbles. Inchon, Seoul—he
saw it all multifaceted, multifragmented as he ran . . .
the damn crazy war and MacArthur the Ego taking a lick-
ing, and the rest of us dogfaces, our mugs frozen, moving
down in the balls-freezing weather, and the staff Lincolns
going by, their chains throwing up muck and ice in our
face—your toes freezing, turning black, and we chewing
ratcrap dry rations and ice cold Spam, feeding your gut
and not too happy to have it. Two days later all those
dead, frozen bodies in the ditch, ours—and the local
gooks in the stubble carrying bundles of straw, watching
your ass dragging by.

On that goddam retreat he didn't think he'd ever get
any life back into his toes or eat hot chow or use his cock
between some broad's legs. Hello, sweetie, Mike is back.

The callousness of losses, the bullshit artists back at
base, a Purple Heart and "good luck, soldier" . . . an
honorable discharge.

Forget, forget he thought, crossing the last set of tracks,
going by a weedy path onto a paved street. He laughed
and sucked air till he was breathing easy, like Mike Brant
liked to laugh. His father used to say in Polish, "If you
don't laugh you cry. Say, *bardzo mi przyjemme*—pleased
to meet you."

He was suddenly feeling good. He had escaped a rousting from those two yard dicks in the freight yard. They
had killed a couple of fruit pickers up the line. He had a

bad night at poker, true, that last night in Seattle, before hopping the Sunshine car going south, but his luck would change. He had that Purple Heart for that arm wound he'd picked up below Wonsan in the wornout war among the wogs, and while he had sung with the rest of the squad, "I got gonorrhea in ol' Korea," he had been lucky—knock wood—to escape it and the old rale, yaws, crabs. Even made sergeant when Bradden bought a farm in a rice paddy—was it Kaesong? Yeah, . . . unlucky bastard. Bradden, all that college education. A Caddy agency back home, and they collected him with a broom to bury.

CHAPTER 2

Eats, said a bright red sign over a dog wagon. *Falstaff Beer* blinked the pink neon sign. Mike shifted his bindle, kicked open the door. It was warm inside the wagon. The usual greasy spoon—a juke box (Elvis?), a row of stools at a plastic counter, a half dozen human behinds in work clothes on the stools, two of them women. A smell of rancid hamburger gook, Lysol, eggs, sunny side up hissing on a griddle.

Mike found a stool and behind the counter, a fat man, needing a shave, but pleasant looking, set down a coffee cup. "Java?"

"Sure, what kind 'a pie?"

"Cokenut, apple."

"Apple."

"Cheese wit the appel? A burger, hum and eggs?"

"No, just coffee and the pie." Mike fingered the dollar bill in the army jacket that still showed where a tech sergeant's chevrons had been ripped off. He unbuttoned the jacket, revealing a gray flannel loggers' shirt, a yellow sweater. He set his bindle carefully between his legs—a crowd-wise man—so it couldn't be slipped away, and he felt delighted to be alive in the serenity of detachment—yet an observer. That buck and sixty-three cents in change, not counting the Canadian dime some joker had put into the poker game, was all his assets. The bindle between his legs held an extra shirt, a razor, comb, two pairs of wool socks, blue jeans, a pair of barley-bucker's leather gloves, a folding knife—called when he was a kid, a frog sticker—some frayed and torn papers held in a paperback copy of *The Thin Man* . . ., letters he had carried a long time, some snapshots of Korean girls, crazy quiff—and a blonde trick he dated in Hawaii . . . a wad of office papers, the honorable discharge, a bill (a legal notice) that he owed on a Ford, long since wrecked and junked outside Cleveland, his Social Security card, oh Christ, that lottery ticket (he took it out of the jacket pocket)—Irish Sweepstakes for a drawing and race run three years before. One corner was bloodstained, and Willie Benzzua and Davey Wasserman had all signed it as partners. Willie had no need of blood anymore and Davey had it made: an official USA disability, drawing a monthly allowance from Uncle Sam and not missing the lost arm; like hell, Davey, he didn't—the best pool hustler Fort Ord ever saw. Davey making a full rack, reciting, "Man is not a mechanism but an individual facing daily disaster."

One of the women got off a stool—middle-aged, a redhead, (does she or doesn't she tint?). Not bad at all for her age, a bit wide in the rump in those pants, but nice knockers, heavy but firm. The slow easy movement of invitation in them. She smiled as she looked at him, a bill and her tab held in one hand. Hope in her smile—hope is the best condition for loving, Mike had always felt.

Her work button and identification picture read *Ruth Welton, Motor-Mite Engineering.*

"Any work for a crane or fork-lift man?"

"Things tight . . . you got a DWU card?"

"I got."

"Maybe later in the week. If that steel plant strike lets up. See you around."

"See you," he said, adding the sweet stud's smile.

He nodded. His problem was spicy small talk *now* to get a hunk of ass or hustle work, feed up, make enough for a good poker game. Maybe later, baby; he had that itch; like trying to scratch his shoulder blades. The coffee was good and hot, real battery acid, the pie a dismal mess of cornstarch, some icky sweetener, soggy crust holding what looked like green goo; that must be the apples. Jesus, Mary and Joseph, not real apples—like that time before the army up in Oregon—he and Davey trimming orchards. Pippins and Baldwins like wine, making out with Fran, the wife of the foreman with the hernia (the foreman had the hernia, not the wife), laughing it up under a hard yellow moon. . . tawny mountains with deep blue distances, drinking Canadian ale, both of us randy with loving and laughing and scratching, and then sleeping under the apple trees—a complacent, shared snoring.

Mike pushed away the pie plate. He was still damn hungry, and he chewed on the last of the pie mess and hunted in his jacket pocket for the makings as he put away the old Sweepstake ticket. But he had used up the last of the Bull Durham makings two days ago.

A weathered old hand all knobs and veins held out a tailor-made, no filter. "Care for a smoke?"

"Thanks." He took the cigarette and a little man—thin, feisty looking, with a week's whiskers and a set of too white store teeth, very blue eyes set in brackets of tanned wrinkles—held a flaring kitchen match to the tobacco. Mike inhaled the pungent smoke. The old man blew out the match and stuck it behind an ear against white hair—what could be seen of his hair—under a cap with a broken beak.

"I alus say a smoke is better than a woman, and a pack

of cigs, when you're shaking for a butt, is to be held higher than hope of heaven. Yep, I'm Smith. . . Wallie
Smith."

"Brant. . . Mike Brant."

The cigarette tasted fine. Still hungry, stiff from sleeping in a freight car, the ceramic smile of Wallie Smith
soothed him.

"Looking for work, Mike?"

"This good union country for it?"

"Shit, it's all fancy dan union halls and press agents
and posing with welfare clients in bingo parlors and some
scut getting a gold-plated tin watch for working his ass
off for the bosses for forty years."

"You don't take to unions, Wallie?"

The old man pointed a hard thumb at a small bronze
button attached to an old brown tweed jacket.

"See that, soldier?"

Mike noticed Wallie had only three fingers left on that
hand.

"An old Wobby, that's me, Wallace Enoch Smith.
Now, *that* was a union. The IWW."

"International Workers of the World," Mike said. The
old coot was delighted by the identification.

"Yeah, yeah," the old man smiled. "The IWW. Those
pricks, the Pinkerton men, they called us the I Won't
Work. . . but we had clout. Shit, yes. Ever read Thoreau?
'I would not run around a corner to see the world blown
up. . . ' Well we blew up mine owners; hell, didn't we
blow up the *Los Angeles Times* that time, that scum
rag?"

"I never heard of anyone doing that."

A wink, a touch of the nose by his forefinger.

"Care for a snort?" The old man tapped a bulging jacket pocket.

"Sure."

"Not in here; Ernie, a good scout, but he's got no likker
permit."

Outside, the mist was burning off, seagulls made patterns. Wallie pulled out a brown paper bag from which the neck of a bottle showed.

"Mighty poor whiskey it is, Mike. On Nob Hill it's Chavis Rivas, but here, what the hell, this panther piss cuts the morning slimes."

It was goddam bad whiskey, and Mike shivered and swallowed. Wallie smiled, his china teeth keeping pace with the rest of him.

"I can get us six hours of picketing for the DWU." He spit. "Not a bad union."

"What's it all about?"

"Walking round for some front cause of theirs. Two hours wearing out leather, an hour off, coffee and sandwiches, a freebee." Wallie smiled, his wrinkled features like heavy, carved mahogany.

"I mean, Wallie, the strike. . . "

"Not a strike. It's a solidarity demonstration against Franco's Spain and the South Africa apartheid—a sort of spontaneous, well. . . , organized thing, see? We're protesting the unloading and loading of some ships from those fink countries. Organized but spontaneous, oh brother."

The old man winked. "Officially it's unofficial, but the seacoast unions are using a little clout against shippers."

Mike's mind was on his hunger.

"Sandwiches?"

"The sooner we get there the better. The goddam rummies and winos might grab off most of the signs— Jasus—a man's either hunting grub or thinking with his *cojones*, isn't he?"

The day had cleared. The bay was impressive, active, the gulls bolder. Mike, on the Bay ferry, found it all busy and arrogant, the wharfs, piers, the traffic on the water. It was a sensory enjoyment to him and brought back the kid images of his first visits to Hoboken, Jersey City, his first boyhood sight of great bodies of water, the old ferry boats with their clattering chains, walking beams that still retained the smell of horse piss—a smell a couple of generations old—the last drays and horses had crossed long ago. The outlines of San Francisco Bay were clearer—levity and complacency—sharper. This is California, you jerk, he reminded himself as he and Wallie Smith walked off the ferry and moved toward a line of waiting men before a dun-colored pier building.

Wallie elbowed his way through the waiting men shouting, "Shop steward, shop steward!" Mike followed; the little bastard was full of moxie. A bum, with no shirt, wearing a long frock coat, cried out: "Piss off, Wallie . . . what were you shop steward of?"

"Cooking Sherry Drinkers Local 102, you rummy."

A depressed-looking man with uncombed gray hair was seated at a desk made from a machinery crate. Behind him were stacked dozens of picket signs in red and brown, attached to husky-looking staves. In Seattle Mike remembered they called them "cop scratchers."

"Hello, Jamie," Wallie addressed the depressed man. "Got room for two fine walkers? This is my old buddy, Mike Brant. Ran the four-minute mile at Yale. Legs of iron."

The man addressed as Jamie made a grimace. "Christ, I thought they had you locked up in some crapper of an old sailors' home."

Wallie sang:

Once you loved with fond affection;
And your thoughts were just of me.
Now you've left me for another
And you care no more for me.

Did a dance step ending with offering the palms of his hands in a gesture of a performer ending his act.

"Frisky as a Barbary Street hooker on Navy Day. No

Wobbly ever ended up in a rocking chair. How about it, Jamie—two cardboards to carry."

"Pier 32." Jamie held up a leaking ball point pen. "Sign here, and you gotta return the signs end of the day. They cost two bucks each."

What am I doing here, Mike thought. I'm a real working stiff with skills, a trade. I don't mooch unless I have to, but now these fuckoffs of rummies and winos, flashers, gutter rats—an old Wobbly. Jesus, the bums, they smell like rotting clams. Do I? *I'm here because I'm here*, as the old song had it—the one my old man used to play on his windup victrola. I'm here because I'm hungry, because I'm dragging my ass, because I'm tapped out.

What am I signing? The right to carry a picket sign, and if the cops are hassling us for the television cameras, I'll have to use the shaft to bust heads. It's like Davey used to say when we were in the Huey copters being moved up against the Chinese at Chunchon, "We eat each other, Mike, and God eats us."

I don't feel like I felt in the army. The G.I.'s life, mean and shitty as it was, it was guy to guy backing you, comradship. Sure, beefing, grouching at the chow, the fucking brass, and laughs, too—when we faced that captain who was making time with the nurses at Taegu—rolled a grenade under his tent flap, the pin out. The bars were fun, even the gyp joints; and the whores were neat and polite Jap dollies, not like the hookers along Bourbon Street or outside of Fort Ord. . . .

This damn pen leaks. (Miss Lambkins, who taught high school art, had an old Waterman and blue ink, and she'd hold my hand and show me how to draw the perspective of a glass). But now it's all a ballpoint world: my mitts need a wash anyway, so sign M – I – K – E   B – R – A – N – T. You're in Cocksys army now. . . just a bum working for cakes and java. The world ends for workers, my old man used to say when high on Slivowitz: "Ends, Michael, when you're worked out, disgarded." My old man was proud though; he'd die in the gutter before he'd lower the dignity of being a good worker. A tire maker—a Polock poisoned by chemical fumes, coughing up bits of lung, a family with six kids, an old grandmother, a rented house with lousy plumbing. At least my old man, he made me finish high school so I'd learn to write easy.

After Mike signed the grimy blue sheet under a sprawling Wallace Enoch Smith (there was no request of an address), Jamie said, "No sluffing off. . . there are TV cameras to take pics, so smile, and no fucking cursing."

Mike was handed a four-foot-high picket sign, counting the stick:

PROTEST PROTEST
STOP SHIPMENTS FROM FASCIST SPAIN . . .
PROTEST
THE RACIAL POLICIES OF SOUTH AFRICA . . .
SUPPORT
THE UNITED HUMANITY COMMITTEE FOR
DEMOCRACY . . .

"Who the hell, Wallie, is the United Humanity Committee for Democracy?"

"Some gussied up dummy front for the commies in the union local. The unions don't mind, soldier. . . government's been trying to knock off the head men as card-carrying comrades for years. But they're too smart for 'em. Now just remember, keep the sign easy to carry over one shoulder, and walk slow. After a few rounds we find a spot to go off and smoke. Look, when we eat, put some sandwiches in your pockets. When they hand out the grub, the freeloaders glom the lot if you don't kick them in the shins. You ever picket and march, Mike?"

"Hell no, and I feel goddam silly. But I'm hungry. What kind of sandwiches?"

"If Terry herself is making them, she'll mooch meat from the restaurant and delis. If it's some mission Christers, it's peanut butter."

Wallie waved his sign and shouted, "Workers of the world arise . . . you have nothing to lose but peanut butter on stale white bread!" His voice registered treble and bass, and he did his little dance step as he moved. His joy depressed Mike.

There was already a crowd on the dusty end of the pier when Mike got there. The rusting high wall of a dark blue freighter was the goal of the protesters. The ship showed no smoke from its lone funnel. Two dozen police carrying long clubs kept watch by a gangplank. Two oilers were on the rail of an upper deck. Stripped to their soiled undershirts, they were staring down at the pickets and some curious people. One spit into the Bay and flipped a cigarette butt at a television truck.

Mike saw the words *La Mujer* on the freighter's bow; a bilge outlet vigorously poured gray-green water into the space between the hull and the dockside.

A tall girl with taffy-colored hair waved to them—hair only partly contained under a dark brown beret. Her blue work shirt was open at the throat, work blues tightly fitted. She was shouting into a bullhorn: "Keep it moving, keep it moving! Fight fascism, racism, keep it moving, keep it moving!"

Wallie banged his picket sign up and down, thumping its stave end on the blacktopped pier floor. "That's right, Terry darling, fight 'em—fight 'em!"

The girl frowned and tapped long, tapered, nicotine-stained fingers on the horn: "Don't sweet-talk me, Smitty, get your old ass in the line."

"Sure thing, Terry . . . hey, this is comrade Brant . . . Mike Brant . . ., Mike, this is Terry Munday, the union organizer of the broads in hospitals and offices."

"We're women, not broads, you hammered-down shrimp."

"Okay, okay. The nurses in white get me horny."

"Brant, keep your sign high. Give us a good howl. We're waiting for the television cameras."

"That needs strength. How about a cup of the brew?"

Mike noticed she had a long expressive nose; temper there he decided. "Coffee and sandwiches, that's all you come for?" She looked at a big watch strapped to a tanned wrist. "In forty-five minutes . . . keep moving! Keep it moving. . . ."

"Shit," said Wallie. "As Emerson said, 'our time is a predicament we can endure if we hold to self-respect.'"

Mike found he felt more foolish than ever marching in a rough oval with the pickets—men and women. Some looked like students. Wallie said, "From Berkeley." And some looked like skid row dropouts—they stank of neglect and cheap alcohol. Some he identified as just people, others exibitionists—earnest shouters against racism and fascism. One old lady with a net shopping bag full of cabbages and two cartons of Old Gold kept shrilly crying out, "Don't eat flesh, don't eat Brother Sheep, don't eat Sister Cow." Kookie old biddy.

All Mike could picture after half an hour of walking and carrying his sign was a good bit of well-done Brother Sheep or charcoal-broiled Sister Cow. He was now so hungry—it was a serious predicament—that he was in pain and drinking great gulps of water too often from a leaky hose. It made him dizzy.

At eleven o'clock Terry relented; he ate seven peanut butter and jelly sandwiches.

There were three of these bossy women working up the crowd and the pickets. Mike studied them as he ate his last sandwich. They were all brisk and loud of voice. They were skilled in rallying the crowd. One was dumpy, with a nice face and silver rimmed glasses, about seventeen. One was on the bulky side (maybe a butch dike—who could figure out?). She had a lot of broadsides printed in blue and red and kept handing them out, adding in a too high voice, "Solidarity, solidarity will defeat the bosses' world."

Terry Munday, she with her bullhorn, seemed as indifferent to the pickets as to the people, using them only as a mass. Mike couldn't blame her: We're a mangy lot, scuffy, and not too interested in protest—but for the students, and they were mostly dogs or a bit wide-eyed.

Terry handed out four cigarettes to anyone within reach. Mike said, "Thanks, Miss Munday."

"You still in the army?"

"Hell no, my tailor is making me a fitting."

She didn't even smile: "We don't want any messing with trouble in the service. They use that against us, subverting the armed forces. Where you from?"

"Milltown, New Jersey."

"Union town?"

"Mostly now, used to be a scab burg with sweetheart contracts."

"Glad to have you aboard, Brant." She patted his shoulder and was off. He said to Wallie, "She pets me like a stray dog."

"Oh Terry, she's too serious. Want to get into her pants? There's maybe a human side there."

"Hell no, she'd bring her bullhorn to bed."

> Go court a tender maiden
> And hope that she'll be your wife,
> For I've been warned and I've decided
> To sleep alone all of my life.

The bullhorn blared out. "Everybody in line, everybody back in line. Keep it moving, keep it moving!"

The sun was low, an orange lollipop in the west, the seagulls seemed less noisy, blue shadows swooping low. Mike's feet hurt, the peanut butter was not too welcome in his stomach now that the edge of his hunger was slacked.

"Got a kip for tonight, soldier?"

"No dough for one, Wallie."

"We'll draw our day's pay, and they pay in cash. No records kept, see, for this jamboree."

"I'd like a steak *this* thick?"

"If you don't mind sawdust on the floor and unshaved waiters, I know a place, Mitch Kelly's, or you can move in with me at Minnie Rothschild's."

"I'll pay my way. I like to be alone."

"I'm a clean old man. There's a song about it . . . "

"I've heard it."

Mike's depression was back. The prolonged circling, walking, the damn radical women manipulating the crowd. He was an ablebodied, card-carrying union man down to carrying a sign on a stick . . . fuck Franco, fuck South Africa . . . and this cheerful old fart with no future but a cheap burial in some potter's field out here. . . . Jesus, it was one of those days he remembered when Moz brought back a fact from history class. There was this Roman emperor who wished all the world had one head so he could cut it off with one sweep of his sword.

Chapter 3

He lived that week in Minnie Rothschild's Hostel, a run-down three-story brick building two blocks from the waterfront. It cost him a dollar and a half a day to share Wallie's small room with its one high window. It contained two army cots, a mirror, one chair, one naked light bulb. There was a toilet down the hall with a showerhead that gave off a tepid rust-flaked water. There were some paper towels over a smelling-of-urine sink. The towels and the tepid water disappeared by nine o'clock in the morning.

Terry Munday had approved Minnie's place for Mike after the first day's picketing. "It's no St. Francis or Top of the Mark, Brant, but they try to keep the roaches down, and Mrs. Rothschild gives you a fifty-cent *mulligan* with meat in it."

"Don't ask what kind 'a meat," added Wallie Smith. Wallie owned nothing but what he had in his pockets and a copy of Conrad's *Lord Jim* and the remains of a volume of *Pepys Diary*.

Mike was annoyed about Terry Munday. He didn't like aggressive women, the kind that ran things that men should. He admitted he was maybe too macho in his thinking; it was a time of his feeling a sense of dismal insufficiency. He fantasized about women, some of the time anyway . . . of women like his old teacher, Miss Lambkins—that was a groovy object of sexual delight, tenderness, the way a woman is in your dreams, a loving relationship, soft, given to conscious gratification. In actuality, he related to the passing tarts of seaports and migratory work camps, the hookers in tight cardigans in tough bars, and casual pickups in bus stations, movie lobbies, or bowling alleys. The dream that had persisted since puberty had failed to materialize.

Wallie Smith sang as he came into the room (*"Get a boy, get a boy, and if you can't, get a clean old man"*) earing only a blue work shirt, carrying a towel lettered Holiday Inn, a bit of soap wrapped in a wad of toilet paper.

"Almost hot water tonight. Now for a good read, soldier, before some shut-eye, or you want to make the gash and hash scene?"

Mike suspected Wallie suffered delusions of adequacy.

Wallie opened one of his two books, reclined on his bed with a thin pillow behind his head, put on a pair of silver-rimmed glasses. Mike thought he looked like a stoned owl.

"You ever read Gibbon, Mike?"

"Can't say I have." Mike was sleepy, and for all his tough body, walking the blacktop on the pier for at least six hours a day made his feet ache, the calves of his legs cramp up . . . maybe because picketing didn't seem honest work.

"Ah, you ought to read Gibbon. The bastard is so clear about the whole fucking shooting match of this world always gone crazy. History, he says, is just the crackpots, the bloody murderers in power, and their cliques having their mind-blowing way."

"You read a lot?"

"Got the reading bug in prisons. I've done lots of time—been worked over by lots of hacks and wardens. Three years in Atlanta for a sweet little explosion of 'dinah' among some Pinkerton men. A year and some extra in 1918 in Leavenworth. Sedition they called it; I was just a kid—for going against what? The J. P. Morgan loans? Fuck the Great War, as we called it. Hard times, mean. I found you can't beat your meat twenty-four hours a day, can you. I latched on to prison reading. It was the better way to wear out time. Hell, I never cracked a book till I was in stir."

"I used to read in the army hospital—Hammett, Chandler."

"That's time wasting. Jesus, I could 'a been a intelligensia. But I never got much of a education, country school in Ohio. Not past the third grade. Couldn't write or read. I printed my letters for a long time. Honest, couldn't write proper."

"I had high school."

"Prison has educated a lot of guys . . . Cervantes, Bunyon, Dostoevski. Sure, books tell lots of lies, maybe most of the time, but it's a game; I like setting myself up against the big geezers. I agree with them, I laugh at them, I say oh shit . . . Say, Mike, if the light bothers you, I'll cork off."

Mike said the light didn't, and he lay back, arms behind his head, thinking of the last few days. . . . Had never been much for seeing the value of unions. My old man got ruined by yammering for and supporting a rubber workers' union. Out on his ass for it, with ruined lungs, and the company or union didn't even pay the last medical bills when the old man croaked, game to the last . . . winking at me just two days before the end, coughing and gasping, "Be a man, Michael. It's not easy, but just stick a thumb up your own ass and hold yourself off at arm's length and see what you are." The rest of his crazy talk was all Polish till he died. The poor don't die nice.

But seeing this coastal union thing up close, it's more than hassling the corporations, kicking the shins of capitalism. It was no featureless mass, just working joes in camaraderie. It gives the guys a right to protest and howl, and it keeps a bit of money in your jeans . . . you can show your union card and be part of the scene among the working stiffs and the migratory workers that follow the threshers up from the Red River wheat fields. And it's a closeness to the girls packing fish in the Monterey canneries. I felt I was too smart for believing—I'm wrong. Sure, sure . . . there are fat cats making a good thing, and I've seen the union governing boards as tight as a bull's ass in fly time in control of the locals. But the unions let everybody have a hunk of the action. At least they share; the corporations don't share, not even much with their stockholders. They just hand out the conciliatory phrases and fire you the day before Christmas.

He wanted to ask Wallie about the local coastal unions, who was on the take, who was playing an honest game? But Wallie was already asleep, his teeth in a glass of water on the floor. Wallie snoring, mouth agap, a little old man in gradual decline. You could read on his face every blow, every slam in the kisser the old Wobby had ever taken—printed there on the weathered skin, the big rummy's nose; it had been busted at one time, you could see that. An old crock ready for what Davey Wasserman had called *Malekhamoves* (the Jew angel of death).

Mike reached for the cord that led to the light bulb hanging from the ceiling, and the room plunged into darkness but for a sort of underwater glow, deep blue,

from the one window behind the cockeyed shade. There
was a rumble of traffic: big eighteen-wheel diesels bringing up the food for the city, trucking from the docks.
Stuff, too, in crates marked Hong Kong, Rio, Cape Town
(the racist bastards). Big wheelers: metal rigs loaded with
Japanese televisions, double-decked carriers with Volks-
wagens, Brazilian coffee bags. You could bet also a lot of
pot and hard drugs, diamonds and watches the sailors and
the dock workers and custom agents on the take managed to get ashore.

Mike yawned. And a half dozen left-wing union locals
could tie this all up, tie up the port, close off the whole
coast. Now *that* was muscle. That was union solidarity—
able to put their own goon squads on the bricks to take
the goons, scabs, and yellow bellies the corporations
would call up. Hell, he punched the pillow—he better get
some shut-eye. Terry Munday was moving them over to
the South African ship with a group of black picket-sign
carriers. Funny, he'd been raised to see them as jigs,
coons, boogs, burrheads: My old man, he had these old
ideas that niggers had small brains and big jocks and
smelled bad, and that they undercut the earnings of
white workers. No, Mike punched his meager pillow
again, trying for a more satisfactory shape—wrong,
wrong (whack), wrong. They were just like any other
working joe; mean or kind, nasty or helpful, greedy or
laughing it up . . . you could like them or not
. . . some were okay . . some were no good pricks
. . . some you could feel were no worse than anybody at
all. Mike was deeply and dreamlessly asleep.

The room, as if relaxing, smelled of old clothes, bug
powder, and damp wallpaper.

The South African ship, the *Gavaert de Haas,* was
loading heavy factory and farm machinery under the ob-
servation of private guards and a force of city police. Ter-

ry Munday, in a tan raincoat, tightly belted, faced the thirty men and women in the shelter of a big earthmover assigned to Capetown. She was speaking with a righteous tenacity: "Now listen good. This cargo is really mostly war supplies. Armored cars, fighter plane parts. We're going to try and bust open a crate marked machinery parts. It's surplus M-16s and machine guns."

"How we going to bust it?" asked a large black man with a fringe of beard, "without gettin' our haids busted?"

"One of the winchmen on deck is a loyal DWU coastal worker."

Someone behind Mike said, "One of them fucking comrades."

"He'll drop a case we are suspicious of onto the dock, hard, to smash it open. When he does, we rush it and raise a ruckus. The press services—all the media—have been alerted."

Wallie blew on his cold fingers. "What makes you think the cops and the goons are just going to stand around there?"

"Yeah," came from several pickets. "What?"

Mike waved a hand at Terry. "Going to be heads busted. Better let anybody who wants to pull away do it before they get coldcocked."

"Look, Brant." Terry kept control of her voice and temper. "Solidarity is the big point. We all know there can be a mean mix-up here. But we've got muscle too. Right!"

"Shit," said someone from the back of the crowd. "Them lefties want trouble."

Terry smiled, put her thumbs under the belt of her raincoat, "You bet we want to attract attention. You don't get no place or any rights or better conditions, not by sitting on your duff in some beer joint crying in your brew how mean they are to you. You, Brant, you Wallie, if you want to stay out, or anybody else, okay, okay. Protect your heads. The Civil Liberty lawyers will see you don't get bounced around in the jailhouse if you're hauled in."

"Hey, Terry," said Wallie. "What kind of cream puffs you take us for?"

Mike added, "Maybe I'm not full of that party line crap, but I'm a working stiff, my old man, my old lady's old man, both got their asses busted a lot."

"I'll make the speeches," said Terry.

"No speeches," said Wallie taking Mike's arm. "Pick up your wood and paper. Workers of the world arise, you're just in time to get your heads busted on company time."

He began to do his little dance and sing:

> He had a million cattle and he had a million sheep.
> He had a million vessels on the ocean deep.
> He had a million dollars all in nickels and dimes.
> Well—he knew it 'cause he'd counted them a
>   million times.

At the pier where the South African ship was berthed Mike felt it was all like a stage set rather than an actual event, so like the times in Korea when an action was planned to impress some stuffed shirt visiting the battle area—a senator and his group, or some United Nations observers in well-fitted, warm coats and packed lunch baskets ready to feed their paunches. For that kind of show some poor sods had to make an attack, just for show, and sometimes there were casualties and a few dead soldier boys.

Terry was in a fine mood, her voice edged with excitement, the bullhorn enlarging her pleas. She looked tough. "Keep order, keep order, don't let them push in between you."

Wallie sang as they moved toward the waiting guards and cops:

I don't want your greenback dollar,
And those things you sent to me.
If your conscience bothers you,
Let it be, just let it be.

There were lots of police and more hard faces, private guards, and some with knobby, broken faces, bulky men who were ex-pugs.

Mike grabbed hold of the shaft of his picket sign more firmly. It would only take a moment to tear off the cardboard lettered, SOUTH AFRICA IS PREPARING TO MASSACRE MILLIONS OF BLACKS, STOP SHIPMENTS TO AID RACISM!

Wallie was shaking his head. "It looks like an arranged confrontation. Hell, this is no protest picketing. A little shoving around, and it's a head busting like you said."

"Got all the signs of it." Mike looked over the activity of cranes lifting cargo onto the ship, caught the looks of hostility from the police. They were shifting from foot to foot as they grasped and caressed their clubs, as if fondling a fetish. That kind of shuffling foot action Mike knew was that of people about to take some rash action.

Wallie lifted his sign high over the heads of two police captains . . . they smiling like babies contented and fed.

"Now, Wallie, get your tail out of this—an old man can break a bone."

"My bones are rubber, Captain McClusky . . ."

"No loitering . . . just legal picketing."

The pickets circled in a tightening oval, moving toward the ship. There seemed to be a closing in all around Mike—a jamming of faces and bodies against the police and goon lines. There was a sense of mischievous hysteria mixed with a quaver of a keyed up mob.

"It's going to be a fucking donnybrook, Wallie. The damn cops are aching for it. Terry Munday should call it all off."

Wallie smiled sadly. "You got a lot to learn, soldier, about left-wing agit-prop."

"What the hell you talking about?"

"It's a lefty setup. They're the ones going to provoke a riot, not the other side."

"Are there guns really in the crates?"

"Maybe so, maybe not. But whatever it is, protect your noggin and nuts."

There was a kind of lion roar, a hurting pressure of shoving that turned to arms waving, signs bobbing up and down. Wallie took his teeth out of his mouth, put them away in an inner pocket. "It's begun."

A new group of men had suddenly appeared with the looks, Mike thought, of broken-nosed, thick-eared gladiators he had seen in an early movie version of *Ben-Hur*. Only these were for real, not apparitions on a screen.

"Who are they?"

"Maybe union goons, maybe gooks from a scab private detective agency. You'll know when you see *who* they hit."

He began to pull the sign off its shaft. Mike followed his action, aware the air was full of menacing screams from the pickets and Terry coming over loud and a bit too shrill on her bullhorn. He had an impression of the crane stopping their load halfway up, of the police whacking away with rambunctious effort, of women pickets shouting, and one hysterical voice way out of control.

CHAPTER 4

Then the new mob were on the pickets. They were clearly company hoodlum, strong-arm men. Mike saw a blackjack flash in the wan sunlight and a thin lanky man go down as the cush struck one side of his head shiny crimson. It was all incongruities. Mike didn't have much more time to be an observer. A wide, dark man with a prominent, pugnacious chin, a flap over one eye, and a length of lead pipe held high was trying to get enough power in the swing of his weapon to crush Mike's skull. It was clear the bastard was clumsy and had had no training either as a parachute trooper or in scientific, jungle, hand-to-hand combat so cherished by sergeants. Mike sent the end of his staff into the man's gut. The man grunted, and Mike struck twice with the side of his wooden stave, once on each cheek. Coming closer, he lifted his right knee hard into the man's balls, and the victim fell away screaming.

The stave was pulled from Mike's hand, and he faced two short, wide men, they with the stance of professional wrestlers, which he figured they may have been. If so, poor ones, for he got one with a hard judo chop to the side of a bull neck. With the other, he ducked under outstretched arms, fists armed with brass knuckledusters and dived at the knees with an old-fashioned football tackle. He brought him down and rolled with the man in a tangle of limbs on the blacktop, the man grunting, going "ho ho ho," and trying for a half nelson; the sonofabitch *was* a professional grappler. That wouldn't do. Mike didn't care for any damaging wrestling holds. He got his teeth into a fleshy ear lobe and bit through; with rage and fury, he severed meat, leaping back as blood came salty to his mouth. The man lying prone on the ground grabbed his ear. Mike was up quickly and kicked the head of the ear-torn man with his heavy work boots: one solid whack (like thumping a watermelon) at the top of head—then a hard heel ground into a cheekbone.

Mike was aware he was breathing hard and felt good. He felt mean and had that tight, easy emotional sensuality of how it had been raiding a village and knocking off Korean natives near Kai Lu Mai, not asking questions of the poor shaking jerks—just clodhoppers, country folk, who didn't give a shit about the war either way. Bad stuff, bad times.

The noise of the battle—yes, it was a battle, dockside—was very loud. People were down and holding injured arms as if they were treasures and precious.

The police were banging away at men, at women; equal rights, Mike thought. One young girl, in panic trying to climb onto an Esso truck was being clubbed down, the thuds of police batons on her thin body making nasty sounds; young flesh and bones being punished.

It's all paranoid, the whole fucking world, as the young medic in the army hospital used to insist. Christ, Mike thought, if Terry's people, she and Jamie Ward and the radicals had planned this, to get pickets clobbered, bloodied, he'd break her ass himself.

Wallie was down, cap off, and covering his few strands

of white hair with his hands, crying out, "Don't hit an ol' man, don't hit a war hero!"

Mike pulled him up and shoved the shaking old man against some stacked bags of Diamond cement. "Get out of this, you old fart."

"Get out yourself, Mike. They're going to toss tear gas."

Mike wiped his face with the back of a hand. "We walked into it like goddam steers into a butcher's shed."

"That's right." Wallie hunted in his clothes. "I hope nobody broke my teeth."

"I'll twist Terry Munday's neck for this."

"Look out!"

Mike felt something solid hit the right side of his neck. A hard club poked his kidneys with a gush of pain. A policeman was lifting his club again. Mike felt pain, deeper, purple. One side of his body seemed without feeling, the muscles all gone to numbness. He kicked the cop in the shins. Then with his right shoulder he drove in and jolted the man's head with the point of an elbow right in the adams apple. The cop gagged, his breath cut off. Mike didn't stay for more because the gas was being released through cannisters. People were bouncing off each other, and someone spun him around as the pickets started running for the end of the pier to escape the reeking vapors.

It was biting, lung-tearing stuff, painful as needles stuck into the eyes, the throat; his stomach protested. Someone was climbing his back and banging him brutally on the side of the head. Just as someone else joined in the attack on his body, he heard Terry's voice, shriller than ever over the bullhorn—hurried run-together words: "That's how they treat the workers here! That's how they support the fascist allies of world corruption. . . . "

The words seemed suddenly torn away, and he began to black out. He fought it on his knees—he fought his head refusing to function, fought going under. The pain was bad; someone was kicking him in the ribs and he seemed to slough off his skin. After that came darkness, and the whole universe black and pinpointed with stars, and he whirling, going, going *deeper under the bed sheet, to the scream of the factory whistles waking the workers for the tire factory, the mills, the unloading of barges on the river.*

It was the end of the world as promised by the factory whistles. There isn't anything else but to wait for the final spin out. And Moz has wet the bed again, and it's sad to leave the little house of my old man. I'll have to get up, and if it's too cold and the water has frozen in the pipes and they have burst, the milk has expanded in the neck of the bottle so that it's poked out a cone of white. . . .

Beyond that, it's too cold in my thin worn clothes to go to school . . . I feel great pain, and the world ends in the burning glare of a big bitch of an explosion . . . there goes my head . . . no . . . *I land on my feet . . . and begin to fold my chute.* . . .

"Hau Yungchi, dang syinsye," the bar girls of Ko Dong say to Davey and me.

The Commandos were scrounging gear in the black market and saluting campaign stars. "It's a hell of a note, Mike, to go and see if some gook clearing can become a scout plane base, with a report of amplification and clarification in triplicate; it's a paper-mad war."

I, treating heat rash, suffering from native black-pajama whiskey: The choppy haze bouncing off the surface of the fruit-green rice paddies made me seasick. "They can't tell from the air if it's practical. Somebody has to go down to see."

Someone had said to send a recon mission with a regimental combat team under some hard-nosed noncoms. So we are the two pigeons set up to go ahead with the engineers, some demolition charges, smoke grenades, and a mixed batch of black GIs and Green Berets. We had only to salute a chestful of Asiatic-Pacific badges, and we were off, headed just above the 4th Brigade of the 25th Division, most of its strength chopped down by malaria, yaws, clap, and being overrun a few times by enemy ambush. The hot poop gossip is that their chicken colonel will get the DSC.

I didn't like what I saw of the Tai Pinh jungle from the air, and I didn't want any part of this helicopter assault, even with bursts from the 20 mike-mike and the 20-mm cannon, to soften things below. Davey was not new to the twenty-man platoons with the MIs we were to land with, having been in billets with them in Su Chow; he'd been drunk there and in trouble with the native junta's Security Group. The chief of logistics had chewed our ass out for it, and then made us a team to go recon the proposed landing base. Even in the air, the anopheles mosquitoes were biting; our ten choppers bunched and dipped, and we came down like beetles around a bit of carrion, and set down in the clearing, tall, thick jungle all around. Stink, too, from some rice paddies, enough to gag a congressman. Davey pushed back his canvas-covered combat helmet. "Shit 'n shinola, what a shooting gallery."

I look around at the landing party, everybody watching the jungle—heat humid on us all; worried over guerrillas.

Morning, dug in. Hot. All night snipers' guns have talked, now a foggy dawn has come up; we are full of GI ration. The enemy is up; we can hear his scouts chattering. Far off in the haze, there is the rattle of iron and the *chutchut* of heavy tanks. Davey grins at me and makes dirty remarks.

We are weighted down. Packs tear at shoulders, the wine swishes around in the water bottles, and we all have three hundred rounds each. Lord, how dirty our hands are and how hot the damn sun. And those silly birds singing. The farmers have left their rice. It's rotting there, and only the red water buffalo remains. The only sane thing, that cow, chewing her cud.

Joe Messer, top sarge, is cursing and lighting his home-made cigarette. The enemy guns are beginning again, rattling like adding machines.

"You look fucked," Davey says. Here come the tanks from our rear. A piping whistle goes up.

The noncoms move our group in behind the tank labeled *Our Pussy*. We hump ourselves across the clearing. A wind meets us—steel and fire. Ahead, nothing. I begin to run. Davey too. Taxi, the Negro boxer, is with us. He throws grenades ahead and ducks as they break like bad eggs. Every time he throws, he winks at us and rubs his great nose with glowing military ardor. "Man, them mutterfukinsons."

The tanks stink. They grind like a wurst machine. The guns begin, and suddenly we all fall down in their shadows with real affection for each other. Ahead is a green wall; it spits and slugs at us. The tank grunts, turns on a dime and goes over to the flank, roaring in high. The bush ducks into the ground like a turtle's head. We cross over it, running. Something red, screaming, mashed, is lying about. Tanks are mean things to lie under.

Ahead a tangle of jungle, sprinkled with red rags. We lie down and hug soil smelling of shit. Rice grew here; a path went down to that ridge that once hid a brook.

The sarge is hot under the collar. His mouth is speaking but we hear nothing. We lie waiting. The enemy has brought up his big mortars and is trying them out on us. I see the left flank go up in a mushroom of soot and flame. Sixteen men, nothing now. . . .

. . . The nurse said, "He's been delirious. Some kind of battle he's fighting in."

The bald, young doctor looked brightly—even if myopically—at the bed chart. "A concussion like that, violent force, really can do damage. We'll take more X rays, test for damage to the meninges this afternoon. But he doesn't seem to have any impairment of functions of the brain. Shock mostly."

"He's still out."

"That's the sedation. Nothing seems to have damaged the medulla oblongata. Respiratory and circulatory systems functioning. No escape of cerebrospinal fluid, the cerebral arteries holding, I'd guess.)

. . . under heavy fire we wait for help. Davey talks to me over the mortar fire while we suffer more casualties. I nod—but who can hear a goddam word? He answers me and winks. We are waiting. I read lips: *There are mines in the jungle.* We are waiting. For what?

I hear hoofs. Water buffalo. A herd of them. Thin clowns with washboard ribs; old with spavins, also young ones. All taken away from the natives. Davey rubs his unshaved face, all red-gold stubble. "Somebody has blown his stack."

The water buffalo are all around us, panting, milling hoofs pounding.

Davey said, "They're going to drive them through the mine field."

Men move among the buffalos; the water buffalo begin to gallop like a dog's ass under the touch of turpentine. Now they are ahead of us, bony rumps in the air, running like mad; someone fires flares after them. The poor bastards toss and foam and show worn teeth and make for the shelter of the wood.

Mines explode. Trees, buffalo, earth and stones go up. The creatures are setting off the mines. We look at each other's dirty faces, sniff, show our dry teeth. Taxi winks, "Better them cats, baby, than us." I try to grin back, my stomach heaves. My stomach gets back under cover. Cordite is around us. I shake.

The piping again. The sarge is tying his fingers together. They are red and limp; we can see the shattered bones. We get up and watch his blood drip on his GI pants. He swears at us. But the noise covers his words, and we are all suddenly erect and going forward. A line of men, the hot wind blowing through our pants. Someplace to the

west, bombing is going on—windmilling Skyraiders, I'd
guess, over the mist. Or maybe the F-105s. The jungle is
very still now. Whistlers pipe us to move on.

All firing stopped. The jumble, the world is all still. We
spread out—hunch under our packs and walk across the
smoking muck as if it were covered with eggs. Slow now.
No hurry. We walk, the steel weapons before us, the hot
day boiling on our tin hats. We walk. We've lost our tank.

We walk into the wood. I imagine faces watching. We
cross jungle rot, game shit, old leaves, and pass around
shell pockets, still warm. A tank ahead. Ours. It is so
still, lurched against a huge palm. The crew sit around or
lie in the grass, as if eating a picnic lunch. But they have
no heads, and their hands are black cinders. The tank is
gutted like a sardine can. We are past the picnickers. I
wipe my face on my sleeve. I can't move. Davey pats my
arm. I find a bush and retch and curse. Little red berries
hang ripe. I pull off a handful and chew. Bitter, but my
mouth is no longer dry. I no longer care. Fears. I've been
falling apart for a long time in this stinking place.

The jungle is dark under foot. The sarge looks at his
bandaged hands and moves us on with a shake of his hel-
meted head. We move in sagging lines, all of us afraid to
talk. No sound of mortars. Suddenly a white buffalo, a
nice old swayback with broken yellow teeth and blind
shiny eyes. He writhes, tries to unknot parts of himself,
his guts coiled red and blue. He stands; Davey lifts his
M-15. Two shots—the old buffalo sinks down. Amen. We
step over him, his dead eyes glazed and staring.

"It's stopped," says Taxi winking, swilling half a liter
from his canteen.

"Why?"

"Maybe they is waiting for us deeper in. The mutter-
fuckers."

That day I get the wound in my right shoulder.

CHAPTER 5

They had sure changed, gussied up, the army hospital at Mukpo; he saw that right away. He opened his eyes, feeling an active mass that he figured to be the size of a tennis ball bouncing around inside his head. The dried blood butcher-shop-stink was gone; the smeared shit-colored walls were robins egg blue. Where was the plywood unpainted ceiling, showing rain marks and the mess of exposed wiring? It's been prettied up; muted pastel walls and a comfortable bed under your back with a stand on which was set a basket of fruit. Someplace there were flowers. And no more hanging fixtures overhead with naked glaring light bulbs. Real lamps with shades. From someplace nearby the schmaltzy sound of Lawrence Welk's *When the Red Red Robin Comes Bob, Bob, Bobbin' along* . . . now dig that . . . all the world of war gone supremely sane.

This was the way to run a war . . . you could maybe now get pissed off at the chow lines, messy dog vomit,

47

even take the grandstanding of MacArthur and his damn
corncob. This was plush; *this* was the way to treat a
wounded hero. But why was his head hurting, when he
had been shot in the shoulder?

"He's blinking, he's awake . . . "
He focused his eyes, and there was a nurse and Terry
Munday in a knitted blue dress lighting a cigarette with a
battered brass lighter and exhaling smoke. Wallie Smith,
too, a darkening mouse under one eye, grinning.
The old man said, "Head like a bucket of ce-
ment . . . "
It wasn't the war of mindless menace . . . it wasn't
the hospital at Mukpo. No, this was California and he'd
been clobbered pretty good in a picketing fracas.
He adjusted his time warp and spoke, not liking his
voice; it was too throaty, as if out of practice. "I forgot to
duck."
The nurse said, "We look fine today."
"You're all right," said Terry. "A couple cracked ribs,
and they took six stitches in your scalp."
Wallie touched his hurt eye. "A donnybrook."
Mike felt gingerly the cocoon of bandages around his
head. Wallie held out a paperback. "They didn't shave
your whole head. Just a bitsy bit enough to sew you up."
Mike read the book title *Of Mice and Men*.
Terry pulled up a chair and sat down. "You were a little
bit, you know, delirious. But they sedated you. Brant, you
snore."
Mike tried to grin. "How do you know, Munday?"
"Stopped in a couple of times and you were corking off.
Now listen, we're arranging something while you're still
of public interest—a press interview. You and a lot of us
were brutalized by agents of reaction."
The nurse looked at her wristwatch. "We need our rest.
Five minutes."
Wallie touched his hurt eye again. "There's a goddam
script."

"Shut up, Wallie. We must use what we have. The city is friendly to us, and we're socking it to them."

Mike stared at Terry. How do you like this broad—all practical politics: so damn earnest, so damn dedicated. Neglecting herself. Attractive, even without too much makeup, but so animated the way she gestured and explained to him that he was a union celebrity, a working class hero, and how he was to talk to the reporters. A cast iron dame; he'd hate to have a hard-on for her. These serious, smart broads, you could never figure them out—how they'd react—as likely to offer to explain Lenin to you as give you a blow job; no never could figure them.

She was talking—yakky, yakky.

"So, Brant, that's the way to play it; why we were picketing, and why we were jumped. Give 'em the whole magillah."

"Huh?" He hadn't been listening to a damn thing. He was still, in some whacked out way, just come out of battle fire and feeling, feeling the desperate situation of a wound carried painfully and fearfully. Did Davey make it? Taxi . . . the rest of the joes? He touched his shoulder, then remembered it was his head this time.

"Munday, I'll say what I feel. Right now I sure feel lousy."

Her mouth bent in a smile, and she patted his chest. "Get well. We have a lot of talking to do. Jamie Ward wants to talk to you. We, he feels, you're an asset to the local."

"Golly gee," he said indifferently in mocking tones.

Wallie winked again and made the O sign with a thumb and forefinger. "It isn't often there is anyone with a head as hard as yours to get busted for Local 104 DWU."

The nurse was back; her satisfaction in her duties, Mike felt, showed too many teeth. On a tray she carried a milky white drink with a glass tube in it.

"We are getting a bit better, aren't we? But we mustn't have too much excitement." She handed him the glass, and he sucked up some bland liquid, chalky and thick.

Terry swung a handbag strap over one shoulder. "I have to go, Brant. Be in touch. We're working to get you injury compensation."

He felt her strong, firm hand grab his, and she was gone. The nurse adjusted a pillow, looked at her watch. "No more visitors. I have to give the patient an alcohol rub and a temperature reading. Two minutes more and your visitors will have to leave."

When she was gone, Wallie moved into the chair. "I've got an alcohol rub for you, soldier."

He held out a pint of Old Forester. "Real posh stuff. Not rotgut from skid row."

Mike took a swallow, felt it warm and move about; it seemed to soothe the slowly bouncing ball inside his head.

"Changed your brand . . . "

"Gift. Jamie Ward. Oh they're courting us." He sang:

> Sometimes I have a nickel,
> Sometimes I have a dime.
> Sometimes I have ten dollars,
> To buy Maggie wine.

"Who's courting us?"

"The lefties. They've used us. You really, and oh the helots have plans. You'll come over fine on the television cameras. A fucking media hero, that's what you are, you bastard, an embattled worker fighting off every man's enemies, and a war hero. I've a newspaper with your mug in it."

Mike took another sip of the whiskey. Wallie handed over a sheet torn from the *Examiner*. Sure enough, there he was, the goddam dope, a smudgy coarse grain photograph of him fighting off a whole mess of goons and swinging his fists—a kind of goony smile on his kisser, like he was doing good on bowling night.

"Want it for your scrapbook?"

Mike shook his head. "What's all this malarkey about being used?"

"The comrades, amigo, have been organizing the West Coast for years. They've done pretty good on the water-fronts. They need somebody to take the punches, to take the socks on the jaw, all for the good of the working man—the union rank and file, of course, Local 104 DWU."

"Well I am a card carrying DWU."

"Sure you are, soldier; give me back the bottle. You're in no condition to get looped. Wow, I am. Here's a bit of advice from an old Wobbly that had his eyes open to dues paying organizations and politics before you were born. No standing still, see? The plan is to move in, organize the stoop labor, the short-hoe people, ginzos and wet-backs that pick the crops and trim the vines."

"Hell, should have done it long ago."

"Oh yeah? Once they busted the heads of the Okies in the Dust Bowl days; now the ranchers and vineyard bosses have become even stronger. They control the sheriffs, own the local courts, and have this storm troop-er field and farm organization, private sluggers with dep-uty badges."

"I've worked crops—it's murder on your back."

"What do you plan, Mike?"

"Get out of here—try and get a job on a fishing boat. Or maybe now I'm in the papers, on TV, I'll get back work-ing a crane or a fork lift."

"Jamie and Terry have plans for you. A couple of frig-ging Machiavellis."

"Who?"

"Set you up around union meetings . . . write speeches for you to make. Maybe Terry will take you into the kip."

Mike grimaced, winced at the pain in his ribs. "I wouldn't fuck her for time-and-a-half with overtime."

He felt vindictive, put upon. The dame had riled him in

some subtle way. She wasn't the dream girl of his fantasy, not a female image in the manner of Miss Lambkins, not at all like the worked over sketch, the secret desire, the perfect pattern of his desires: Jesus, I'm thinking like a goddam soap opera. He picked up the paperback *Of Mice and Men*.

"I read it in the army hospital. A lot of bleeding heart hogwash, but the ranch and farm stuff was real."

"I'll bring you something else to read. But you're getting out. You want my advice: Get as far away as you can from this port. Union politics is not for everybody. Oh you're no dope—you got a brain behind your dial, but you're a puking innocent."

"Don't bet on it. I've seen something of unions; we'd all be up shit crick with no paddle if the unions were weak kneed and polite. But I don't go much for the lefties' way of yelping and yelling fascist and pointing up corporation dirty ways." He propped himself up on his elbow in the bed. "Give me another snort." He drank. He felt light in the head, and gabby. "No, the way, Wallie, to get things done is to be *like* the capitalists. Use their savvy, their skill in handling the newspapers, taking on the law. They have this public relation gimmick and use it right."

"If you can't lick 'em, join 'em?"

"Just use their own methods against them. Study how they get results. Beat them with their own weapons. Organize the hell out of them for the workers' benefit so it's an equal share, for them, for us. See?"

"You're a cheap drunk, soldier. Three swallows and you're the straw boss of the whole fucking show?"

"Yeah." He sank back on the pillow, sweating. His heart was thumping away like a fresh caught trout out of water, his head aching worse than ever. "When I was hungry, drag ass broke, it came to me—what's power? Huh? Power is using money."

"That's news."

"Be seeing you, Wallie. I'm bushed."

"Power is using money? I'll carve it on stone."

Wallie put away the bottle and adjusted the sheet and blanket around Mike's chest. "What you need, mister, is a hunk of ass, something solid, cozy in the hay with you. Nothing like it to give a man a feeling the whole shooting match is all worthwhile. Unless, like me at my age, it's finding a gutsy bit of reading."

April 19, 1952

Dear Ma,

Don't you go paying too much attention to that newspaper clipping, the one the nosy Mrs. Malvenk sent you. Just because she was once our next door neighbor, and now lives up in San Rafael out here gives her no excuse to upset you. It was nothing much, just happened to be in this picketing scene and they took my picture, or pitchur, like Moz used to say when a baby.

I'm fine, believe me, a little knock on the noggin was nothing compared to the clobbering I used to collect playing high-school football. I'm out and about, eating good, taking fine care of myself. I have this job as a checker on a pier. I mean the unions along the coast are real strong. I'm with the Drovers and Wheelmen, the DWU, and they have clout and are beginning to try and organize the migratorys and the vineyard hands. Pa, if he were alive, the old man would have liked our style of action. Remember how he used to talk about the old days of Gompers, Tobin, and John L. Lewis and the United Mine Workers and hope the rubber workers would have that strength, only they never did. I live at a nice place, well, fairly nice. Once I get settled to what direction I'm going, I'll see about more room. I share space with this crazy old coot, no teeth, a rummy, but good to talk to. He's either the biggest liar ever or he's been around and, as Pa used to say, had "got his lumps." He read a lot of books in the clink as an IWW.

I really think the old boy—his name is Wallie Smith—is whacked out—all those years of nothing but reading in stir. But he's funny, always jigging, like the St. Vitus dance Aunt Maude's girl Nancy used to have. He's always tap dancing and reciting crazy poems. He says the DWU has plans for me. They like my style. Well I've come round to thinking, Ma, that the way unions are moving, they are the thing for me. I'm no dummy; you never raised no dumb bunny. In the army intelligent tests I did okay, and I'm seeing how the rank and file are steered for their own good, how bargaining strategy and power plays are really done.

Poor Pa with his talk of Eugene Debs and the steel workers' strikes at Pittsburgh and Gary, the Pullman strikes, the trouble in the Paterson silk mills; that's all so much junk from the past. Now unions are real big with solid planning and meetings. They don't bring in Federal troops no more, or pimply kids in the state militia. It's big business; only the creeps think everything in unions in the past was better, like hell—I'd like to see the International General president in a pressed suit, smoking a dollar cigar. We have brains now, running things in the locals. I feel someday we'll be using methods like General Motors or U.S. Steel. Scientific power with press agents like for movies and cigarette brands on a really big scale.

It's a kooky country for what Wallie calls the Big Sell for dog meat and cornflakes and shit like that, sold through Madison Avenue. And I feel the image of unions can be made to shine like your kitchen on a weekend when we kids had to walk on newspapers you laid on the floor.

How are you? Sorry I got carried away in the pier riot; maybe they dislodged my brains in that army hospital (that's a joke, Ma) and I'm off to cloud cuckoo-land. Don't work too hard as a nurse in that dinky hospital. Someday I'll come out to unionize all hospital workers, and you can say "that's my son the doctor tamer." How is Moz? Still a pool hustler working his way through law school? Tell him that's the great racket; the damn lawyers are like sharks, living it up, screwing the clients. It's time the working stiff had better legal help on his level. You tell Moz I'll beat his tail off if he doesn't finish that law course

to pass the bar exams. He can live on his skill with a bil-
liard cue only so long, then somebody he's promoted into
a game with a little side bet will conk him with one.

I'm observing and watching and learning. Frisco (they
hate you to call it that) is an exciting burg. I'm attending
classes nights in the Labor School. Notice how I'm writing better and even know a little of what grammar is—
things I should have learned in high school but sluffed off.

Took a girl to a union dinner for some big muck-a-
muck in the Marine Cooks and Stewards Association at
the Sir Francis Drake Hotel and she said I had to learn to
be couth. Terry Munday is all right but she's all het up
about the class war and the brotherly radicals who ache
for the rights of the guy in the street, which is a crock of
shit. We got to talking of the fake trials in Russia and
screwing Joe Stalin, and she said they weren't rigged trials. I got drunk, just a bit sloshed—no fall-down-drunk
stunt. Don't you worry, Ma, I can handle the sauce—and
so we yelled at each other . . . real yelling, and she left
in a huff, and I sat in the park and cooled off. I haven't
seen her since, and don't want to. I mean, I don't go
around knocking women as just for home and kids, but
when they are lefties, they swallow whole anything the
Ruskkies send out. I feel it's like the horse manure Lind-
bergh used to put out about the Jews and the power of the
German air force, and how they would win. Hell, Ma, I'm
my own man, and I listen and I look, as the old old railroad sign at the crossing past our house used to say—*look
and listen*—but I don't rush to no new action without a
lot of thinking it out.

I miss you. I always do. But for Moz I never did cotton
too much to the other kids. They were either too old or
too busy doing their own thing. I think I'm maturing;
hell, at twenty-four I should be. Now I'm out of the war,
meeting new people in the middle of the fracas to unionize the whole West. I'm learning to think about more than
girls or sports or just having a good time. I want you to believe that, Ma. I've changed.

Maybe you could come out here to see for yourself.
They need trained nurses, and the ripoff of the fancy doc-

tors of the Nob Hill crowd is something. If you like sunshine there is L.A., a fink town, run by a newspaper they say—the newspaper, it got blown up in 1910 by some steel union boys. There are real orange trees with real oranges. I like Frisco better. It's more like a real town. L.A., as Fred Allen said the other night, is a good place to live if you're an orange. Remember how you used to give me half an orange to suck when I took medicine . . . and rub my chest with goose grease and tie it up with a flannel cloth. Well, my chest is fine, my shoulder is fine, my head is fine, and all of your wandering boy is fine. If all goes well, maybe I'll hustle home for Xmas and beat Moz in arm wrassling.

> Always with lots of affection,
> your loving son,
> **MIKE**

CHAPTER 6

Mike wrote to his mother once a month—at least he tried to make it every month. He felt it was the only tie to his past that he wanted to keep tight and warm—a sort of continuity of generations. It was true he related very little to his brothers and sisters, but for Moz—Martin Brant, future attorney at law. Perhaps, he figured, maybe because they shared the same bed in the little house as kids. Moz was two years younger and the last of the children Ma had. The others were nebulous to Mike; Jacob who had been lost in an explosion of a Greek oil tanker off the Cape of Good Hope; Willie who was in Alaska working diesel caterpillars as an earth moving contractor, married to a half-Indian dame, a big spender who kept him in debt; Netta who had married a drunk and ran a fried chicken stand in Florida.

Then there was whacked out Herbie up at Attica—ten to fifteen—for interstate transport of a stolen car with

manslaughter attached, and Bobbie doing well in England
with a string of hat shops.

And little gravestones, too, at Drood Memorial Park, of
those kids who didn't make it: whooping cough, TB, and
a mysterious drowning of Margo, an older sister, maybe
murdered up at Lake George.

Yes, Ma was the only one that counted, and if Moz
didn't get deep-sixed hustling a pigeon over a rack of
balls . . . the kid, he was twenty-two, would make it
bigger than any of them. Moz, he had the moxie and the
grace of a Gene Kelly with his walk and his way with the
broads, Mike thought. Maybe I'm as smart, but I lack the
education.

After Mike had mailed the letter and come back to
Minnie Rothschild's Hostel, he sat smoking his pipe. He
had given up cigarettes a week ago, and it was hard getting used to a pipe but he persisted. He did have his old
man's stubborn streak. So here he was sitting on the cot
in a small, sleazy room, drinking Wallie's booze; the letter to Ma had been a kind of cleaning process, a thinking
out of his situation. He was no dummy about his setup.
He knew the left wingers had used him, the riot had been
planned, but it had been for a good cause, even at the cost
of six stitches. His part had attracted attention, it had focused, Terry Munday had said, on the conditions of Franco's Spain and white South Africa's racial attitudes. Not
that he was crazy over the Negros, but for a buddy like
Taxi in Korea. In high school there had been jigs and
boogs, and if you screwed a high yellow you told yourself
it was for a change of luck. There was a load of prejudices
you grew up with: Like when the micks, they called you
a polack and asked "How do you break a polack's nose?
You hit him on the elbow ha ha, when he has a finger up
a nostril."

No, he saw the workers differently now. They were all
on one side of the wall: micks, hebs, burrheads, hunkies

or swenskis, mackeral snappers, rednecks, peckerwoods or mud sills.

On the other side of the wall were the tony folks: the bosses, foremen, the big shot lawyers, the shysters, the jaundice-eyed judges ready to toss you the book if you didn't belong to their country club; the board of directors, trustees, the vice presidents with the gold keys to the crapper; (Jesus, I owe Wallie a fresh fifth) the college grads with their Phi Beta Kappa keys on thin gold chains; they're on the other side of the wall too—and the crumbums who could order wine by French names, and all those contingents of long-legged cunts in their summer dresses, in sexy lace shorts knocking a tennis ball's brains out.

(I'm getting drunk—I've got to lie down.)

All that delicious upper class ass . . . he had actually seen them as a caddy at Fairlake Country Club. He had even knocked up a society chick from Berkeley when on leave from Fort Ord—he looked real classy in his tight-tailored army threads, a top sergeant, six foot two, a good head of brownish blond hair and all his teeth in a row like piano keys. Jesus, those nights at the Fairmont Hotel with Miss Society—it taking all his dough won at poker, and pawning his camera, and his wristwatch presented to "The High School State Champions" on the football field.

(He killed the fifth, took off his shoes.)

Only it turned out he wasn't the only one banging that society quiff. Miss Society had decided to blame it on an Oakland stockbroker who had a weekend place in Carmel for a shackup; and so shaking her fine high class ass, she had left Mike to take her place among the horse shows, pedigreed dog turds and Republicans. He had shipped out a week later, on orders cut to get some good sergeants to Korea, as the United Nations fuckup of a police action was going badly.

(I'm drunk.)

He tried to knock out the pipe into an abalone shell he had picked up at Fisherman's Wharf; discovered he had a beauty of a hard-on. You never get over thinking, Davey used to say, when it was fine and good and satisfactory, something so special in pussy.

If he weren't a bit drunk he could take his erection down the line, get his ashes hauled at Daisy's place: good laughing girls there on high heels— *so* high—girls mostly-out-of-work cannery hands or beginner browns tired of being waitresses. But hell, after the just-fading memory of Miss Society and all that class stupping at that room service hotel, even if *so* long past, no, no ten dollar trick in stale bedding.

Wallie came in carrying a Safeway supermarket bag, did a little dance step and patted Mike's shoulder.

"Don't be sitting there like Rodin's Constipated Thinker pressing for a crap. Get your best duds on; there's that shindig tonight for Walter Reuther. Remember? He's getting the Amalgamated Meat Cutters and Packing House Workers Award . . . good booze, friendly women."

"I'm in no mood."

"Come on, you're down to make a little speech."

"No shape. I had a little drinkee."

"Yeah, I can see that, but Terry set this up."

"Did she?"

"Look, soldier, she's sorry about that mean mouthing in the hotel, and she's getting to like you. She said that wasn't easy. You lack political savvy, she said."

"Going to set me up again as a patsy? Get my teeth knocked out?"

Wallie took from the paper bag an electric hot plate, six cans of baked beans, four of soup, a loaf of French sourdough bread, two cakes of Palmolive.

"We'll be living like an old married couple now I mooched this hot plate."

"Liberated it, I'd guess, Wallie."

"Well it was doing no good in a closet at the Y. I was working as a swamper there, mopping up the halls and there it was, forgotten, neglected. Remember Huck Finn liberating watermelons and corn on the cob?"

"I never read Huck Finn."

"No shit, never? I was in solitary up at Q, and I had this paperback copy of ol' Huck, and the trustee, Wendell Ford, an old United Mine worker, he gave me this flashlight to scare off the rats; and I tell you, Mike, I never had a better time in stir, reading ol' Huck. God, what I'd give today to find anything as balls busting to read . . . I washed your shirt at the machine down in the cellar. So I'll make some coffee, shine your shoes—we're off tonight to the ball, Cinderella."

"You're crazy, Wallie, you know that?"

"Took you a long time, soldier, to find out."

"Let me sleep a couple hours."

That was the trouble, Mike decided, about a clean old man; he was always wringing out your clothes after a trip to a washing machine, just like a goddam overattentive wife.

It was a hefty printed program of attending union brass, handed to Mike at the Frémont Hotel ballroom. Between conventions the big labor unions held honorary dinners like this. This year's honored guest was the Puskin (Eli James) the gum-chewing, German-Greek ex-coal miner who headed the International. With him was Soren Verner, of the LBO (Labor Brotherhood Organization) and the heads of several independent groups like the Dock and Shore Brotherhood; the Association of the Original Locomotive Engineers and Firemen (now the Air and Land Transport Association, a majority of its member pilots, jet mechanics, field crews of airlines); and the Allied Theatre Guilds, which covered certain sections of talent in film and radio and television, including dancers, designers, announcers, actors and news anchor people.

The long rows of tables were gay with bunting of the

various union groups—slogans and logos of the DWU, the LBO, the WNUSA hung from paneled walls. Like Wallie said: "Battle flags in old castles I once saw pictures of."

Many of the people were in evening attire: men in black tie, their necks irked by constraining collars. Some of the women adopted better and wore shoulder-revealing gowns. Those who were not in formal evening attire, Mike noticed, were shunted clear to the side. Unions were no longer run by louts in caps, that was clear. A felicity of pleased expression was expressed on many faces.

"What the hell are you doing here, Wallie, and me?"

"Getting a big feed, and as for you, the Puskin wants to meet you."

Christ, Mike felt panic, awe, and a sense, too, of questioning, why are they making such a fuss over me? . . . a patsy, as Wallie thinks. Or maybe it's true as that bitch Terry Munday puts it: I've got something. Ma used to say I had a good head on me, and I've learned by observing. Only Terry Munday, she made me sound like I was a new toy wagon, with fresh red paint on it.

Wallie looked at their admission tickets and led him off to the right where some rougher types were drinking whiskey out of big tumblers, and waiters were setting drinks down with a hint of contempt for people not in formal evening attire.

Mike sat down in an atmosphere dominated by cold cigar odors, spilled drinks, a table of eight jolly men and women living it up . . . a table far from the raised platform holding the long table of big shots with its flowers and extra wine glasses. Impressive people up there: big and bulky, or thin and foxy-looking. Even a few women. Terry was in a pale yellow gown; good shoulders Mike had to admit, for such a cold bitch—boobs well hung, an orchid pinned to her right tit. And just two-three places on the right from her the boss, heading the International

WNUSA and its new affiliate, the DWU. The Puskin had a hard face, a fringe of reddish hair, eyes blue as glacier ice, and the jaw of a bulldog. He was chewing gum since he gave up tobacco.

There was Jamie Ward up there chewing the Puskin's ear—Jamie in too tight a starched shirt sitting with the trustees of the locals of the coastal unions . . . all the fat boys looking, said Wallie, sipping whiskey, looking like the parents of Porky Pig . . . "That would be the Meat Cutters on the left," he whispered. "You could get two dollars a pound for them, butchered out into fat, red, prime cuts."

Boisterous tranquillity still held most tables.

After a hotel whiskey in a glass, mostly ice, and weak, cheap whiskey at that, Mike noticed there was a band playing dated Irving Berlin. Except for the Musicians Union, the labor organization members weren't too crazy for the newer Elvis stuff or the prancing and wailing that the kids were jiving to.

On the platform a man with a paunch and serious features, his thick eyeglasses reflecting overhead lights, was making a speech, reading it from sheets of paper, feeding his text directly into a microphone. It sounded to Mike, over the din of glasses, the drinking and eating of the first course of fine large shrimp and very good crisp rolls, that the speaker was explaining open-end grievance proceeding of some rebel local and a federal investigation of a controversial health pension plan. No one seemed to be paying much attention to the speech—laughing, talking, the tone turning raucous, people visiting each other's tables, all with much touching of shoulders, slapping of backs. "Organizers mostly," Wallie said, "of trip hammers, brewing, distilling and textiles, and the flashier—the mob-connected—oh *yeah.*"

The speaker finished, there was little applause, and the orchestra in red hussar jackets began to pace *Star Dust* for dancing. Several couples got up to dance, and waiters served salads.

Mike saw Wallie filling his pockets with salted nuts from a bowl, while singing softly to himself *As Time Goes By*. On Mike's right, a plump lady, dress and hair very red, a large handsome nose, gave him an elbow in the side—a solid nudge. "You WNUSA?"

"No, DWU."

"You should wear your button, Mr.?"

"Brant. I shoulda. . . . "

"I'm Nell Goldrose, head of Hairdressers Cosmetics Local 105 . . . a gala tonight, eh?"

"Looks it."

A waiter set before him a dish of half a chicken not too well plucked free of its pin feathers. The waiter dripped some brown sauce on it.

"Never mind the sauce." (Too late.)

"It's *Sauce du Perigord*." (No "Sir" added.)

"Up yours."

Nell Goldrose said, "Class, I always feel class counts in hair health. The affluent parvenus, they don't understand that."

As a wine waiter appeared, she covered her wine glass with a hand on which two gems glistened. "No thank you, no wine, I'm acid, wine doesn't agree with me. Flatulence . . . you an organizer, Brant?"

"Just now I'm a dock checker."

"Yes, well, San Francisco is such a romantic port of call. It's very democratic, isn't it?"

Mike took a chew of the tasteless chicken; the *Sauce du Perigord* hadn't helped.

Nell Goldrose said, "Never eat in hotels if you can avoid it. It's all computer controlled merde."

The red and gold menu listed *Delice glace a la creme de noix* (translation under the text: ice cream and walnut liqueur). Wallie was slipping some dessert spoons and forks into a jacket pocket. Mike shook his head when the old man picked up a salt shaker.

"Stick to ashtrays, Wallie."

"They allow for this, soldier. It's all on the tab."

Mike was feeling cheerful; he had to get out more, not sit in his room. The small shaved area of his head where the stitches had been put in was neatly covered by hair combed just so. He saw his reflection in the shiny coffee pot set before them. Not a bad face; you could call it handsome if you didn't want Clark Gable. Ma had a good, smooth skin color. "Early American farmyard," she used to call her complexion. Add Pa's high, polack cheekbones (maybe a touch of Magyar invasions) to all that, and I'll do. (You'd never know I'm drinking too much to-day . . . how many hotel whiskeys in me by now? Who's counting?)

The air was thick with cigar smoke, the musk of women's perfume, and antiperspirants on their moist skins, was warming up as they ate. The men were a bit more gamy ("The silent fart is on the wing," Wallie said.). More couples were dancing, and the ice cream was melting, and the coffee was weaker. Wallie took to singing to himself, then nearly falling from his chair. The people at tables were beginning to feel overfed and some refused a second dessert. But the trays of little cakes with union labels done in colored icing held the attention of those still sober. The wine glasses stood neglected, partly filled, while Scotch, rye and martinis were ordered from the bar. The union locals were picking up the tab.

Mike accepted a cigar from one of Jamie Ward's boys passing them out from a redwood box. "Compliments of Dockside and Shore Local 503. Only one each, you muzzlers. Jus' one."

Mike fingered the cigar, pushing off its cellophane wrapper but didn't light it. His confidence was disintegrating—he sat with a petulant expression, brooding.

Nell Goldrose had been talking—her mouth close to his ear—even through a speech by a woman with too long a nose and heavy upper arms—arms like turkey thighs,

Mike decided. The woman had talked of transitory class solidarity plans—and pressed for a political slush fund of seventy-five cents a month per union member. When there was no applause from the guests she added, "Voluntary pledges, of course."

Nell Goldrose said, "Une génération, des perdues . . . you can't get good girls to train as cosmetic sales people or hair colorers. Never call it hair dye, I keep telling them. But unless you want niggrah chicks, the white bitches would rather work the lobbies of the hotels for johns . . . I mean I've nothing agin niggrahs but with their oversexed home life you never know—infections I mean, they could pass on to the clients."

Mike was aware of a hand on his shoulder. He half turned to find Terry Munday was looking down on him. She didn't appear quarrelsome. The evening had melted her usual austerity.

"Hello, Brant. Having fun?"

"Up till now."

She dug her fingers into one of his shoulders. "You still sore over our argument?"

"No, I'm not sore."

CHAPTER 7

Later, he tried to figure it out. What started here? A dance? There was music, some tune he remembered from an old Cagney film. Jesus, I'll knock her back on her heels—surprise her.

"Miss Munday, you dance?"

"Pretty good." She lifted one eyebrow as if to doubt his question.

"Pretty good?"

"For me, mister."

The tune, he had the name of it. . . *Strawberry Blond*? . . . a corny, happy nostalgia movie with gaudy beer saloons, fist fights, high button shoes, wasp waists, all like it never was Ma had said. But nice, very nice, even if what could a girl like Olivia see in a mug like Cagney played.

"I'm waiting, Mr. Brant."

Mike stood up and took her arm as they walked around people moving about, to dance, to go to the *gents* and *la-*

dies, to visit other tables. The dinner was becoming un-buttoned. Terry said, "This Walter Reuther is some guy. I mean he stands out among the big shots and roughnecks in the locals."

"I didn't notice. Which one is he?"

"Two places past the Puskin on the left." She blinked her eyes. "God, those cigars can kill when they get wet."

The smoke was thick, the heated air, gamy.

Reuther looked, Mike thought, a bit stiff, but pleasant, a guy who had learned how to mix, how to make it with any kind of people. No apprehension about him—or if any, he hid it in public.

"He's honest and direct, and he runs a tight ship."

"I thought he was autos." It wasn't much of a joke but he had to put this dame down a bit.

"Oh shut up and dance," she said. They were moving in among the embracing couples, and Mike's dancing felt he was doing it right—head back, spine limber, the way he and Moz had practiced dance steps and attended high school dances. One summer as waiters in Atlantic City they worked their way through all the new dance steps, came back as experts to the club, *The Lost Cherry,* the gang on River Street had started in Chink Connor's cellar.

Terry Munday danced nearly as well as he did. No awkward turns, she had that grace, that knowing swing of hips and arms; she put her feet down right, swung her legs in time. Not just the Arthur Murray klotz stuff for stiffs but all of her really danced. Was this the dock lefty or her twin sister? He felt her warmth, picked up the way she followed as he led in more intricate movements—a kind of test he put her through, with a lift of a heel, a pointing of a toe, an ass wag, the two of them, his thigh to her thigh.

"You're good," she said head against his cheek. He was dominating her—she breathing a little, winded.

"You've got it yourself."

"Um um," she just nodded. What the hell had he been

scared of? This wasn't the hard-shell Munday, the union
hot shot, the tough-tittie organizer. She was just a broad,
and he knew broads. He pressed closer. She was built as
Moz used to say of a well stacked babe, like a brick out-
house. She was human after all. A girl, like any girl.
Maybe a bit old for him—say twenty-eight, even thirty.
But careful or you'll find yourself getting the hots for this
bimbo, and what you don't need, Mikoloj Brandicki, is a
dominating bitch. This Munday has all the earmarks of a
balls breaker, a man eater. Still it is a challenge.

"After this dance I want to take you to meet the Puskin."

He swirled her around, a perfect union of two dancing
bodies knowing their stuff. He was almost an adolescent
again, dominating an evening at *The Lost Cherry Club.*

"You mean, Miss Munday, The Eli James Puskin!"

"Stop clowning, you bastard. You never know what's
good for you."

He stared into her half-closed deep-blue eyes. No sense
of humor, he thought. Serious all the time, smart; knows
the ropes, but not a million laughs. Very sure of himself
now, he settled down to enjoy the rest of the dance; he
hadn't been in emotionally sexual action for some time;
a nice armful, a good clean smell of something that reminded him of apples stored in a dry attic.

The Puskin was certainly impressive. When Mike followed Terry to the big table, the man gave a hard shake of
Mike's hand. Not a fat man, the Puskin—seemed tall, so
you felt power in him, and also a sly cunning. As a journalist had written, "There was the slyness of a hundred
generations of Greek peasant in the Puskin actions of
hungry field people who had found the city streets hard
to press living from and had used their cunning to survive

"You're the young fella got clobbered?"

Mike inclined his head to show the shaved area and the
red welts of the stitches on his head. The Puskin admired
the healing wound.

"Well, Brant, we've all taken it in the past, and also

given it back with interest. You'll do fine, fella, just
fine."

"I try, and. . . "

But Mike was aware he was being pushed aside by a
discreet hand on his elbow, being steered away. Jamie
Ward filled the gap, presenting an old man with bushy-
white eyebrows like caterpillars.

Jamie said, "Chief, this is Harry Gottlieb. One of the
real old-timers. . . wrote for Daniel DeLeon's paper *The
People* in 1891, a charter member of the International
Brotherhood of The Dray and Street Union in 1899."

"Welcome, Gottlieb. It's folk like you that planted the
seeds that brought labor a harvest."

"He's a bit deaf, Chief, so. . . "

"I said it's folk like you. . . "

"I can hear. Glad to shake your hand, Mr. Puskin. I remember the day John L. Lewis, when he fought the an-
thracite operators, and all the United Mine workers getting killed like flies by the scabs, so this day the Iron and
Coal police they. . . "

"Interesting, damn interesting, Gottlieb. . . we'll talk
later, eh? Jamie, get him some cigars."

"Big Bill Haywood, he once. . . "

As Terry led him away Mike said: "Quick but sweet."

"Don't be getting cynical, Brant. He'll remember you.
Now get me a big drink. I've had two and don't feel a
thing."

"You a lush?"

"No, I don't drink as a rule, except for special events
like this. You know, you're not such a shit after all."

"You know how to flatter a guy. I'll buy you two drinks
for that." (It was the line he handed out at *The Lost Cherry Club*.)

An hour and a half later he had helped her out of her
gown, seen her naked on the bed, puzzled but assertive at
this turn of events, waiting for his direct sexual atten-

tion. It was not that Mike was surprised at this private drama; the whole evening was cockeyed. Even if he had never had trouble getting into a girl's pants without too much lamentation and protest, it was just he was surprised this was happening with a woman like Terry Munday. True, sure they were both a bit whacked out on drink, and they had been maudlin and accusing each other of things all the way to Terry's place, of being opposite types, "oil and water," Terry had insisted.

Two rooms, two stories up, she lived in a bay-windowed, narrow house top of a hill. . . . Talk at first how much they resented each other and what shitheads they thought the other was. . . laughing too, Mike remembered, and feeling their liquor. . . but then kissing, eating noses in the cab, grabbing each other here and there . . . all the time a quickening cadence of their desires, and she inviting him up for one for the road.

Then, in the lamp light looking at each other, he knew and she knew that they had come to fuck. And more than that, just something else between them was deeper. But just what Mike didn't know. The velocity of the way everything was happening was exciting. Why he was attracted more than ordinarily to a woman taking off her clothes he didn't try to figure out. He shucked his pants and unbuttoned his shirt. Terry had a hell of a build . . . once you saw her jaybird naked. The body was long and well hipped; no boy shape out of *Vogue* here. And when he held her skin to skin and rubbed her belly and her tits, she moaned: "Oh hell, oh hell, Mike."

"Oh hell what?"

"You're a mean bastard . . . why, why?"

"Why what?"

"Why do I want you . . . gotta have you?"

She put her hands between his legs, cupped his balls— set a moment of fear in him, but already he was aroused so much that if she had said no, no, not with you, he knew he couldn't have moved off, gotten off the straddle of her in this bed, aware as he was they were as yet antagonists and deprecators.

She must have read his mind, he figured, for she said, "Christ, it's you," and she pulled him down over her and they were at it. And the whole moment assumed for him a gratification of dominating her, of having her under him, of entering almost as kind of a punishment of her pride . . . a humiliation of her former cold professional approach as an organizer, of her maybe seeing him a tramp worker, somebody to use. But as he thrust into her, and she lifted her ass, moved her hips in slow motion to function as part of this so natural process for both of them, he knew he was obsessed with her. It was clear too he could see on her open mouth, lips wet, the stare of her desire-glazed eyes that they were full partners in equal rights to this passion that had overtaken them.

The defenseless moaning sound reached him—and then as they both felt the rise of the reciprocal sexual moment, near climax, she sank her teeth into her lower lip and arched her back to its final bow. They came, they quivered, he related fully to their giant shudder that seemed to separate flesh from bone. Her orgasm was not one prolonged sensation but rather like little leaps of sensation that ran from cunt to stomach to fingertips and moved her body in spasms as her naked heels acted as spurs stabbing the bed.

The doubt in Mike had drained away, the idea of punishment, of domination, was gone. She was voiceless under him; they could hear their efforts of breathing, at first struggling for air, then calming, and then they lay side by side, for the moment sated, in the small bedroom on the too narrow bed, the light from the night table lamp just gilding their bodies, illuminating a section of wallpaper (roses), a framed photograph of girls picking oranges— they on ladders, a mountain in the background.

On the night table Mike's vision registered a bottle of

aspirin, an ashtray lettered *Pine Inn, Carmel,* an electric clock with a blue plastic body and a moving red minute hand. Mike watched it race around the dial: *Time, time, you old gypsy man*—he had recited that poem in the fourth grade.

He felt Terry's hand grasp his elbow, grip arduously—possessively?

"Who would have thought . . . "

She was still a bit short of breath but there was a tenderness in her voice he had never heard before.

"Not me, honey, not me." He didn't say it mean, he just said it naturally as the tail of this inevitable sequence of events. "I'd as soon, Terry, have kicked your ass as kiss it now . . . that is, when the evening started. Shows you the effects of booze."

"I wasn't that drunk, Mike. No, I just was, well like I was standing to one side and watching myself go along with what was happening . . . and you?"

He put his arm around her, kissed her cheek. "These things happen, honey. It's any way you want it now. A one night stand, or we can put a floor under it."

"That easy for you? Women have spoiled you, Mike. I can see that."

He grunted, flexed his legs, nuzzled her cheeks. "Maybe I'm worth spoiling. I don't make any claims. Like the song says, doing what comes naturally. I've got no fancy words."

She tossed herself against him. "Let's stop the act. You're right for me. I'm right for you. I am, I am, aren't I?"

He had a vague idea the mind in love does not act—it conditions the action—but he could not express it. He kissed her mouth, holding her for some time; he kissed her neck, shoulder, mouthed a fine tit, pressed his head between her breasts. She explored his body, lips, hands, making discoveries, a lightly tingling sensation—putting a pressure here and there.

He said, his voice half muffled against the warmth of
her skin against his mouth, "We'll find out how right we
are for each other. It's come all so quick. . . me, you
. . . this making it like this. So?"

She laughed. "All I need to know is what do you like
for breakfast?"

All the time she had been handling his dong, and he
was aroused again. So they clung together with even a
stronger drive, an urge deeper than before. But at a slower
more controlled pace. There was in Mike the tiny
thought. Am I falling in love with this bimbo, is this one
of those things where you go gaga, cross-eyed with love,
with loving? But he didn't take that thought too far for
they were engaged, fully, physically. He was feeling su-
perb sensations, not new: he had been at this since four-
teen. But feeling them deeper—even if this wasn't the
dream princess of his fantasy built on the foundation of
Miss Lambkins, high school art teacher, no—this was
reality—certainly a lover squirming sweatily under him.
So alive, earnest, and a great tenderness came over him,
even if perhaps against his will. It was no time to analyze.
Just to be, yes, soldier, to feel stronger, react passionately,
and let all problems, dilemmas, doubts go hang.

Later they slept soundly in each other's arms on the
too narrow bed, and the last thing Terry whispered in a
husky voice was, "We'll have to get a bigger bed, a much
bigger bed."

Mike awoke an hour before dawn, and he could not ori-
ent himself. Where the hell was he, and what was he?
Was he eight-years-old and the factory whistles were
blowing, announcing the end of the world? Had Moz wet
the bed again, the damn little bastard, the stinker too
lazy to get up to pee in the cold john . . . no it was not
Moz's tepid, wet piss. It was a warm, naked woman. She
had that deep, relaxed breathing of someone who had
been well taken care of and was in sleep or in her body re-

membering and enjoying what had been happening. The hash and gash scene, but there was no smell of pot. And it wasn't the factory whistles of a New Jersey mill town, but the hoot of ships in the San Francisco Bay moving past buoys and signaling the Oakland ferries to watch their step. He was a couple thousand miles from home, and Ma wouldn't come and wake him for school and hang the damp sheet out on the line before she put it into the washtub.

He felt a stranger in a stranger place, a wanderer with no roots seeking the bodies of women to test himself in the bullshit of macho. The woman: Look at her, he thought. She feels sure of me, she has snapped her snatch like a bear trap around me. No . . . be fair—you know what about her? Terry Munday. Not bad, not bad at all. I feel good with her. I admit it. I feel a kind of protection in her not being a kid. Hell, at my age—she's maybe five, six years older. Does it matter? Something more than a lot of drinking happened. Am I scared to admit something? What was it Wallie said: "A steady life with a woman is like seeing an elephant . . . all right to look at, but who wants to own one?"

Mike got up, went to the little bathroom with its drying girdle and stockings on a line. Then he found a can of Yuban and a percolator. Terry came awake to find him standing there with two cups of coffee on a tray, some toasted danish, and a pot of strawberry jam.

CHAPTER 8

For the next few days Mike couldn't decide if he were spooked or bemused; his own terms in his mind were, I'm either daffy or trapped. But maybe it's what I really want. I don't know, but I like it. When he decided on an action and packed his few things in the room at Minnie Rothschild's, Wallie shook his head as if he had lost any lucidity he had ever had.

"Shacked up, eh? Well I'd have introduced you into womanizing on the coast with a more fun gal than Terry. But don't get me wrong, she's class all the way, even with her Marxist mumbling. In fact she's too good for the like of you or me."

"You, you goofy old mutt." Mike inspected a frayed shirt and decided to leave it behind.

"Why not me? I dance, I sing, and best of all I remember better respect for women. Hell, they don't have to be beautiful no more, just patient." He broke into his crackle of a laugh, slapped Mike on the shoulder. "Good luck, soldier. I'll keep the extra cot just in case. We'll stay in touch?"

"Sure, sure, why not?"

The old man shrugged, clicked his set of teeth together: "Jamie Ward seems to think the DWU would like to use you as a field organizer. You have the heft, the looks of a simple jerkoff who'd like to get his head busted."

"You think I'm not smart enough to take on union work?"

"Oh you're smart—but full of hope and piss. It's a snake pit, organizing, believe me; I've been in and out of it like a fiddler's elbow. Unions are a goddam pecking order of fat cats and every prick in the international organization trying to knee you and get his boot in your face as he tries to climb up the greased pole before you to the top."

"But it means a decent organization for the workers, the working joes. . . ."

"Dream on, boy, dream on."

"Better hours, fringe benefits coming to those who lift them bales." Mike laughed as he folded his raincoat. "Jesus, you make me talk like a jerk-to-Jesus street corner spieler."

"Well listen to yourself sometimes. Emerson said, 'Beware of what you desire, you'll get it.' "

"If what I want don't come in too big chucks, I'll swallow it." Mike held out a ten dollar bill. "For a couple of fifths to cheer you up."

"Me? I'm always cheerful." He did his little dance step and sang:

I hear the train whistlin', it'll be there on time,
To take me to Nashville to serve out my time;
The steam from the whistle, the smoke from the stack;
I know you'll be true blue until I get back.

"You ought to be on television."

"Listen, Mike, I'll dance at your wedding."

Mike gave the old Wobbly a hard look. "Nothing like that . . . you need anything, just call."

The old man looked miserable in a sudden change of mood. "Sure I will, bet on it. I'm not proud to take hand-outs." He crackled the bill. "A couple of finiffs sure look good." He turned to face Mike, a trembling irritant in his voice. "I never give much advice, but I know solid stuff when I see it. In some ways you're not dry behind the ears yet. In other ways you've got that lumpiness of being aware of things, of having some kind of special ability, and a bindle stiff's idea of how to get from here to there. Don't interrupt me, Mike, I'm talking. I've seen a lot of guys like you—roughnecks but full of bounce. Well, maybe not a lot, a handful. Young Jack Dempsey, John L. Lewis, Woody Guthrie, George Meany, the Puskin Jimmy Hoffa, Cagney. A kind of clock spring tight wound, a fuck-you toughness, and the world as their oyster. Jesus, soldier, be careful."

"Of what, Wallie, of making something of myself? I don't carry any ambition to be president or a movie star. I'm an ordinary guy who wants to better himself and not be ashamed of what he does."

"Don't bullshit an old bullshitter; you know what I'm saying."

They parted with a handshake. Alone, the old man sat, sagging, head down, feeling his years suddenly, feeling the past a crock of ashes. He didn't usually let himself drag ass like this; always laughing and scratching, he used to express as his idea of life. Now? He didn't feel like reading from his small supply of favorite books, not even his pet, Pepys. Better try a tune:

I've counted the days, babe, I've counted the night;
I've counted the footsteps; I've counted the lights;
I've counted the minutes; I've counted the stars;
I've counted a million of these prison bars.

Mike and Terry went down to a discount slock place and bought a wide studio bed with a good mattress and springs. She insisted he take a present of two good sports shirts and some underwear. "You can't go through life in work shirts."

They also brought a few bottles of red wine and two pounds of short ribs, which Terry cooked up fine with sweet and sour sauce. Mike mixed a salad of garlic, blue cheese and iceburg lettuce to which he added a coddled egg. Grinning and touching, they ate well and laughed and looked at each other's greasy mouths and laughed again. Drank up a bottle of wine. After which they smoked—he his pipe—and talked the banal audacity of lovers. Both were still a bit on guard. Then the evening and the testing of the bed.

Morning. The day was sunny and they went for a walk along the Embarcadero at North Point, bought a bottle of gin and four, huge, scarlet crabs steaming from a big pot, a long French bread. They came back to Terry's place— on the stairs up, reeling and shoving each other about with their hips, happy as grigs (what the hell was a grig?). In some way Mike felt they were getting used to each other, testing each other, enjoying the willful process of being a pair. They made love, seriously aware of their new feelings for the first time. Hilariously, the second time. He had to admit, if this was being truly in love, he hadn't known real love from a cockeyed Chinaman.

Mornings, he went to his job as a checker on an unloading dock; Terry had a job helping edit the DWU labor paper, *West Winds*. Afternoons, she was busy organizing office women into a union, badgering waitresses in greasy spoons and trash food joints to seek the solid protection of union membership.

Mike was coming around to a better understanding of the DWU world, the inner tensile strength of union organization: the heads (often fat cats), the fanatics, the dedicated powerhouses, earnest workers for better conditions. He was aware of the con men, the slow-downs, feather bedding, gold bricking. He told Jamie Ward, while they waited to unload a South American freighter, "It's like everything else, big business, political hoopla. Some play it straight, some could hide behind a corkscrew."

"You're right, Michael, my boy. But what counts are that work conditions get better, pay fairer, fringe benefits keep coming to the right people. Hat in hand you get nothing. Eyeball to eyeball, you'll get a dollar cigar sometimes."

Mike accepted advice. Jamie was a wise one, a knowing one for all his look of desolate depression; he nursed a persistent ulcer, had a son in Folsom doing five to ten for willful homicide. Mike didn't feel he should burden Jamie Ward with too many of his own ideas. Jamie, who had been helpful, had gotten him this job.

"And learn to have a blind side."

"Yes, a lot of the Bay workers goof off."

A certain amount of cargo was looted. There seemed to be a sort of loose rule that a limited amount of dockside containers would be broken open; watches, radios, rolls of cloth carried off.

"As long as it doesn't go beyond a certain point," Matt Hedrick, the security guard boss, told Mike, "we wink the eye to it. That is, the shippers, the insurance lads, the consignees, the union, too—just see it as sort of a tip. The shippers and receivers now have their customs swindling too. False bills of lading and all that."

"Yeah, yeah—but. . . ."

Matt took a chew of tobacco off a plug of Copenhagen, fitted it into one cheek, thought, spit and smiled. "It's waterfront tradition."

Mike laughed to show he understood a checker's limits. "Hell, I wouldn't go against tradition, Matt. Why it would be like saying there's no God."

"Everything within reason," said Matt, ambling away

to where some men were unloading Japanese cars off the *Hokusai Maru* onto a trailer carrier. Wallie had told Mike, "Dockside stealing is simplified; no taking of anything one or two men alone *can't* carry off."

Mike himself in his wanderings had done a bit of minor pilfering: milk bottles off a morning stoop, a newspaper without putting down a coin he couldn't spare; once when hungry in the Kansas City airport he'd lifted a briefcase off a drunk—it contained a soiled shirt, a box of Golden Age corn chips, and two copies of *Playboy*, annotated and improved in red ink.

One had to accept the way of the world, he told himself; a way that is usually not moral or legal but necessary for survival, if one had worked out a code that tried to live without doing real harm. And one didn't become an outlaw. Ma had the right idea (I'll write her about Terry and me tonight—that will set her back on her heels). Ma always insisted to him and his brothers and sisters, "You respect people, don't look down your nose on anyone lower than you; if you have to take anyone, let it be corporations, insurance companies, the government of bastards that bleed us. So if you must help yourself, why pick somebody that is carving you up."

As Wallie had put it (Ma would have liked it) quoting from some French writer, "Behind every great fortune there is a crime."

Mike didn't discuss all this with Terry. She was, he saw, as he got to know her better, a dedicated party member, swallowed all the left-wing bull, even read Lenin, *The Daily Worker*. She had more personal quirks, many of which he liked. She feared dark places, unlit rooms, and was like a little girl as she clung to him in fear of thunder and lightning. She was vain about her feet, the shoes she wore; and her feet were not small, not large either. She insisted she could spit in the eye of the world, "no abdication of the will in me," and yet there were times during her period when for two-three days she became deeply depressed, brooding, hardly talking, becoming a formidable obstacle to a relationship—making little moaning sounds.

Other times she was more daring than Mike: leaping off the cable cars before they stopped, talking to strangers, carrying on intimate, long conversations with bums, waiters, and waitresses. She liked long, long walks. Mike didn't; he'd been on the road too long, had hiked army fashion till his heels were blistered.

Before reporting for work she'd often roust Mike out of the kip at dawn for walks, meeting the city still in its night mist, hearing the lonely hoot of tugs, the snort of a newspaper truck dropping off the morning edition, seeing the night-shift workers' shoulders sagging, emerging from buildings, power plants, city service structures. He paced himself to the *clop-clop* of her well-made walking shoes, that major vanity—and him, still funky with sleep, head turtled into his uplifted coat collar, coming along yawning, teeth together, the first pipe of the day hanging from one corner of his mouth. He'd be thinking of the warm bed left behind, Terry's body; he was getting to know it like an old neighborhood back home. He was puzzled by her, delighted with her. If she was in a good morning mood, they'd breakfast at some early opened diner on a pot of coffee, huge platters of ham and eggs . . . or Canadian bacon . . . or even a small steak at times, an egg on top. She was a good feeder, ate cheerfully, with relish. She damned, she said, a fear she might get fat, and he'd turn to other girls. So she'd skip the pie or cruller Mike usually finished off a breakfast with. They'd part for their day's work, she running off, fine legs flashing. Sometimes, not too often, they'd feel so horny and compliant on a walk they'd get into a hallway and make it standing up, he unbuttoning, hiking up her skirt or dropping her jeans—once in a deserted gardenhouse in a little park off Golden Gate Avenue, and once they were ordered off from under a Nob Hill porch by a real butler in a white jacket, carrying a feather duster.

"You can jolly well bugger off the two of you."

Their life together, as two months passed, had its serious side. Terry had plans for a union future. On a Sunday morning of rain and salt wind they had not risen until eleven; they sat in their open robes—she had bought him a red flannel one and stitched onto it the word *Potentate*. They sat with a three pound Sunday newspaper; they only intended to skim through its scattered-about sections. They heard church bells and the wet tires of morning traffic. There was in the place the odor of last night's beer revel with Wallie and Jamie and four strangers who, by the looks of them, were oil field roughnecks.

Terry let her robe gape open, extended her naked legs. "I'm going out to organize the field workers in a week."

"What the hell do I do? Play with myself?"

"You're part of the plan, buster. Jamie has gotten a DWU agreement for you to go out, look for work as tractor driver at one of the big vineyards, meet with some of the field hands who are trying to get a union going. Not easy, as the wetbacks and the Spanish-speaking labor are scared."

"Why . . . they have the right to a union. The NLRB says so."

"So has a fish to water, but if there is no water? The ranchers and farmer owners are hiring hoods. There are vigilantes, and the damn sheriffs and country cops are on the take on the ranchers' side."

"I don't know enough about organizing."

"Me and Jamie will teach you in a couple of days. There's nothing to it, if you know how to protect yourself."

"Don't want you to go. They hacked up a nigger woman pretty good in Imperial Valley, when she asked for a union vote in the tomato fields."

"It caused such a stink they'll not try it again, on a woman."

"Terry honey, why split up what we got."

"We have it because we take chances, because we have a job to do. Don't we owe the union something, don't we? I mean that's how we made it together."

"Oh fuck it," he said, rising angrily, pacing the worn rug, his feet seeming to try to grip it as if he had claws, trying to firm up the implications of their relationship.

"You know what's out there in those crop belts? It's redneck sheriffs with baseball bats; it's company dicks, scabs, hoods, Pinkertons. It's shotguns, 12-gauge, loaded with deer shot. You're a city girl, Terry. Here there is some kind of protection. At least there are reporters, city ordinances, union lawyers, the ACLU."

"I've been out there. I went to organize dairy farms near San Diego, got a vote taken anyway."

"You lost?"

Terry nodded. "They scare-boogered the help, most of them wetback Chicanos who could get deported. But I know the road, the fields up close, the packing plants."

She held out her hands, palms up. "I still have scars from the canneries, the packing sheds." She stood up and put her arms around him. "Stop pacing, Mike, it makes my headache worse. Don't you ever get a hangover, sweetie?"

"Just a little hammering between the ears and over the eyes. It was a neat party." He kicked aside the comic section, the sports, and the TV folder from underfoot. "What would you like? Bed, lunch out at Sheppi's? But no goddam hike."

Terry laughed, turned to the rain moving down the window panes. "You lug, if we start now, rain or not, we'd be past Sausalito and into the big trees by nightfall. No rain reported up there. I've never been laid under a redwood tree."

He grabbed her arm with his two fists, grinned. "You know, lady, that's your problem? You got no shame."

"That's right, mister."

They got into the studio bed, thumped around in a

cheerful, earnest frenzy, then slept and woke to find the
rain stopped. They dressed, went to *Fu Lee's* on Kearney
Street and ate *Tim Shun Chow Yu* and *Lung Ha Fu Yung*,
shrimp fried noodles with Kiren, the Japanese rice beer.

"I'll have to diet for a week," Terry said.

"I like wide hips."

She insisted they walk over to the Kung Chow temple
on Pine Street, where she bought and lit two joss sticks to
burn for good luck for both of them. The priest was
pleased with a half dollar Mike slipped him. He didn't
bow or act at all like Charlie Chan, just nodded, and said
cheerfully, *"Ni syihwab cha ma?"*

"What'd he say?" Mike asked.

"Do we want tea."

"No, I don't."

"Ha yung chi."

"That, Mike, is good luck."

Mike bowed to the slim old priest. "Good luck to you,
too, pal."

It was that night that Mike Brant decided to also go out
and try to help organize California field workers. He
couldn't bear to think of not being near Terry. Like so
many men trapped in love, he had resented this image,
but he was not a man given to too much brooding over
the inevitable. Not at this time of his life. Jamie Ward
gave him a list of names to memorize, and then destroy
names of field workers who were in a union already, secretly as yet. Also he handed over a small Smith & Wes-
son six-shooter, but Wallie advised him not to carry a
weapon.

"That's all the tin badges need is an armed organizer,
and they stomp you to death in a cell."

Mike pawned the pistol for ten dollars and bought himself a western style John Wayne hat.

One virtue of Mike's living with Terry, one advantage
beside the sensual satisfaction, was an intimacy with the
inner working of the union locals, organization, and

procedures. It could be, he thought, a vital turning point in his life. For he had, up to the time he'd come to San Francisco, carried a sense that he was an outsider compared to men and women who had college degrees and knew how to speak with grammar, who had not in childhood felt hunger or doubted the fairness of things. They, the educated, had slept in middle-class style, alone, throughout their adolescence. He had doubted in the past he could ever have the amorphous social power of those who lived above the depressed standards of Ma and Pa. Terry said vulnerable, diverse influences had kept him apart from the fullness of existence.

"Most college grads come out stamped from the same cookie cutter."

Now, with Terry and Jamie's help, he saw the world of unions from close up; he sensed he was as good as any man in them, even better, as his perception of himself grew, and the dreams, the fantasies, the frustrated ambitions surfaced in him—all of it, not as way out as he had supposed. He became self-assertive but not loud. Jamie Ward was pleased at how quickly Mike could grasp in detail much of union procedure in organizing new locals.

The two of them were drinking boilermakers; a shot glass of whiskey dropped into a schooner of beer, drinking at the bar of Indian House Motel, Jamie explaining, "You see, Mike, you have to know how to press your way to get what's the best for the union. You start with the small firms—put a finger to their eye—or with a management that to keep in business needs money coming in. It has to capitulate to DWU organizers to survive; a strike means ruin, so we get a closed shop. Any strike or lockout will break their balls."

"But we'd go against the big boys, some of their agreements. I mean we're part of them, and you've led workers through their picket lines."

"Here's the gimmick on that; the employer sees us as a

friend, and when we come to bargain he's easier badgered. We stood up against the International. Hell, we made more progress starting some bargaining with a dispute between various locals than breaking heads. If a picket is a rival from another local, remember—treat 'em as an enemy."

"It isn't as simple as I once figured. Locals fighting each other."

Jamie held his stomach with both hands, winced. "I better go easy—my ulcer says what the hell are you drinking? The worst problem is local autonomy held by some half-assed local slobs. I've broken a few of them, off the record, of course, supporting corporations to stand against union demands. Sounds bad, eh? But in the end, the corporations let in my local of the DWU, a closed shop. And every son of Adam there pays dues to us."

Mike took out his pipe, blew through the steam.

"Maybe that's why, Jamie, you have an ulcer. All this horsing around not letting your right paw know what your left one is doing."

"As long as you're loyal to your union local all you have to figure is what's to the good, what's to the bad. Sweet justice, the law doesn't belong—it's for the rich only—and remember, Mike, money is the source of all power, including union power. Dues, pension funds, fringe benefits, that's the socko, the knockout blow in pressuring to see wages rise and benefits pile up."

Mike lit his pipe, slowly puffing pungent white smoke.

"What can you, the DWU, get from farm workers? They're dirt poor and out of work half the year—jalopy tramps."

"Millions, if we organize them properly. We never have gotten close to a farm union. The time is ripe. Usually it's some half-assed gringo organizer hating the barrio Mexican who gets clobbered by the rancher's strongarm boys . . . or flanked out by the sheriff's men. You pick up Latin boys to do the yelling."

"I've been beaten up myself. I don't like it." Mike looked at his watch. He was meeting Terry and Wallie for dinner. "You ever been clouted, Jamie? Worked over, but good? Piss red for a week from jabs in your kidneys from a police club?"

"Look, I got more scars than a twenty-year preliminary ring bum. But we're attacking the farm and vineyard organizing differently now. We're sending mass organizers into the Fresno district, Imperial Valley, Orange County, other heavy crop and grape country. And at harvest time. We're showing our own muscle to the tomato kings and bottlers, and we have our farm lobby talk big with the National Labor Relation Board. We have a batch of eager-beaver lawyers standing by. Also a lot of the bleeding heart folk ready to cry in public. We have one problem. Recruiting."

Mike laughed and stood up. "You damn right have. Who's going into the fields and hope he can duck?"

Jamie nodded, no smile on his face. "As long as you understand that."

"I can take care of myself. It's a man's job. Not for women."

Jamie pushed aside his beer schooner. "Terry is tougher than both of us. That is, when organizing. Besides it's the field hands and vine workers who get the worst of the reaction when organizers show up. Even if. . ."

"Don't tell me it's for their own good in the end."

Jamie put down some bills, nodded to the bar man. "As our friend Wallie would quote from his readings in stir: 'The wounded deer leaps highest.' "

Mike brooded for the next few days. Sure, he had found confidence, shelter, in the local of the union. A sense of purpose, the first time since the war. He was no innocent, life was no game like Red Rover played summer nights under street lights at street corners. It was more like making your punches count, covering up to protect yourself from the return blows. Now he wasn't back-packing, not with Terry making life more than it had meant in the past. Self-esteem was better than a punch on the nose anytime. Could he stand the heat?

A hard-nut union organizer called for some kind of creative temperament if one was to succeed.

Waking early, Terry snoring slightly beside him, he'd think he had a lot to learn. But hell, look at the men who had made it, no more educated than himself: Gompers, Debs, Lewis, Reuther, Quill, Bridges, Hoffa, Meany, Verner, the Puskin—not a goddam Ph.D. among them, no Phi Beta Kappa keys dangling from gold watch chains.

Sleep lost, he promised himself to penetrate the hazy, still mysterious relationship in the system on the union side, the employers' side. Ma hadn't raised no stupid son. He rose to make the coffee. He felt better when the three of them were eating at the Xochimiclo, chomping *Mole de Guajolote* and *Cuauhtemoc*—Terry gagging on the spicy chili sauce.

It was their last night before Terry went off as a field worker to spy out the vineyard worker's attitudes. Mike would follow as a tractor operator a week later.

Wallie showed them how to drink tequila properly; a quick suck on a slice of lime, a lick of salt from between his thumb and forefinger, then he gulped the firey brew in one quick swallow. He looked from Mike to Terry, clicked his teeth together. "Well my advice, amigos, is if after a few days it looks like suicide take it on the lam. They shoot horses don't they, and organizers?"

"Jesus, Wallie, we're not in the shoot 'em up days of the IWW, or the union head busting of U.S. Steel. We're in the 1950s. There are official boards in Washington watching."

"They busted the heads of lots of Okies when I was younger."

"Sure," said Terry, "but you got yours still whole."

Mike decided he didn't care for tequila or even the

pulque Wallie insisted they try. "The damn Oakies are ranchers—land owners now, own lots of farms and some run vineyards. You'd think they'd remember how it was once for them."

Wallie grinned, his teeth gleaming too brightly:

> The night I came home drunk,
> As drunk as I could be,
> I spied a hat on the hat rack,
> Where my hat ought to be.

"You give a hungry dog a little meat, soldier, you try and take back even the bone, you're going to get nipped. Hey, no use wasting that tequila, I'll finish it for you; waste not fear not."

He looked about him, an old man in doubt. "I may mosey up to the fields. Look for a lecherous old tomcat, and if I believed in the Shop Foreman upstairs, I'd say God bless."

He swallowed the drink quickly with a jerk back of his head.

Mike and Terry spent their last night together in talk, in bittersweet loving, in trying to sound cheerful. Near dawn they both slept fitfully with much turning and tossing. Outside a thick congealing fog closed in. It was Terry who made the coffee, heated the danish. Seated close together, smelling of sleep and lovemaking, sipping their coffee, he decided they were sentimental slobs. Worst of all, he didn't really feel bad about that or ashamed of that antimacho stance.

BOOK TWO
TERRY'S VINEYARD

CHAPTER 9

There is a road life and there is a car life for the homeless, all along the magnificent road systems that California had and was still building. The rootless road life moved slowly with a pack or suitcase and dusty shoes; thumbs held out begging to be taken up by the passing traffic, away from the broiling sun. The car life seemed suspended above the world, moving at a steady speed, controlled only by state troopers if they barreled by at more than sixty-seven miles an hour. The car life felt superior to the road life and hardly noticed flattened platts of hide and hair, dried discs that had been small animals that crossed at the wrong time.

Coming east along the highway from Salinas to the San Joaquin Valley, Terry had been lucky. A lumber rig carting pitch-pole pines for a new telephone line at Hollister had taken her part way, and then a chicken rancher had dropped her into the hot afternoon sun at Mendoca. Here

Terry was to meet the Carters (secret organizers of the Field and Ranch Workers Union). They were picking fruit that summer all the way from the Imperial Valley up past Bakersfield and into the Fresno fields. They worked oranges, lemons, avacados, lettuce, melons, and the final three weeks on grapevines, before all the fruit tramps and migratory workers drifted down to Monterey to drink cooking sherry, patch the trailers, and stay alive, till the next crop, by working in the fish canneries.

Already two weeks on the road, Terry was tanned and weathered by the sun; her blond hair was cut short and worn over the forehead. She wore just enough lipstick to show she had a little vanity. Enough vanity to feel somebody in a bar would stand her to a double bourbon, or ask her for a dance in a joint, while a trio ground out the real New Orleans style. She herself preferred sentimental ballads sung by Italian ex-barbers.

Standing in the powerful California sun outside the Mendoca Star Motel, Terry looked a migratory worker in her tight, blue-denim jeans, cut rancher style, her white, man's shirt all held together by a wide black leather belt set with Indian silver decorations. She wore the usual heavy, Hollywood sunglasses, and at her chukka-styled, ankle-length boots lay her bindle, a skillfully knotted, rolled-together blanket, raincoat, horsehide jacket, canvas carryall, all packed and strapped to fit over one shoulder, easily lifted into place or dropped in a hurry.

Terry hunted for the Carters' jalopy among the passing cars. All around her the fruit crews were coming in for the grape harvest, in baling-wired crates, homemade trailers, cut-down trucks, ancient Packards and Caddies that went back to almost unknown eras of motor design. It was that way, she knew, all up and down the San Joaquin Valley from Salinas to Fresno. Everywhere the Kings River and the big irrigation ditches brought in the water, wherever the crops grew, there had to be somebody to pick them. Bindlestiffs were dropping off the freightcars, the truckers were lifting up hitchhikers. Any where along the cottonwood-fringed bottom land and under the cement bridges, you might find some fruit pickers, organized into a cozy little group, with a spider skillet on a fire of old, broken-up crates, cooking a meal. Tomorrow they would sign up for a picking, crating or processing job. In a few weeks the valley would be empty of its ripe harvest. The crews would move south again to the melon and celery fields and the citrus groves. A hell of a pick-me-up life. And the union getting no place.

Terry hunted in her jeans for a smoke and found the last, bent, king-sized cigarette in a crumpled pack. She struck a kitchen match with a broad thumbnail that had once been covered with nail polish of fire-engine red, and set the tobacco on fire. She stood in the strong sun inhaling the pungent smoke, wondering where in hell the Carters were. They were to have picked her up hours ago. Max Carter was a wino, sure, but a solid old-time organizer; Liz had the brains and weight to keep Max in line. Their secondhand Ford had only 40,000 miles on it, not counting whatever had been turned back on the mileage reading by "Honest Harry, the Best Car Buy in Bakersfield."

Terry felt sad. The sun was hot. She had no watch, but her expert eye tested shadows and told her it was after three.

She had talked to Mike in Fresno; a phone call arranged for her. He was having a hard time. "The Associated Crop Farmers' goons were making trouble, beating up organizers." She hoped he didn't get hurt. She had said, "Easy, easy, Mike." He said, "See you at the Big Mesa Farms in a few days."

Meanwhile, here she was marooned. She could take a bus, but that was outside the pattern of a field worker.

She had enjoyed taking drinks with Mike. Now she felt she needed one—if only to remember how it had been between the two of them. She touched the secret little pocket under the wide Indian belt. Two twenties and a five in dirty, folded bills. She looked across the highway, past the huge fruit carriers that passed by pulling trailers of crates and stinking up the road with their rigs. A sign read: *Ronny's Bar and Grill, Cabins for Rent, TV, Chili.*

Terry lifted her bindle expertly onto one shoulder and crossed the road, passing between two wildcat rigs that were going down toward Alcalde where a new oil strike was reported. Her father had been one of the best of the roughneck oil crewmen before that crown block fell on him and smashed him into the Kelly Bar. The little raunchy lawyer from L.A. had managed to bilk Terry out of almost all of the insurance the company was supposed to pay her for Dad's death.

Terry opened the door of Ronny's Bar and went in. It was nose-biting cold from both air conditioning and the smell of chilled beer. Two long distance truckers with big shiny serge behinds were chomping dripping segments of pie and watching the ball game on the TV set on a shelf over the cash register. A sick-looking, redhaired waitress was wiping the counter. The barman was studying a racing form.

Terry slid her bindle down to the floor and got up on a bar stool.

"A bourbon."

"Over rocks?"

"No, with a chaser."

She knocked back the drink in three fast gulps and closed her eyes before taking the chaser. The water tasted of mud and frogs, but it was cold. She risked a dime in the jukebox meter on the bar, and listened to Bing Crosby sing "It Was Only a Paper Moon."

"Care for a lift, sugar?"

It was the taller of the truck drivers. His upper teeth were outlined in gold, his little blue eyes almost lost in red angry flesh weathered by road glare. He wore a union button.

Terry shook her head. "Not this trip, Mac."

"Just askin'."

You bet you were, Terry thought. He and his ape buddy would certainly like to get her in the front seat of their two-ton rig and gang up on her in the sleeping compartment over the truck cab. Truckers were all a little crazy from long hours of hard driving.

The truck driver threw down some silver, took a fistful of toothpicks out of a jam jar and said, "Lousy fruit bum."

He went out with his relief driver, and Terry ordered another bourbon. She hadn't meant to. She teased the second bourbon a bit and took it slowly, sip by sip. She put a dollar on the bar and the cash register rang up: $1.00. Four bits a ball is what they charged on the highway.

"Another shot?"

"No."

Terry inhaled the cold, conditioned air, got her bindle, and went out into the dusty hot bite of the California sun at its afternoon worst. Everything was coated with a film of gray dust. The shadows were very black, and the highlights on buildings and billboards at the crossroads of the sun-punished town were too bright to her eyes, even through the thick sunglasses.

The Carters weren't coming . . . maybe they were in jail . . . organizers often got framed and tossed into the clink. They were hours late. They had been just up the line, fifty miles to the north, crating musks and red hearts. If she hung around waiting, she'd miss the hiring lines tomorrow.

Terry needed a ride. She stood on the shoulder of the road, aware she was well stacked; her can was neither too large nor too small. Her long legs in the tight denim were the kind the pin-up hounds liked. Skillfully, she chose a not too fancy car, a four-year-old medium-price job with a homemade waxing, driven by a little man with glasses who wore a sewed tweed hat; a conservative who wouldn't try to out-wrestle her.

He let himself be thumbed down, and she ran up to the car and tossed the bindle in the back among some frayed leather sample cases. She slid quickly in beside the driver and banged the door shut. Never give them time to change their minds.

"Thanks."

"I'm going through to Monterey."

"That will do. I get off before the town."

"Picking?"

"That's right, picking."

He pulled out a pack of filter tips from under the sun visor, put one between his teeth and held out the pack to Terry. She took one, and he lit her smoke before his. A gent. And he had shaved that morning.

"I don't usually work this part of the state. My territory is north of Frisco. But the salesman that has this section, his wife died last week. Healthy as a bear, then suddenly a lump under the skin, you know, and the doctor says it's too far gone. Twenty-two, with two kids. Tough."

"Tough," said Terry, enjoying the smoke. "When you have to go . . . "

"Ben, that's the salesman, is all broken up about it."

"You married?" Terry asked, figuring it might save a lot of motions later on.

"Yes, seven years. We live in Carmel. Artistic town, full of nuts painting and messing up clay."

"Sounds like a ball."

He didn't make a pass for thirty miles. Passing an open-pit gravel loader, he gently put one hand on her thigh. "It gets lonely on these routes."

"It shouldn't be. Seeing it's not your own route."

He looked at her closely through his glasses. He was a little on the thin side, not too bad a head, but going bald. Most likely was class president in his high school, good to his mom, cheats a little on his wife who's head of the PTA.

"It's still lonely," said the driver.

"What about your wife?" Terry said. She pushed his hand off her thigh.

"I've got an expense account. Take care of an air-conditioned motel room, shower, television."

"Class," said Terry. "Real class."

He was a likeable little bastard. If she could con him for another hundred and thirty miles, she'd be near enough to the hiring lines to brush him off without him getting mean. Years ago, before she got political and was a young crop picker what did it matter if she shacked up on a couple of good Beautyrests with coiled springs, got a shower with real clean hot water, and a good dinner on a real tablecloth.

She had done it with strangers when looped on a little grape, the record player grinding out a mountain ballad. Jesus, she sure cried when a ballad was low and sad and some galoot had a bottle of vino. And the mood was on her, mellow.

At first, after Dad was killed by the crown block on the rig, she kind of felt it was a lousy thing to be doing. Later, she got some sense, and didn't like it much with these pickups. The quickness with their fast line of what they'd do for you, come morning, and how cold the old bag was they were married to.

Now Mike had come along, and she wanted to settle down on some little place. Grow chickens, run a lunch counter, pump gas. Jesus, to have a house and a guy legally on record. To racket around again in love with a big mug who thought the two of you had invented it. She wasn't getting any younger. Around the eyes you could see the little lines and her belly was getting a little slack. No . . . better stay in union work. Mike had a yen for it now. (There was that hand again.)

"The name's Jack. Jack Williams. . . . "

The motor division card attached to the steering wheel read: William Jackson. But it figured. He wasn't going to take a fruit bum into a motel and give his right name.

"Jack."

"Don't think I don't respect you, honey, just because you thumbed a lift. I mean, I know just because you're a migratory—I mean, that doesn't mean you haven't got self-respect. You know what I mean?"

Terry put her hand over his. At least that would prevent its roving. "Sure, Jack. My name is Terry."

"There's a pint in that yellow pigskin case. Help yourself."

She pressed his hand. "You're driving, and the damn tin badges around here just smell a burp on us that isn't as pure as Ivory soap and you're in the can for six weeks. I like you fine, Jack, but not as a cellmate. Your wife wouldn't understand, or your boss."

That kept him silent for twelve miles.

"How'd you become a fruit worker, honey?"

"When my father was killed in an accident seven years ago I couldn't stay put or work indoors . . . better two hands on the wheel here. There's a police trap 'round the bend. The whole fink town lives off the fat fines. The judge is the cop's father-in-law, the turnkey is a son, and the bailsman is a creep who runs the only garage; they always conk your motor with an eight-pound sledge while you're in court shelling out."

"Thanks."

It was getting on to dusk, the sky the color of the inner skin of a wine grape. She decided she was near enough to the vineyards. She said in a casual way, "I get out at the next light."

"Wait a minute, honey. We had plans."

"You had plans."

He didn't fight it. He wasn't the type. He just said sadly, "A hell of a lot any of you care. Just use a guy."

The light was a hundred yards ahead. Terry put one arm back to grab her bindle. "Okay, Jack." The car groaned to a stop. The man leaned over and opened the door. "Get out." She slid out quickly—bindle and all.

The car shot ahead in the oil reek of a badly needed cylinder job. Terry stood by the roadside in the gathering darkness among neon-lit cabins, gas stations, and the red signal towers of a branch railroad line.

What had that fancy shrink screwball in La Jolla called her? . . . "an unmitigated romantic. You live in reality and desire dreams made by Marx."

No motel tonight. She'd camp out under some railroad bridge up the line and invest in sliced bacon, a few eggs, bread, and a pack of smokes. Just one pack. "Unmitigated romantic?" It had just cost her a good bed, a fine dinner, booze, and Jack.

Shouldering her bindle, Terry looked at the too bright supermarket on the crossroad. Not for her. They'd accuse her of shoplifting and tear apart her bindle. Down the road was a little lopsided Mexican grocery. She started for it, carrying the bindle close and dragging her chukka boots a bit. It had been a long, tiring day. A lot like all her days when she went out organizing. Maybe she and Mike could make it for a night when they met.

She felt the trouble with Mike was that he was still starry-eyed about organizing, still the earnest young guy who had gotten the call; he was like some skid row wino who found Christ. But she liked him for that. He was hard, he was no fool, and he'd been hit often enough to know existence wasn't a bed of roses. There was something special about him, Terry thought as she hunted a good spot to sleep—something that was a bit different from the usual young organizer. He was studying situations all the time, watching, observing, not scared, not even taking care of himself, but wanting to discover—wanting to find out. She wouldn't have fallen for him (she certainly didn't want to when they first met), if he hadn't interested her, made her wonder how is this guy put together . . . what's his head full of?

Wrapped in her blanket and raincoat, sleeping under a bridge, Terry dreamed of all the migratory workers in one big union . . . the pickers of culls, the weeders, trimmers, packers; city faces, country faces, young punks, high school girls puking in the morning with their first pregnancy; all of them either from across the border, legally or as wetbacks, or out of the towns, hoping to live cheap, live hard, work, and have a few laughs. Even to fall in love. They came by whatever would carry them to the picking fields. They rode the rods, hid in empty freight cars, a lot of them women and girls. Women on their own, taking care of themselves, living the tough setup of the migratory worker. Not such a pleasant dream.

Even when she added the horsehide jacket to her blanket and raincoat, it was still cold under the railroad bridge. She muttered in her sleep . . . Mike was bending over her, laughing and wrestling her down with his stance on the bed. The angle of the dream turned, and she was picking limes, in the world of the pickers again, and tomorrow they were hiring. She would be there with the first, for the valley and the ranches and the vineyards. The mood and the color of the rich fertile valley stained her dreams. In the fields the planting and cultivating was over. The harvest season was here. Now came the fruit pickers and the packers, marching along a road carrying blankets and pots. Nobody asked who they were or wanted to know their secrets. A migratory worker has a pair of hands, a set of muscles. . . . The dream blurred, grew full of noise.

CHAPTER 10

Some bluejays with raucous voices broke the skin of her sleep. Terry awakened to the louder sound of a fruit freight clanging overhead sending a shower of cinders raining down on her. She sat up and stretched, and got out of the blanket and her raincoat. The jays flew off, still shouting, and the string of cars went vibrating down the branch line.

There were some old packing cases and thin boards nearby. Terry built a little fire under the cement and got out a paper of bacon and her frying pan with the folding handle. While waiting for the fire to burn down to cooking embers, she looked around and saw a termite-eaten shack down a path among the bushes. There was also a dripping faucet. She'd wash up a bit, find a sheltered place for her morning needs. She went off, whistling "The Isle of Capri," a short length of blue towel and a cake of soap under one arm, loosening her belt as she went.

* * *

She had just disappeared behind the shack when a wild-looking young girl, who had been huddled behind a pile of railroad ties twenty feet away, came up. She peered around the campsite and walked with wary steps up to the bindle and the bacon laid out in the frying pan by the side of the blazing wood. She was in her teens, wearing overwashed, thready, yellow jeans, and a man's brown sweater—much too big for her, with two buttons missing. Her short cut, deep, red-brown hair was in disorder over a pale face that might have been pretty, if the child didn't look so desperate, frightened, and underfed. She glanced in a foxlike way around her. She touched the frying pan, then pulled back her fingers. For two full, mouthwatering minutes she sat looking at the rashers of cold bacon, at the half loaf of bread in the pack, the red labels of two cans of tomato soup. Hunger at last overcame fear. She seized a strip of white bacon and. raw as it was, began to chew it desperately, fully engaged in the task of trying to swallow the rubbery raw strip. She reached for the bread, tore off a corner, jammed it into her mouth, added another raw strip of bacon and, squatting on her haunches, gasping and desperate, chewed and chewed. Dismally frightened, she felt the choking lump in her throat tighten and pack down until she could hardly breathe. A curt voice from above her said, "You crazy or something, eating raw bacon?"

The girl looked up to find Terry standing there, her towel held like a whip, a weapon. "What kind of game you playing?"

"Nothin'. I was hungry," said the girl.

"You alone?" Terry looked down at the busy highway below the bridge.

"Yes . . . this yours?"

"That's right. Where you from?"

"I'm on the road," said the girl, too frightened to chew her mouthful of food.

"What's the matter with you—lost all your marbles?"

"Don't call the cops."

"You're no picker."

Terry put the frying pan on the fire. The rasher began to hiss and curl. She stared at the girl. "I'm not going to beat you or work you over."

Terry took out two eggs wrapped in newspaper and broke them, letting them fry with the bacon. From a pocket of the leather jacket she took out a switchback knife, flipped it open and hacked the bread in sections.

"There's enough grub for two."

"I'll pay you back when I get work."

"Sure you will."

"Smells good."

"I'm Terry Munday."

"Pleased to meet you. I'm Ginny. Ginny Wolnik."

"Ginny, go down to the faucet there and wash your hands . . . good."

"Wash?"

"That's right. You might do a bit with the ears and neck too. Take this towel and soap."

"I don't need to wash."

"You do if you eat here."

"I got a comb."

Terry watched the girl walk down to the shack and shook her head. This kid was about as much of a picker as Terry was Queen Elizabeth.

Ginny came back fairly clean and sat down as Terry handed her a fork.

"Here, I'll eat with the knife."

"Thank you."

Ginny grabbed the fork and began to eat like a wolf after a hard winter.

"Tastes just fine—not like at . . . "

"Like where?"

"Other places."

"Don't gulp it, kid. You'll cat it all up."

"Not me."

"Where you really from?"

"I'm . . . I'm . . .," the girl began.

"Skip it, if you're on the lam."

"I'm not running away. I came to get a job picking."

"Better take off your give-away label."

Terry pointed to the pocket of the yellow jeans and the heavy, painted letters C.C.

Ginny tried to cover the letters with a hand. "They don't belong to me."

"California Correction. Right, Ginny? You want to get picked up?"

Terry leaned forward and began to cut off the pocket and the letters with her knife. "No use advertising." Terry tossed the detached pocket into the fire.

The girl stopped eating, her mouth all greasy, and began to sob. Terry let her cry. She calmly took out a cigarette, lit it, and sat puffing it until the girl stopped weeping.

Ginny wiped her face on her sweater sleeve and sniffed a few times. She said, "They beat me. Miss Randall, she used to twist my arms and laugh. She's the ward matron. She used to back me up and let me have it hard in the stomach. She liked it. It gave her a bang—the old bull dike."

"Okay—you don't have to tell me anything else, Ginny."

"Look, I've been scrubbing wood floors." Her small hands were red and raw.

"How old are you? Sixteen? Seventeen? And already on the lam. If you were smart, you'd give yourself up. You'd have a roof over your head, free grub, and medical attention. Here in the picking sheds all you get is the foreman crowding you into corners."

"I think I'll go now. Thanks for the food, Terry." She stood in panic and looked around her.

"I'm not chasing you." Here I go again, thought Terry. I can't let this square kid go around getting into trouble. Besides, they'll pick her up soon and take her back where she'd be safe behind bars, if the dikes in the pad would leave her alone.

"Sit down, Ginny. You're too young and dewy to trust out there with the fruit wolves. Want to be my picking partner?"

"Sure, if you want me." She sat down eagerly.

"I don't want you, but I've got you." Terry began to wipe the frying pan with old newspapers. "We'll get to one of the vineyards bright and early."

She began to repack the bindle taking some thin dollar bills to button into her pocket, then looked at Ginny and added a safety pin to the pocket. "You weren't in for stealing, were you?"

"No. My father and mother were killed in an auto wreck. I ran away from the home they put me into—an old lady who didn't feed me. Then they caught me and locked me up. I bit a cop."

"Good."

"You been a migratory long, Terry?"

"It's no honor, kid, but it's a free outdoor life. Short dough—some fun—and no questions asked."

Terry looked around for forgotten gear and swung the packed bindle up on her shoulder, motioning Ginny to follow her.

"We'll get down on the road and get a lift to the vineyards. You let me do the talking."

"Sure." Ginny nodded.

They began to pick their way through rocks and buffalo grass to the road. There was a lot of traffic. Giant logging trucks carrying sections of redwood logs as big around as a cottage vied with produce and milk trucks hauling for market. Passenger cars in a hurry going in either direction wove between the trucks, taking chances in passing the twelve-wheel, heavy carriers.

It was another hot day and would continue that way till dusk. The weather was usually the same in the fruit and vegetable country. In the far distance Terry saw the lofty black mountains and the tawny, amber hills where there was no water. There were lonely black trees here and there, trying to make a go of it on arid ground. Terry loved those lonely, wind-twisted, thirsty trees that went on year after year, adding a twig, a few buggy leaves, but always surviving. In their sooty trunks she suspected was hidden away the thin sap of life.

Now, with this girl along, maybe it would be easier to talk union to the crop workers and tone down the farm and ranch owners' rancor. Organizing was still dangerous.

Ginny was holding back. Terry looked at her and motioned her closer.

"Come on, don't give yourself away with every look."

"So much traffic."

It was going to be a mean, dry day. The sun was already slanting up, and yellow dust clouds in the distance marked the back roads where a big red caterpillar job was plowing, pulling half a dozen gang plows along—the birds following to catch any turned up worms.

Off on a brown side road Terry observed a white cottage and a hay barn and wire fence. A collie was running back and forth beside a baby in a crib under a fig tree. A woman with a blue cloth tied around her head came out and tossed a basin of water on some flowering bush. She stood there a moment, wearing a striped housedress and nothing else. She arched her body and smiled at the baby as if she owned the world.

Terry looked away. Domestic scenes were too corny to take. That woman had everything: a kid, a dog, about fifty acres of black bottom land, a husband to support the place and give her more kids. She heard Ginny's voice at her elbow.

"Listen, I ought to keep moving."

"Sure, if I bore you, move on, Ginny."

"It isn't that. If they catch me—and Miss Randell works me over again in solitary, I'll kill somebody. It's mean."

"You need money to travel."

"So long . . . I'm goin', Terry. . . ."

"Look, we decided to be picking partners, remember?"

"I know, but I'm afraid to stay around here."

"It's as safe here as any place. When we get work tell 'em you're nineteen or twenty."

"Don't I look it?"

"No."

"I'm still growin'."

"And say this is your first job out of high school. That's why you haven't a Social Security card."

"All right."

"Your name isn't really Ginny Wolnik?"

"No, it's . . ."

"Don't tell me. Use it . . . it's as good as any in case the cops check the work sheets."

They had no luck all morning. Around noon an old chicken farmer with a tremor in his large hands gave them a lift down to the Big Mesa Vineyards. He let them off by a dirt road leading down between tall blue gum trees to a big red processing plant. Terry looked Ginny over. What a partner! No luck in her.

But Mike was some place around here. He was picking up five hundred union broadsides at a printer's in Stockton. The DWU was beginning its drive to unionize the district, starting with the workers at the Big Mesa Vineyards.

The printer in Stockton was a woman: Rose Kleinsohn. The little shop, *Fast Fine Printing—Rosie's Reproduction Center*, smelled of turps, gear grease, and old paper. Rose herself was old, but large, with a reddish wig she wore pushed back on a too wide brow. She held up, in ink-stained fingers, a broadside for Mike to look at. Her voice had a boom, but a jolly tone.

"Eh, will that knock the bosses on their *tocus,* I ask you?"

Mike studied the large bold letters on cheap yellow paper:

FIELD WORKERS DO YOU KNOW YOUR RIGHTS?
FARM LABOR DO YOU KNOW WHY YOU NEED A UNION?
The law says you can vote for a union . . .
so vote for the FIELD RANCH WORKERS UNION, DWU.
It is your right
to fair working and living conditions,
to your demands for health, welfare,
improved working hours, sanitary living quarters.
JOIN THE FIELD AND RANCH WORKERS UNION NOW . . .
organizing all field workers in California.
Carry the union card.
It is the Labor Relations Board ruling
that you and your fellow workers can be part
of the DWU and have a Union!
SIGN UP . . . SIGN UP . . . SIGN UP . . .

Mike reread the broadside. "It will do, Rose, do fine. Just pack 'em up."

"Pack 'em up, like that? . . . No . . . I'll roll 'em up—five hundred in a blanket and tie it tight with straps, so no one will know you're carrying them."

"There's no law against it."

Rose snapped an army surplus blanket open. "Boychic, there's no law you have to eat, but people eat. You find yourself in a tight corner with these, you throw the

whole *magillah* away fast. The Associated Crop Farmers'
Nazi police find it, you'll get your arms and legs broken."

Mike watched the large old woman distribute the
broadsides on the blanket over the composing block and
then roll it tight.

"It's like the old days when Nat and me were organizing the New York shops for the International Ladies Garment Workers Union for that Dubinsky. But out here, we
came here when Nat was a lunger, but it didn't help here,
the sun, he died . . .and so I print fire sales and wedding
announcements. Now, Mike, be careful. You can't leave
here till dark, and my printer's helper, Xesus, will drive
you part way."

"Rose, there's no danger . . . you're full of ideas it's
like it used to be."

"Let me get out the slivowitz, and you'll tell me, my
held, how it's changed."

As they drank the plum brandy Mike told Rose a little
about himself, a little about Terry. The Mexican youth,
Xesus, working a poster press in a lean-to out back, was
singing:

> The Comintern calls you
> Raise high the red banner
> In steelhard lines to battle
> Raise the sickle and hammer!

Mike said, "He's going to get in trouble."

"Xesus? He's still living like the CP was still something out here. Believe me, it's all in the past. Also, the
big unions are getting rid of the Jews as too impractical
dreamers for justice. You aren't anti-Semitic, Mike?"

"Hell no. My war buddy, the only man I'd ever trust,
he's a Jew . . . Davey Wasserman. I don't judge people
by anything but how they effect me and what side they're
on."

"Good. I don't burn up anymore. I rest on my old values. My sons, they live in Trenton, in Philadelphia. A dentist, and the other a dairy farmer, no less. Up to his navel in cow *dreak*. My daughter, Naomi, a dress designer, very fancy, flies in her nose. Me they ignore. The old Red Front Mama, a disgrace, a shame to them. They go to temple, their children are called Cedric and Fredrick and Nancy Belle and Fiona. I ask you, for them, not me, I want a better world? I ask the dentist last year when I saw his Nixon button, 'You circumcised yet?' "

Later she fed Mike a steak, a potato pudding, and they sat on the back porch of the shop sipping slivowitz, looking over fields where men were plowing with gang plows pulled by huge tractors, and the wind tore at the tops of the rows of bluegum trees set out as windbreakers.

"Steinbeck—Steinbeck country, they call it. It's all, Mike, as romantic as getting your teeth knocked out. Watch your step at Big Mesa . . . they got the worst labor record for any vineyard around."

"We have a couple organizers inside—a good man named Lopez—and we're not making any noise yet."

"I wish I could go along but my feet, the veins look like road maps. Ah, when I was a *firebren* on Delancey Street, sixteen years old and organizing the Embroiderers, Pleaters, Tuckers, Stitchers, Tubular Piping Workers . . . Local 66 . . . well, let's drink . . ."

It was twilight when Mike and his bindle and the rolled blanket containing the broadsides got into the rusting, Ford pickup, and the Mexican boy, Xesus, coughed through his hand-rolled cigarette and said, "Solidarity, solidarity."

Rose had packed them chicken-fried veal sandwiches, and the night was clear; someplace far off a dog barked, and Mike felt they'd have to kill me first to get these broadsides away from me.

CHAPTER 11

The farmers and ranchers' private police, the local law-men in shiny boots, wearing flat brimmed Stetsons, tight belts with pistols in oiled holsters, patrolled the main roads around the vineyards and crop fields, turning back anyone in a jalopy or camper they didn't like the looks of, or identified from photographs as radicals, ACLU, "bleeding hearts." At first they were ordered to make a U-turn with a wave of the arms, then a truncheon was used to direct them to "back up and git." Those few who insisted on their right on a public highway, got rousted, and one or two who stood fast got a few days in the over-heated jail as vagrants. "No sweat," as the local chief, Matt Bowers, told the vineyard managers.

Cars passed Terry and Ginny on the Big Mesa side road, but a lot of the pickers were on foot carrying their bin-dles, pots—even babies, indifferent to flies and heat rash. They were all caked with the orange dust of the dry roads, tanned like leather, and broken up into tribal groups or newly created menages and gangs, male or female, or even into creeds. A large sign, with a smaller one beneath it, and several postboxes were nailed to a redwood fence. The larger sign read:

BIG MESA VINEYARDS CORP. No. 2.

The smaller sign was the one Terry read out loud to Ginny: PICKERS AND PACKERS WANTED. MEN AND WOMEN.

Two Latin girls joined them at the signs. One was slim, tough, and very pretty; the other was plump and dark and carried a guitar. Both girls had blankets and gear. Terry said to them, "Where they hiring today?"

"Down by the packing sheds," said the slim one. "They call me Nita. This is Angela."

"Mitch Buckley of the Mesa Vineyards is hiring today," said Angela. "We going there. We show you."

"Thanks," said Terry. "I'm Terry Munday. This is my partner, Ginny."

"Pleased to meet you both."

Ginny just nodded a greeting.

They all started down the dirt road to the big buildings. The oak and cottonwoods swayed leaves in the warm wind. Pickup trucks carrying open boxes of grapes passed them going toward the town. The girl who said she was called Nita stopped to pull a stone from her shoe. She was wearing high heeled silver slippers.

"My name Nita Vargas . . . everybody call me Round Heels. American Joke. I Mexican."

"I guessed it," said Terry.

"We been up near Fresno picking greens. Angela very good guitar player, not such good picker."

Angela grinned. "Too much bending over in the fields all the time."

"That's the main idea in picking," Terry said. "This Mitch Buckley, good to work for?"

Round Heels shrugged her shoulders and accepted a cigarette from Terry. Angela turned down the smoke, and Terry didn't offer one to Ginny. Round Heels lit her cigarette with a book of matches lettered: *Pepe's Grand Chili Parlor.*

"If you're pretty he hires you first. And you not talk union, catch?"

"A wolf?"

Angela nodded. "Thees feller Mitch big shot football player one time at Stanford. He tell me all about it last year. Going to play for the L.A. Rams, he said."

"You know, always trying for a touchdown," Round Heels added.

Ginny said, "It always this hot?"

Angela grinned. "This not hot. Wait till we out in the fields."

Big Mesa Vineyards No. 2 was part of a wine bottling combine called *Banko Wines.* It produced millions of gallons of cheap grade wines under fancy labels and with modern packaging. Mesa No. 2 was several thousand acres of fast producing vines. The grapes were crushed and barreled here, then shipped in tank cars to be bottled and processed at the main plant near San Francisco. It also sold crated grapes to smaller distilleries. It contained a huge processing and bottling plant for a popular western wino trade wine, *San Joaquin Gold Label,* a powerful, fortified, cheap wine favored by winos seeking a low priced drunk. It was made of the crushed skins, stems, and seeds of the grapes.

The four girls joined a milling crowd of men and women in front of a three-foot-high loading platform near the main building. A tall, very wide young man with short cut blond hair, a fat mouth, and deep-set dark eyes was standing on the platform.

He wore an L.A. Rams football jersey, carried a clipboard and papers. He looked down at the pushing pickers while smoking a three-inch cigar, holding it in his teeth. Every few moments he would flick the ash off the tobacco and yell.

"Stop pushin' or I'll stop hiring for the day."

"Sure, Mitch, sure," someone shouted.

"You heard me. I said stop the shovin'."

Round Heels waved. "Hey, Mitch boy!"

Mitch ignored her and looked at his clipboard. "Now, I need two more vine trimmers, some loading platform hands. And a lot of bunch pickers. Good clean pickers."

Round Heels said, "Let's get over to the side and come up by the weighing scales. He'll hire us. What a build on him, eh?"

They followed Round Heels' shapely back and her wobbling high heels up to the side of the loading platform and up three steps to the weighing scales. The crowd began to push forward again and cry out:

"I ready to work."

"Six lugs an hour is easy for me."

"How about me?"

"Hey, me and the old lady."

Mitch was pointing and nodding. "Okay, Chico, on the boxes. You there, platform mover. Hello, Joe—vine trimmer."

He turned, dropped down to the ground from the platform, and came over to the group. "Hello, Round Heels; back for the fat pay and easy life?"

"You no mad I trip you into water ditch last year?"

"That's just unfinished business, doll." He winked at Ginny. "Say, who's your friend? Where you from, honey?" He felt her shoulder through her shirt.

Terry said, "We've been down south . . . Imperial Valley . . . we're expert pickers."

"Friends," said Round Heels.

"That's right," said Mitch, "one big happy daisy chain."

Mitch motioned a thin, blond boy to take over the clip-board and the hiring.

"I can use all the pickers I can get." Mitch held out a pad. "Sign here, and then when we get to the camp, the bunk boss will take names and issue bunkhouses."

"The bugs still there—in the bunkhouse?" Round Heels asked.

Mitch looked Ginny over. "How old are you, honey?"

"I'm, I'm nineteen."

Round Heels laughed. "Mitch, he afraid of jailbait. The state John Laws, they're strict about tasting quail."

Terry said, "I'm over seventeen, in case anybody is worried."

Mitch remained in a good mood. "All right, you girls, into the station wagon. I'll run you up to the bunk-house."

Mitch pointed to a dusty station wagon lettered *Meso No. 2.* They crossed to it, Ginny hanging back a bit. Mitch asked her:

"You want the job, don't you?"

"Sure," said Ginny.

"Well then, you got it." He turned to Ginny and took her arm. "You ride with me up front. You ever pick grapes?"

"I've picked fruit . . . lots of times."

The car started off in a snarl of gears, puffing up road dust.

Mitch said, "Lots of wine to make. Big place. Our own spur line and shipping platforms, winery, presses, and box factory, and no paying union dues—free enterprise here."

"You one smart foreman, eh?" Round Heels said.

Mitch said, "A little respect. Personnel director, girls, not foreman."

They were climbing up past packing sheds, past box

factories smelling of wood shavings, past the processing plant and its sour, fermenting odor. Beyond were dusty pines and a more rutted road, below it was a big watering pool with steel sides and rows of small, pitch-roofed bunkhouses, very old, paint peeling, standing on unsteady concrete corner posts. The station wagon drove up to the row of bunkhouses. Men and women were active at little outdoor fires, cooking evening meals.

Mitch stopped the wagon with a snarl of brakes. "Second bunkhouse is empty. You girls can have it."

"Furniture's so old," Angela said, "even the worms don't want it."

"Mattresses thin as pancakes," said Round Heels.

"You can get some mattress cornhusks from the shed. Ginny, if you have any problem, come to me."

"Thank you," Ginny said.

Terry sensed Round Heels had something on Mitch. The Mexican hot shot was possessive with him. He was giving her a light brush, but he wasn't being tough about it.

The station wagon pulled away and the girls dropped their bindles on the hard packed earth.

"Not too bad a place," said Angela. "I like it better than paying rent, cleaning house, or beating rugs. Who cooks?"

Terry pulled out the frying pan. "I'll start. Who wants to run to the company store and get some bacon, cheese, doughnuts, white bread, and some cans of soup?"

"Who's the millionaire?" said Round Heels.

"Me," said Terry, pulling out her bills. "You can all flip your share back payday. Stretch this as far as it will go at the store. I'm the trusting type."

Round Heels folded the money into the front of her shirt. "I get something extra free, don't worry, *amigos,* the old free enterprise system, yes?"

Ginny looked over the interior of the bunkhouse and

came back to the girls. "It's better out here unless it rains." Angela shook her head. "Wait till you've picked a few dozen lugs of grapes."

Round Heels went off to the store on her wobbly slippers. Terry and Angela, old hands, began to gather large, fire-blackened stones for a cooking place. Far off several tractors were pulling in loaded lugs of grapes. On the horizon someone was burning old vine trimmings. Way off, almost lost in space, there were the rigid backbones of some very impressive mountains. More and more people were coming in from the fields.

"Not bad," Terry said. "But we'll bunk and cook in the open on nights like this."

Angela was idly plucking her guitar. "Sometimes it make me very sad always moving place to place. How you?"

"Sure. Where you from, Angela?" Terry asked.

"I come from Italy, when I was little girl. Folks all dead, their jobs all in mills all day. I come from family of farmers, so I go back to farms." She played a sad chord and put down the guitar.

"Round Heels related to you?" Ginny asked.

"No. I meet her in Riverside in an orange grove. She gave a cooking sherry party with a gang of winos, and they left her behind. She not much good when she drinking. She Mexicano. Where you two from?"

"Around," said Terry.

"What around what?"

"Around."

Terry was busy building a stone fireplace on the ground. "No place. Everyplace U.S.A. Ginny, help me build a fire. Angela, go get some water from the tap. Run it till the rust is gone. Steal us a few more stones on the way back."

"You've been picking a long time," Ginny said. "You know the ropes, Terry."

"I've built more campfires than Daniel Boone."

Soon dozens of little cooking fires were burning in front of the bunkhouses.

Terry asked, "Very nonunion Big Mesa vineyards?"

"Damn big, fucking nonunion."

"How do you feel, Angela, about unions?"

"How I feel? I feel, yes, I feel no? If they let us, I want union. But you get on black list, you never pick again, never."

"There is talk of union organizing again. Would you join if it looked as if the law backed us?"

Angela whistled and said, "The law? The law is lousy cops, them Gary Coopers in the cowboy hats and the guns big as their cocks, they hope, on the hips. That the law. The law work for the owners."

"The National Labor Relations Board in Washington should decide the real law for the workers."

"In Washington? That too far away. I learn always stay way from law, they break your goddam ass, right, Ginny?"

"I, I never had me much to do with the law."

Terry decided to lay off union talk for a while. It wasn't going to be a cinch, that's for sure. Maybe the older folk would be easier. They knew more, had suffered a lot. These young kids were still sassy and fiesty.

"Times are changing fast," she said. "Things we never hoped to happen are happening."

"Oh sure . . . you like Elvis Presley, the new kind of music . . . shaking his balls?"

Round Heels was back, with packages, and the pan was soon full of bacon frying and bread toasting, and near it a pot of soup steaming. Ginny laid out tin plates. Angela was cutting bread. Terry was writing on wrapping paper.

"I'll keep book, and we'll settle up later in the week. Round Heels, that bacon is as crisp as it will ever get."

"Smell good, huh?"

Terry divided the food, and all started to eat with a
good appetite. A hound dog barked across a row of trees.
Late birds shot across a sooty sky, snapping up moths as
they flew.

They were all healthy young women, and all were very
hungry.

It was a busy, animated camp scene at the bunkhouses.
Two large brown women were feeding babies at plump,
hard breasts, while they drank wine. An old man was removing burrs from a mean-looking dog, and several
young children were playing television cowboys, running
wild among the cooking fires. It was a mild evening. A
low moon would be out soon, and here and there an oil
lamp was lit. There was no waste of stringing electric
wiring to the bunkhouses.

A teenager with a great oily head of black hair combed
high in front and into ducktails in back was playing a
portable radio. He snapped his fingers and rolled his
naked brown shoulders to a recording of lyrics that had
meanings under the first meaning.

An old Indian-Mexican with white hair and a white
moustache was sitting barefoot on the concrete steps of a
bunkhouse sucking up red, sharp wine from a bottle. After every swallow the old man would say to the boy with
the portable radio, "That is right, Chico, live when you
can. It rain soon."

"That's right, Daddy-O, get slopped."

"Respect, Chico."

"Sure, you twacked old boozer. Man, you old cats kill
me. Don't you like to share the vino?"

"Alone is best for drinking, Chico."

"Look, man, I mean don't you care for chicks or kicks
or tea no more?"

"Chico, you find out only the bottle, she is good."

"I know, it rain soon."

Some of the workers were lighting a last cigarette and
wrapping themselves in blankets and looking up, arms

folded under their heads, jackets for pillows. The babies cried.

Angela dropped the empty tin dishes into the bucket and sat on a box that had once held baked beans, hugged herself, and inhaled the scent of a mock orange bush doing its night work beside their bunkhouse. "It's nice in the open with the smell of wood smoke. I want to cry."

Round Heels opened her shirt, took out cigarettes, chewing gum, and a candy bar. "You cry, Angela, and I leave you. Look what I swiped at the store for us."

"Not crying! Just happy. You got a family, Ginny?"

"No, my folks were killed on . . ." Ginny paused, "on the Ridge Route one night. A truck skidded into their car."

Terry asked, "What did you get out of the insurance company, Ginny?"

"The funeral people took the money. They say silver handles—solid—on the caskets."

Terry yawned. "We better hit the hay. Work call early tomorrow. Ginny, you go wash the dishes."

"Play us some tunes, Angela," Round Heels said.

"Let's drag the mattresses out here," Terry said. "The bugs could use some fresh air."

Angela began to play her guitar. Her hair undone and falling over her half-nude shoulders, she began to sing softly an Italian song.

"Hits you, eh, *amigo?*"

"Sure does."

"That was beautiful," said Ginny as the music stopped.

"Pretty as a punch in the nose," added Round Heels.

"What's it say?"

"It is about love and wine," said Round Heels. "What is more better?"

"It's really about a boy and a girl," Angela added.

"One of each, that's nice." Round Heels giggled.

"They are sad," said Angela. "Sad and in love. Sad life is short, and sad love passes. Is *very* sad song."

"All good songs are about love," said Round Heels. "Love is a very sad business. But very wonderful, huh, Terry?"

"I bet you pretty good at it."

Angela stretched and yawned. "Some day I find love—a big, fat, rich Armenian. And sing no sad love. All fun and dancing. Love be one big ball of a party."

"Good night, ladies." Terry tossed ashes on the fire. "Happy picking tomorrow."

The fire died out to one last red coal.

It had been dark when Mike swung off the oil rig that had given him a lift. Big Mesa Vineyards lay just over the next ridge. No use reporting for the tractor job till morning. Jamie Ward had given him the address of a joint where the union organizers had a connection—an understanding with the Negro owner of the place. The word black was not yet in use—in fact a black man would have resented it.

Mike came into a cleared off and bulldozed section of ground. Here stood a gas pump and a low pineboard and fieldstone building with a long narrow sign outlined in red and blue neon: *Willie Moon's Dixieland Jazz Ribs Beer Dancing.*

Several battered cars, a shiny white Cadillac, and two little rump-jolting English jobs were parked on the blacktop in front of the building. The sound of a trio taking a solid chord of "Chinatown, My Chinatown" came to Mike.

"Real King Oliver style," said a fat man as he set a station wagon in place.

"Oh, that Moon, he's in the groove tonight," said a girl with the fat man, rearranging her wrinkled jacket.

"Just remember you're with me tonight."

"I am?"

"Get rid of the roach," said the fat man.

She took one last drag of the cigarette and flipped it down. The man looked at her in disgust and walked over to the glowing butt on the blacktop and ground it into small fragments under the head of his sports shoe. Carefully, he kicked the bits away letting them fly in all directions.

"You're chicken," said the girl. "Charlie Scott is chicken."

"You're damn right, Marge. I don't want to do any Federal time."

Mike grinned and went inside.

Moon's was a long ranchhouse style building . . . inside were exposed rafters, wagon wheels wired for electricity, a large, low platform where three wet and expressionless Negroes were hard at work jazzing the music. Moon himself, three hundred pounds of him, was at the battered upright. ("Shat man, yo' can't play no real hoehouse jazz on no Steinway, nohow.")

His shaven black head was beaded with sweat, and playing, he concentrated: eyes closed—shaking from side to side. The dance floor held a dozen couples. Some small tables held a dozen more partners, and maverick strays of both sexes. There was a redwood bar and two waitresses, tall-legged high yellows called beginner browns, who were busy serving beer and glasses of rye or bourbon. It was no place to ask for Scotch or mixed drinks, with or without a pink cherry.

The smoke was getting thicker, and the smell of cooking grease, restroom disinfectant, and body powder filled the place.

Marge waved greetings to people she knew. Mike figured they were field bosses, secondhand car dealers, mink ranchers, smalltown businessmen, a sleazy lawyer, several girls from picking gangs. Several of the men ignored her greeting.

They sat down near the bandstand and ordered rye. After two rounds Moon joined them. Mike took a seat at the next table, ordered beer.

"Yo' sure ain't been around, Charlie, in body or spirit."

"Busy at the vineyard," said the fat man.

"I keep sayin' there's one cat knows the real jive, understands the Jelly Roll Morton piano style. That Charlie Scott." Moon turned to Mike. "You like it?"

"Sure. Can I buy?"

"Sure. Join us."

After a round of beer it was all very cozy and there were introductions.

Moon wiped his heavy damp neck with a yellow silk handkerchief. "Later a few of us go jamming in the cabin out back. Some nice sessions goin' there late at night. The real gut-bucket New Orleans stuff. Not for these yere squares."

Charlie said to Mike, "Moon played with Bunk Johnson."

"I gigged with everybody worth a kick in the can."

"My brother Moz, he collects Louie, King Oliver discs."

"How about that!"

Mike bought another round, and he studied Charlie Scott closely. The man was on a list Jamie Ward had given him, his name marked: *Very doubtful—once interested.*

Moon said suddenly, "Hey, look at me, how ol' yo' ofays think I am? I'm seventy. Still jivin'."

Mike felt he would have to study Charlie—maybe trust him.

Mike listened to the sound of a valve horn taking a glide and a riff with "Oh, Johnny, Oh." The drum sticks did a press roll on the traps, followed it down and improvised their own pattern. Then someone on the piccolo took it away into a flare-up.

Charlie Scott said to Mike, "You been giving me the goo-goo-eyed all-over-look all night. You freakish?"

"No, I'm no jocker. I'd like to talk to you. Let's go take a leak. It's safe."

"Shit, I can take care of myself. I'm no gunzel."

* * *

The john was small, piny smelling. They stood leaning toward the urinal, flies open.

"Jamie Ward gave me your name."

"Jamie, huh? Hasn't his ulcers killed him yet?"

"Not yet. He felt you might . . ."

Charlie Scott zipped up and waved a hand. "No, I wouldn't. If it's the ol' union fuckoff, not me . . . no."

"You were a hell of a good man, Jamie said."

"A stupid jerk. I got my head busted, yeah—got a big hospital bill too, and no sonofabitch 'round Sacramento would hire me to handle no machines for a long time."

"You work a fork lift at Big Mesa. I'm going to run a cat there."

"Well, mister, stay away from me or I'll test a valve wrench on your noggin. I need the bread, see? Marge is knocked up, and I'm still making payments on the car." .

"Jamie said you could be trusted, Charlie . . . anybody jockeying machines that's for a union?"

"Go find out. Mike, don't count on me. I'm chicken, ask Marge."

Mike left it at that. He'd work on Charlie. It was having a woman pregnant on his hands that made him rabbity. Jesus, he'd been lucky with Terry.

They went back to the main room. Mike had a few more, and the jazz lovers moved into the back as Moon closed the front joint. They were in the low-ceilinged cabin behind the joint. An electric light bulb, painted red, was hanging from a wire in the rafters. Everybody was on the floor, or on two studio beds. There were six of them listening to the funky music; and the air sharp with reefer smoke. One of the beginner browns had passed out on the floor. Moon was playing the horn, his great, black bulk shiny in a small chair. He bent way over, blowing for himself, woodshedding, making sounds he maybe heard in his mind and was not putting out the way he wanted them to come out.

The drummer was a mean-tusked, razor-scarred buck, and looked stoned. But he could handle the sticks, the whisk, and the Chinese blocks like no one Mike had ever heard before. Everybody was pretty far gone. The place smelled, he thought, like a henhouse.

"Oh, dicity, uppity folk," sang the drummer, "stay 'way."

Charlie Scott was snapping his fingers, his eyelids half down like window shades. He had a tan butt smoldering from his fat lower lip. He was trying to whisper. "That's the way the breaks come. One day you're high on the hog, next year you're breaking your tail, and then you're stuck out here in the tall weeds with the half-assed fruit bums . . . up shit creek and cold as Kelsey's nose."

Only it wasn't coming out that clear. A fat blonde escaping from the top of her beaded evening gown was singing in a wonderful way, Mike felt; made you think of Billie Holiday and Bessie Smith; only this was not a recording.

> Rubber tired carriage
> Kansas City hack
> Took poor Albert
> To the cemetery
> And forgot to bring him back.

Mike left just before dawn. He pushed union broadsides under the wipers of any cars still left in the parking area. He left them in any mailboxes he passed. He settled in at last at the Pioneer Motel, bushed.

CHAPTER 12

Terry stirred in her sleep; the cool field wind near morning had a chilly nip. She rolled over and tightened the blanket around her. An owl hooted as it hunted mice under the vines, and the beat of a car engine grew louder. She came awake, listening to the owl, the car, and someplace the heartbeat of a laboring pump bringing up water. The car motor stopped. Angela was sleeping on her face, snoring. Ginny lay very still and the moonlight made her features into patterns that showed the child that lived in the girl.

There was the weaving clatter of very unsteady feet and Terry half closed her eyes. Round Heels came around the corner of the bunkhouse, her hair over her face, her feet almost beyond control. The girl held on to the corner of the building, then stumbled over to her mattress and blanket and sat down. Terry wondered if she were ill. The motor of the car grew louder and went away, and she knew the kid had been out with somebody; it was noth-

ing to bother Terry. Among pickers one didn't question
moral patterns or hassle about what one wasn't asked.
She sure looked sick. Terry could smell the sour sweat,
the odor of rye, and a certain sweet scent that wrinkled
her nose. Tea.

She watched Round Heels fall back on the mattress
placed on the ground, mumble something that made no
sense, and pull the blanket partly around her. In a moment she either slept or bombed out.

Terry readjusted herself in her blanket and closed her
eyes. Who could blame the kid? There was no future at
all in picking, unless the union improved things, and no
place to go when you were through picking—or too sick
to make the rounds—or too broken up by women's diseases or stiffening joints. Terry believed, or tried to believe, live when you can. Terry had a lot of trouble with
her conscience in working out a pattern that satisfied the
big chunk of decency, moral values, and romantic nature
that controlled so many of her actions. Jesus, she'd better
keep an eye on Ginny. Nothing wrong with her except reform school, no parents, and this lousy job, as long as it
lasted. Terry brooded, wondering would she see Mike tomorrow?—and fell asleep quickly and didn't dream.

A packing plant down the road blew off steam with a
shrill scolding at seven in the morning. It repeated its
moaning note fifteen minutes later. By that time the
pickers sleeping in front of the bunkhouses were up.
They were sticky-eyed, feeling their stiff joints, making
mouth gestures of disgust for the night's aftertaste. The
tacky babies were howling for breast milk, the young
snotnoses were making rackets with two mongrel dogs.
The workers were lighting little smokey fires or moving
with rags and towels and bits of soap toward the two faucets and the row of privies behind the pepper trees. Scattered fragments of old, yellowed newspapers floated un-

derfoot. There were many flies, and at this hour their bite hurt. Wood smoke and coffee and the smell of wine barrels flavored the day.

Terry was up and folding her blanket, dressed for picking, a dark tan man's shirt shoved into her tight denims.

"Come on, Ginny. Get in line at the faucets. And race down to the johns before they get too popular. I'll make the sandwiches for lunch. Angela, nudge Round Heels."

"I tried, but she not move."

"Turn her over and keep trying."

Ginny sat up and hugged her knees. She felt worried, but somehow pleased at this new excitement around her. Dogs were barking, kids rushing underfoot, and the smoke of morning fires suggesting black, black coffee and something solid to keep one going till noon. It was going to be a hot day. The sun was already warming everything that had cooled off during the night.

Round Heels stirred under Angela's pushing fingers and opened one bleary eye. "I wanta die. Die right now."

"You look like hell."

"Angela, I feel it. I don't think I wash."

Terry said sternly, "You wash if you bunk with us. Come on, I'll get some hot coffee and grub ready and make sandwiches for lunch."

Angela and Ginny elbowed their way to one of the faucets. They splashed their faces wet and used a bit of soap. Sharing a grimy towel, they wiped themselves fairly dry. Round Heels came up to them rubbing her eyes.

"What happens now?" Ginny asked.

"We get our work slips."

"Picking grapes sounds like clean work."

"Sure, fun for old ladies," Angela said. "Like drinking tea."

Round Heels was splashing water over her face. "You crazy? Field work gives you muscles in wrong places." She slapped her rump. "Ten years and nobody want you! I get me an inside job, packin'."

Terry was waving some yellow cards. "Come on, they need the water for the crops. Here are your work tickets. We all start picking in the north two-hundred-forty."

Angela nodded. "That's fine field. The grapes big and good to pick."

Round Heels looked at her work slip and frowned. "Hey, Mitch said he'd give me an inside job."

"I'd rather be in a field," said Angela, "where I could run from the big lug."

After a quick breakfast the girls walked toward the field. A tractor passed, pulling a row of low box wagons. The driver waved to them.

It was Mike, a pipe smoldering in one corner of his mouth.

"Hey," said Terry, running over to the tractor.

"Hey, yourself. How you been?"

"Worried. Everything . . ." She was wide-eyed, earnest. "Everything is fine."

Mike looked off to the two girls watching him and Terry. "I see you have a couple of friends."

Terry nodded. "Kids . . . Angela, Ginny, Miss Heels . . ., this is an old friend of mine . . . Mike Brant."

"He not so old," said Round Heels.

Terry said, "We worked the docks together down in Frisco. Lots of picketing."

"That will get your tail busted," said Angela.

Terry said, "We are sort of forming our own work crew."

Mike nodded, leaned over, whispered: "I've got some union broadsides for you back at the Pioneer Motel."

"Hey," said Round Heels, "maybe we ride—we don't talk so much."

Mike nodded and pressed Terry's hand.

"Girls, give you a lift?"

Angela grinned. "North-two-forty."

"Hop in. I'll take you as far as the water cutoff."

Round Heels shook her head as the girls got onto a drag behind the tractor.

"I gotta see Mitch."

"You keep out of trouble," Angela yelled after Round Heels as she ran off.

Mike drove the tractor with the skill of someone who loved machines. He turned his head around to talk to them.

"A great day for picking."

Ginny nodded. She seemed to have more color and a greater interest in life. "It's healthy, isn't it, working outdoors?"

Mike began to move the tractor up a dirt ramp. "All off. See you after work." Mike handed Ginny a pair of cotton gloves. "You haven't picked before. Wrong kind of roughness on your fingers. Here, you better wear these."

"Thank you. I'll see you get them back."

Terry picked up an empty lug box and said, "Pick up a crate each of you and follow me."

All around them the pickers were busy detaching the grape clusters with small clippers and laying them with care in the boxes. The work had started.

Mike drove the snorting tractor to where he was to pick up a train of three drags being loaded. Big Mesa was a smart, modern outfit. They grew hundreds of acres of grapes on native roots: Sémillon, Savigny, Muscadet type grapes, dark and white grapes. They took good care of the vines, spraying, sulphuring against pests and phylloxera.

Charlie Scott was seated on his fork lift near a loading point—ready to load trays as Mike came up.

"Hung over, Charlie?"

"I'm not singing and dancing." He looked to right and left. "Now you just leave me be, Brant. I'm no stoolie, no company fink, but I want no part of what you're doing."

"Sure, Charlie, sure . . . seen Manuel Lopez around?"

"Went to a cock fight yesterday. Must be drunk some-place."

Mike saw the ground around the vines was dry and fine as powder. The weeds had been chopped out between the thousands of vines growing in rows. The sun beat down.

Terry, wearing a man's hat she'd picked up someplace, and the girls all wore dark sunglasses. There was a baby blue sky with white clouds (drawn poorly as if by a child) overhead. The air was already too warm for comfort, but it was a clear day with just a dusty haze to the south where they were burning bush on a hillside. For miles around the green fields the black vines were laid out in rectangular patterns—falling away toward the roads or climbing up near the hills. Mostly it was flat, fertile land. In the country, Mike figured, thousands worked in the fields. Great gangs came in covered trucks from the bor-der, under evil-looking Mexican *patrons* who exploited their simple and ignorant countrymen. There were also wetbacks, nationals who had crossed the border without permits, and who took the lowest pay and ate the worst food and were hunted down after the picking season and dumped back across the border.

There were whole families in the fields—white-haired, silent people who kept to themselves. These were the last of the Okies, who had come in the '30's when the Dust Bowl blew away and the great depression was on the land. They were a dull, staring folk who could re-member cops beating them down with clubs in the tar paper Hoovervilles which used to dot the river bottoms where their kids had died with sore mouths, the United Ranchers feeding them pig slops and giving them blows on the head. All this their sad eyes told Mike. Now they just picked or later sat in front of the bunkhouses with horny, worn hands.

As the old man who handed out the lug boxes told Mike: "It's a living." It was vittles—ash cakes and a hog

jowl—and the old woman and the kids could go to town
and belt away candy at Woolworth's and take in a picture
show. But the vitality, Mike saw, was out of the last Oakies. The young ones had gone into the army and learned
to eat white bread and like rock and roll. The gals were
doing up their snuff-colored hair and talking sass to the
old ones, getting jobs inside and horsing with the half-
breeds in the coke parlors, and riding in hotrods to drag
races. "A hell of a note," the old Okie told Mike. But they
didn't speak much. Just picked.

Terry had her group at work. Angela began to pick and
load. Ginny watched as Terry explained the process. "It
takes little brains, Ginny, just some moving of hands and
piling up the grapes. You lose the clippers, they take off
two bucks pay."
"It looks fun."
"You clip a long stem, you handle with care, you don't
bruise, and you lay the bunch easy, so it don't crush in
the lug box."
"Sure."
"You do it."
"Like this?"
"You ruined the grapes."
"Can I eat 'em?"
"You'll get the trots."
Angela said, "It's somebody else's fucking grapes. Who
cares?"
They worked for half an hour.
"I'm getting blisters," said Ginny, stripping off a glove.
"The badge of the fruit picker," said Terry. "Welcome
to the club."
"How many lugs do we fill today?" Angela asked.
"All we can. The more we fill, the more we get paid.
Where's your picking partner?" Terry asked.
"Round Heels? Promoting. She's very good at promot-

ing. But this time I think she gets trouble. Mitch has his eye on Ginny."

"You talk too much," Terry said.

"My back hurts," Ginny moaned, standing up straight and stretching her arms.

"Poor folks got no backbones. Just arms. Pick."

Terry wiped her face with one arm and pushed back her hat. "*Only* your back? Look, partner, we don't complain unless a leg is coming off or the top of our head melts."

"It's hot enough."

Filled lug boxes were being pulled toward the packing shed. Round Heels had wasted most of the morning looking for Mitch. She found him near the warehouse; he was checking a list of lumber lengths on hand.

"Hello, Mitch."

"Get back to the fields." He seemed to have a bad head too.

"You promise me. I want an inside job. Fields ruin my skin, *amigo*. You want to spoil my complexion?"

"I'm busy. Get away before the manager bugs me."

"You never too busy for makin' love."

He threw down the list in anger. No dame ever seemed grateful anymore.

"Want me to run your ass right off this ranch?"

"Maybe you like Ginny girl, huh?"

"A guy is entitled to a change."

Round Heels started to claw Mitch's face. He grabbed her arms and twisted them to her side. He wrestled her into a helpless position.

"We had fun, we had our laughs. You bitch, if you want field work, go ahead. If you have any fancy ideas, try Madame Wald's cathouse in town."

He flung her aside and picked up his list.

She shrugged. "Sure. Give us a smoke, sweetie."

"Get going." He tossed her a half pack of cigarettes.

"Keep 'em?"

"Keep 'em."

"I'll get in a good word for you with Ginny." She cut her throat with a finger gesture. "A *real* good word, shithead."

She went off muttering. Mitch pushed his hair back into place.

A blue and white car, waxed to a shine, came up the drive. A stocky, middle-aged man with a weatherworn face drove. The car carried no fancy lettering or special lights, just a sign on the windshield reading: Sheriff's Department.

The car came to a stop, and the man got out. Mitch waved to him. "Hi-ya, Sheriff."

"Hello, Mitch. All set on your work crews?"

"Just short a few pickers. Got your eye on anybody real bad, Jake?"

"No one in particular," he said as he took some photos from his pocket. "Just the usual heads and mug shots that came up from Frisco and L.A. Take a gander. Hire any of these characters?"

Mitch took the handful of photographs and began to move through them quickly. Picking hands were hard to get at times, and yet the vineyards had to play ball with the law. It was usually just petty stuff. What he saw wasn't impressive. Weak faces, cruel faces, but none that looked smart enough to be real dangerous. Drunks, petty hoodlums, car looters, shoplifters, wife beaters. He stopped: Here was that Ginny Wolnik, labeled Louise Jenkins.

"Any big time stuff?" he asked casually.

"Jumping a car's wiring, rolling a drunk, small time punks."

Mitch held up Ginny's photo. "This the drunk roller?"

"No . . . a kid who went over the wall at the female correction center at Twin Peaks. She'd be better off where she could be taken care of. Information on the back."

"If I run across any of 'em I'll let you know. Can I keep this set for a while, Jake?"

"Sure." The sheriff lowered his voice, took out a folded copy of one of Mike's DWU broadsides from an inner pocket of his western cut jacket. "Seen any of *these* around?"

Mitch unfolded, read, and whistled. "Nope. Where?"

"All along the highway, pushed under windshields of cars."

"What do you figure the cocksuckers are trying to do?"

"I figure, Mitch, I better swear in some deputies, and maybe Big Mesa should ship over some security guards. The DWU looks like it's going to try again to organize the pickers and trimmers."

Mitch refolded the broadside. "Shit, Jake, they got their heads busted but good last time. They're not coming back for more of the same."

The sheriff sighed, wiped a funnel of sweat off his nose. "You don't know organizers . . . they got support, got the spick priests and civil rights bleeding hearts, and there's talk of a table grape boycott. You just keep your eyes peeled, Mitch. You spot anything, like outside people coming in to talk to the field hands, just buzz me, and we'll make some vagrant arrests."

"I'll not let anybody leave the place after work."

"No, no. Let 'em roam in town. I got some boys planted in bars to see who they talk to, who's handing out the union printing."

"Care for a jolt of grape?"

"Not while I'm on duty."

Jake Fry, the sheriff, turned away, then stopped and turned back to face Mitch. The man's face was expressionless, but Mitch felt the cold blue eyes boring in on him. The goddam Jack Mormon was a moral man. He'd hate to have the old boy work him over with shoes on down at the sheriff's office. Jake Fry had the reputation of a man who liked to knock you around when you didn't answer promptly.

"And, Mitch, try to stay out of trouble this year."

"You've been hearing gossip."

Jake put his face close to Mitch's. "I've been hearin'."

"What you driving at, Jake?"

"The law likes to see girls workin' for a livin'—not screwing for it."

Mitch gave a mocking laugh at the idea. "Sheriff, Mitch Buckley doesn't have to force anybody into the kip."

"That's nice, Don *Youan*. Watch yourself."

"I always do, Jake."

Mitch nodded. Goddam Mormons got all their jollies at home, all that holy happy nookie serving their stud like he was God, a horny God.

CHAPTER 13

When the sheriff's car was moving its dusty way down past the blue gum trees, Mitch let a twitch of fear and rage run across his face. He scratched his armpits, staring openmouthed at Mike's union broadside. Somehow Jake always knew when there was trouble brewing—also of any underage picker being chased, or a big crap game at Cap Farley's. Jake Fry, the son of a bitch, had something cunning in his thick, not fat, body. He didn't take payola either. He let Cap Farley's dice game alone, but Cap had upstairs protection.

Mitch put the photos and the broadside into a pocket. He crossed to the row of white cottages where the top help, the vineyard manager, Moss Contrall, the processor, Ed Weintraub, the foremen, and plant-machinery managers lived. Mitch had a room of his own behind the cottage of Nils Hansen, the tanker trucks boss. He let himself into his bedroom-living room—a square, hot room of knotty pine, with a sagging brass bed, fumed oak wardrobe, and the smell of Flit. He switched on the fan in the ceiling, got out a quart of grape brandy, new and raw, and took a big swallow. Mitch looked in the small wall mirror and admired himself and his looks. His confidence and his courage returned. He hung Mike's broadside on a nail on the wall. Hell, he'd take care of that. He caught a phantom forward pass, pushed back his hair at his tanned temples, and wondered how he'd look with a moustache. He took another belt of the grape brandy and sat down on the bed, looking down at the old copies of *Sports Today*.

The season playing pro football with the Los Angeles Rams had been fine. They had sure courted him—wall-to-wall cunt. The manager had built him up in the half-assed press they had there. Then the touts at Hollywood Park hadn't come up with a good winning streak for a couple of months. Ten grand he still owed the big bookies, and they were leaning hard on him.

Mitch was rather proud of owing that much to the horse-book muscles of L.A. Anyway, the young punk from the bookies in the Beverly Hilton one day had offered Mitch a chance to make good and carry a big paper bag of pot north to Frisco. So the Rams got wind of it, and whammo, he's out on his can.

Mitch took another drink of the grape brandy and closed the bottle and put it on the dresser. He'd bust a few union organizers, show Big Mesa he was the stuff of leaders. He tore up the union broadside.

The sun stood high in the unwrinkled sky. It was noon, and the fields and vineyards had become unbearable. The burned pickers and field hands knew noon was only a short break before taking on the rest of the roasting afternoon. Relief would come when the disc of white sun slipped, like a coin into a slot, in the west.

Terry's group had stopped their bending and picking over the low black stems of the vines. Slowly, in the dry, heated air they moved with dragging feet to the shelter of

pepper trees and poplars that lined the fields, or into the
blue shadows of trucks parked here and there, or to the
mercy of a stretched canvas shelter from the never-failing
sunlight.

Terry, like a good field general, had found a deeply dug
out bank topped by a tool shed, one wall of which threw a
triangular dark shadow. She, Ginny, and Angela took
from the greasy paper bag tuna fish sandwiches, several
hard boiled eggs, and some loose salt twisted up in a corner of an old *Time* magazine page.

They drank rubber-tasting water, delivered warm by a
hose attached to a distant outlet where twirling sprinkler
heads were trying to keep a field of lettuce from burning
up.

Ginny took off her shoes and rubbed her naked toes.
She wore no stockings. "My dogs are killing me."

"How are your arms?"

"Terrible. How do you keep on this picking?"

Terry began to finish a half of a sandwich. "It's the system. No work, no eat."

Angela looked off toward the vineyard buildings. "Here
comes Round Heels."

"A lot of help she's been today."

Ginny, after sucking on the hose, fell back into the
deeper shade, gasping. "I can't eat."

"You better. And don't drink too much water. You'll
get sick."

"I am sick."

"Stop playing baby. I haven't got time for it."

"Yes," said Angela. "It's Round Heels all right."

Terry looked down the patch. "She looks plenty mad."

Round Heels walked up to the group. She sat down and
scowled. "I *hate* grapes! I hate everything!"

"You hate to pick 'em," Angela said.

Far down the field a whistle blew.

"Back to the Muscadet mines," said Angela.

Round Heels refused any of the food. She sat on the

ground and threw handfuls of dirt around. She kicked her worn heels into the earth. She buried her head on her arms and looked up at them with tired eyes. "Damn it, nobody cares, nobody asks you wanta work, you wanta cut grapes, nobody."

Angela handed her a clipper. "You got a lotta catchin' up to do."

"I go pick in the next field."

Round Heels went off. Angela shrugged her shoulders and went after her. Ginny watched them go.

The sun moved with the afternoon in the overhead sky and leaned far to the west as Terry and Ginny filled their last lug box. Their legs were trembling, their hands tingling, as they walked slowly toward the path that led to the bunkhouses.

"I'm eating dust," said Terry. "I wonder if there's any real cool water around . . ."

The sound of a powerful motor filled the vineyards, and Mike and his tractor mounted a ridge before them. He lowered the pitch of the motor.

"Come on, I give round-trip service."

"It's better than walking," Terry said as they mounted the dray behind the big red monster.

From the fields the workers were moving, the ache in their bodies showing in their slow pace. At the bunkhouses Ginny got off the dray.

"Thanks a lot," Ginny said.

Terry said, "All I want is a deep, deep bathtub."

"You gals can use the irrigation ditch north of the storage plants. It's almost out of eye range." Mike pointed in the proper direction.

Terry pressed Mike's arm as the girls went inside the cabin. "Can I see you tonight?"

"You bet. I'm at the Pioneer Motel. I'm borrowing Charlie Scott's car. Pick you up in an hour by the packing shed. How is it?"

Terry grinned. "A worker's ache all over. You know, I

keep forgetting field work is goddam hard. Listen, don't take chances, Mike. Somebody said there was a police car here this afternoon."

"Sheriff hunting some kid got out of correction school." He looked at Terry closely, winked. "It's that kid with you, isn't it?"

"Lay off her. We can't send her back to that creep joint. Have you met any people with union on their mind?"

"I've talked to six men Jamie Ward gave me the names of. They're mostly hot for it, but wary. Charlie now, he's worthless, scared. There's a weekend hoedown party in a couple of days, some kind of company setup. We'll plaster the cabins with the broadsides, get them around while the party is on."

"Mike, Mike, I need loving . . . tired as I am, even just to hold me, hold me tight at that motel."

They spent the night together in a room smelling of insect spray, made easy love, not too violent, and Terry slept. Mike watched her sleep, and in the main house of the motel some rodeo people were having a party—a big wild brawl by the sound of it. Mike lay a long time not sleeping, listening to Terry breathing. . . . He drove her back early in the morning and went looking for Manuel Lopez who was reported to be in jail for running a cockfight.

That afternoon, after a day's picking, Terry was stripping behind the bunkhouse door. "Wear your underwear. It's not formal."

The irrigation ditch was a long, cool stretch of water lined with women in all stages of undress and bathing outfits, bunching up to go into the brown, slow moving water. Angela was there in a slip, and Round Heels in torn shorts and bra.

Round Heels said as she looked at Ginny, "They're letting *anybody* into the water now."

"What's the matter with you?" Angela asked.

Terry said grimly, "Maybe she wants a real sixteen jewel punch in the nose."

Pushing Ginny ahead of her, Terry got into the water. It was cool, but not cold, after a day in the sun. Around them the bathers were splashing, dipping, and snorting, kicking up brown heels. Peace, peace, Terry decided, as she swam out.

The feel of water after hard work was a comfort. Several of the older Mexican women bathing in the ditch wore long night dresses that clung to their huge buttocks and big bellies. The younger girls wore as little as possible. One young blonde lost her drawers and calmly rolled over and over in the water in the nude, exposing her white flanks. Most of the girls were hard-muscled, tanned, shiny skinned and a little underfed. A few were heavy breasted, bursting with tribal fertility, and big in the rear. Remarks ribald and lewd were passed in Spanish and dance hall jargon that puzzled Ginny. She wiped water from her face and said to Terry, "If Round Heels wants trouble, I'll give it to her."

"Don't do anything crazy. She's just hung over."

"I was pretty good at the correction school in taking care of myself."

"Sure you were."

"You had to fight to get anything to eat, to keep a chair, fight off a dike, or to hold on to your weekly chocolate bar. I can hit."

"Don't, unless you have to."

Terry floated on her back, arms relaxed, her hands locked behind her head, her long legs spread-eagled. The ache in her breasts was soaking out. It was good to float here and forget the girls and the hard day's picking, to let the reek and sweat wash out of her. Terry was beginning to feel the calming process—the numbing of her locked muscles and of the pain in her hips. And these girls? Ahead was only the cannery or a waitress job in one of those dismal dogwagons or roadside rests with an amorous Greek boss pinching and breathing garlic in your face, or the cannery foreman thinking a free beer was an invitation to Liberty Hall. Jesus, if these girls could only break out of it somehow.

Terry turned her body, saw the length and smooth curves of it, the grace and hunger of it. Also, she got a look at Round Heels moving in on an unaware Ginny, splashing in the deep, middle water of the ditch.

Terry cut ahead of the Mexican girl with a powerful stroke and got to Ginny's side. The kid didn't look so bad now with her face red from sun, her hair washed clean, her little white teeth showing as she laughed. She wasn't as thin as she looked in clothes. The arms were shapely, but hard; the breasts were small, very round, firm; and Ginny had hips and a nice can. The type of developing young girl that drove certain kinds of men a bit crazy. A little more filling out here and there and Ginny would be a beauty.

"Stay away from Round Heels. She's mean. Can you swim real well, Ginny?"

"Sure. I'm part water rat."

"Duck her if she roughhouses you."

Ginny was swimming like a seal, hand over hand, swimming well and enjoying it.

"It's great."

Round Heels began to splash around Ginny.

"Want the whole pond?"

"Just the part I'm in."

"You don't like the work with us wogs and greaseballs?"

"I didn't say it."

"You don't have to. I got it . . . fucking WASP."

"Aw, go soak your head."

"Smart, eh!" Round Heels shouted.

"Don't push me."

"You tender, chicken?"

* * *

Terry watched, wary. The kid would have to learn to take care of herself. Terry saw there was something she didn't know about Ginny. She saw the girl was riled up and her temper on the boil; then the mouse turned wildcat and the weakness turned to fury. She couldn't make it all the time, but after long suffering and being put upon, she got that glare in her eyes and her mind started to spin off like the countdown on a rocket. She could do damage then, and inflict pain . . . only she couldn't sustain. . . .

"I don't start trouble," Ginny said.

Round Heels shouted, "You're pretty cheap twat, I think."

Terry said, "You shut up talking like that!"

"She can't make me stop talking."

"Break it up, you two," Angela said, swallowing water in her excitement.

"She's been making dirty cracks," said Ginny.

"Not just cracks. I bust your nose."

Round Heels turned and backhanded Ginny, a slap that sent her under.

Terry shouted, "I'll snatch you bald!"

"No ganging up on me!" Round Heels yelled.

"I'll take her!" Ginny shouted, blood dripping from one corner of her mouth. She was glassy-eyed with rage and shock and was grimly determined. Terry was amazed at this new Ginny; those correction schools must be, she decided, *very* tough.

"Watch out, Ginny."

Ginny grabbed Round Heels by the hair. "I can handle two of you, Round Heels."

"I'm ready," said Round Heels, butting Ginny in the stomach. Ginny swung Round Heels around by her hair. Round Heels tried to thumb Ginny in an eye, then grabbed her by her underwear. She began to tear it off of her.

"Leave 'em alone. Let 'em fight it out," Angela said.

A ring of wet girls and women formed in the water. Ginny had Round Heels down under water. Terry grew worried. Round Heels came up spattering and tore Ginny's slip, then grabbed her in a football tackle and stomped her down under water. Ginny came back, legs kicked out; Terry, with two women, came barging in. Clothes, fists, and legs flew. Spray covered the water as the fight became a free-for-all. Round Heels had Ginny's head on the bank and was banging it on the ground. Ginny turned over and grabbed her just under the arms and whirled her around. Round Heels bit Ginny's hand. Ginny roundhoused Round Heels a blow that sent her staggering out onto the bank and down on her naked legs.

"Let 'em fight it out."

"Boy, what a sock!"

Both girls were naked, shiny, and streaked with mud in the sinking sunlight. Ginny pulled back a hard little fist and sent the Mexican girl down. She leaned over and pumped blows fast and deadly on Round Heels' head. With her sharp elbows she drove off anyone trying to pull her off. Ginny had a mean look of hate and power on her face as she delivered one last deadly chop to Round Heels' jaw. Round Heels went over on her back. Out.

"Break it up! Here comes the hiring boss."

Mitch came and stood looking down with pleasure at the naked, wet girls panting on the ditch bank.

"Knock it off. Everybody out. Jesus, crazy broads!"

Coming out of the water, Terry grabbed his arm. "I want Round Heels run out of camp."

Ginny held up a bleeding hand and tried to cover her pelvic section with a wet rag. "She bit me!"

Round Heels sputtered into life, ignoring her nakedness, "I like almost drown. They try to kill me!"

"One more rumpus, Round Heels, and you can pick up your time and go."

Angela moaned. "I swallowed a gallon of water in excitement."

Women ran up with towels and blankets to cover all

nakedness in sight. Mitch crossed to Ginny and looked at her hand. "Better bandage it, Ginny."

He watched her cover her little, hard, applelike breasts with Terry's towel. Her pubic hairs were like fine spun-gold. In her rage and battle fury Ginny was more desirable than ever. He liked them when they would mix it up and put up a little struggle to the roughhouse of his violent sex play.

"That's bad bleeding, kid."

"I didn't notice."

"Teethmarks all over it."

Ginny readjusted the covering of her nakedness. She was slim-legged, coltish, not yet graceful, but full of an innocent lure for Mitch.

"I'm still bleeding," Ginny said.

"Come on. I'll run you over to the office and fix it up."

"She said things I don't take from anybody."

Round Heels seated on the ground, wept, "I'll snatch you to bits, you baby-faced bitch!"

Mitch helped Ginny into the station wagon and drove off. Terry sat down and put her head in her hands. She said to Angela, "This is a real trouble camp. I can smell it."

"Who you say stinks?" said Round Heels, staggering to her feet. "She take Mitch from me, the lousy little cock-teaser."

Terry got up and swung a haymaker and knocked Round Heels down.

Angela said, "Oh boy, oh boy. . ."

Terry turned sadly toward the bunkhouse. "She made me lose my temper."

Angela looked down at her friend. "You stink for a fighter."

Later, trying to sleep, Terry sampled the night sounds, unable to calm down. The night was dark, the gasoline-engined water pump never stopped coughing and gurgling. Somewhere small night creatures hunted each other for food among the deserted vines. Terry could hear the hunters strike, the delayed cry of agony as claws or teeth came through fur or feathers, and then all was silent. Out there in the fields a battle for survival was also going on. The rules were simpler, Terry thought, the results the same. She had to shake these blues out. She had come through half a hundred crises in her time. What the devil was the matter with her tonight? In the bunkhouse behind her she could hear Ginny sobbing. Well, if Ginny had decided to stay here that was her own problem. Terry sighed.

Where would the girls go after she was gone? The field hiring must be over by now. It was always either too many jobs or none. Nobody ever knew except the ranchers, and those bastards wouldn't give you a free smile. They liked this confusion in the hiring pattern.

Terry sat up, the old itch to gamble on her. It didn't break out often but it was like booze or loving with some people. When she wanted to throw dice, or bet on a nag, or play red and black, or draw twenty-one, you'd think it was the only worthwhile thing in life. Jesus, the wonderful time up in Harold's Club in Reno when she was really hot with the dice. Four sevens in a row, and she had let all the winnings lay. What a pile of silver dollars she took away after the fourth roll. Stopped just in time.

She went outside into the night. Nearby was the old man with the white moustache worn old style, the wino who bunked with Chico. He was writing a letter on the steps of his bunkhouse by the light of an old stable lamp. It was a letter, she knew, written at least once a month. He proudly let her read it:

Governor of California.
Why do not sleep?
Is it because you do nutting about us who
lived in the fields like the animals, and

those who 'lected you to office now is
nutting. Will nutting be done to better our lot? You
make good sounds on the radio you love us all
you say but the law is against us. They beat
us they no one care for us . . . dios que da
la llaga, de la medicina.

The old man signed it: *A true Christian*. He then folded the letter and put it into a grimy envelope. He addressed it and added *personal* in one corner.

Tomorrow, he told Terry, he would buy a stamp, a nice
clean one with bright colors and mail this letter. Now he
felt at peace. He had a few drinks left in a hidden bottle.
He would not be caught short in the morning. He adjusted his blanket on the thin mattress and lay down, and
Terry hoped he thought of his wonderful youth and the
hardships of a long life, thought of faces long dead; last of
all, of himself and how he would not be here for long.
Then he slept.

Terry looked over at the old man. The workers slept all
around her or huddled over small fires.

Chico, who seemed to know everything—even about
talk of union action—had told her there was a crap game
going on every night behind Cap Farley's general store
and hardware shop on the main road. . . . Maybe she
would meet somebody there who would know of the union talk, of Mike. She looked in the direction of the unlit
bunkhouse. Ginny had sobbed herself to sleep.

She knew (Mike had told her) that Cap Farley's storage
shed was the secret meeting place of those field worker
leaders who were planning to announce the formation of
a union. Cap was an old-time longshoreman who had
moved out into the country and was the man who kept
the DWU informed of the reactions of the local ranchers
and farmers to talk of forming a union local among the
migratory workers.

She could meet Mike there, and as she prepared to leave she looked at the old man, thought of Chico and other youths, of the tired field workers around her, and she wondered, with such troops, did she and Mike have any *real* chance?

As she left to pick up a ride or catch a bus in the direction to town, the great, glass-lined metal tanker-carriers, twelve wheel rigs, were moving out of the vats section of Big Mesa, carrying their five-thousand-gallon loads of wine that had been processed, fermented, its sugars and yeasts turned to alcohol. Moving it toward the bottling plants where it would become *Mesa Vin Rose, Great Mesa Riesling, Royale Chablis* and *Beaujolais, Grand Mesa Muscadet* and *Sauternes*. The tankers, like a row of motored elephants, moved past her, red taillights on.

BOOK THREE
THE CLOUT

CHAPTER 14

Manuel Lopez had only one of his front teeth missing. He was a broad man, and unlike most Mexican-Americans, he was also tall.

He appeared suddenly at the Pioneer Motel, and he sat with Mike, smiling, his legs in his cowboy boots crossed, at ease.

"I have been for two weeks in the calaboose. It was the cockfight. But my best chickees they didn't catch. A friend has them."

Mike studied the man. He was more Indian than Spanish, and more Negro than Indian. More cheerful than depressed by the appearance of him.

"We needed you here, Lopez."

"Mister Brant, I am here now. I have some of the best men now agreeing to talk union in a good way the workers will understand."

"What do you think? Will there be enough on our side to impress the vineyards we are ready . . . mean it?"

155

Lopez looked down at his broad, square-cut fingernails. "Understand so many are what is called wetbacks. Illegals, eh? They fear to be deported if they make protests. You don't know the hell of Meekico . . . a few rich ones there have grabbed everything what the revolution of 1910 gave us. So there is nothing for the people left."

"Don't worry. Here they need pickers, they need workers. They have it fixed with the authorities no one, not many anyway, will be sent back. The ranchers, vine growers, they need us."

"So, I hope."

"Forget your damn birds. At least until we get something done."

"But of course. To you the chickees they are something foolish, no? But what have we? Women with too many the children, too little food we can get . . . and then we pack up and get the hell out, to the next field, the next vineyard, the same shithouses, dirty cabins, bugs, dirt . . . and the *patrons* who bring us to places for jobs, they take their big cut. So if some of us fight the cocks and bet a little, it's the pleasure we have."

"Okay, Lopez, I guess I'm too keyed up. Sorry. We'll be in touch." Mike held out a ten dollar bill. "For the kids."

Lopez laughed with his remaining big white teeth showing. "I myself would do this union thing for nothing. You know dot, but the women they scold, they keep us from the bed, eh? They want to eat meat, the kids are always hungry for eating; *ol amigo su vicio.*"

He put the bill away. "I go."

They shook hands and the big man left.

Jesus, thought Mike, a good man . . . but how many like him?

Later, after dark, Mike had other visitors at the Pioneer Motel. Jamie Ward and Wallie Smith, the old-time IWW member, had gotten off the nine o'clock Greyhound, parched and rump-sprung. They now sat drinking beer in

Mike's room: Two six packs of Millers rested on ice cubes in the bathtub.

Jamie looked irked and hot, claimed he had heat rash. Wallie was amused, looked smaller, in a too-large, brown windbreaker and square-toed workers' shoes.

He said, "Jamie here thought I'd fall by the wayside, he did. Well, I've had to prop him up all the way. Mike, you look healthy as a year-old heifer . . . still on the tit."

Jamie took a packet of rubber banded brown envelopes from an inner pocket. "I was sweating blood carrying these. Anybody suspect, and I'd be maybe DOA."

"I doubt it, Jamie . . . what are they?" asked Mike.

"Besides some personal letters for you, injunctions the DWU got out of the Labor Council in Sacramento—and writs issued by Judge Benton Wallace. Injunctions and writs against any rancher or farmer refusing to let his field workers freely vote on a union . . . legal documents against refusing us permits to recruit on a ranch or farm. Injunctions . . . oh hell, read them yourself."

"A little dynamite," said Wallie. "Like we used in the old days, and . . ."

"You shut up, Wallie. We're going into this legally and properly. When, Jamie, do we use these injunctions?"

"Spoke to Dick Seabrook about that. He said to leave it up to you."

"Ol' Dickie, letting others do his work," Mike said. Mike had no liking for the president of the DWU. But there he was, "good ol' Dickie Seabrook," and would be there. Old union bosses never fade away in the DWU.

"Never mind. We talk tonight at Cap's with the union demands committee I've formed."

Mike rubbed his unshaven chin. "Now I haven't written any names down but, Jamie, make a note of the union committee: Ramon Tamayo and Farrico Rojas, Manuel Lopez, they as chairmen. All solid Mexican revolutionary types. Jules Madden, Pete deValera, Diaz Guzman, as field watchers. Now I want some of the women mentioned: Alicia Gongora, Lolita Hernandez, Mary Moore, and oh, Terry Munday."

"How is Terry?" asked Wallie.

"Working hard. We'll maybe meet her at Cap's."

Jamie had been writing in a small notebook. "What about Charlie Scott? He is a hell of a good man—*was* anyway."

"As you said, wishy-washy now . . . but he's no problem, I mean no snitch. He may even be a help."

"How do you plan to begin?"

"We will serve legal notice and copies of these papers to six of the vineyards in this district, demanding a national labor election board to vote on representation. We know damn well their answer—'fuck you'—so we send the final injunctions and call for a strike . . . and begin picketing."

"Can you get enough pickets?"

"I've got thirty-eight promises . . . but once we announce a strike, we'll get good support."

Jamie shook his head. "Thirty-eight pickets from a couple thousand field hands?"

"That's just from Big Mesa, as of now . . . we'll get hundreds. I intend to demand a union vote at Freeman Farms, Avellaneda Winery, Monks Walls Bottlers, Golden Rose Distilleries. I'm hearing reports on how many they can put into picket lines tonight."

Jamie closed his notebook. "We've got a publicity group working out of Fresno and cameramen ready, and there will be a press conference. We can't depend on the *Oakland Trib,* but the *Bee* will cover it, and the two wire services will most likely send reporters. Congressman Miguel Cortez will make an appearance in the picket lines—and maybe a couple of liberal television actors and a movie star."

"If they get clobbered," said Wallie, "you'll make the afternoon papers. Even if only a tomato in a pretty kisser."

Mike set down his beer glass. "What do you think, Jamie, can we win this time?"

Jamie decided against another beer. He sat on the bed and thought. "As good as any try we've made to create locals. It all depends if all the vineyards and farms are picketed hard enough and stand to lose a crop. And if the law doesn't stand too far away when there is violence, or joins in against us. How's the situation here?"

"The sheriff is kind of fair, but not mad about unions. He has run out a few organizers . . . small fry. The local police are in the ranchers and farmers' camp in all ways. You can't bank on local cops to help keep down violence. The state troopers may be fair, *if* the governor presses them. I don't see the state guard coming in unless there is sabotage and killings. Jesus, Jamie, it's complicated."

"Play it by ear, Mike. We'll keep up a yelling and hollering from the coast—goose the Civil Liberties boys, and try and get TV and the press involved."

"Another beer?" asked Wallie.

"Lay off, we're going to Cap's and I want you, Jamie, to stiffen the spines of the men we're meeting there."

Jamie nodded. Mike wished the two men were more excited.

Cap Farley's store on the highway: one unwashed window held farm tools and an amazing supply of different sized pipe wrenches. The other displayed sun-faded, empty breakfast food boxes, a cat with two suckling kittens and a sign reading: BEER ON ICE.

As Terry entered she saw no change in the setting . . . the interior of the store was hung with an aging stock of farm tools, fly-specked posters for weed and insect killers, cake mixes, cattle foods and frozen TV dinners.

Great gouts of garden hoses half unrolled, like plastic snakes, threatened the passerby.

Terry waved to a yawning clerk working over a *Daily*

Racing Form who motioned to her. She pushed open a well oiled door marked "Keep Out." She was in a wide, narrow room which still held tractor parts and long lengths of copper pipes on racks on the wall.

There was a large, green felt covered crap table with the proper markings on it under a big square of tube lighting. There were two poker tables and a faro game. Half a dozen ranch types, their pickax-toed boots still gray-green with dry cow dung, were involved in a lazy crap game. It was early yet. Terry went over to watch the faro dealer, put her dime into the Coke machine, and sat drinking the damn poison, as she always called it. She had once read in a Digest magazine that it could dissolve a set of false teeth left in it. She didn't know anybody herself who washed their store teeth in Coke.

A couple of characters wearing linemen's climbing irons came in and gave her the eye. A fat man with an old-fashioned, linked, gold watch chain across his paunch took up the dice and ran two sevens before he crapped out. The play was getting better. Someone was smoking a terrible cigar.

Terry went to the dice table. She put down the half empty Coke bottle and went over to the table. There were several piles of silver dollars in front of the table boss, and he was adjusting a half-dozen bills before pushing them down through a slot in the table to the drawer underneath. The stickman, in his green shade, shoved the pair of dice in front of Terry and she threw down a bill and blew on the dice and said, "Don't hex me."

She rolled a nine and made it easy after three rolls, took half the winnings, and rolled five and made that after two rolls. Several of the ranchers began to place their bets. Terry lacked the true gambler's spirit; she pulled off half and more every time she made the roll. She wished Mike would show up. She was jumpy with the union ready to move.

She saw Mike come in, then Jamie Ward, and Wallie

Smith. They acted as if they didn't know each other. Terry handed over the dice as Mike came up to the crap table. "How's it going?"

"Not bad."

The stickman, under the green half-moon of his shade, had dead-gray eyes, hair like spoiled hay, and large, loose teeth. He pushed the dice at Mike. "Give it a try?"

"Sure."

A first roll, he got a seven. The stickman said, "Make them bounce off the back cushions."

"Okay."

"House rules."

"Sure, Mac."

Another seven, and the stickman piled up the silver. All of the ranchers were encouraging, placing bets to follow a string of passes.

"That's rolling!"

"Keep 'em happy."

He made five straight passes in a row. The stickman rolled his eyes at the pit boss standing by. The stickman pulled in the dice and examined them.

He put them away and threw in another pair. Mike hefted the dice to see if they were loaded, quickly checked the numbers to see they weren't an unmatched pair that would crap out, felt the corners. They weren't tapered.

He threw a four. Everybody relaxed. The ranchers pushed back the Stetsons on their heads. He made the four easy. The next roll was again a seven.

Now there was great excitement. Everybody was piling silver dollars and bills onto the table betting for or against, making odds, and taking a quick course in math and the laws of chance, and following it with their money.

Mike decided to pull out two thirds—*after* the next roll . . . let it ride just once more.

Someone behind Terry said, "Hi." She half turned. It

was the little man with the glasses, the joker going bald, the salesman who had given her the lift and the romantic pitch when she had thumbed a ride with him.

Terry frowned. Tight lipped, she picked up the two silver dollars in the groove in front of her.

"The name is Jack, remember?"

"So?"

"Listen . . ."

"Get lost, Jack. . . ."

He kept taking her arm, and she kept shaking it off.

"I mean, I've been looking for you . . ."

"Don't."

Mike had given up the dice and came over. Jack moved away. Mike took her arm. "A fink?"

"No, a joker who gave me a ride on the road."

"We've got a meeting going."

CHAPTER 15

Terry followed Mike out through a side door. Outside were Jamie Ward and Wallie Smith, who had preceded them.

Wallie said, "Looking fine, Terry."

Under the one low watt bulb hanging over the door Wallie looked, she thought, like a troll in the *Blue Fairy Tale Book* she had once owned. "You look pretty fair yourself, Wallie."

"Come on," said Jamie, "less chatter. This is no coffee klatch."

Mike led the way around a pile of overaged lumber, past an empty chicken run, and up to a low metal-sided building set on cement blocks. A crude sign in red paint read: STORAGE   NO ADMITANCE.

Mike tapped twice and the door opened a bit, and a Latin face framed in shiny black hair peered out. Mike's group slid into an area of piled-up grain sacks, the smell of crop dust and mouse dung. One work light was on overhead. Six men stood around a work table by the side of a big Fairbanks scale. They were men from Big Mesa, mostly Mexican-American, mostly middle-aged—Manuel Lopez among them.

Mike made introductions, and Jamie shook hands. The men were nervous, passing a bottle of grape brandy around. *"Guerra a muerte!"*

Jamie pointed to two benches. "Let's squat. Now, men, we're about ready to go. We're hitting six of the biggest vineyards in the district."

"And they hit us," said someone. "Bloody."

"Don't dare . . . we'll have reporters, cameramen, and the sheriff isn't a bad man."

Someone made a foul oath in Spanish and added, *"Justitia, mas por mi casa."*

Mike said, "Don't be so downbeat before we start."

"Is all right for you the men say, Senor Mike," said Lopez. "You start it, you move on. They say, we have kids maybe and some pots tied up on the back of a beat up Buick. I say to them, but we stay if no *la cosa marcha*, and we no get the clubs punched into the kidney so we piss blood, 'scuse it, Senorita."

Jamie took out a newspaper clipping. "It's not like the old days, Lopez. They know it. We have official Washington muscle behind us now. Listen, we just won a big one against the Sea Prime Canneries. This is from this morning's paper." He slipped on silver-rimmed eyeglasses and read:

UNFAIR LABOR PRACTICES RULING UPHELD
SEA PRIME FIRM LOSES APPEAL COURT ACTION

A National Labor Relations Board ruling that Sea Prime Canneries was guilty of unfair labor practices was upheld by the U.S. 9th Circuit Court of Appeals.

The ruling stems from a two-year-old dispute with the DWU's Cannery & Packers Local 301 union that began when the union charged that the company fired a number of prounion employees shortly before a union certification election was held.

The last two years the three hundred and forty-one-member union has been on strike, and the Federal Court order demands that the company return to the bargaining table, reinstate fired employees, and pay lost wages of the striking union members.

The NLRB found Sea Prime had "engaged in a course of action designed to frustrate bargaining and provoke a strike."

The NLRB had charged Sea Prime with using unfair labor practices and then attempting to conceal those practices "by interfering with the testimony of witnesses at a board hearing."

The federal court supported the NLRB finding that the DWU union did not engage in an economic strike for their own gain, but were responding to provocation and "unfair labor practices" by management and were therefore entitled to reinstatement.

David Glasston, president of Sea Prime, said he plans no appeal and "will comply with the court order."

Union officials had estimated the back pay could cost Sea Prime $500,000.

"Two years?" said someone.

"Half a million dollars," Mike added.

A man with red hair, one cheek deformed by a chaw of tobacco, raised a clenched fist. "Up the rebels, I say. If they did it to Sea Prime, we can do it to Big Mesa, and in less than two years."

"Good," said Jamie. "We want you, the stewards, to stand ready to pull out as many pickers as you can when they refuse our demands. We've got the evidence on their unfair labor practices. We'll start proceedings—so it's . . . ."

There was a small scrapping noise outside, and Jamie stopped talking. Mike said, "Terry, go look around. If it's all clear, just tap twice."

"And stay as lookout," added Jamie.

Someone turned out the overhead light. Terry slowly opened the metal door and went outside. It was cool, a slight night wind ruffling nearby leaves on young trees. A mist seemed to be walking across plowed fields, and from the highway came the whine and grind of the big rig moving into the night—heavy twelve and sixteen-wheel diesels.

Terry saw a cat clawing among a pile of empty soup cans. The creature looked up, eyes luminous in the dark. Terry made a gesture, and the cat turned and ran. She felt chilly, lifted up the collar of her jacket, and tapped twice on the door. There was dew on its metal surface.

It was all unreal, this night world, like when as a child she used to go with Dad, driving all night in his camper to some new drill site, ready to spud in a wildcat well. She remembered sitting by his side wrapped in an Indian blanket as the night landscape rushed by, dank and blue, broken only by an orange square in some late farm window—outside the world all the undersea tones of a fish bowl.

Now, she had that unreal feeling again. She sat on an empty Bud beer keg thinking of her life. How politics had grabbed her, and radical ideas, and how earnest she had been for the cause. Now she was with Mike and it was good, and it was bad, too. Her interests were divided. There was even a lot of doubt as to where it would all lead . . . where was Marge getting with Charlie Scott . . . pregnant, and Charlie a loose-spined character.

Terry laughed, hell, she *also* was pregnant. Two months since her last period. The whole entire Big Mesa world to her seemed fertile, not only the fat Sémillon and Sauigny grape vines. Half the married women pickers were carrying a little or big growing packet up front. Mrs. Lopez, the joke was, almost needed a wheelbarrow, she was *that* big up front.

Terry thought, should I tell Mike? Or get rid of it? She had had one abortion four years before, caused by—did it matter who had caused it. Now it was different. How different? She thought about it a long time. Got no clear answers.

After an hour the meeting inside broke up, and the men came out one by one and melted like animated ghosts into the darkness.

Jamie seemed depressed as usual. Wallie, a bit high, had a bottle in a brown paper bag in a coat pocket. Mike was pensive.

"I'm full of hope, Jamie. They're solid."

"I hope so. Now, Mike, better not go back to that motel. Never know if there isn't a spy in this group. Me and Wallie will go to a Ramada Inn. Terry, good to see you again. Look great. . . ."

Wallie pulled out an unopened pint from another pocket. "A little gift. Doesn't it say in the Ingoldsby Legends, 'we've drunk down the sun, boys, let's drink down the moon.'"

Mike took the pint. "Get going you two. Me and Terry, we'll go to the Indian Penny Inn for the night. I've already signed in there."

"Looks good, the fight here, I think," said Jamie, and he and Wallie went off. Mike put his hands in his jacket pockets, made a grimace, and looked around at the night scene: "Looks good, he says? I'm not so sure."

"Let's get away from here, Mike. I'm cold."

"Wallie's booze should warm us up." He hugged her to him. "I'm jumpy as a turpentined cat. I need you, Terry girl. Jesus, I need somebody close to trust."

"I'll get so close to you, mister, I'll be behind you."

It was an old joke, and they laughed as they got into Charlie Scott's car, borrowed for the night.

Between them they killed part of the pint before they came to Indian Penny Inn. Mike drove the car up under the wooden Indian sign and up to a row of cottages, all with Indian names. They got out of the car, and he put a key into a door labeled "Crazy Horse."

Inside it was the usual low-priced motel room, full of stale air, dead flies, and moths on the window sills—knotty pine walls. There were two sagging beds with red cotton covers stained with old experiences: A place marked by drink, cigarette burns, and hasty lovemaking. The night table was scarred by white rings from wet glasses. There was a cloying sweet smell of jasmine and cesspool cleaner.

Terry stood and watched Mike bolt the door, push a suitcase off the extra bed, and come toward her. His eyes were gleaming in the light of the room's single lamp with its yellow shade.

Terry, too, was aware of warmth and some desperate need for love. They hugged and held each other close. When he began to undress her, Terry helped him. He was all trembly with lust and love. First, off came her wide black belt with the Indian silver, then slipping down the tight jeans, pushing off the boots, his hands feeling so right and strong on her thighs. With his own shirt and pants off, he was remarkably brown and hard. Sitting on the bed, she in her panties and he in his shorts, they finished the pint. There were moments when they didn't talk but kissed and rubbed against each other.

"You believe it's us here, Terry?"

"It's us."

The bottle between them added its own acid bite to the close, funky atmosphere of the room. Mike made promises. He spoke intimately of his strong hopes for the DWU and his hopes of making her understand how their love would be. She said little. She was a woman who needed no vocal love patter. There was a thin wedge of fear of the coming events in Mike, and he needed her, needed the sexual assurance that he was still vital and a man.

The room seemed to melt in the cozy intimacy of the two of them. Lovers sweating in the little room, the windows closed.

He unbuttoned her shirt and when her fine breasts tumbled out, she too felt of his pleasure in her without reservations. She submitted to her own desire and his demand.

They made love on the two beds pushed together. He was a marvelous lover. He could be tender, and he could be brutal at just the right moments. He could be slow, he could be quick. In her own simplicity Terry was direct and earnest, in her passion strong and violent, aware of the final commitment one made at such times. She took joy, big and well-made, with a bronze body amazingly white where it had been sheltered from sun. He was aware of the fashionable mode for slimmer, more boyish women. Terry and her ample ripe curves, her well-formed hips, her firm but large breasts suited him. He made the ritual gestures, the sensual worship to all of her that came naturally to him. Mike was not sophisticated, not jaded, not badgered by clinical texts of emotional blocks or fixations he had never heard of.

It was an hour before dawn when they fell away into the exhausted sleep of sated and satisfied lovers. The trucks passed outside. The room shook as the heavy traffic of wheels and trailers took up the haulage of fruit and vegetables on the highway.

She had decided to hold off telling him she was pregnant. He'd feel bad that their precautions had failed, and he had to keep his mind on the coming strike.

At the early dawn the sun hit broken bottles behind the cabins and turned them to jewels. There was a standpipe near the motel running water with a bubbling sound into some field. Terry awoke to a feeling that she too, in some daffy way, was part of the theme of watering the arid soil. Mike was already up—naked as a jaybird—rubbing his face, looking in the motel mirror. He decided he could get by without a shave.

"No time for it."

"Time for breakfast?"

He came over and kissed her, holding her very close. She loved the man, his eyes twinkling.

"I'll pick you up at six o'clock," he said.

"Sure."

He bunched the taut, milky skin of her stomach in his fingers and the touch of him to Terry was like a sudden drink taken without eating. She got out of the bed, nude and brown and white where the weather had never touched her. "I got to shower."

"Hurry up. We'll have breakfast and I'll drive you back."

Suddenly she wished there was no strike coming up, that they were not here to unionize farm workers. What a betrayal of ideals and principles love is —or, she thought, was it some subtle chemical change in my body busy making a baby?

She showered and put on her denim jeans and shirt. Mike dressed, even wearing a necktie. They went out to the coffee shop and ate a big breakfast: juice, grits, eggs, sausages, lots of coffee. He looked at his wristwatch. They drove out to the vineyard. He drove with one hand and held hers with the other. She gripped his neck with her fingers. It was all great, and it was very early. The blue shapes of little birds in the gum trees were darting in a pattern that seemed to go in loops around the insects they hunted. The leaves were trembling in the morning breeze, sounding like thin brass plates as they beat together.

Mike stopped the car by the loading platform. He looked important in the early sunlight. Terry kissed him.

He ran his hand over her back in possessive pride, and she hoped he was really proud he had her.

The car made a U-turn as he headed for the tractor lot . . . gathering speed, and the dancing dust rose behind it. Jesus, she was jelly all over, itching and hollow . . . everything is rolling in the sky.

She lacked the full vocabulary of emotional expression for deep felt ideas put into words. It was as if daydreams, crazy, goony dreams were the law of the land. She had been thirsty, and now she was fed. She had been lonely, and now there was somebody who gave a damn. She had been unsatisfied; now there was a sense of security all over her, like bees hovering near their hive.

Terry walked slowly to the bunkhouses. The pickers were still asleep. She sat on the cabin steps till the work whistle sounded. The people came awake. Ginny, by the doorway, was sleeping on her side, mouth open. Angela came out of the cabin doorway, hair in her eyes, mouth slack.

"Hi. You up early, Terry."

"You look, Angela, as if you fell into the grape crusher."

"No top to head. It ache. Got any aspirin?"

Terry got her two pills from her bindle. Angela sat by her side, holding her head. "Oh, maybe I die."

"Not from that you don't die. Not right away."

"Say, Ginny is doing all right. Mitch fix it. She is going to work in the packing shed."

"Well, it's no skin off our nose, Angela."

"I feel worse."

"Want some breakfast? I'll knock up some food."

"No food. Just lot of black coffee." Angela gagged. Chico appeared from the road, carrying some firewood; he was bright and cheerful as he dropped wood.

"Morning . . . need some firewood?"

Chico built the fire. Ginny came awake, sat up and yawned. She seemed listless, as if sleep had not rested her.

"Another hot day."

Angela winked. "It cool in the packing shed."

"Yes, sure, guess it's better working inside."

Terry watched the frying pan smoke and put in the last of the bacon. "You're nuts to go there, Ginny."

Chico took out four eggs from his pockets. "Thought maybe, Ginny, you'd like fresh eggs. I didn't steal 'em. My landlady sold 'em to me. Okay, Ginny?"

"She can't cook," Terry said, taking the eggs. "But watch me turn 'em sunnyside up." She broke the eggs into the frying pan.

"I don't like the idea, Ginny," Chico said, "you working in the packing sheds."

"What's wrong?"

"I don't trust Mitch."

Terry said, "Who does? Here, Ginny, eat."

Ginny stood up. "I don't want any breakfast." She walked off toward the vineyard buildings.

Terry shook her head and admired the eggs hissing in the pan. "I give up. But I'm not playing mama cat any more. Sit down and have some of your own eggs with me."

"I sure will," said Chico.

"My old man used to raise chickens."

"Say, there sure is talk how we go on strike for a union. You know anything?"

Terry looked up. "Chico, don't gossip . . . wait for events."

The sheriff's car was parked by the packing shed. Mitch was leaning against the open door. He had shaved and put on a yellow suit with a brown bowtie.

"The way I see it, Jake—it's not just passing out broadsides . . ."

"What's on your mind?"

"Sheriff, I think I have a lead on one of the organizers."
He held out a police photograph of a young man with a
scar.

"Him."

Jake Fry looked up at Mitch, carefully studying his
face. "What about him?"

"He came in early this morning and asked for work.
When I asked too many questions he blew. Went in the
direction of the river. I looked up an old file, Roger Pan-
kin, DWU organizer three years ago on American River."

"I'll alert the Highway Patrol. See anything of the
girl?"

"Not a hairdo here that even looks like her."

"Mitch, you're being helpful." The sheriff drove off and
Mitch went into the packing shed. It was long, dusty, full
of crates and tables. Ginny came out from behind bundles of unmade boxes.

"Hello, Ginny. That was our sheriff. Old Eagle Eye
Fry."

"I just came in. He's after me?"

"That's right."

"You didn't—?"

"We got a bargain, don't we, Ginny?" He touched her
arm and then gave it a tender pinch. "Don't we, baby-
skin?"

"Oh sure, Mitch."

"That's my girl."

"How'd he know I'm here?"

"Got a phone call, some unknown woman's voice saying you were here," he lied.

Ginny went limp. "Must have been Round Heels.
What'll I do?" She shook. He steadied her with his hand.

"Honey, I wouldn't let you down."

"No?"

"Of course not. Now, Ginny, you can help me. You
know I may look like a big man around here, and I am

with the crews, but my boss Mr. Mangin who runs Big Mesa, he's worried over radicals, troublemakers. Now, this Terry, what's her name? She ever meet people, not just social talk—you know, in whispers?"

"Well, she meets this tractor driver, Mike . . . I saw them looking at some kind of poster talking real low."

"Union stuff?"

"I guess so."

Mitch rubbed his chin. "Now, kid, you're in trouble . . . but I don't want you mixed up with any of them commies. Who else is part of . . . I mean who do they talk to a lot and whisper together?"

"Oh, some of the field hands, pickers, but they all look alike to me. And there were two men, they met down the road by the bus stop . . . yes . . . a tall, thin fella never smiled, and a little runty guy doing a dance step, honest, and joking."

"Workers here?"

"No . . . I mean I've never seen them picking."

Mitch rubbed the back of Ginny's neck with rough affection, using the palm of one hand. "You're really all right, kid. Don't worry . . . I told the sheriff I didn't think you were around this part of the valley."

"I better give myself up. No. I'd rather die than go back to the 'Walls,' and the solitary cell."

"You broke out, huh? That's bad. You can't just walk back and say 'I'm sorry.' They'll make it so tough you'll wish you were dead."

Ginny turned bitterly away. Her shoulders sagged. "I wish I were dead right now, Mitch. Maybe I'm crazy to trust even you."

"Don't say that to ol' Mitch."

The pulleys that moved the fruit past the packers, the whine of saw blades making box sides, the automatic nail punch of the press putting sections of forms together, all started at once. Girls began to fill the crates quickly with specially pressed grape juice. They were for the refrigerator cars. Men hammered on the crate tops of juice-filled cans. Mitch said to Ginny's ear above the din, "We made a bargain. It's a fair deal all around, isn't it?"

"I'll keep my part."

"Sure you will. We'll have a ball."

"Yes, yes—but *how?*"

"Tomorrow about eleven you slip away from the Saturday night party. Get in the car. I'll be behind the bunkhouses. I'll hide you in the old winery. Then I'll give you some money Sunday and put you on the Frisco bus. Make up your mind. It's freedom *or* solitary."

Mitch turned and walked away. Ginny stood and watched the boxes pass. Grape juice for people who didn't like wine.

The work in the fields was if anything more torturous than the day before. Terry was picking with Angela. Round Heels had never made it. She had been unable to stir off her bunk. All morning Terry picked and nothing mattered; the hot sun, the choking dust, the sickening smell of crushed sweet grapes that in time got all the pickers down. Terry ate little lunch. Angela went to see how Round Heels was doing and didn't come back.

Terry sighed—it's too early for morning sickness, isn't it? *No!*

CHAPTER 16

The day ended in a fearful mess of a red sunset. A light wind came up from a new direction. The live oaks overhead, full of hard, bitter acorns, scarcely moved in the breeze. They were old trees and very tough, much mutilated by boring insects, knife play, and unscientific trimming.

Terry washed her hair at the faucet and sat by the fire drying and combing it. Ginny, in a low mood, came from the packing shed and sat at her side.

"How's packing?"

"Work is work." Ginny remained sad-faced and scowling.

"That's right. Listen, kid, I'm pulling out soon. Maybe in a few days."

Ginny's face brightened. "Are we?"

"Don't give me a hard time. I can't take you."

"But why? We're partners. Listen, Terry, you gotta take me."

176

Terry shook her head and tied a blue cloth band over her hair. "There comes a time when a girl has to think of herself."

"I'll be no bother. Honest."

"No. I'm going off."

Ginny nodded and sank her head on her thin arms. "Sure, sure . . . a guy . . . with a guy . . . that tractor driver."

"Maybe at the party you'll cheer up."

The migratory families looked forward to Saturday night, with no Sunday work. There was a big fire under the old live oaks beyond the bunkhouses, and people got a little high on cheap vino. Everybody who could make it, made it. Even babies, kids, and the stray dogs. The hot shots with freshly oiled hair took the girls up into the groves of young trees that would someday be an orchard. The older folk kept drinking red-eye, while the women fed the babies at their breasts and took on a bit of booze themselves, nibbling on store-bought pizzas big as wagon wheels. The kids threw stuff on the fire or went off to bushwhack the coupled lovers among the young trees. Everyone hoped there would be a good fight and that no one would pull a switchblade.

The Big Mesa vineyard owners furnished nothing but the free space and the old lumber or rotted tree limbs for the fire. Most of the workers in the bunkhouses had managed to wash in more places than usual and their shirts were crumpled but clean. The few serious card players were in a group by themselves. The dogs finally had to be tied up as the excitement of coming events mounted and people rushed around.

Mike found Terry by the fire and motioned for her to join him under one of the live oaks in the shadows. Lopez was there. Both men wore bulky leather windbreakers.

"Now look, Terry, me and Lopez, we 've got the union broadsides under these jackets." He unzipped a few inches and pulled out a small wad of yellow sheets. "You try and pass these out to people you think you can trust. The union jumped the gun at Oxnard and already have pickets out."

"They hunt us?"

"Hope not," he smiled. "There's talk the sheriff may try and arrest some of us. He's been prowling around here since sunset."

Lopez said, "I don't worry 'bout that. But my fighting cocks don't know where is safe."

Mike ignored Lopez' lament. "We're going to plaster the huts with these, and Jamie is already alerting the media and the wire services of our demands on Big Mesa."

"The demands so soon?" asked Terry.

"That's it—blast-off time. We call the union meetings at all vineyards for tomorrow. No work Sunday . . . and we'll be passing out these sheets at the churches—some of the workers may go, too. So, Terry, pick you up around midnight by the storage sheds, and we'll go hide out at the Indian Penny Inn till morning. Now, if I get picked up, Jamie will see about bail and lawyers."

"Goddam, don't get clobbered again."

Mike nodded, and Terry went back to the party feeling miserable.

Some dogs, not tied up, were running wild and barking at the assorted kids who drove the animals to wild frenzy. Running underfoot, they showed their teeth, ready to bite on short notice. A lot of the kids got slapped by total strangers who didn't bother to see whose whelp they were giving the back of the hand to. The kids didn't mind; they felt they had earned the blows, and went on howling and shouting to earn more, feeding the fire, roasting franks.

Branches and logs were set around the pit where the fire was already going with smoke and sparks. People once shy or wary were beginning to come forward for the fun, carrying a jug or a packet of food in oily newspapers. Chico of the ducktail haircut was in charge of the fire.

Terry tried to eat a fish sandwich.

Around the fire about thirty workers had finished supper, cleaned up, and were gathered around in an odd hope of amusement. The party spirit had crystalized—a few were slightly tight on wine. Round Heels and Angela had an early start on the drinking as Terry and Ginny joined the group.

"Hello . . . I got cigarettes, you got matches?" Terry said. Her offer of store-bought smokes was accepted by some of the group. Round Heels ignored them; she and Angela, on the other side of the fire, were sitting next to a couple of young guys drinking vino, making obscene gestures at Ginny.

"Stay clear of them."

"They're just trash," Ginny said. "My mom always said stay clear of trash."

"To some folk we're all trash, if we're pickers."

"Take me with you, Terry. I won't get in the way. I'll sleep by myself."

"No . . . can't."

"You'll be sorry when what happens to me happens."

"Oh shit, you're not my problem. I've got my own."

Round Heels and Angela stared at them across the fire. Angela said, "Shake up some music. This party's dead."

The man seated next to Round Heels put his arm around her. "Hi."

"Hi yourself, amigo."

"Hi, chiquita . . . how you doin'?"

"Don't chiquita me." Then as she looked at the bottle the man handed her, she added, "Salut!" She put down a tremendous swig.

Someone turned up a portable radio. A dozen couples made an unenthusiastic effort to dance. The kids were throwing more wood on the fire. Ginny looked around, saw someone on the edge of the crowd. Chico stood there with the man Mitch had said was the sheriff. Ginny reacted without even thinking it over. She rose suddenly and faded back into the crowd before Terry could stop her.

"Hey . . ."

But it was too late. Well, let her go, Terry felt.

Someone brought more Mexican food wrapped in newspapers. Chico unpacked it and tossed the newspaper aside. Terry picked up a section of crumpled newspaper and smoothed it flat. Most pickers didn't often read a newspaper; world shaking headlines meant nothing to a migratory worker, and if he read a newspaper at all it was to puzzle his way through the comics. Terry read:

TROUBLE IN VINEYARDS HINTED
STRIKE MAY INVOLVE FOREIGN LABOR

To avoid rumors of strike talk in the vineyards the Department of Immigration offices in California have stepped in to try to settle disputes involving Japanese, Mexican, and American farm workers. The Labor Secretary had asked the Immigration Department to go along with a ruling of his department. Immigration agreed, apparently setting a precedent for the removal of all foreign workers from the job if laborers strike; in Oxnard maneuvering is going on, including a picket line formed in front of the Immigration Department offices.

ISSUE COMPLICATED

The Drovers & Wheelmens Workers Local 7 of Oxnard set up the picket line at noon. They charged that imported Japanese laborers are being used as strikebreakers. The issue is complicated by the fact that the Japanese are here under immigration laws and under jurisdiction of that department, whereas the Mexican braceros are here under jurisdiction of the Labor Department.

Today there was a ruckus at the ranch of Les Batsuda near Oxnard. Workers walked off the job. Jamie Ward, representative of the workers, said they quit in a demand for union recognition and a contract. Rumor persists that Big Mesa and others will be struck next.

* * *

Chico was at Terry's shoulder. "How do you like that? I'm the union organizer here, and they start without us."

Without finishing the article, she crumpled the paper and tossed it on the fire.

"This kills our surprise, damn it." She handed Chico her wad of broadsides. "Get these around. Where did Ginny go?"

"You ask me, I think she went to meet Mitch the macho . . . very much the big scorer."

"She's only fifteen."

"Like they say, they big enough, they old enough."

"I have to find her."

Terry looked around her. The fire in the pit behind the bunkhouses died down a bit. The heavy drinking had started. Round Heels danced. Terry asked her about Ginny.

"Who?"

"Ginny?"

Round Heels had noticed Ginny slip away from the party and go up the road that led to an old winery. It brought back memories of all the little trips she and Mitch had made to the old winery the year before. Nobody ever went there anymore but lovers, lovers seeking privacy. It had been replaced by the new modern plant that bottled wine and crushed grape juice. "She go up by the winery . . . maybe meet Mitch. A good place for lovers; adobe building with walls two feet thick and dark corners where a couple move in a mattress and a few bottles of grape . . . yes . . ."

So that's how it was, Terry thought. Ginny and Mitch, they were going to make out in the old winery . . . sure, . . . she caught a glimpse of a slight figure in the shadows of the old winery road.

Terry saw the sheriff watching her. It was no time to go after Ginny.

Ginny had gone alone on the dark road, not too sure

that Mitch's promise had any value, but the horror of seeing the sheriff had driven her on without much thought.

Around a bend of the old road was the station wagon.
Mitch was seated in it, taking a drink from a bottle. Too
practiced a hand to show much pleasure, he just waved to
her.

"What's the matter with you?"

"Nothing. I came like I promised, didn't I?"

"Sure you did."

"You said you'd get me away."

"I will."

"Do it."

"How's the party?"

"Who cares? Let's get away from here right away."

She got in beside him. He took another drink, offered
her the bottle. She shook her head.

"I hate it."

"Look, I got you away from the party because the
sheriff is there, just waiting to raid it . . . going to make
arrests."

The car moved off into the inky darkness under a hood-
ed moon. The winding road led upward. Ginny sniffed,
inhaling the scent of bruised sage and the smell of some
night animal, pungent and sharp. Ahead, the road ran
white under the car lights that Mitch had turned on to
avoid hitting great rocks by the side of the road. Not far
ahead was the shape of the old winery building and its
giant oaks gleaming in a sudden burst of moonlight. It
was quiet. Serene. The station wagon, with lights
dimmed, pulled up in front of the winery door and
stopped. The lights went off. Mitch got out and looked at
the building.

"We hide here till morning; then cross the ridge to the
101 Highway bus station."

Ginny got out of the car, shivering. "Sure is a lonely
place."

"That's the idea of a hideout, honey."

"Let's go over the ridge tonight."

"You crazy? It's just a trail."

Ginny pulled away, realizing the full impact of the situation. "Mitch, I want to go back. Changed my mind."

"Don't be dumb. I'm taking a chance protecting you."

"They going to arrest Terry?"

"Whoever Jake thinks is making trouble."

"Let me warn her."

He gripped her arm. "You crazy kid . . . want to be picked up?"

"They'll get me anyway."

"You let me worry over them. Get inside."

"Mitch, please, no."

"What the hell do you want?"

"Give me a little time to collect myself."

"All right, but *inside*." ·

He grabbed her harder; she said, "Just a little time."

CHAPTER 17

It was not just the sheriff and his men. The town police were also there, massed by the packing houses. There was a county station wagon with wire glass windows for transporting prisoners. Below, on the highway, state trooper cars were flashing green and red lights, and Terry could hear the sound of sirens. Most of the pickers and packers around the dying fire had gone off into the night to wonder, to fear; children cried and someone kicked a dog that yelped in pain in a descending crescendo of sound.

Terry, Angela, and Round Heels were surrounded by police flashing lights in their eyes. The women stood against the side of the station wagon. The police captain was young, with a too long head and large hands and feet; without being aware of it, he kept grabbing his tight crotch.

"Now I want your names, your social security numbers."

Terry said, "You want to charge us? You just give us the usual warning and state our crimes. You can't third degree us here."

"Look," said the police captain, "I kin do whatever I want to protect private property and keep order . . . see?"

Round Heels smiled, tried to touch his arm. "What's all this 'bout, huh?"

The sheriff came over and spoke to the police captain: "Okay, Buck, I'll take it from here. . . ."

"Come off it, Jake. It's my jurisdiction. One side of the land is inside the town line."

"Shove your jurisdiction. Out here it's county."

He turned to Terry. "You know your rights. You'll not be abused. You'll get a right to call a lawyer or make one phone call. Now for identification." He motioned to an officer with a Polaroid camera and flash gun. "You Terry Munday?"

The flash went off and Terry felt huge purple rings fill her vision. And a big black blind spot sat in the center of her vision.

"I am Terry Munday, employed at Big Mesa Vineyards."

"We all is," said Angela.

"You are an organizer, Munday, for the Drovers and Wheelmens Union, defying injunctions against making disturbances at any Big Mesa vineyard."

"I work here, that's all I have to say."

Round Heels asked, "What's all this injunctions crap?"

"All right, Munday, get inside the wagon. We'll book you formally at the station."

"You haven't charged me with anything real. What the hell kind of a frameup is this?"

"No frameup, Munday, believe me. I work to the letter of the law."

Terry turned and broke free of an officer holding her by a shoulder. "Look, uphold the law against rape. Mitch

Buckley has taken a fifteen-year-old girl up to the old winery. Well?"

The sheriff scowled. "*What* girl?"

"The runaway. Ginny doesn't know what she's doing. She's scared."

The sheriff stomped a foot on the dust. "The sonfabitch! He told me she wasn't here." He turned away from Terry: "Walters, Cronkwald, you go up to the old winery. And if Mitch is up there with an underage girl fooling around and it's—it's bad, you bring him in. And the girl, don't scare her . . . she's a runaway from a home. I repeat, don't scare her."

"Thanks," said Terry. "I suppose you'll tell us now you have daughters that age."

"No, Munday, I don't. My late wife and me we never had any kids." He shook his head. "We're looking for a James Ward, a Mike Brant and. . . ." He looked at a list and began to read off a list of mostly Spanish names. "If you know any of their whereabouts you'd be doing them a favor to get them picked up. Hotheads—local deer hunters and such—are forming a vigilante group, and . . ."

"And you don't want trouble."

He motioned Terry to get into the station wagon. Round Heels yelled, "Hey, what about Angela, me—ain't we just as dangerous?"

The sheriff laughed. "Not this trip, girls."

He got into the front seat by the driver and turned to talk to Terry behind him. "I've got no horns, no cleft hooves, Munday. My father was an Okie, tractored out in Kansas. We came out here in a jalopy and stayed; had a hard row of it. So you see why I want to save your friends getting into the hands of the ranchers."

Terry said, "You're breaking my heart, Sheriff."

The police captain stuck his head in. "I'm not forgetting this jurisdiction invasion, Jake."

"Well, Buck, why don't you just bring in Mitch Buckley—I'll share a rape charge with you."

It was a tense Sunday. The distant corporation heads who controlled Big Mesa had been served, again, with legal papers demanding an election, and their lawyers had given up golf and weekend boatings to try and invalidate the order. It was clear that the Big Mesa Vineyards would defy the Labor Board orders and that the five other major vineyards in the district would support Big Mesa. Already, extra security guards were being moved in, heavy wire mesh was being nailed over windows in the management buildings. Workers moving in and out of the vineyards were checked by men with pistols on their hips and a harsh tone in their voices. The pickers and field workers were mainly apprehensive, even as the stewards that Mike had appointed moved among them asking for support on this demand for an election. Many held back, some were leaving, packing their few belongings: a stained mattress, some folding chairs, a collection of pots, a spider skillet, a washtub, loading them onto some bailing-wire-repaired wreck of a car—hurrying from what was coming.

In the red brick City Hall building of Sky High, which contained a courtroom, a jail, offices of the police, and two prisoners, an unSundaylike excitement had taken over. Terry was in a large cell called a tank. Here, a drunken old woman slept and mumbled in some strange language; a young whore read a movie magazine.

Terry had been in a heavy sleep between periods of nightmarish waking. In one corner was a small sink and a cracked toilet bowl gurgling loudly. The two-tier bunks had no sheets.

Terry sat up, tossed off the gray blanket smelling of Lysol. The young whore waved. "Hi, good morning."

"Good morning." Terry looked at her left wrist, remembered her wristwatch was in the brown paper bag along with two rings and her handbag in the police locker. "What time is it?"

" 'Bout nine-ten. We get java and cakes." The young whore leaned against the green painted bars and yelled into the corridor. "Hey, what about scuff?"

The drunken old woman whined in her sleep. The young whore said to Terry, "What's the charge? You don't look like no hustler."

"Don't know."

"Uh huh . . . you must be one of them field-stooping broads. Hell, why does any dope go into them fields. Backbreaking."

A trustee appeared in worn gray overalls, carrying a tray with a coffee pot and some danish. "Here you are, ladies."

Terry felt better after two cups of hot black coffee. She couldn't face the cakes, not with a touch of morning sickness on her.

"Not bad, not bad at all," said the young whore cheerfully. "It's a good hoosegow. You don't have to put out for the turnkey, and they feed you fine . . . you wouldn't have a spare twenty?"

"Twenty dollars—not on me."

"I'll get this fine, see; a twenty . . . I can pay it back in an hour—turn a fast trick. I don't usually get run in working the bus station . . . copping a joint in the bowling alley. But this fuckin' strike talk, see, they're a bit goosy, clearing the streets, and. . . ."

A police sergeant appeared outside the bars with Wallie Smith smiling at his side. Wallie did a little dance, reciting:

> The judge he'll take all your
>   money before he will rest.
> Then tell you "plead guilty,
>   I think that it's best."

You go to the judge and he
reads you the law,
Damndest old judge that you
ever saw.

Terry said, "Hello, Wallie."

"You're getting bailed out."

The sergeant held up a clipboard. "You're being released. Just sign you were not mistreated and your belongings returned to you."

"What was I charged with?"

"Just sign." He held up the clipboard, and pushed it
through the bars.

Wallie grinned. "Public profanity. Some kind of local
ordinance against dirty words."

The sergeant said, "The bail of fifty dollars is your
fine."

"Who put up the bail?"

Wallie winked. "People's Legal Defense League of San
Francisco."

Terry signed. The young whore said, "What about me?
Don't I rate any legal defense as people?"

The officer said, "Not the same thing, Flora."

Outside in the sunlight, after gathering her belongings,
Terry asked Wallie: "Where is Mike, Jamie?"

"They're busy ducking tin stars." He elbowed her.
"Hey, look!"

The policemen were escorting Mitch Buckley across
the lawn, his wrists handcuffed. One side of his face was
badly bruised. Terry rushed over to him. "Where's Ginny? Where is she?"

One of the policemen pushed her. "Get away, lady, the
prisoner just had a preliminary hearing."

Mitch stared at his shoes. He seemed numb, unable to
articulate.

"I want to know, officer, where the young girl is,
named Ginny . . . ," yelled Terry.

"Lady, this is a statutory rape case, and impairing the morals of a minor. We can't discuss it."

Mitch lifted his head; his eyes were bloodshot. He wet his lips. "The lying little bitch. They got her stashed away some place lying her goddam head off. It was nothing . . . , just horsing around. She fell, that's how her drawers got bloody. Whoever done anything to her, it wasn't me, and . . . "

"Shut up." They moved off, the two policemen manhandling Mitch to hurry along the path to the jail.

Terry shivered. "Sonofabitch, and that poor kid."

Wallie said, "They got her at the county hospital. She's beat up but isn't badly hurt. Of course rape is no picnic if you put up a fight."

"I'd like to kill him. Where is Mike right now?"

"Easy, easy, Terry . . . he's doing his job. We're painting picket signs . . . bringing in coffee machines, lots of sandwiches. It's no friendly town, Sky High. The damn Deer Hunters Club is polishing their rifles. A real vigilante set of no good bums."

"I want to talk to Mike."

"Later, later . . . he's laying low."

"Why? I mean he has rights!"

"Well, the Big Mesa people have a warrant out for his arrest—claim that he and Lopez stole some tractors. A lie, but they could keep Mike from running things if they toss him in the can while the strike is on."

> The jury you get's a hell of
> a crew.
> They'll look a poor prisoner
> through and through.
> The sheriff he thinks he's a
> real big shot.
> I'm telling you, boys, he's
> the worst of the lot.

It was near dawn the next morning. Wallie was driving

a Hertz Rent-A-Car. Terry had contacted Mike. Wallie drove fairly well, just a bit given to hitting ruts rather than avoiding them on the neglected back road. Terry sat arms folded trying to remember some old trick of remaining calm when one wasn't calm.

Mike Moon's Dixieland Bar and Grill came into view, looking scabby and shanty in the daytime. It didn't open till dark, and there was no sign of life about. No cars but for two battered heaps that most likely could never roll off the blacktop parking lot again.

Wallie drove the car past Moon's and off a narrow trail into a little woods, went through the second growth timber and weeds to the back of Mike Moon's cabin. From the kitchen of the main building he heard the clatter of dishes and the ropy laughter of Negroes preparing for the night trade.

Terry followed Wallie to the cabin door, and he tapped lightly with two fingers. There was no answer. Then they heard at last the hiss of flat naked feet on the bare cabin floor. The door didn't open. Moon's chocolate thick voice asked, "Who that?"

"You know who."

"Oh that who."

A chain guard was pulled back, a bolt released, and the door opened a narrow gap. Wallie and Terry went in quickly. Blinds were down, and it smelled of coupled sleep and unwashed flesh, almost making them gag. Moon, wearing only green silk shorts under his overlapping belly and smoking a cigar, faced them. In the bed behind him the beginner brown slept soundly in a tangle of her own hair with no covers or night clothes. Moon pointed them silently toward the kitchen. They followed him into the tiny slant-ceilinged room, most of it taken up with a table covered with empty gin and beer bottles. Drunken flies buzzed feebly at a length of sticky paper hung from a light committing a casual suicide.

"Yo' is sure raising hell. Radio been talkin'."

"It's all a frame. You're our friend."

"I ain't no white man's friend. I'm one coon that ain't no handkerchief head."

The black man sat down in the only chair and shook his head. "I plays for yo' ofay cruds. I earns my tricks and vittles from yo', but I'm a bigot."

"Where's Mike Brant?" Terry asked.

Moon grinned. "Sometimes I'm a bigot for unions. There's a ole mobile home about hundred yards down trail. Yo' is welcome."

Terry followed Wallie through some mule brush and onto a dim trail lined with trodden grass. The mobile home was painted a dun-mat color and its door was open. She heard the click-click of a typewriter.

Inside they found Jamie bent over a portable typewriter and Mike, smoking a pipe, marking off with a red crayon a map taped to a wall.

Mike turned and Terry ran to his arms. She said tearfully, "Get rid of the damn pipe. You big lug . . . I worried."

Jamie looked up. "You cost us fifty dollars bail."

"Oh shut up." She hugged and kissed Mike. "Things are getting mean."

"Honey, we know. But it's going to go fine, isn't it, Jamie?"

"Just fine." He scowled and went back to his typing. Wallie hunted up a beer can in a tray of ice and sat in a low chair sipping his beer and tapping his toes on the floor of the mobile home.

"Fine for who?"

"Mike," said Terry. "They're bringing in goons as security guards, and there's a local Deer Hunting Club I hear about that's vigilante."

"We know, we know. We've filed official notice of signs of violence, and we're prepared."

"How?"

"Tomorrow we'll have six vineyards out on strike. Hundreds out to picket."

Jamie pulled a sheet of paper from the typewriter. "Big Mesa, they'll keep some workers active. Scabs. And they'll keep shipping out in those tank trucks. We'll not be able to close them up tight."

"We'll see."

Terry said, "I'll take care of the women's section, set up a first aid station and. . . ."

"Nope." Mike knocked dottle from his pipe on a window sill. "You stay here. We got a walkie-talkie set up from here to a place where Lopez is at a phone. You and Jamie will keep typing events as we relay them—then our PR setup in Fresno will see we get some kind of fair media coverage. It's going to be a nasty, balls-kicking strike."

Wallie said, "Bring in your own muscle, soldier. Violence now, that's what the news cameramen love. All revolutions attract attention by violence."

"No," Mike said. "I'm going to run this without that on our part if I can. Firm, sure . . . no namby-pamby politeness, but no head busting by us."

"If . . . if . . . ," said Jamie.

Terry suddenly felt she had to cat up the coffee and went out behind the mobile home to retch. God, this having a baby was no picnic.

Mike followed her out. He stood eyeing her as she bent over a bush. She said, turning to face him, wiping her mouth with a handkerchief, "I guess I'm not used to jail food."

Mike said slowly, "My old lady is a registered nurse. I've gone on her rounds at times."

"So?"

"So I know morning sickness when I think I see it."

"Crazy," said Terry. "Crazy."

He went up to her. "Jesus, you're pregnant."

She felt his arms go around her. "What a hell of a time for it, Mike."

"A great time, any time . . . yeah! I think it's great, just great."

"Do you?" She searched his face. "You do?"

"Happy as a grig. Me, I like the idea of being a pappy, but in your condition now . . . "

She broke free. "Now you want to pack me in cotton-wool and put me on a shelf? No you don't, Mike Brant."

"Listen. . . ."

Inside the mobile home Wallie asked, "Any whiskey?"

"Not for you, Wallie. What's going on outside?"

"Love talk." Wallie grinned. "Listen to the bickering."

"Oh?" Jamie was reading over what he had typed. "How do you spell ingratitude? Look who I'm asking!"

"I – n – g – r – a – t – i – t – u – d – e. Easy, Jamie."

"You a damn college boy?"

"Sure . . . Folsom, Sing Sing, Leavenworth."

CHAPTER 18

The DWU's attempt to organize the field workers produced a strike that lasted two weeks—fifteen days to be accurate. It began with mass picketing of vineyards; it led to shouting and shoving battles with some workers who wanted to continue picking in the vineyards. The police of the town of Sky High were on the side of the owners, and they used tear gas, roughed up the pickets, arrested them, even assaulted them, when out of range of the news cameramen. It was the television coverage, Mike insisted, that kept down the violence, perhaps even killings. For the vineyard owners were determined to keep the union out of the fields.

They had appealed the Labor Board ruling in Washington on several, clever legal grounds and had taken full page advertising in the large California newspapers, mostly nonunion publications, pleading for *Free Rights For Free Americans*.

* * *

On the second day of the strike two container-tank trucks were wrecked; someone had released them during the night and overturned them in a gully. Big Mesa claimed it was union sabotage; the DWU issued statements saying the trucks were old rigs, not in use, and that Big Mesa had wrecked them to blame the union.

Both Jamie and Mike were patroling the various vineyards; Mike was in constant danger of being picked up on the false charges of stealing tractors from Big Mesa. Lopez, who had been jailed on the same charge, was freed when the Civil Liberties lawyer proved he was in the Stockton jail at the time the warrants stated he had stolen the cats. He was under arrest at the time for promoting cockfights. He said to Mike, *"Para todo hay remedio sino para la muerte."*

Mike had grown a moustache, wore dark sunglasses and hoped he'd not be picked up. "What the hell does that mean?"

" 'Everything will out right unless you die.' "

A bootleg phone line had been connected to the mobile home behind Moon's place. So Terry did hear from Mike from time to time.

"Honey, it's getting bad," he told her. "We had a truck ram the pickets at Monks' Distillery . . . three hurt, one bad."

"Are you all right?"

"I'm breathing and talking. We have pictures of the truck incident. Now you get some text on it from *our* side. The damn newspapers, they called it faulty brakes. Faulty, my ass . . . how you feeling?"

"I'm too busy to feel. We're printing a newspaper in the field. True facts, and on a cranky photocopier."

"I mean, you *know*."

"The little mother? She's fine. Tossing her cookies every morning, just like in a soap opera. Mike, I'm all right. Just don't you get your head busted."

"I'll try. Take care of my kid."

"Our kid. What the hell am I, just an egg layer?"

* * *

By the end of the first week the vineyards were at least forty-five percent back into activity, hiring every vagrant, bindle stiff and skid-row person they could, moving them in big buses with steel mesh-covered windows, herded by police and sheriff's crews escorting them through the picket lines.

The sheriff had warned the local group of Sky High deer hunters they would be treated just like any other trouble makers if they interfered. But they booed him, and a dozen of them, in hunting caps, took their rifles out to the clearings by the Boojoh River for target practice. One night they caught Chico pushing leaflets under the windshield wipers of parked cars. They shaved his head, stripped him, covered him with molasses and chicken feathers, and ran him down Main Street. They tossed him onto a truckload of crated tomatoes bound for Los Angeles. Chico managed to get off twenty miles down 101 in spite of a broken nose and telephone the union offices in San Francisco.

Some of the press coverage of the vigilante actions pointed out that Chico had a record as a school truant and had broken into a bakery two years before to steal six loaves of sourdough French bread.

At the beginning of the second week, as Mace and tear gas were heavily used, Mike called a meeting of ten strike leaders in the mobile home. It was crowded, and the smell of stale, unwashed clothing and tobacco smoke drove Terry out into the open.

Mike looked unhappy in the dimly lit interior.

"We are not doing so good. More scabs are moving into the fields. We have had fifty-two arrests, and bail payment has now gone to over twelve-thousand dollars. We are asking for funds from WNUSA . . . haven't gotten an answer yet."

Lopez made a fist, waved it. "Them fancy dans . . . they just good for talking at fiestas, smoking dollah cigars."

Jamie held up a report. "No, no. Soren Verner of the LBO has pledged us six-thousand dollars, and he talked on *Meet the Press* the other day, saying the Labor Board was backing down in its demands for a fair election."

A man with a patch on one cheek said, "He didn't come out for the national boycott on table grapes."

Mike said, "That may be illegal to advocate that publicly. Now, violence is growing. They are going to try like mad to lure you into counterviolence, and we'd be licked. They have the police, the sheriff, and maybe the state troopers on their side. They say they're fair, but when a picket is being rousted they look the other way."

"Yeah," said Wallie, "and arrest the picket."

"Protect yourself, but don't let it get into a real donnybrook."

"How the hell," asked Wallie, "can you save your gourd from being busted and not hit back?"

"Sit down, Wallie. We haven't got the manpower to clobber them when it comes to a battle royal."

Lopez asked, "What about our president, Dick Seabrook? Why he not come to lead a picket line?"

Jamie Ward picked up a telegram. "He's been down in Florida looking over the orange pickers situation. He'll be here in two days and will join the pickets at Big Mesa. We're going to try and get three hundred into the picket lines there. We're going to have new and bigger signs. And State Senator Montez and Father Velasquez have promised to join in."

There was a cheering and Mike stood up grim faced. "Now don't get caught with any chivs; and anyone carrying a pistol is on *their* side. Don't have any weapons but the two-by-twos of your picket sign. They'll railroad you to ten years in Quentin or Folsom if they find a weapon."

"Can we win?" someone asked.

Mike shouted back. "What the hell do you think we're here for! . . . if not to win! It's hard, sure, on you and the women and kids. But they're hurting too . . . Big

Mesa maybe can take the losses in grapes rotting in the field; many of the tanker trucks are not moving, some drivers not wanting to pass the picket lines. But the smaller vineyards are hurting so bad the banks may move in. Keep your chins up and, Christ, yell loud. Don't show any glum mugs to your people. It's bright-eyed and bushy-tailed, goddam it, all the way."

Jamie added, "And pull out any drunks and keep them out of sight when Seabrook is with the pickets."

Lopez made an impolite noise. "Ole Dickie Seabrook, him and his two hundred dollah white linen suits and always the smiling. . . ."

"Just a nice figure of a man," said Wallie, "but you boys keep electing him." He sang in exaggerated buffoonery:

> Tell me how can I ever stand it,
> Just to see those two blue eyes.

"Meeting over," said Mike. "We'll pass out the picket lineup for the big scene with thw DWU president. Now, get out of here one by one, and don't all take the same way out to the main road. And don't act like you're a plant growing under a rock."

Mike felt depressed, tried not to show it. Wallie began to fan the foul air and tobacco smoke out of the door with a blanket. When Terry came in Mike and Jamie were bent over a manifesto, as Jamie called it, to be issued and passed out during the visit of the DWU president. Terry wanted to force Mike to get some sleep, but she just sat with Wallie listening to some hootenanny music on a small radio. Her hopes for the strike had been high, but now she had a sense of foreboding; she blamed that on her condition. She just wanted to hide away some place and let nature take its course with her body like, as she had read in a *National Geographic* in a dentist's office once, the way a mother bear lays up all winter in sleep and births her cubs in the spring.

Mike rubbed his eyes and yawned. He felt some inner insulation. "I hope this is going to turn the tide. Dickie Seabrook is a good front, looks respectable as an undertaker, and he's got a great line of malarkey to feed the press."

"Get some shut-eye," Terry said.

"There's a lot of night left for that."

And there was, as Terry saw through the open door. A dark night with a network of clouds, a faint hint of a moon with qualms about exposing itself. All nature, the whole damn universe, Terry felt, is going on its way, indifferent to us. No hatred, no amiability to our own crazy dance here below . . . , and she was awakened two hours later by Mike, having fallen asleep in her chair. Mike was kissing her cheek. "Get to bed."

Over the struck vineyards, morning came brightly. Lopez had collected a kind of a band for the big doings: field hands with "gitars," two drums, a silver-plated cornet, and several singers fluent in both Spanish and English. "*Olé, ojalá la DWU!*"

Jamie had arranged for cars to meet Seabrook at the Sky High airfield. Senator Montez was driving down from Sacramento. The priest, Father·Velasquez, would hold a mass in the Church of the Holy Mother for those strikers who would attend, and after blessing the strikers, would lead them in a procession of choir boys and church members to Big Mesa.

Mike had decided noon was the proper time for the big event. Sky High and the county had refused the DWU a parade permit. Jamie was still in Judge Bramberger's court debating the legal decision on the matter of the permits.

There was a festive air all along the road in front of Big Mesa. Chili stands gave off odors of *cuauhtemoc* and *orijoles*; hotdog and hamburger vendors were busy. Cola bottles and cans were emptied. Those pickets who had good clothes wore them; Round Heels and Angela had wide ribbons of red and green, the colors of the DWU farm workers (and Mexico), and were handing out lengths of ribbon for the women to tie into their hair or wear as sashes. A kind of demoniacal possession obsessed the younger pickets and incited the stray dogs.

Sheriff's cars and state troopers on motor bikes moved up and down the road, bullhorns active in a tough-toned exhortation. "Keep the legal distance apart. Do *not* block the roadways into the vineyards. Do *not* interfere with those going to work. Keep the legal distance apart."

Officers were pacing about or standing in formations stroking their clubs in almost erotic gestures with their hands. The officers carried cans of Mace attached to their pistol belts. On side roads various official cars were parked, some with extra police and deputies, others containing shotguns, handcuffs, first aid kits. Police short-wave radios gave off growling orders to various units. The sun was high; there was no breeze. From the road one could make out the bent backs of those men and women who still worked the overripe acres of vineyards. Already most of the grapes were past their prime, the leaves turned orange and brown.

Security guards patrolled the fields led by huge dogs on chain leashes. The pickets sang, *"Donde esta la verdad esta DWU!"*

Mike was out of sight—hidden away upstairs over an eating place, the *Arroz Mexicano,* watching from behind a lace-curtained window with a walkie-talkie in contact with picket captains. There was a roaring cheer down the road from the town, and four black-booted motorcycle police appeared on their bikes, then an open car with Dick Seabrook in white linen, his white hair done dramatically, ruffled, he waving, and by his side sat Jamie Ward and an observer of the National Legal Defense League.

The police and sheriff's men began to link arms to push

back surging workers not in the picket lines; the pickets
began to march with a faster step, waving their signs,
singing in Spanish and in English. Terry had a bullhorn
and was encouraging the young girls to sing louder.

Someone fired three shots at the crowd. It was never
known just who fired the shots. They were fired directly
at the crowd massed near the Big Mesa pickets. Only two
shots took effect, hitting a young girl in the arm, grazing
the head of an old man.

At once there was a rushing about, people flinging
themselves prone on the hot, road surface, police beginning to stomp about, weapons and clubs held ready. The
pickets massed, some still singing. Then there was a mixing of strikers and police, all shoving. A club began to
beat down on heads with the regularity of a piston; picket
signs were used as weapons. Soon stones, bottles, and
empty Coke cans were in the air.

Picket captains tried to retain order, shouting into
their horns; orders were bellowed out. "Don't break rank,
don't break rank . . . don't provoke the cops. Don't
fight back!"

It was useless advice as the sharp bite of tear gas filled
the air. Then Mace was released. Coughing and retching
people huddled in a mist of gases. There were more shots;
state troopers arrested three men in hunting jackets. In
the rush away from the fumes, several children were
trampled. Some tenacious pickets coughed and held their
ground.

Mike was downstairs, rushing into the roadway, trying
to get the fighting pickets back in order. The sheriff and
the police captain were shouting their own orders; a great
cry of apprehension and rage rose from the women, while
howls of anger came from the men. Some youths seized
an unattended police car and tried to overturn it by rocking it. Clubs rained down on their heads—but before they

fled, the cap was off the car's gas tank and a burning newspaper did its work. The car began to burn with a dreadful intensity, making a fireball of prodigious size. Two cameramen were clubbed by the sheriff's men— their cameras smashed. The sheriff began to read out the riot act; a Pepsi bottle caught him on the side of the head and he went down in a circle of his men.

Mike, seeing homicidal conditions, tried to talk to the police captain, who was tugging the back of his jacket into place.

"For Christ's sake, pull your men off the people."

"Who the fuck are you?"

"I'm one of the people in charge here."

"Like hell you are."

Mike was pulled aside by two police who jabbed their clubs into his kidneys, guns fired. . . . It was at this moment that Wallie Smith and Manuel Lopez were shot at close range by pistol bullets. Whether the shots were fired by the police or the sheriff's men or by some of the deer hunters mixing with the frantic crowd was never fully determined. There was talk that Wallie and Manuel had been picked out as leaders by the police—but no evidence was ever produced.

Wallie fell—his small body offering no resistance to gravity; he half rose to his knees holding his torn-open chest together with both hands. And he did try to sing, Angela said later, as she tried to help stop the flow of blood from his body with her scarf:

> Whistle, daughter, whistle,
>   and you shall have a cow . . .
> I cannot whistle, mister, I guess
>   I don't know how . . .

Then he died with a shake and a shiver.

CHAPTER 19

With the killings and the law officer's attack on the pickets and strikers, followed by arrests and harrassments, the back of the strike was broken. For all the angry talk of other unions joining in, it was finished. Jamie Ward was arrested and Mike disappeared into the hill country with several warrants out against him. The strike committee members were either in jail or running. Dick Seabrook, at the first sign of trouble, had been moved out so fast by the police that he found himself in Fresno before he knew it. Senator Montez' car never got to Big Mesa; it was stopped by police outside Willowbrook and detoured in circles. Father Velasquez' group was dispersed—the choirboys getting their asses whacked.

Nothing was left but to bury the dead.

Two days after the battle, or riot (it had various names in the press), a mass was held for the dead men, Lopez and Wallie.

"It isn't much of a church we go to," Chico told Terry, his head shaved, nose broken, face crisscrossed with adhesive tape. "Hasn't got a basketball team, they don't play bingo."

The Church of Santa Maria was of mustard-colored adobe with a red-tile roof and a small, dull bronze cross. It was set among several roadside businesses behind a big Standard Oil station. When Santa Maria had been built by Spanish-speaking field hands seventy years before, it had stood alone among the bean fields. It still held services for Mexican-Americans. The migratory workers, defeated strikers—a few rehired—were gathered for the funeral mass. The field workers, pickers and packers, collected worn coins, one by one, to pay Father Velasquez. The caskets rested before a bank of fluttering yellow candles on the altar.

Terry entered the church with Chico and they sat down on hard, backless benches. The place smelled like a henhouse.

Terry said, "Not many people." She looked over the fifty or so brown faces, weathered by field work and sun.

"Lots would have come, but they're afraid."

"*Asperges me, Domine, hysoppo,*" said Father Velasquez.

Terry wished she could pray, send up a cloud of requests for herself, for Mike, for the beginning of the child under her ribs. She grasped Chico's hand. "You sure Mike got away?"

"He's going over the ridge to Casa Grande. It's out of the county."

"Alone?"

"He's got good maps, and our people, Spanish-speaking, along the way, will take care of him. This Casa Grande is . . . was a railraod town. Used to be a repair junction when the steam trains were big stuff. People there will help Mike get to San Francisco where our lawyers can bust these charges against him."

There was a droning sound from the women in the

church. The men sat silent, defeated. Would they get work again in the vineyards or would the law hassle them out of the county? Outside two sheriff's cars watched the church.

Terry asked, "Was Wallie a Catholic—I mean this mass for him . . . ?"

Chico made a grimace and touched his hurt nose. "Maybe, maybe not. But what does it matter. It's the respect. We know he died for something."

Terry looked to where Lopez's widow and children sat, up front. The children were restless, the wife, dark, firm-chinned, staring at the two coffins, at the priest going through the ritual of the mass for the souls of the dead. An old man, that priest . . . brown and thin in the orange candlelight.

Terry had a foolish thought: who would care for Lopez's fighting cocks?

Jake Fry came into church, politely removing his Stetson, followed by a police matron who held Ginny by one arm. That caused a small sensation. She was scrubbed, combed, loosely dressed in faded hospital gray. Not a cruel dress, but impersonal and officially tasteless. Terry nodded to Ginny who looked up expressionless and pale. The field-acquired sunburn on her nose was peeling. She and her escorts sat down front. There was no whispering as the priest approached the coffins.

The priest dipped his whisk in holy water and sprinkled the caskets. On them lay a few dying flowers, sent, as a big card read, from "Field Workers' DWU." The priest recited, "Thou shalt sprinkle me with hyssop, O Lord and I shall be cleaned."

Someone began to sob, breaking into hysterical cries. It was Mrs. Lopez. Angela was down front by the coffins, weeping, rubbing her eyes, becoming distraught. Two Mexican women were holding her, each gripping one arm. Father Velasquez held up a tinny-looking gold cup, the ciborium holding the wafers. Chico explained he had once long ago been an altar boy and that the chalice was for the wine.

"*Confiteor Deo omnipotenti . . . vestri omnipotens Deus . . .* "

It seemed so sad and futile, so far from the reality of dying. The Latin and the incense depressed Terry. Several half-Indian acolytes flitted around in their white frocks, picking their noses, dropping more incense over the hot coals of the thurible, and swinging it three times over the caskets in the form of a cross.

Terry watched Ginny's face. She had become placid again, the way she had been when Terry first met her. The vitality and the courage that had come up with a burst of energy in her were gone. They had examined her at the county hospital, Terry had heard, and issued a cold official report on her condition, full of clinical details. She would be taken back to the correction school.

Chico shook his head. "Poor kid, what a rousting."

Everyone up front bowed his head. The horny-handed field workers, the stoopers from the picking fields, all were awed by death, except the old, white-haired wino who didn't care anymore and was against priests for political reasons. He had come to pay his respects to anyone who could face up to the futility of existence.

Terry watched the old man, his arms folded, head up, staring at the rain-stained ceiling. The front of his tattered jacket bulged, and she knew he had the remains of a bottle of vino there and could hardly wait to get outside and take a good belt of it.

The priest had lifted his arms. There was a clatter as almost everyone knelt on the hard stone floor for the blessing.

"*Benedicat vos omnipotens Deus, Pater, et Filius, et Spiritus Sanctus . . .* "

Chico took out a bundle of thin paper leaflets from a pocket. "Gotta give these out at the door. Our side of the strike."

Terry turned toward Ginny and went over. Angela was on her feet, eyes popping.

Ginny looked strange with her hair combed down straight, wearing the ill-fitting gray institution gown. "You all right, Ginny? They treating you good?"

Down front Angela's lament was cut off in a half scream as Father Velasquez delivered a hard slap to her face and briskly gave her some orders in Spanish.

Sheriff Fry looked at his silver railroad watch. "She's being taken care of . . . Miss Raspe here represents the Juvenile Division."

Miss Raspe nodded. "Judge Hyde's order."

Terry asked, "You're not sending her back to that place?"

"That's for Judge Hyde to say. You seen the trouble she got herself into runnin' loose."

"None of it was her fault."

Ginny didn't change her expression or utter a sound. Terry colored and got angry. "Why don't you blame the goddamed football player?"

"We have him. He'll get his."

Miss Raspe took Ginny's arm. "We must get back now, mustn't we?"

Terry didn't join the workers filing past the caskets. As she came out of the church, Chico, standing there, handed her a leaflet. "Here you are. Don't let this happen again. Make the growers . . . ranchers . . . deal with the DWU."

The day had become windy. The thin cottonwood trees in front of the church were bending in the crisp breeze. The sheriff's duty car stood by the curb. A state trooper's car, siren and red lights on, whined its way up the road and stopped by the sheriff's side.

The sheriff crooked a finger at Terry. "Mike Brant is a

fugitive from justice. Anyone harboring or aiding is breaking the law."

Terry felt terror, was near panic, sensed she might faint. With effort, she answered: "Fuck you," and walked off to where Angela waited for her. They were sharing a motel room. A trooper, full of menace, approached Chico who quickly turned and ran off.

Mike was making slow but steady progress across Big Wolf Ridge, being helped by some herders—hay harvesters—friendly to the field workers' cause. But as he got into wilder country, he worried over a radio report he had heard in a sheep herder's camp: Several parties, a new item stated, were combing the hill country looking for Mike Brant.

A manhunt, he knew, brings out long-hidden, deeply buried emotions in people. They take on a pattern of belief in law and order and the course of justice in order to hide their lust to hurt and kill. A manhunt gives them the right to run down and seek out and feeds their desire to destroy.

Mike's flight into the hills was a clear call to all sportsmen. The broadcast of the sheriff's search made citizens with old Smith & Wessons or Colts in the bands of their pants ready to take a pot-shot, even despite the stern warnings of the sheriff that he'd hold every one of them for illegal interference with the law.

The state troopers were searching every car that tried to run the barriers set up on roads leading to the hills. The deer hunters gang had managed to break through on old trails overgrown with weeds and Johnson grass.

A closed-truck TV unit was broadcasting from near Big Mesa. An excited young Ivy Leaguer was speaking into a pickup mike and trying to get some of the field workers gathered around on the roadside to say something. Most turned away.

* * *

Jamie Ward, looking ill—his ulcer was bothering him—when he came to see Terry at the motel, said, "Mike should be at Casa Grande by tomorrow sometime. I'm out on bail and I'm leaving pronto before they re-arrest me."

"He's all right?"

"I hope so. You're to meet him there. We've got a car to take you around the ridge. But we have to be damn sure you're not being followed." Jamie broke down, clutched his side. "Poor Wallie . . . and here, it's all over for a while."

"I suppose so. What about the workers?"

"They'll move on. We're getting a lot out of jail. Some will go back to the vines. A hard strike to lose, but we'll be back someday."

Terry discovered she didn't care anymore . . . she just wanted to get away, to find Mike . . . .

The dogs were Mike's big danger. He had made a run down and across the hills behind the brush, and he had thrown off the dogs. There was a stream trickling between the rocks. They would expect him to use it to throw off the dogs. He'd use it all right, but he'd go *up-stream, not* down. It wasn't easy. He slipped often and hurt himself, but he went on. After a while he came to rock, smooth and wind-worn. It would be hard to pick up a scent here. He walked across the bald expanse of yellow stone shot with crystal streaks and came to a belt of planted trees. Below was a plywood cabin and a dirt road going east. He stopped, flopped down, and thought. The cabin was boarded up. Not in use. There was a lean-to behind it, and he saw several red, empty gasoline cans. If there was a car stashed in the lean-to he was in luck. But nobody left a car behind in a boarded up weekend cabin.

He went slowly down to the shuttered cabin. He didn't touch it. No use leaving anything that could be used to show he had come this way. Not unless he had to. If not a car, maybe a motorbike.

The lean-to held a canvas-covered shape. He pulled off the heavy, gray cloth. Under it was a beat-up hot rod job used for drag racing. Some young punk had spent hours on it. Lowering the body, taking off the fenders, putting in twin exhaust pipes. The key was not in the switch but Mike knew how to pull the wires under the dash and twist them together to bypass the ignition switch. He unscrewed the tank cap and sniffed. There was some gasoline in there. How much he didn't know. There was no gauge on the dash. He found a four-gallon can in a corner half full of gasoline. He poured it into the hot rod.

Mike washed his face and hands in brackish water seeping into a barrel set into a spring. He added a handy, fancy, sport cap, ornate sunglasses. There was a set of dirty white cotton overalls, and he got into those. He took out some maps and studied them. The dirt road was hard to find. He found it. It led through Wolf Ridge to a cement factory at Stone Crossing. Here he could take a secondary road to Casa Grande. With luck, he'd make it. Meet Terry.

After awhile he got the motor turning over. In a cloud of blue smoke he put the hot rod onto the dirt road going east. Mike had broken his wristwatch in the scuffling at the picket scene, but he guessed it was mid-afternoon. He shivered with anticipation at the idea that he had a good chance to make it.

His hands felt swollen and the hopped-up-car was a little difficult to handle, if one didn't know the tricks of the heap. Someone was firing a gun far off on the ridge, at rabbit shadows in the brush most likely. That was fine. He came to the secondary road and surprise: He waved cheerfully at two state troopers watching from a crossroads a hundred feet ahead of the dust clouds over on the ridge.

In his Joe College sports cap and white coveralls, driving this fancy junkpile, he could risk it. He shouted. "They got him boxed in up there."

They waved back and Mike turned the hot rod toward the cement works.

His first panic had passed now. This was the worst hassle he'd been in yet. But he'd Houdini himself out of this one. Now he knew how the victim of a hunt felt. How the vixens and the little sand-colored foxes panted when the hunters and the dogs moved upon them with no mercy in their teeth or weapons.

Terry had slept badly; she worried all night, imagining dreadful dangers to her, to Mike . . . Chico would pick her up for the roundabout trip to Casa Grande. If they ever did get together, she'd tell Mike, "Drop out, we're making a baby."

CHAPTER 20

Near morning there was a hint of rain in the air that failed to keep its promise. A pump someplace near the motel was still sucking up water from a deep well, the noise breaking into Terry's early morning sleep.

Those last fragments of dreams persisted in which she saw herself in an orlon housedress in the cozy living room of a small house; Mike was across the table, carving a chuck roast. She saw herself go to the kitchen to see if the blueberry pie was browning properly in the oven. It was a magazine picture house, in Technicolor. As in many of her dreams, she was able to see several facades of her life at once. Tying the climbing vines of dime store roses to a wall trellis, drinking beer from ice-cold cans in a rented mountain cabin, Mike in shorts, flyrods in the corner, and the portable radio playing early Bing Crosby. The lonely, insane lament of a train whistle in the night of her dream made her feel good, she in bed and Mike in her arms, and everyplace a warm grouping of the valid

213

things in the universe that made her one with the greater pattern or plan of existence . . . the shrill, noisy sound of the pump woke Terry inside the fetid bunkhouse.

She lay listening to the pump. Something was wrong with its inner plumbing. It needed oiling or a bearing had worn out. She had no knowledge of what was wrong, but she could hear it protesting, banging away at its duty. Just as she had done for so long.

Outside she heard the clatter of movement from the fields behind the motel—the clash of pots on early breakfast fires. The workers were getting ready for the fields. She looked out the window and judged it was about seven in the morning. A long hour before Chico picked her up.

"Jesus," she said out loud.

In the nearby field she found Chico and the old man boiling coffee over a small fire and toasting stale two-day-old bread.

Chico looked up. "Hi . . . a good night?"

"They find Mike?"

The old man soaked some bread in his black, sugarless coffee. "Hunters still after the wolf."

Chico nodded. "Too wild, all along the ridge."

The old man put the wet bread between his toothless gums. "When I ride with Pancho Villa in 1913, 1914, we were hunted, too."

"You big liar," said Chico. "*You* ride with Pancho Villa? You've flipped."

"No."

"Yes."

"*Somebody* ride with Pancho Villa. Why not *me*? So one day they corner us. Me, Pancho, and Ignacio Pontores from Baja . . ."

"Oh sure."

"We get very drunk and say, let us die shooting. We came out shooting."

"I bet."

Terry paced nervously. "Are we going?"

Chico pointed to a small battered truck nearby with a panel on the door reading: *Mardone's Fruits Vegetables.* The open back was piled high with bunches of carrots, crates of lettuce, bags of potatos, and the green watermelons.

"We are going to be small farmers. The old man is window dressing. You will wear jeans, an old straw hat."

"We being watched?" asked Terry.

"Not sure. We go in ten minutes."

There was hardly any traffic when they started, except for some milk-container rigs and a highway crew cutting weeds. The old man was still rambling on about his riding with Pancho Villa.

"I tell you, Pancho, all of us, we were trapped after stripping some fat *comerciante* of his money, and we had the federal *comandancia* on our tail. A hundred men, firing, and we get out because no one think we crazy enough to try it."

"Maybe you lie a little bit. A hundred *hombres?*"

"Very little lie."

Terry looked at the old man. "You think Mike should come out fighting?"

Chico shook his head. "They'd murderize him."

"What else?" said the old man. "It is the time, then a clean death is the best. No capture by evil men, the howling of lawyers."

Chico produced a vacuum bottle of coffee. He filled the old man's cup. "How do you like this old cat, Terry; dead sober on coffee, giving advice. You should hear him when he's stewed. He's even better."

"I always better than you, Chico."

"Who is he? Your old man?" Terry asked.

"He no my son."

"He's nobody. I just travel with him for laughs. He's nobody."

"Nobody," said the old man, beginning to roll a hand-made cigarette from brown paper and some loose crumbs of tobacco he dug out of a jacket pocket.

Chico held a match for the old man. "You're a mean old cat."

They passed a vineyard where workers were moving to the fields; the tractors were dragging out lug boxes. But the rhythm and the pace of the entire vineyard was off. There were workers missing, still afraid of the law officers.

"Three things you cannot hide," said the old man, exhaling plumes of white smoke from bronzed nostrils. "The sense of courage you show the world, a mountain, and a man riding an elephant."

Ahead of them the heat shimmered off the highway, turning the view above it into a kind of crazy mirror sideshow, of rippling and distorted images. Terry smoothed her stomach. Did anything show yet?

From *Interstate News Service*:

UNION LOSES GRAPE FIRM ELECTION
DWU CHARGES CALIFORNIA'S BIGGEST
VINEYARDS WITH UNFAIR LABOR PRACTICES

Two months after a failed strike the DWU field and ranch workers were overwhelmingly defeated in a secret ballot election to represent workers at Big Mesa Vineyards, California's large grape-growing company, according to vote totals released today.

DWU officials charged the company with unfair labor practices and said the election was influenced by the makeup of the work force, which the union said was 65% illegal aliens.

The vote conducted Monday was 900 for no union, 673 for the DWU and 172 challenged ballots or votes that could not be counted until the eligibility of the voter could be verified.

No incidents were reported, although Big Mesa Vineyards was at the center of a violent confrontation in a bitter strike led by Mike Brant.

This is obviously a very significant election," said Orto Waldman, vice president of the company, "although we can't say that because they lost here the trouble makers will lose everyplace. So, growers beware."

Waldman said a "rapport and mutual respect" existed between his firm and the real farm workers. He said the company's campaign was based on telling workers DWU representation would cost them 3% of their wages in dues and less freedom through union hiring-hall procedures.

Waldman said by law the company could make no promises about increased wages, but that company workers average about $1 an hour—10 cents a box, he said, and it was easy to pick about one box each 20 minutes.

James Ward, a spokesman for the DWU, said more than 100 unfair labor practice charges against Big Mesa Vineyards would be filed with the Agricultural Labor Relations Board.

Mike Brant could not be reached for comment. Ward said Brant was on his honeymoon, having married after the strike.

BOOK FOUR

THE CONTENDER

CHAPTER 21

The young man who got off the Midland Express at Kansas City's Union Station in the spring of 1955 was dressed in neat blue suit with a nearly invisible gray stripe, on his head was a homburg of a very dark shade of blue. He carried a briefcase (clearly new). In the left hand, however, he held a suitcase, rather battered, from which some old labels had been scraped off.

He was slight of build but carried himself with the surface confidence of a much larger man. The face was thin, long, handsome, with a bit of wariness built in. It was the eyes that gave it character; very large and very blue—eyelashes (his own) that looked pasted on, they were that long and curved.

As he walked briskly through the station toward an exit, he looked about him. It was a busy scene of arrivals and departures; the airlines had not yet cut too deeply into railroad travel. The echoing structure smelled, he thought, of peanut shells, pigeon shit, and train-machinery grease.

He walked around a black man pushing a huge broomful of floor debris before him. Near the exit the young man saw a familiar figure smoking a pipe, standing by a newsstand looking over the display of magazines. He called out, "Mikoloj!"

The man turned—a copy of *Newsweek* in his hands "Sonofabitch, the kid brother!" They met, embraced, heads laid on each other's shoulders.

"You're putting it on . . . "

"All muscle, Moz, all muscle. Jamie, my kid brother, Martin. Jamie Ward."

Martin (he no longer thought of himself as Moz) was aware of two men with his brother: this middle-aged man with a pessimistic face—pain that seemed etched into its features rather than a mood just put on. The second man was built wide and solid with a rather stupid face, a healed scar on the right side of his mouth, giving him a lopsided grimace.

"So," said Jamie Ward, "Mike has been talking of you. Welcome to Caysee. Starker, get the car."

The big man left without being introduced. The brothers kept beating each other's shoulders. Mike appeared very happy. Martin smiled; he was not given to public display, but went along with the expected male game of heavy jolly greetings . . . and he felt suddenly more confident . . . not the usual put-on public front but an actual release of some pressure.

"How's Terry and the kid?"

"Absolutely dandy. We've got this fine place . . . you're staying with us till you settle in. I've been damn busy deputizing . . . getting progress off its ass. If there's anything I need it's somebody who knows the damn tangle of legal mumbo jumbo."

"Yeah," said Jamie Ward, seizing the suitcase against Martin's wishes.

"I always feel, Moz, use the law . . . if you can beat them in the courtroom, fine. If not . . . "

Martin nodded as they walked out into the sunlight. Mike was a bit different. He'd learned to talk differently. He seemed to be able to pick his words better . . . and express himself with a kind of hard dignity. He was dressed casually yet neatly in a gray suit, a bit tight across his big chest, and the shoes were expensive: shiny brown leather with a gold-colored, small buckle on each. The cufflinks on the pale yellow shirt sleeves were small red stones; the wristwatch a heavy instrument . . . a pale silver dial with lots of items like date and month and day as added information — even a red stopwatch hand.

Jesus, Mike's wide fingernails were trimmed properly, and there could be a colorless nail polish. There was a touch of tough class about the man, and a look of purpose, even a qualified hardness—not as he had been back home, just a tough Polak kid.

"How's Mom?"

"Like always, Mike. Still going out on special, terminal-case nursing assignments—still playing church bingo."

"My old lady and old man, Jamie, were pushovers for small games of chance. Anything with big odds against them."

That, Martin decided, was more like the old Mike.

Starker was standing by a large dark blue Lincoln—a bit out of date, a '49 job, but well-polished. He held the door open and Jamie followed the two brothers into the back seat. When they were moving away from the station, Martin looked back: "Was that the place the G men hit the mob that tried to get some most-wanted prisoner freed?"

"That's the spot," said Jamie Ward. "J. Edgar Hoover's shitheels grandstanding. Real shootout at the O.K. Corral. The mob is still pretty well-set in the town, Moz; and the old Tom Pendergast machine, it plays ball when it has to."

"How are the DWU locals getting along?"

Jamie Ward frowned. "We got problems."

Mike smiled. "Situations, Jamie, sound better than problems. You can face a situation easy. A problem— now *that's* a problem." He laughed . . . the soft laugh of a man who knew his strength. "Didn't you teach me that, Jamie?"

"There's a lot I didn't teach you . . . like taking on too much."

"There is no way no how to take on too much, unless of course you don't feel you can match it for size. Moz, I'll fill you in later. Right now, I want to show you your office. You like a secretary with a big ass? Quantity not quality?"

"As long as she can spell. I've got to get acceptance to practice law in Kansas. There'll be an examining board of a bar association to meet?"

Jamie answered softly, "No sweat, no sweat at all. Judge Kresh is a hell of a sweet soul and Olden and Dunnigan—that's our legal eagles in union court matters— will give you the ground rules. You're in like Flynn."

Mike dug an elbow into his brother's ribs. "You'll like Kansas City. It's on its toes, and we've got our foothold here . . . "

Martin studied his brother. "Not like the Frisco docks or the vineyards?"

Mike frowned. "I was just a young punk, wet behind the ears then. I felt all good men would support the worker in need of a living. Me wanting to do it with no violence on our part, no shove. They socked it to us, but good."

"Here it's different?"

"Here, Moz, Martin, *I'm* different. I may have scars inside and out, but they taught me a lot." He grinned. "I've kicked my frustrations aside. How you like that talk, frustrations?"

Jamie said, "You'll be putting your hands on your hips next."

"I talk to the Elks at lunch, make speeches, or address some organization like the ACLU. I have to be more than a mug talking sloppy. I read when I have time. I listen to the fancy-talking jerks on radio and TV. Know what I mean? I didn't take an education when I could of—like you did—when I had the chance."

"No, you didn't."

Mike tapped his brother on the chest. "We're going to be a great team."

"If you don't get run out as in California."

"Look, I learn. I'm no preliminary bum anymore, I'm a contender."

Martin had to admit Mike looked confident and had the tone of voice to match it. But had Mike changed, grown? Time would show if it were all a facade, or behind it all Mike had the stuff, more than hard compulsion or a vicarious desire for power.

Mike's quizzical eyes were on him. "Now I don't let the old desire to fight rush in, not without thinking which way the wind blows. Yes, the DWU has a foot in the door here, like I said. Hell, a whole leg—right up to our knee in the doorway. This is a big time town. Big in packing houses, wheat, machinery, *and* politics. That's the name of the game. Going to unionize the county to the hilt. Hell, these cow-paddie lawyers, wait till they see a real eastern, University of Pennsylvania law school kid at work. Moz was highest in his class, Jamie."

"Second," said Martin grinning. "Nobody can be as good as you think, Mike. And these local firms are fancy dans . . . they represent Ford and General Motors, Standard Oil, and the Central Pacific."

"And the International WNUSA, the LBO . . . , but I'm talking locally. The Puskin, he's very fancy in Washington, but he's letting a lot of locals we should be holding in the Middle West go to the LBO. Hell, the right way has to be, you organize solid *here* and then spread east and west. I'll give you the setup later. Right now, I'd rather be up against U.S. Steel than take any guff from the Puskin and . . . "

Starker turned his head, showing them a bit of his right profile. "That green two-tone job been behind us two blocks."

Mike laughed, didn't turn around. "Starker, nobody is following. You're getting goosy." He turned to Martin, "Some tin-horn cheapy tried to push his paper local against Spinelli's hotel suppliers and waste handlers union and got gunned down. A small timer."

Starker bunched his shoulders as if testing his muscles and touched his left arm pit. It was clear to Martin the man had a gun in a shoulder holster there.

Jamie settled back after a look. "The green car turned off to the President Hotel."

"This is a good town," said Mike, knocking out his pipe into a silvered ash receptacle by his side. "Everybody knows the score. I'll have George Spinelli explain it to you. Everybody tries to accommodate, that's it, *accommodate*."

"Accommodate," echoed Jamie Ward sourly. "You married, Martin?"

"Not so far. I like them. I treat them fine. But Mike, he's the married man in the family. How's Paul?"

"Two years last May. Lots of teeth, and maybe we'll have him set on the pottie some day. Got Mom's mouth and chin. You know, determined . . . sees the world from an advantageous view."

Yes, Mike had changed; using works like that: determined, advantageous.

Downtown, Main and 12th Streets, were busy, and they drove along on what Jamie Ward called the tour: past the Civic Center, along the Kansas River bottom, the stockyards, the industrial district, the muddy Missouri River, then drove back along Grand Avenue to an old red-brick building, walked up a chipped set of stone steps. Over a 1924 doorway was the emblem of the Drovers & Wheelmens Union, and under it the letters *Services & Machinists Local 203.*

"Once a schoolhouse," said Mike. "We're affiliated nationally with the WNUSA, but they have their own place past the Federal building at 9th and McGee Streets. This will do for the time being. Nothing fancy."

Inside Martin found painted, hospital-green walls, old-fashioned, frosted light fixtures, lots of battered paneling. They passed a thin girl with brass-colored curls typing on an old Royal, and went into an office with a deerhorn hat rack, several cattle auction broadsides as decor, a colored view of the meeting of the two rivers which Kansas City depended on. There was a glass-top desk, two gray metal files, a small safe under a side table. Mike pointed to the only other chair. "Sit down; Jamie, go get our special files."

When the two brothers were alone Mike inspected a rack of well-smoked pipes, picked one up, leaned back in his swivel chair.

"Jesus, I need you, Moz."

"Let's forget the Moz. It's Martin now."

"Moz or Martin. Kid, I'm fighting for my life, my existence here. No, no . . . I don't mean I'm in danger from any goons. I mean I'm doing things here the Puskin and Sorren Verner of the Labor Brotherhood Organization doesn't like at all."

"I'm confused, Mike. Isn't the DWU part of the WNUSA?"

"Affiliated is the word. And they're the bastards that want the Middle West kept low key . . . stabilized. I'm fighting them."

"I mean, Mike . . . if everything is cozy . . . "

"It's not 1892 when Samuel Gompers set up the first big unions. Hell, ten years later there were strikes against Carnegie by the Association of Iron, Steel, and Tin workers . . . lockouts . . . bloody heads. But now I see bolder leverage pressures needed and a controversial health and welfare plan. Get this: I'm going for open-end grievance procedures, locally."

"You want full, personal control out here?"

Mike stood up and walked to the window, walked back and tapped the files, looked up at the cattle auction broadsides taped to a wall. "I want to organize everything not fully signed up around Kansas City. I want to get the locals not happy with the old labor statesmen to come in with me, into the DWU. That's all."

"That's *all*?"

Mike smiled and winked. "That's all. I've got the local of the meatcutters stockyard people, the machinists in the pipe and pump industries on the verge; coke and gas maybe soon. The boys don't like the way suppliers and warehouses do things. Hell, there's petroleum, hydroelectricity, laths, trip hammers, breweries, distilleries, cotton textiles, mineral corporations—all in sight. My mouth waters."

"What have you got? Don't bullshit me."

"Hotel suppliers, food processors, warehousemen, car repair men. And not paper locals either, with hardly any members. I've set up plans for a political slush fund of seventy-five cents a month, a member."

Martin nodded. "Voluntary pledges of course?"

"Of course. I'm careful now there are twenty-six injunctions from the Department of Justice across the country against various union officials."

"Where do I fit in?"

"Study the indictments. Put them into easy language. I'll use them to show up some of the captive locals and welcome them into the DWU."

"Going against the national organization?"

"Against? Look, what's the national . . . a ten-million-dollar, gold, sandstone building in Washington; a fancy, rent-free penthouse terrace for the Puskin's ornate offices, three bars, the works of Irving Stone and Hubert

Humphrey in a thousand-volume law library; a chef, a sauna, masseurs, sexy female employees. Hell, even a deep freeze meat locker kept full for the general president and the board."

Martin eyed his brother closely. "You're going to blast the high living and low benefits of the rank and file."

"You bet your sweet patootie some reporter will. I know a few. If reaction is right I'm calling out six unions of maintenance men and car parts suppliers people . . . *against* the inclination of the general executive board."

"They'll remove you."

"It will be wildcat strikes. Remove me? Wait till you go through some files I have. No, they'll maybe use strongarmmen against the wildcat organizers. But we'll be ready for that. They want no public stink. The fat boys know they're vulnerable . . . that they're dragging their feet with the biggest industries for better contracts. Lousy health and welfare plans . . . no real pension set-up, or paid vacations, medical care."

"You think you can pull it off?"

Mike sighed. "I'm not too damn sure how far I can go. I'd hate to put my own hard boys on the bricks. Now look, don't stare at me, Moz—Martin. I'm serious. I want real worker benefits and solid resulting negotiations. I remember the old man and his fink union. I know the fucking the average working joe gets from his fat cat union international. I'm going to change all that . . . going to try."

"You'll have to use muscle."

"If I have to I have to. So a bloody nose . . . a little shove to push."

"Like Starker?"

Mike gave a crooked grin: "The Starker Glitz? Isn't he a lulu? He's a Polak sailor . . . had been wrestling as a Jew wonder boy from Israel. He's really a Catholic from Warsaw. A bit thick between the ears."

"Your bodyguard?"

Mike frowned and looked at the pipe, rubbed its bowl against one side of his nose. "I take care of myself, but the Starker, he's impressive, and Jamie, he's a bit rabbity about a roughhouse. Now don't let Jamie Ward fool you with that sad, hound-dog look of his. He knows where everybody in union politics is buried. He knows labor history; the mess of the Coeur d'Alene strike busted by Federal troops. His old man worked with Eugene Debs and helped organize the American Railroad Union—a hundred fifty members in 1894. Just ask, he'll tell you dates and figures. He'll show you how to set up bail forms and legal papers if any of the pickets get arrested. Also a list of judges to plead before—pleading the men and the company judges to avoid—we own a few judges, that is, favors returned for the political people we support. It's all done with trust."

"I can see that," said Martin ironically.

Jamie Ward came in with several bundles of red cardboard files and set them down on the desk.

"There's a bit of code on names involved, Martin," he said, "but I'll key you in. Mike protects certain connection sources."

"Spies. I have some people stashed in the Washington headquarters of the WNUSA."

"Trustworthy?"

"No, but handy. *Capisce?*"

The phone rang. Mike picked it up. "Yes, yes. Sure he's here. Now simmer down. I'm just getting him settled in here. Okay, we'll be right over." He covered the part of the phone with a palm. "It's Terry. Give her the glad talk . . . here he is, Terry, shiny-eyed and bushy-tailed."

Martin took the offered phone: "Hello, Terry."

The voice was loud and clear, just a bit irked. "Hi, Moz. Don't let him hold you there. Take a cab if he wants to stay. So, how's it been, lawyer?"

"It's been good so far. I haven't done much
. . . clerked for a New Jersey judge for eight months,
represented the Perth Amboy Waterfront Association.
But you don't want to hear all that."

"You're damn right I don't. I'm up to here from your
brother with union doings. Got a girl back East?"

"Not too many."

"I mean serious . . . a good working girl."

"How about a Jewish princess, heiress to a junk dealer's fortune, with a million dollars? Seriously, Terry,
don't bother. How's Paul?"

"Bouncing, teething. Look, I've got a seven-dollar roast
in the oven, and tell that bastard Mike it's our wedding
anniversary."

"Want to talk to the bastard?"

"I better not. Just get him here in an hour. Good to talk
to you, Moz."

"Martin . . . "

"Martin . . . "

He hung up. "The missus has a bee in her ear."

Mike was lighting the pipe. "She thinks I don't know
it's our anniversary. I've got a case of Mums in the car,
and there's a ton of roses on the way. I've got a call coming in from Detroit, and then we'll be off and running.
How's she sound . . . I mean you only met her twice."

"She sounds like you're a lucky guy."

Mike grunted. He was studying some papers.

CHAPTER 22

It was a two-story, dun-colored colonial house set back from the street with several small maple trees, much damaged by dogs, and a lawn that was never in good health this Kansas summer; it was, Mike explained, a good middle-class neighborhood, and he had put down five thousand dollars borrowed from the DWU Aid Fund at a low four percent interest. The house had cost twenty-eight-thousand dollars. The mortgage would run twenty years at six-and-a-half.

"But I expect to be out of here," he told Martin, "in a couple of years—find something better by West Terrace Park."

Martin said, "It looks very livable." He noticed the fairly good six-year-old pale yellow Chevy in the open double garage—a bicycle hanging from the rafters; some old chairs, a radio leaking wire entrails, a trash can.

Mike said to the Starker, "Be back in three hours. I

have to be at the Muelbach, meeting with some of the Mercantile Bank and Trust people and the Finlay Engineering College dean. Get the car washed. But first bring in the champagne."

"Washed this morning," said the too-solid man.

Mike led the way past a kiddie car, kicked aside a local sales throwaway.

"The Lincoln belongs to the local but you use it when it's free." Mike pulled out a key chain, selected a key, and opened a white front door with a half-circle, stained-glass fanlight.

Inside it was still light enough to see a living room of some good furniture: two oversized lamps topped with pink silk, reproductions of Van Gogh, and a rose period Picasso, an Andrew Wyeth. Steuben glass stood about in the shape of a seal and bull.

"It's Terry's taste. I have a den . . . hey, the old man's home!"

The woman who came out of the dining room seemed to Martin too mature to be the Terry he had met three years before. The hair was set too tightly into a matron's nest of twists; the dress set well, but was strictly a rack job he guessed: J. C. Penny's or Monkey Wards.

But the face had the right smile, a bit plumper maybe, the eyes a bit over made-up. Still it was the old Terry in a new setting.

He kissed her cheek. She smelled of baby piss and roasting beef—some new kind of bath powder as she hugged him.

"Better than the grape fields, eh?" She rubbed the back of her brother-in-law's neck with firm strong fingers.

"It's all right, it's damn all right," Martin said holding out a little pink package tied with a green ribbon. "Happy anniversary. Just some fancy, smelly toilet water. But Chanel."

"Good boy."

Mike held up a larger package with red bows over gold

paper. "You thought the old fuddy-duddy he forgot? Right? Right."

"Who reminded you?" She smiled and kissed Mike on the mouth. "It's good to be remembered." She felt the box—saw the sporting goods label. "You didn't!"

"The hell I didn't." He turned to Martin. "Would you believe a solidly married lady who wants rollerskates with high white boots, would you?"

"I would. Terry, they have a good rink in town?"

"Past the Kansas City Art Institute off beyond Warwick. You skate?"

"Like the wind."

"He's a goddam wiz." Mike was looking over messages on yellow slips left by the telephone on an end table. "Jesus, can't that dinge learn to write better?"

Terry said softly, "Watch it, mister. Good help is hard to get."

"Charlie knows I love every joint in her black body . . . you believe it, Moz, she's named Charlie." He stuffed the messages into a pocket and turned to the Starker standing with the case of champagne in his arms. "Put it down, Starker, and go get the car's oil changed."

He grasped his brother's arm. "Come see the kind of kid me and Terry here made."

"He's being bad," Terry said, following them down a hall to a room, painted white, with two windows and heavy wire mesh grating over them. There was shiny white baby furniture with trolls and elves and butterflies painted on. A blond baby sat, bibbed and stubborn, in a high chair and a thin black woman was trying to get the child to swallow a mess of green mushy vegetable matter—pushed into a mouth turned away and cheeks stained with the mess.

The black woman said, "He's got his mean streak on tonight, Miss Terry."

"Hello, Paulie." Mike made a mock gesture of a blow

on the baby's stained chin with a closed fist. "This is
your Uncle Moz, only we have to remember the dignity
of his law degree—he's Uncle Martin. What do you think,
Martin? Mom's nose and mouth?"

"Terry's too." Martin came closer, the baby spit up and
his bib got messier.

"Thanks," said the child's mother, wiping the chin and
holding firm the small, blond head trying to move out of
the range of the cleaning process.

"I could ram in some more, Miss Terry."

"He eat the puree of beef, the carrots?"

"That he liked."

"Then he's had enough. Go see to the kitchen, Charlie,
and I'll put him to bed. You guys go and have some
drinks. Tonight, honey, it's champagne all the way.
Charlie got me that big set of crystal goblets."

It was a good healthy dinner. Not gourmet food maybe,
Martin felt (he had been, during his college years, invited
to some Main Line estates and down to Delaware when
they needed an escort for some of the girls he was screwing—the hosts never suspecting maybe he was the son of
a Polak tire worker and a New England registered nurse
who took terminal cases). A too-thick pea soup, but
tasty, flavored with thyme, the roast sliced thin, done
just right, the corn pudding, the vegetables a bit over-
cooked—two kinds of pie: apple and lemon meringue.

"Who told you, Terry, I like lemon pie?"

"Mike dropped a word that way . . . have another
slice or Mike will gobble it. He's getting fat."

"Not fat . . . solid." He opened the first bottle of
champagne, the cork popped politely, and they drank the
bubbly pale yellow wine, smiling at each other. Mike
said, "Deceptive stuff . . . it gets into your legs." He
lifted his goblet. "Terry, I think I'm going to let you stay
on."

Terry looked flushed and very handsome, Martin
thought. She had helped with putting away the martinis,

produced after all before the dinner. She seemed in a loose, cheerful, thoughtful mood. "You better, you big stiff, with the assets I have in my name."

"Not much, honey, not much. But we'll do all right. You see, Martin, with all the Federal Justice Department jerkoffs trying to get injunctions on every union boss around, it's best the whole kit and kaboodle be in Terry's name . . . house, car . . . do we still have a bank account?"

"A little one. I bet, Martin, you thought heads of locals were rolling in loot . . . like the fat cats?"

"That's the impression."

"Twelve Gs a year," said Mike. "A car, of course, reasonable expense account. But hell I'm not in it for the money. I could run a trucking company or a packing plant's personnel department for twenty thousand a year. I get offers. No . . . I know what I want."

"I want more champagne," said Terry. "And a mink coat."

"Here's the bubbly," said Mike, refilling her glass. "You'll do with a cloth coat like that prick Nixon offered his wife."

Charlie came in with a large, white square cake, its icing decorated with red and blue; big pink roses of colored sugar and some red lettering set among candied orange rinds, dates, and figs in glazes, studded with shelled nuts.

"Where'd that come from?" asked Mike.

Charlie shifted the cake onto the table, read the inscription: *"Happy happy anniversity to the best of them, Mike and Terry Brant, from everybody in Services and Machinists Local 203, DWU."*

Mike smiled at Martin. "And nobody twisted their arm either."

"Get the big, blue-edged plates, Charlie. We'll freeze what we don't eat tonight."

"Never mind that, Terry. What's left I'll take down for Jamie, the Starker, and the staff."

Charlie turned her head. "I hear the child. He's not getting to sleep."

Mike stood up. "I'll go to him."

Terry nodded. "Thanks, it's been a big day. I'm bushed."

When Mike was gone, Terry slowly sipped her wine. "What do you think of big brother?"

"I hope you don't mean that in an Orwellian sense."

"Oh that book? I never had time to read it. You know I used to read a lot . . . I mean Will Durant . . . tried Faulkner. But I've let go. Getting sloppy."

"Hell no, Terry. You look great."

"It's the Helena Rubenstein. I don't know, Martin. What do you think of Mike? Level with me."

"He's changed. He's confident—a little less noisy. He's learned to talk better. I mean the mug is still there, that's part of him. But he's thinking things out, got plans, ambitions."

"He's got this drive. But I wonder. You know for Kansas City, the Middle West . . . it's still Boss T. J. Pendergast's territory. Ol' Harry Truman, he got his old gang leader, Tom Pendergast, a pardon when Tom went to prison. I never could go for Harry Truman as the noble, common man. Hell, he's got his nose in the local dirt like all of them. He's giving the country a snow job."

"You still a Marxist, Terry?"

"Huh? I guess in principle. But I look at what the shits have done in Russia and China . . . I . . . pour me another glass. It's our night to howl."

"As Mike said, this stuff sneaks up . . . trips you."

"That's all right. I like to get sloshed once in awhile. Mike's in trouble. The executive council of the national don't like his hand on the door. His ideas of autonomy of each trade, and over and under the table negotiating. And there's the mob stuff—labor racketeering here, too, is thick as jam on bread."

"I noticed the Starker had a gun, and the heavy wire mesh in the kid's room . . . "

"Mike is overcareful. Maybe he's right. But he likes a fight, and I was raised fighting. Christ, it's good to have you here, Marty."

"You happy?"

Terry pushed her half-filled glass away, lowered her head, lifted it, looked closely at her brother-in-law. "Happy? Yes, sure. Set, contented. Mike's too busy to go roaming in the gloaming." She laughed. "There was this crazy professor . . . she was doing some kind of scientific study on labor . . . how many times a day a worker wipes his ass or something. She propositioned Mike."

"She did?"

She took a sip of wine. "Know what Mike told her?"

"What?"

"He said, 'Lady, even if I wanted to make it, the logistics can't be worked out.' The logistics, he told me. He thought it was a laugh."

"Logistics, that's pretty good."

Mike was back. "He conked off after I sang at him a bit. Hell, we need another bottle."

"I've had enough," said Martin.

"I've had more than enough," said Terry. "But what-the-hay . . . every day isn't my wedding day. One more drinkee."

"You're looped," said Mike laughing, opening another bottle.

"A bit shaky in the wings." Terry began to weep. "I feel *so* out of things. I mean it's the house, the kid; okay, okay, we've been all over that I know."

"I'll take you to Chicago next month. A meeting. A remembering of the police massacre by the Chicago cops Memorial Day—shooting of three hundred pickets of Republic Steel. Back in '37."

Martin looked at Terry, winked. "That should be a barrel of fun."

Terry was sniffing back tears, giggling, wiping her eyes with a napkin. "A million laughs. I can see it from here."

"We'll get away, do the night spots—Palmer House, go out to the races. You like that, figuring odds on ponies."

"Tell me what I like . . . I like ponies, I like Paris, I like Rome. Ever play that game when you were a kid, Marty?"

Martin said no, he was hustling in the pool halls as soon as he could hold a cue.

The next few days Martin spent meeting union lawyers, mostly getting to know Kansas City, the various segments of it, like an orange, parts all able to separate themselves—yet be part of a whole.

Mike was busy; rumors were printed in the *Kansas City Star* that labor unrest was about to strike the city: "Wildcat strikes are being planned; the national union chiefs in Washington condemn the hotheads." Statements by the Puskin appeared with an AP byline: "The ruffians and crackpots will not be able to shake the calm understanding of the WNUSA and industry."

On the six o'clock news on television the Puskin spoke out—lean jaw firmly set: "Kansas City is a prime example of cooperation between the working man and big business, and we shall clean our ranks of those malcontents who ruffle the feathers of the wheels of American industrial progress."

The Puskin was a man to mix metaphors to make his point: "We sit today on the point of a dilemma." The LBO statement was made by Soren Verner on *Meet the Press*. Verner, a placid-looking Swedish-American gentleman, responded to the questioner from the *St. Louis Post Dispatch*: "The Labor Brotherhood Organization—the LBO—has strived for many years to bring labor peace to the Middle West; and certainly now the unions will not toss aside their part of the bargains we pledged to support."

There was no mention of the DWU locals, or any that Mike Brant controlled. He did do a morning appearance on *Good Morning Caysee,* facing a sleepy girl on television who kept searching her notes for some interesting questions to ask. When she asked, "Are you Mr. Brant, the man behind the rumors of wildcat strikes being planned?"

Mike insisted:

"Now, dear lady, I don't claim to dictate the welfare of the workers. They are themselves vocal as to their working conditions, aware of failed promises, the lack of a true mutual trust between them and some employers. The workers elected me, but they speak for themselves—like at the moment through me. They can elect someone else if they want, as their spokesman. And I'd support him. I've been a worker myself since I was twelve years old. I've worked crops, I've been a longshoreman, I've driven tractors. I've always felt there is a hell of a—pardon me—a great difference between the working joe and the big boys in the national union positions in Washington who come out to pat our heads once or twice a year—to okay their own pensions and private suites. Wildcat or not, a strike is *always* based on a grievance ignored."

Martin noticed this statement of Mike's was not reported in any of the city's newspapers and was cut from the noon roundup of city items on *High Noon News.*

Martin, on foot, in taxis, in the borrowed Lincoln, he with the curiosity of a boy, found Kansas City the fascinating hub of a vast network of railroads, with a huge changing population selling and buying horses, mules, cattle. The grain and food processing, machine and auto, and truck assembly plants had no one big union gathering them together. These unattached locals or weak paper organizations were in the process of being taken over, or fighting off those who wanted to represent them.

The garment manufacturing plants were often open

shops; the workers in the sale centers of the great markets in food stuff and in warehousing were interested in the DWU, *but* with a wariness.

Martin went shopping with Terry at Harzfelds, at Adlers. "That's what I am, Marty, a shopper—to get away a few hours from Paulie's diapers. Sweet kid, isn't he? The like-lead hours of being a housewife gives me the willies. It's shopping, soap operas, or baking one of those damn cakes you see being made of doctored flour; waiting hubby's return so he can say, 'Hey, this is sure good cake, sweetheart.'"

They were sitting in the bar of the Drum Room at the Hotel President, drinking gin gibsons, after viewing the Thomas Hart Benton Memorial at Benton Boulevard and St. John Avenue, and after buying something in blue for Paul at Chasnoff and Mindlins.

Terry motioned the barman for a refill, then changed her mind. "Never two before six o'clock. That's a rule. It's fattening. You know, Marty, I'll send back most of what I bought today. A sterile routine."

"Why doesn't Mike give you the women's locals to work with—typists, nurses, laundry workers?"

"Would you believe it, he's old-fashioned? Scout's honor—he feels a wife is for home work only."

"I think maybe it's more than that, Terry. He isn't that square."

"Tell me, lawyer. I'm a prisoner of baby shit and Pablum."

"He doesn't, I think, want to move along too many union fronts at once. He sees maybe, perhaps, he can drive a wedge for local autonomy through the service and machinists' locals he's controlling. Once with a success there, he'll move in all directions—expand his clout."

"What if he becomes a cropper?"

Martin shrugged, smiled. "Mike was always good at picking himself up, dusting himself off, after a fall."

"I'm not that limber no more; maybe it's because of

Paul. I've become a goddam mother type." She grabbed
Martin's arm. "I'm scared. I don't show it in front of
Mike. I'm Terry, the fireman's child—no fears showing.
But I get this feeling, like a dream I used to have when a
kid: I'm lost, see, and wandering, and nobody knows who
I am when I ask . . . and I dream sometimes, the last
couple of months, I ask Mike who I am, and he looks at
me and shakes his head . . . doesn't talk, walks away."

"In a dream we invent character's actions—the real
person doesn't invade our sleep. Freud."

"Screw Freud. Barman, we'll have that refill."

They drove home in the beat up Chevy, tipsy and
laughing all the way. Martin wondered if Mike understood Terry at this crucial stage of their life together. He
wondered if his brother knew of her fears. She appeared
as vital, as alert, as Martin had imagined her to be from
the small knowledge he had of her from a couple of previ-
ous visits. But there was a deepening kind of probing of
herself going on. One could almost call it a despair.

Martin came to the conclusion that Mike was a lousy
husband. Maybe fine in the sex department (even there
one wasn't sure), but dedicated now to his progress in the
dangerous, savage infighting of union politics—of making contacts (and enemies), of seeking support from perhaps questionable quarters. Mike Brant, always on the
go, always with pockets full of notes; Jamie Ward at his
elbow to remind him of something crucial; the Starker
going off with Mike in the Lincoln for nightly, late-hour
meetings. Martin, trying to sleep in the spare bedroom,
would often hear the car returning, and he'd look at his
watch; it would usually be two-thirty, three o'clock in
the morning. There would be voices from their bedroom
and sometimes loud words between Mike and Terry.
First whispers, then a shouting, then silence. Or steps,
light steps; Terry going down to the bar? Martin would
wait for her return trip—would often lie listening till St.
Stanislaus (Polish) and St. George's (Serbian) church bells

summoned the pious to early Mass—and he'd also hear Kansas and Missouri railroad cars—mile-long freights sounding as they approached the Kansas City Livestock Exchange and stockyards, with thousands of animals for the morning slaughtering crews at their concentration camplike posts.

One morning Martin awoke to the sound of loud words (blows?), and Mike slamming the door in a rage as he left. Terry locked herself in the bedroom, and Charlie fed the baby and made ham and eggs for Martin. "They always make up. They both feisty."

Martin took a taxi to the DWU offices. Mike had been too much enraged to remember him. He didn't see Terry to say good morning before he left.

CHAPTER 23

The first walkout came on a Monday, all outside the Kansas City limits. Most of the workers at Stevenson-Kirk Services in Bellmer went out, and ten pickets were walking with signs calling Stevenson-Kirk Services, *"Unfair to service workers."*

Stevenson-Kirk offered crews of men and women who cleaned offices, washed banks of windows for business places and factories, carried off trash in great bins, waxed acres of public floors. For three months Mike had been negotiating with Stevenson-Kirk for a new contract; a wage increase of sixteen percent, longer lunch hours, a stronger medical insurance program with the Stevenson-Kirk Services to carry a bigger percentage of the costs.

Mike hadn't pushed too hard. As he explained to Martin, "A strike puts a certain kind of fear in the employer who depends on contracts. He's easier to handle when he can't perform services and no new billing goes out. His contracts with big industries, banks, department stores in the city are all invalid as long as the strike lasts. So he's a bit more willing to give in for a better deal with the union."

"But suppose he uses nonunion help."

"Not on city contracts," Mike smiled. "He may have a few old hands who will get spit on by the pickets, get some cars scratched, a few tires slashed. But he can't fill the ranks with real help who know the routines. He may hire some rummies and loafers. But he's up shit creek while his contracts seek maybe other firms or put in their own services. There he's a loser for good."

"There will be injunctions against the DWU."

"I expect it, and I expect you to fight them. That's why I'm staying outside city limits. So you tie them up with legal mumbo jumbo, get injunctions against Stevenson-Kirk for violation of fire laws endangering the worker's health."

"So you think this will be settled soon?"

Mike looked at the picture of his son Paul set in a silver frame on his desk, the child's image smeared with cake from his second birthday party . . . his small fists imbedded in the mess of cake, a paper hat with the large number *two* pasted on it on his round head. "Martin, I didn't give a plugged dime about Stevenson-Kirk's Services. I want them to act foolishly . . . try and carry on, rough up the pickets. Then a dozen wildcat strikes will come out. Not just the DWU locals, but the WNUSA auto parts suppliers in Greenmoor, the LBO warehouse units, and lumber yard people in River Point—the tanners who will stink up the county with unused hides at Centerville. Chemicals too. You know how much crap goes into packing house products? And I've stayed out of Kansas City, so there is no violence here to upset people."

"What if there are no wildcats in support?"

"Let's wait and see."

At two o'clock the Kamisky Tanners and Leather Workers local in Willowby Junction was proclaiming solidarity with the Stevenson-Kirk Services. Martin never knew if this was a true spontaneous strike or had been engendered. George Spinelli called Mike. George had statewide contracts for his trucks to carry off the offal and more messy stockyard wastes—the surplus chemical by-products, the greases, the rancid fats, the bones—to rendering and soap plants.

George, born Giacomo, was a polite, well-educated Italian-American, not at all a roughhouser, even when he went bowling with Mike. George fancied himself as resembling an actor, Ricardo Cortez, and was a man who liked well-tailored clothes, avoided two-tone shoes. His father, Fanguella, had been a "Moustache Pete;" one of the old-time Kansas, grand bootleggers of the Prohibition days who had raised and educated four sons, loyally supporting the Pendergast machine, which saw he got contracts for gravel and sand, winning bids for city and state road and street construction work.

After George Spinelli called Mike, there was the spreading of the strikes . . . a lockout of the Fernwall Leather Processors in Oaktown; they having an agreement that in a strike against Kaminsky Tanners and Leather, they would show a solid front against union tactics.

Mike didn't come home that night.

Orden, Dunnigan, Rashe, and Cosimo, the lawyers who represented the DWU, were a large law firm of seven partners, twenty-two lawyers—an army of clerks, apprentices, researchers and makers of torts and briefs. The firm was on two floors off Washington Square, where the partners' vast offices could look down on the equestrian statue of General Washington, he calm in the saddle—"The horse," as Herb Orden (senior partner) said to Martin, "knowing who was holding the reins."

Herb Orden was a short man in his late fifties, with a
great loss of hair, too much nose, and very strong white
teeth. His office was of polished walnut with a collection
of Frederik Remington western color prints. Herb Orden
was a horse owner who raced midwestern tracks under
his own colors, hoping to breed a horse to win the Ken-
tucky Derby.

"Jesus, Mike is taking on a lot. Twelve arrests of pickets so far today."

"We don't want to bail them out right away. For anyone arrested, to sit a few hours in the jail and appear before friendly judges, makes drama."

Orden admired for the thousandth time the picture of
The Fight at the Water Hole. "Pete Kresh is a judge of
sense and sensibility—that honest Lionel Barrymore
face."

"What about the County Board of Health regulations
being flouted?" asked Martin, ignoring the cut-glass decanter of Scotch Orden was pointing to.

"Flouting? That a Penn Law School term? Well now,
we could stir up Kaminsky, but old Aaron Kaminsky,
sure he's retired with the *goyem* in Palm Beach, but he's
also solid with the party fund raisers. Know what I mean?
Kick his boys a bit, sure, but don't break all their teeth.
Condemn their plants."

At two o'clock on Tuesday, the Hilton Gasket and
Manifold Foundries at Topwaha Lake, suppliers of parts
to the local assembly plants of Ford and General Motors,
were out—not too large a firm, not the only supplier.

An hour after a walkout of the Welders and Metal Cutters Local 2 in Unity City, Martin received a report of a
bloody affair at Gate Two near the metal storing sheds.
Two strikers were run down, hurt, not killed, by a six-
wheel Mack truck; the driver was badly beaten, had his
leg broken; the Unity City police had arrested six pickets
for "intent to commit murder." The truck driver was not
held.

Mike was present on the scene, shaking a finger at a police captain, seeing to the ambulance for the injured, ordering an added twenty men into the lines. "We are peaceful," he addressed the shouting men. "We don't seek trouble; we're lawful and know our rights. We fought for them, didn't we, in Europe, Korea. Never mind what the national union big shots claim. This isn't a wildcat as we see it—it's a protest; it's free Americans, and you Mexican-Americans back there too, using your rights to protest and seek out full value for your services."

Martin, and Orden, and Dunnigan were busy as the action grew rougher; violence was common. The employers were fighting back. The law firm's labor expert, John Cassady Dunnigan, had to fly back from Saratoga. He was a Catholic power in the state, a Knight of Malta, not just a Knight of Columbus, getting hopes of a Federal judgeship.

It was clear the law could bend, be blindfolded, and still appear to resemble justice.

By Wednesday morning it was the pickets who were getting the worst of it. Their cars were dented, their tires slashed. Three pickets were assaulted by club carrying strangers in Sally Sands' Steak and Roast Beef Diner. The union delegate and grievance chairman at Kaminsky's had his picture windows in his home smashed near Swopes Park. His wife and two children were cut by flying glass. The sister of the editor of Union News in Kansas City was mugged by two blacks who took nothing from her but her hat, yelling, 'Your mutterfukkin' brudder is next."

Mike, freshly shaved and barbered, sat in his office listening to the noon newscast on a small television set. He sat facing Jamie Ward who had a black eye and a torn coat sleeve—Martin examining a file of arrest reports, George Spinelli, a picture of good tailoring—a fraternity key on his watch chain, sat on a corner of Mike's desk swinging a Bond Street shoe.

Mike turned off the television set. "All right, George, you tell me why it's a new ball game."

Spinelli nodded. "It's what we both know."

"Mob goons?"

Jamie Ward tenderly touched his hurt eye. "From the Purple Gang flown down from Detroit last night."

Spinelli nodded. "I'd say that the employers are laying heavy dough on the line for power. Mike, your own boys don't stand a snowball's chance in hell against professional muscle."

"You're not telling me anything new. Jamie, you think the International—maybe the Puskin—is backing the employers to kick my ass?"

"God forbid, Michael. Against their own rank and file?"

Martin tossed the reports on to the desk. "If the big union bosses want Mike off their back, why not? He's a troublemaker who offers local autonomy to the unions here . . . better contracts than before, with the padding for the employers removed. Sure I'd do it if I were the Puskin being shown up."

Jamie turned the television on low. "It doesn't have to be the Puskin. Say, somebody in his inner group—one of his boys who don't tell him everything. After all the Puskin is a labor leader who eats lunch in the White House and gets scrolls from the B'nai Brith."

The television screen came alive with a mass of pickets being beaten by an attacking group of hard-looking men in black jackets; the police were shoving at the edge of the crowd; picket signs fell, fists flew, men were stomped on the sidewalks.

"George?" Mike said.

"Detroit hoods, all right. That's Batsy Wako pushing his way up front with that cush . . . well?"

Mike stood up, his face calm, the freshly shaved jaw-

line twitching a bit. Martin knew that sign. His brother
was just about at the limit set to the control of his temper. The danger signal was out.

"Yes," said Mike simply to George Spinelli. "Yes."

Spinelli nodded to Jamie Ward to follow him out of the
office. Martin stared at his brother who was breathing
hard. With a sweep of his arm Mike sent everything on
his desk crashing to the floor. "The bastards. They've
forced me to make a deal with mob hoods."

Martin bent down and picked up Paul's picture, glass
unbroken. The television screen turned into a football
game, and an announcer's voice took over: "From political violence in the Middle West, we turn to violence on
the football fields as the battle goes on as to what two
contenders will play in the Pasadena Rose Bowl annual
championship game come next New Years . . ."

September 30, 1955

Dear Mom,

Called you last night but you must have been out on
one of your terminals. I know that last issue of that rag,
Life magazine, must have upset you. But look at it the
right way. It all certainly made my organizing work national. Yes, sure I take a bow as a national figure myself.
What the magazine story got cockeyed was all that malarkey about squads of mobsters roaming the streets and
turning the countryside, the city, into a "blood bath."
What a word.

Industry and labor can now come to the mat even stephen. I mean we both have the shove and the power to
take each other on, no holds barred. See? And if they play
tough, why we have to take our cue from them. It's called
practical logical relationship. They can't let us get too
much ahead, and we can't let them feel too raunchy about
being able to go beating our brains out whenever they feel
like it.

What really happened was fighting for a better break for
the working stiff, and less crud from the fat cats who run

the unions at the top. We won . . . anyway we're winning, and the press and the magazines don't report it fair; we're not the big advertisers. So there were some arms and legs bent, and we made it come out just a little better for our side. We had them by the short hair, Mom. The firms needed to continue taking in money to pay for their plants and bank loans. And every day we blocked off their fulfilling their contracts—their life blood—they suffered. We didn't go after the big boys, DuPont or Standard Oil or Sears. No, just the fellows that serve them, make parts, always sweating, panting to get contracts. One bad season and it's the shithouse for them.

We're revising contracts, letting some men and girls go back to work. Not all at once, but in bunches while we're sweet-talking each other over conference tables.

The real bastard, Mom, is our own DWU union president, the chairman of the board of high livers—Dick Seabrook and his pals. We're not getting all the rights for the locals we asked for, but we're getting the right for them to vote for the DWU as their representative and have their dues paid direct into our treasury by the employer, and we decide *what* the national gets.

I'll say this for the Puskin, he knows he's been in a fight, and we here didn't get scare-booger when he said on the news broadcast that he was thinking of running the DWU out of the WNUSA. He's grandstanding. He wouldn't dare. So just remember what I did was for guys like the old man who never had a real union with balls. Lots more to do. A hell of a lot more. I'm not sitting on my duff; in this setup, you go up or you head for the ashcan. I'm meeting in Chicago soon with a whole raft of locals, their heads, and I've got me a plan—one Moz worked out, for interrelationships among all the midwestern locals that can become part of our charters. And I also see a lot of locals who don't like the sharp end of the stick they are now getting in the eye from the old-line boys. Moz is kay-okay. He's a real legal whiz at seeing the law as full of loopholes for us.

As for what you used to call "the quality," he's handling the high class shysters, their lawyers, and their fancy gab with kid gloves (with an iron horseshoe in them); Moz, he's going to do all right.

With me up to my ass in vital things to attend to, fences to mend and a few to tear down, he's keeping Terry from giving me a hard time. I don't know where you heard she's on the booze. Not at all. We do a little social drinking when celebrating. She gets a bit gay—fingersnapping at some of the affairs with a bunch of stiffs at a banquet. And who can blame us? They're Dullsville from the word go, but we have to put in an appearance.

Paulie is growing like a sand lot weed. A sweet kid, bright, too. We have him in walking shoes, and he wobbles from side to side like he had the crabs. But he's filling out, has some teeth, and me and Terry, we're thinking of having another baby. I mean, you know, an only child, they get spoiled, and Terry with a full family will feel set in life, the way she always wanted.

Why don't you come out and live with us? None of us are getting any younger. I know you have the rest of the kids and their families all around you. But I feel now, or soon, I'll be able to do all I ever wanted to do for you and couldn't. Your work of watching some old geezer croak is no way of living, and out here, they have very fancy hospitals and high-priced doctors . . . if you wanted to take a case now and then.

Terry and Moz—he wants to be called Martin now— would certainly make you welcome. You're too proud, like to have your own way. I know that, but did you ever think we might need you? I still blow up sometimes when a head of steam is building up in me by some pressure of my work; I dream I'm a kid again and Moz has wet the bed, and the factory whistles are blowing in early morning for the workers to go to their jobs. It's like the feel and sound of the world coming to an end. Of course I've outgrown all that nutty stuff, but when there comes a touch of it, Terry calls it "the Old Nostalgia Waltz." She has a whacked out sense of humor sometimes.

She sends her best. I am fine, a bit rushed, but I just had a physical with the insurance company doc—nothing to worry over. The local DWU is taking out fifty thousand dollars life and health on me as a sign of their gratitude. But I don't expect anyone to collect on it for fifty or sixty years. Moz is really spreading out, kicking up waves. I try to get him to write but you know these goddam intellectuals—our fault we educated him—he's buzzing about with fancy society broads at country club dances and furnishing a flat. I'll chew him out to keep in touch with you.

Your loving son,

MIKE

P.S. Forgot to ask . . . I hope the fancy weeds I sent you Mother's Day were fresh.

Martin was hardly having all the heavy social life Mike wrote to his mother about. He had been to some of the country clubs—not the most desired clubs yet; he was very busy trying to see that the legal end of the strike settlements were as rosy as Mike expressed them. There was a great deal more turmoil and confusion than calmness, and Martin learned to dislike his profession even more.

He made a note in a journal: "The legal bickering, knifings, even unethical, illegal conniving by the law firms for both the unions and industry is like two bandit gangs in a face-off—reaching a pitch that to me is almost Elizabethan melodrama. The doublecross is normal: the running up of expense money, fees for doing nothing, and bills for luxury entertainment are beyond reason. Shakespeare was so right about us lawyers."

Herb Orden spoke to Martin after a hard day of getting very little done but talks of golf scores, taxes. They were drinking and eating at the Golden Ox. "You learn too soon, Marty, that the big bastards, they judge a lawyer by his fees. You stick it to them good and deep, and they think you're the Einstein and Green Hornet of the law courts. You play it square and on the level, and you're in a one-room office with unwashed windows, taking cases from people who fell off a bus, or found some broken glass in a coke bottle. . . .

"Like the steaks here? Top cut. What say we get our ashes hauled? The corporations have these call girls on salary, and we could nip in and out on the cuff."

"Not tonight, Herb. I've got some briefs to look over." It wasn't that he couldn't use some shack-up time; Martin was feeling a neglect of his usually active sex life. But besides being rushed with legal work, he never consorted with whores. He felt a man, a well-hung male, true and virile, never got to paying for it. Or as Herb Orden did, put it on the cuff. Martin felt a decent, well-set-up, mannered man could find himself the right sex partner among better class women: adventurous wives, alert women in executive positions trying to prove they were still baby-dolls. The female population that lived life as an active man did—moving from parties to beds, from singles bars to theatre lobby pickups; using business conventions for casual sexual pairing, never launching long enough into an affair to think of it as something one wanted permanently, or getting stuck in a situation that could result in love.

Right now Martin was eyeing Millie Warner—a chit from the University of Chicago's advanced Social Science, Arts, and Humanities—she doing publicity for the DWU during the crisis. Fancy glasses, (a girl's eyes seemed captives of promise to Martin when under glass); a trim not too narrow ass, no tits to speak of. Millie Warner had a way of tossing her head of ginger-colored hair around like the models in the cosmetic ads. Martin had a date with her for the weekend—a trip in her MG to Arrow Lake Park fifty miles from Kansas City.

They had spent an afternoon getting to know each other better at the Nelson Gallery of Art on Rockwell Road, looking at the T'ang horses ("pronounced *Tong*," she said). Millie was working on her Masters, writing a thesis on "Workers' Statues in Chinese Ceramics."

Be nice to score with a scholar, Martin figured.

Mike was a deeper, thornier study Martin set himself to. Big brother Mike who gave you a slap of reconciliation when you crossed him in some argument, cruelly efficient, full of affectionate teasing when in a good mood.

Martin lacked the driving, rugged force of Mike. Martin had been the sensitive, delicate one of Mom's litter, given to colds and ear aches as a child—the only bedwetter in a large family. He was more intelligent than Mike, he felt, but Mike had this really monomaniacal energy and seemed insensitive to subtleties (not true, Martin told himself—he just hides it better). There was a proud conscience in Mike, for all his hard-trampling exterior. In the secret kernel of his brother, Martin felt existed a frenzy of senses, for all the astute opportunism that surfaced. Martin made a note:

> You can almost taste the avid expectancy in Mike . . . not like so many of our dismal background, tied to withered dreams. No, Mike Brant knows how to hide his bitterness, his anger, when it could do him harm (Mom called this "swallowing your toad"—those times when things went very wrong, and you had to face up to unpleasant facts).
>
> But it seems Mike has gained much from his strike involvement. I saw George Spinelli get a check for funds marked "survey research," which set a lot of Spinelli's people with tough faces—when he paid them off—to getting drunk in little bars and go picking fights in the Fairyland Amusement Park at Prospect and 75th Street. The Kansas City Star reported they got mean over some nasty remarks, among other things about the Kansas City baseball team's chances of winning the league pennant. Maybe so.

As Martin was doing the final packing for his weekend, at six-thirty in the morning, Mike came in, yawning,

mussing up his hair, now beginning to salt a bit with silver. Mike was in his crummy old bathrobe; a frayed, faded blue, even though he had, as Martin knew, a very fine
silk one Terry had bought him two Christmases ago.
Mike was in need of a shave. He was carrying an extra
large coffee cup, a favorite of his, with a pattern of impossible flowers and painted on it, the words "Big Daddy."

"I could'a slept a week. You off with the school girl?"

"I'm off."

Mike took a roll of bills out of a pocket. "Here, have
yourself a time. You earned it. We all earned it. If you
have time between the stupping, write me a speech for
the Chicago get together. Ten hot minutes—a couple of
Henny Youngman zingers."

"How deep are you in with the mob?" Martin didn't
look up as he asked this.

"Not your department, kid. My nose is clean."

"They blew your nose for you, didn't they . . . and I
hear we have ten of them on the payroll."

Mike picked up a houndstooth sports jacket. "I always
look like I'm wearing a horse blanket when I wear something like this."

Mike turned and went out. Martin finished packing
and found he had the roll of bills shoved into his sports
shirt pocket. That was Mike, even since they were kids:
you do as he wanted, and he enjoyed rewarding you.

CHAPTER 24

The man from the national headquarters had phoned from the airport to say he was coming over. He was tall and thin, produced a short barking cough as soon as he entered and saw Mike behind his desk. Mike looked up. "Do I need witnesses to this?" Mike glanced at some notes on his desk. "Sit down, Mr. Remaken."

"No witnesses."

The man sat down, gave again his barking little cough. Mike thought he had the face of an expensive dog.

"What the hell did you think you were getting away with?"

"Before I answer that, did my friend the Puskin send you?"

"Let's not get chummy, Brant. I'm here to tell you, none of this is official; anyway off the record. You're a stiff-necked young punk and they don't like it."

"Who is they, if it isn't the Puskin?"

"I didn't say *who* but I'm giving you the *why* with no

257

trimming." He leaned forward and gave Mike a strong searching look, as if trying to penetrate to some secret that might be on Mike's face. A hint from the way he sat: easy, wary, a half-smile on his lips; but the smile seemed pasted on.

"You've put the organization into a nasty fix. You're upsetting the good will, the trust, we took years to build up here."

"You came here, were sent here, to tell me that?"

"No, I came here to tell you the people who think enough of the union movement to protect it, say *this* is as far as we'll let you go. Dick Seabrook, not you, runs the DWU."

Mike stirred his shoulders, inhaled deeply. "You're not going to stand me in a corner, call me a bad boy?"

"Don't play coy, Brant. Nothing official is going to be made of this. It's wildcat action, and we will never see it any other way. We don't want to force the locals to take a step back—set off a fight among ourselves that can give the outside satisfaction."

"Very right there, Mr. Remaken."

"You don't know what's right, so don't go off in that direction, thinking we approve."

"We . . . you . . . they . . .?"

"It's been decided, the national is going to stand behind you and the action *if* it's ended properly."

"What's the weenie?"

"The what?"

"The catch! 'Take what you like,' my Mom always said, 'and pay for it.'"

"Yes." The man paused. It was clear he found his task distasteful. "The council wants it—wants you to announce that you have brought the wildcat strikes under control. That the action is against the best . . ." He hunted for a word, "the best for the interest of the union and the community."

Mike lowered his head, rubbed two fingers against his

lower lip, looked up. "I'll buy part of that, that I end the wildcats, but the gains stay . . . *I* stay."

"Naturally."

"Fuck naturally, I want something in writing from the Puskin that I am the director or whatever title he wants to make it—that I'm running the DWU here."

"That will be the day when the Puskin writes you such a letter."

"I don't give a shit who writes it, as long as I have a text, a protection."

The man smiled for the first time. "You damn well know a letter or not, we can tip you out of our basket."

"I know that, Mr. Remaken. But if you do tip me out like a potato out of a sack, I can show *something* to the rank and file when the new strike begins, and this time we'll call them in Kansas City, close the stockyards, stop the auto assembly lines because of no parts and—"

"You're threatening the national council?"

"You bet your sweet patootie I am. You top brass want to save face. I want to hold on. It's a Mexican standoff. I've got everything to lose, but I have a lot to gain. You lick me now, I don't go up the chimney like smoke. I'll still be here—a troublemaker busted by entrenched big shots."

The man stood up; he didn't seem fazed at the situation. It was clear to Mike that Mr. Remaken had faced such tough situations before. Most likely he was the Puskin's best troubleshooter; he had been dickering for a deal, the best he could get.

"The cards are on the table, Mr. Remaken. You play the hand."

"You'll get an official notification thanking you for settling the strikes. That what you want?"

"*And* what I mentioned."

The man seemed to relax, his cough sounded softer. "You're pretty sure of yourself, Brant. I've seen them come and seen them go. You could have a future with the general council—replace Dick Seabrook some day. But no, you're the loner, the man who can handle himself, win on his own."

He shook his head. "You can't, you know. Where are the Yids who started the big garment unions—the boys who got beaten up in the underpass at Ford? Big Bill Haywood, where did he end up? The Wobblies . . . the commie unions that held the waterfronts . . . the electrical workers locals? All had a smell of it and ended where?"

"You're so right, Mr. Remaken, about them. Can I buy you a drink?"

"I have to catch a plane to the coast." He pulled out an old-fashioned railroad watch. "You sound as if you have more sense than we thought. I expected some wild-eyed young radical full of liberal ideas and loony changes. You're an opportunist with an edge of purpose. Yet you really like the workers. A strange contradiction."

"You a head doctor, a shrink, too, Mr. Remaken?"

"I'm a judge of people. That's my job, that's why I'm sent out. It's going to be interesting watching you."

"You'll cry when I fail?"

"Why fail? We would not waste time on just anybody. The union can use you. You've got gall, drive—and you've run things damn well."

"Is this soft soap part of our deal? Do I come in out of the cold and kiss the ring?"

The man stood up, looked at his watch again. "I don't like you, but I can report you're good at what you try to do. I don't give advice anymore. I found you young bastards don't take it."

"But *if* you did give advice, Mr. Remaken?"

"If I did, I'd say, 'Mister, digest what you've bitten off, don't go for the whole hog.' Can you call me a taxi?"

"Better than that." Mike pressed a lever on his intercom. "Sally, have Starker drive the gentleman to the airport."

"Don't bother. Just a cab."

"No bother, the local owns the car."

Mike held out his hand. The man cocked his head to one side, then offered his hand.

When Remaken was gone, Mike sat as if in a trance. He felt sweat pour down his rib sections from his armpits. He kept his hands from shaking by clasping them together on his lap.

The national, they had come to *him* to make peace. No matter how you sliced it, *they* had made the peace offer. It was a victory; it tasted damn bitter.

After awhile, feeling more under control, he pressed the intercom. "Sally, did you record all that?"

Sally's voice sounded glum. "He said, the man, it was all right to give him the tape. I didn't, and he just opened the drawer and took it. I'm sorry, Mr. Brant. How'd he know?"

"God, Sally, knows everything."

While the national board, the Puskin as general president, accepted Mike Brant's actions without too much joy, they were not yet fully aware—nor was the Middle West—that here was a major personality dominating labor. Mike was rated, if not a revolutionary, a potential voice for dissidents . . . a voice strong in contractual strategy. He was later to admit to Martin that he had done nothing so very new in mounting the wildcat strikes. "I just combined a lot of power maneuvers into fast sequences, where before it was done bit by bit with the generals in the castle behind the lines never in full contact with the front line troops."

His steering of the rank and file in the series of walkouts had been viewed as grand strategy by outsiders, but he himself knew how close it had been to collapse.

Mike now set up a standard for grievances and the facing of complaints. He avoided inaccessibility; he learned when to delegate authority and when not to delegate.

Martin felt in Mike a genuine concern for the workers, concealed under the ruthlessness of Mike's procedures, even if the paradoxical complexity of the man forced him to become more and more a player of roles.

After Martin returned from an addled sensual weekend with Millie Warner with a firm conviction of not becoming involved with her again (while amorously active how can one relate for two days to a girl in bed who insists that "in labor legislation, darling, one must note the automatic changing structure in the economy . . . oh my do *that* again, yes, just there . . . *um!*").

The labor conference in Chicago would be the big test, Mike told Martin as they left the Civic Center after a luncheon meeting with the Chamber of Commerce and the new local's officials and the old local's top people who were celebrating a solidarity—worker and commerce.

"As the Puskin sees it I'm going to run things with kisses on my face for what I did here, but they'll be looking me over. They don't like my leverage pressure. I'm no labor statesman like Walter Reuther, and I don't know too much as to how a welfare and health plan works. I'm going to bring out an old war buddy of mine. We were in the Korean War together. He's got a hell of a head on him for figures."

"Old buddies, Mike, don't always pan out. How many snotty kids we ran around with in Milltown would we be happy to see today?"

"Davey is an insurance actuary. Know what that is?"

"I got past the fifth grade, Mike."

"Tell me, I don't know for sure." Mike laughed as the Starker drove up in the car.

"Basically it's the figuring scientifically of percentages, balances, rules of loans and interest rates—a kind of charting of a project—its advantages as a policy from all angles."

"Thanks, Martin."

They got into the car and Mike leaned back and got out a pipe but didn't fill it from his pouch. "We have to move fast. It's costly all this setting up of locals, and the dues coming in aren't covering it yet. Still, still . . . there's Cleveland, St. Louis, where we have connections. Join 'em or push 'em out. I want the DWU to take over all that can be integrated with us in the Middle West."

"How far, Mike, how far do you think you can go before the national gets the roof to fall in?"

Mike laughed. "By the time they're ready to pull the roof down on me, I'll be building an organization of stone."

"You had how many martinis at this lunch?"

"Yeah, yeah. You're right. Look, I'll need you in Chicago with Spinelli and Jamie Ward."

"Jamie knows the ropes."

"But he's an old timer—a John L. Lewis type—he sees industry, big business like all those radicals do, as the enemy. I see the corporations as *our* cows—our bulls, to use, to study, to copy. I've said it before, but I see now how right I was. The way they do things, move in, take over, sell a product, twist the Federal Trade Commission's balls. Oh, there's a lot to learn from them, the way they deflect the course of the law for the good of their progress."

"And from George Spinelli you learn something too?"

Mike pulled out the stem of the pipe and blew through it:

"As the stud said to the dame on top of him, 'who's screwing who here?' The mob families aren't what you think or *Time* magazine thinks. It's got its muscle; it gets things done in the dark. But it's legit now in many ways. It has the best lawyers; the government can't get any place with them but for maybe putting some front stooge in the can on income tax. They own hotels, car hauling, contracting agencies, beach fronts, Nevada casinos . . . and hell, George is second generation dago, a gentleman,

Stanford—a Phi Beta Kappa—collects art. Jesus, you should see the stuff on his walls—dots and drippings, and honest to God, a picture made of sewing old burlap potato bags together."

Martin shook his head. "He's still a mob front. The taxi war up north with cabs and bodies in the river and those four men they found hanging on the meat hooks in that packing house . . . must have taken them six days to die . . . like hotdogs stuck on forks."

"Come off it, Martin. George Spinelli never personally handled a hit in his life. Me—you—we saw too many Cagney and Eddie Robinson movies as kids, playing, remember, 'you dirty rat, you killed my brudder,' and 'ya-ya, I'm taking over the East side, see!' . . . That's all gone. Anyway, I know you feel I'd goose the devil as long as I knew what I was doing it for."

Martin decided Mike was talking too much, not so much from the drinks at the lunch, but because he wanted to convince himself in this querulous mood that he was right.

Martin wrote in his private journal:

Mike has these quicksilver moods where he insists white could also be called black. He is brilliant in handling situations, but nonintellectual. To him now, after his victory, all is power relationships. He has been uncouth but ethical; old moralities still break through or he wouldn't be trying to justify himself.

For all his contradictory streaks Mike has a disciplined, agile mind. But that facade of inexhaustible energy, could it hold up—showing in public no frailties?

Everything for Mike is direct cause or effect. He's not much given to a sense of abstracting—always sure he'll find the proper, positive decision someplace. And that hard learned philosophy of his: "Get on top or somebody will get on top of you."

* * *

Martin was aware Mike did understand, or was beginning to understand, how to perpetuate power. But the new mob alliance understood power even better than Mike did, and had been at it longer.

Martin gave up trying to penetrate into the inner Mike. Better he devoted more time to the speech Mike was to give at the Chicago gathering of local and national labor leaders. Martin sketched in his mind a statement on democratic unionism in solving internecine, interunion squabbles—the policy discussions laid out to avoid jurisdictional fights. But was any gathering much beyond window dressing? Mike would just have to play the labor conference by ear. Martin had a shrewd idea his brother was making alliances with other central states union locals, seeking to have the DWU dominate the Midwest and the Southern states.

To Martin that could only mean organization by coercion, well-coordinated violence, where Mike went past traditional boundaries of the All States Councils. It was clear Mike was pushing the DWU to centralized, area-wide bargaining.

Mike seemed to ignore the old boys who slept at their posts someplace as president and chairman of the DWU: old Dick Seabrook, deaf, addressing high school graduating classes in his declining years, liked to be introduced as "the elder statesman of the union movement." Parker Amphorin of the union welfare and health plan, so busy in real estate and vineyard deals he never even remembered meetings.

Mike could push them aside any time he wanted, when he controlled just a bit more of the DWU locals. Then . . . when? . . . Martin didn't care to guess. He took Terry and Paul out to the Swope Park Zoological Gardens, and the three of them looked at the elephants, smelled the lions, enjoyed the antics of monkeys. They fed Paul ice cream and gooey cake. Mike and Terry had lunch at the Green Parrot after they delivered Paul to

Charlie, who frowned, saying, "The chile sure looks feverish to me . . . seeing them animals crowded in isn't healthy."

It was a good lunch. They drank white wine and had a brandy after the white fish and hot bib salad. Terry was in as fine a mood as he had yet seen her. Her tendency to contradiction was under control.

"It will be good to get off this cow patty for a few days."

"It's not a bad town, Terry."

"I didn't expect Paris or Disneyland, but if you've been here two years, you know it's still frontier in Caddies and golf carts. I'm going to get me a whole set of new togs at Marshall Fields, have my hair done by the best fairy in town, and wear your brother down to a nub with demands of loving."

Martin said, "He'll not fight you there."

Terry twirled the stem of the brandy glass. "I guess what I say, it's all in the family. Mike, he's all worked up over his goddam organizing. I'm living with a guy who's forgotten there are two sexes."

"Not the Mike I know."

"*Chicago, Chicago,*" sang Terry, "that toddling town."

That night the child Paul began to hold his ears and scream. He had a temperature of 103 degrees. To get a doctor, it took a little shouting on the phone by Mike. The signs showed a deep infection in the left ear. The treatment was penicillin powder. The penicillin powder blown into the child's ear brought the infection down, and some shots of the antibiotic helped. But it turned out Paul was allergic to the stuff, and the fever was soon high again. George Spinelli got a specialist from the Kansas State Medical School who found a new substance that didn't affect the allergies. Mike, Terry, and Martin let their faces relax, and Charlie went to the Holy Mother of Christ Church and lit a candle in her heart's gratitude.

The shock of the ill child seemed to make the world of unions, strikes, and settlement unreal. It wasn't until the third day of the illness that Terry said. "You better go to Chicago without me."

Mike, in exasperated fear, said, "Oh hell, his temperature is down. He's better."

"He's too pale, and Doctor Zimmerman says we have to watch he doesn't develop a bad reaction to the new antibiotic."

Mike looked over at Martin as the three of them sat at the breakfast table—a soughing wind in the trees outside in the bit of garden—a tin-colored sky signaling that perhaps it might rain. Mike put down his coffee cup.

"What do you think, Martin? Drop Chicago?"

Terry answered instead. "This is a big thing for you. For Christ sakes go and let me alone with the child."

"You were so . . ."

"I know, I know, I was looking forward to it. Now don't kick it around, Mike, or throw something. Marty, get him out of the house. He wants to go, he has to go."

Later Martin, as he packed, wondered if Mike would have given up the Chicago trip. Paul's fever was down, and while pale, he seemed alert enough. When Mike went in to say goodbye to his son, the child was listening to a swing version of *Mother Goose*. Charlie turned off the record player as Mike looked down onto the small boy in his little bed.

"Pop is going away for a few days, Paulie. What would you like me to bring you back from Chicago?"

"Bow-wow."

"Doggies have germs Mama says."

Charlie set down a batch of recordings labeled *Tiny Tots' Tales*. "Get him a wind-up dawg . . ."

Paul reached for and held his father's hand. He looked from Mike to Martin. "Don't let them hurt Paulie's ear."

"No, no . . . go away bad pain," said Mike.

Martin thought: It's like a scene from Dickens at his worst.

The dozen local officials from Kansas City had a parlor car all to themselves on the River Cities Express. Jamie Ward had found four players—a hillbilly band—among the Tanner and Leather Workers Local. They had two guitars, a banjo, and a country flute and were animated with such tunes as *The Union, She'll be Comin' Round the Mountain*, and a dirty version of *Frankie and Johnny*.

George Spinelli, splendid in traveling tweeds and a small Italian hat with a tiny red feather in its brim, had seen to the case of whiskey, and even the three women from the Typists and Graphic Local—and a girl who had organized the law courts' shorthand experts—all were drinking highballs.

The dining car waiters continued bringing in trays of sandwiches, ignoring the swaying car. Martin observed Jamie Ward hadn't changed his dour expression but kept on repeating, "Feeling no pain, here's cheers everybody . . . feeling no pain," until Mike insisted Jamie lie down before he fell down.

CHAPTER 25

The Mike Brant-Kansas City group were staying at the Palmer House; the convention would begin its meetings in the main ballroom of the Hilton at nine o'clock.

Already there were gatherings of union groups in the hotel suites. Some short and stocky individuals, some hardly looking, to Martin, like union leaders—more like bookkeepers, he insisted.

He shared a suite with Martin. George Spinelli was in another room across the hall with two young men sporting duck's ass haircuts and loose tailoring of too loud a pin stripe: Dom and Tony seemed to lack last names. They marked up horse sheets and spent a great deal of time contacting bookies for results at Pimlico and Hialeah.

Mike surveyed the suite's living room: the baskets of fruit, television set, the piano. Martin studied the cards with the fruit. "Why the piano?"

"Came with the suite. Frank Sinatra had it last week, I hear . . . I like the speech you wrote—but make me sound more like a mug . . . not like Ed Murrow."

"Don't worry, you don't . . . Tri-State, Comet Insurance sent the fruit."

Mike grinned. "Everybody loves me. I'm doing some TV show today . . . what the hell is it called? . . . the Kup Show?"

"Very big."

"I'm on with a Gabor sister . . . the fat, little one, and Congressman Vertell, and some writer named Robbins. Ever read him?"

"Just tell him he's a genius and be sure to let some of the others talk."

"I'll be all right." He hunted in his pockets. "Dammit, I lost my best pipe. Is there a Dunhill in this burg?"

There was a discreet tap from the hall door, and Mike held up a hand stopping Martin from opening the door.

"Yes?"

One of Spinelli's boys was heard. "Mr. Brant, there is a Mr. Wasserman out here."

"Davey!" shouted Mike, motioning Martin to open the door.

The figure that came in and stood there smiling was at ease, eyeing the young Spinelli hoodlum with amusement. Davey was dapper in the best sense of the word. The first thing Martin noticed was that the visitor's left arm was missing—the well-pressed, empty sleeve carefully placed in the jacket pocket. The jacket itself was a sporting item—bold color with a check pattern, but carried off well against the dark, handsome face; a head of heavy black hair, thinning at the temples. There was a bamboo cane held under an arm pit. The entire figure was one of grace, not hauteur.

Mike cried out. "You fucking dude. Martin, meet Davey Wasserman, the greatest crapshooter the paratroopers ever put into the field."

Martin heard a city voice of a variegated distinction, earnest, liquid. He liked the man at once. "You're the kid brother." Davey's handshake was firm. Martin noticed a cufflink that was not linked, and he reached for it. Davey shook his head. "How the devil do you think I'll be able to open it later?"

"Sorry, Davey. Wasn't thinking."

Mike was pouring Scotch into three glasses.

"How has it been going, Davey?"

"Going, gone, going again. It's a hustle. But I'm having fun."

"To all dead friends, good paratroopers all," said Mike lifting his glass.

Davey nodded. "Cocksmen, goofoffs, pals."

They sipped their drinks. Mike asked, "Still in insurance?"

"In a way. Been hearing good things about you, Mike. Who'd have guessed it, eh? . . . when we were knocking off the poor wogs that we'd some day be here drinking seven-year-old Scotch. Who?"

"A refill."

"No, I've got some people downstairs, but we can get together later on your proposition."

"It's settled. You're coming in with the DWU."

"What can I do?"

"Set up a watertight welfare and health plan. Big dues will be coming in from the employer and employee— contributing to health, welfare, pensions. Millions, soon."

"Billions," said Davey, setting down his glass. "If you don't fall by the wayside, Mike. Christ, do you realize investing big money is a headache." He turned to Martin. "There are six Federal indictments out right now on mishandling of funds. And they're peanuts."

Martin said, "That's why Mike is shaky on details. I can handle the legal stuff, but banking and investing isn't my side of the bed. What do you know about all of this

. . . no offense, but Mike jumps to conclusions about situations, people."

"Oh shut up, Martin," said Mike. "Davey and me, we've done everything together but make love to each other."

"Now, now," said Davey, holding up a pacifying hand. "Martin's right. I was three years with Westward Ho Insurance; industrial coverages, assets, charting liabilities, investment portfolios, group coverage for workers, injury compensation, retirement plans. After that, a year with Woofin Enterprises handling their real estate, building programs, overseas holdings."

Martin nodded. "I know of them . . . they're into Reno, Vegas, the West Indies—in land speculation, gambling casinos."

"Sure, look at their stockholder reports. I wrote them, and I'm proud of them. You want to know, I can guess, are they mob connected?"

Martin said, "You saved me asking the question."

Mike said, "Where aren't there some tie ups?"

"The Schiro family," said Davey, "owns some interests in two West Indies casinos, hotels. The Pirrones had a small holding in Vegas—downtown keno parlors. I don't know if they still do. The Calogero brothers are developing marinas in Florida and around the New Orleans area, and on the West Coast. They all own a bit of Woofin Enterprises, which is well thought of. It's been investigated and found legal and solvent."

"Cut the crackle," said Mike. "Davey, you want the job, you got it. Work me out a plan for a real, honest to God welfare, health and pension plan, and we'll kick it around. Fair enough, Martin?"

"I hate to rattle you two lovers but who's going to handle the insurance policies for the rank and file . . . who's going to collect commissions on all that? I have to make this all legally palatable."

Davey wriggled the stump of his missing arm and smiled. "I'd recommend Westward Ho Insurance—they're AAAA, above board. Later, if *you* want to form an insurance association, it's also legal."

Martin asked, "Who will get the commissions on the premiums from Westward Ho?"

Davey pointed to Martin, then to Mike. "Not me. You decide. You can plow it back into the local's union treasury, or you have anybody desiring to open an agency to handle all this?" He turned as noise came from the hall-way—the sound of the hillbilly band. "There are a cluster of show girls across the hall."

Mike shook his head. "Keep it low. I want to call Terry. My kid, he's had an infected ear. You have any kids, Davey?"

"Two some place. I've been married twice, both times tossed out on first base. My mother found me a kosher princess . . . dull, lazy—result, one little girl, and I left. Second time at bat, married a shiksa from Vassar who wrote copy for *Vogue*—found her one New Year's night copping the joint of the golf pro at Southampton during the festivities. Got a son. Maybe he's mine. How old is Paul?"

"Nearly three, and I *know* he's mine . . . you guys go ahead. I'll meet you at the bar downstairs."

When Mike got through to his home, Charlie tried to tell him something all jumbled until Terry came on.

"What's with her?"

"She's excited . . . she lit some candle in a church, made a prayer and it worked . . . Paul is fine because of it."

"Is he?"

"He's still pale but his ear seems to be healing up. He doesn't want to eat, but we're coaxing him along. Did you promise him a dog?"

"Let me talk to him."

"Don't be crazy. He's in no condition. How's the gathering?"

"Loud."

"I can hear it. How sober are you? Wish I was there."

"Next year in Miami."

"You're too good to me."

"What?"

The hillbilly band was active just outside the door. Mike put a finger into one ear. "*What?*"

"I said have a good time. Not *too* good."

"Yeah. I'll call back in the morning. Bye."

"Night."

Mike wondered if Terry was a bit looped—had a few. For a moment there he had a recall of their early days together. The first good nights on the coast, the first walks, talks along the waterfront streets and the times of some routines trying to organize the farm workers . . . the whimperings of pleasure when they made it so good together . . . the insinuating caresses in the open fields.

Nothing lasts . . . nothing at all . . . always change. Those first years so grand and brief. Then to go moving on, to drive, to do . . . to find out for sure that grim truth; if you lift your hand to do good you could get it bitten.

Mike put the telephone back on its cradle. There was profane, exasperating shouting in the hallway. He touched his back pants pocket to check his wallet—his inside pocket for his speech, touched his fly (all zipped), adjusted his tie's knot in a square of a mirror.

The phone rang. It was Davey Wasserman. "Gung ho! "Come on down . . . the paratroopers have landed and have the situation—42—32—30—well in hand. Like times, Sergeant Brant, in Inchon and Seoul!"

"Be right down, you goldbrick. Order me a double Chivas Regal. Like old times."

Like old times? No . . . nothing is ever like old times. As Mom used to say; "and never were."

There were two other major conventions in Chicago at the time: The Young Presidents Under-Forty Society and forty thousand followers of the Sama Kai, a new religious order that ran auto rental agencies, vegetarian snack food shops, laundries, and believed that God was living quietly some place near Aspen, Colorado.

In the files of the news services there still exist glossy prints of the photograph of Mike Brant being cheered in Chicago by the assembled labor groups at the end of his speech. He stands there, younger than most remember him, large and clear, clutching in one hand the text of a speech he hardly followed. His damp hair is flowing loose over his forehead; the chin is thrust forward as if in challenge, nostrils flared. It is only the eyes that to one viewer seem to belong to another person. Martin, sitting nearby, felt they were glazed by a kind of trancelike stare, and he thought of some desert prophet held in suspension by the awe of his visions. But Martin had been drinking with Davey Wasserman, George Spinelli, Jamie Ward, and some assorted labor people whose names he did not remember.

Mike had spoken well, (a "firecracker," said Jamie Ward). He had worked on, developed a roughhewed style, had practiced a clear speech pattern, and his gestures were few but carried conviction. Mike did have a habit of pinching his right earlobe, tugging at it as if it were an aid in finishing a vital sentence, when reaching some pitch of effort. He was seemingly unaware of it. In time this odd trait was to become sort of a trademark.

He had discarded the text of the speech completely near the end: "I will give it to you straight and clear and with no backtracking, no excuses. American labor must enter the political arena, not as we have in the past by

passing out money, shaking hands with a candidate and
hinting, 'see our side.' No, we can attack, dismember,
and flatten the enemies of labor to the ground. We have
to remain even with the clout of big industry—big business, big, oh so damn big, corporations. We have to stand
just as high and solid as those who now control the nation. No more going to beg for our rights, no more sitting
in the back of the economic bus, no more making a curt-
sy for Federal agencies handouts as favors. We are labor,
we are workers, and we are voters. You bet we are! United we can elect, and vocally we can demand our fair share
in an economy where the stockholder, the banker, the
politican are favored over the working man *and* working
woman. Let's not overlook the ladies! Women's rights ar-
en't just so they can wear pants or refuse to do
housework. Woman, too, is part of the whole picture of a
hundred thirty million worker-voters. Watch the Drovers
and Wheelmens Union prove labor is on the move. Don't
just follow us, march at our side in the forefront of where
the action is going to be!''

It had them on their feet, men with cold cigars in the
corners of their mouths, a few women with make-up
melting . . . cheers, whistles, and shouts rising over the
regular cadence of applause. Davey nudged Martin as he
pounded his hand on the stained tablecloth. "That's the
stuff to give them."

"Great speech, Marty," said George Spinelli, searching
faces around the ballroom for their reaction. "Great, just
great. Really socked it to them."

Martin watched his brother's face, picked it out in the
glare of the flashbulbs going off. He wondered if he would
ever know Mike fully—from smooth astuteness to im-
passioned earnestness.

"It's the way Mike delivered it . . . what he said was
well . . ."

"Damn it," said Jamie Ward. "It's the way John L. Lewis used to pound it into them."

* * *

Martin sat down. No use expressing anything about what was after all such true and tried stuff in Mike's speech. What was clear was that he had, in twenty-two minutes, captured the attention of American labor gathered in Chicago and that, with the notoriety of his actions in Kansas City—his handling of the wildcat walkout—he was now a man to be reckoned with by the higher echelons.

Mike shook hands, waved to the crowded tables. He pushed away the mikes of two networks and walked slowly, shaking hands back to his table. Here again, he took congratulations, applause, without speaking. He sipped some soda water Martin handed him, dried his wilted shirt collar with a napkin. He made some ambiguous answer to Spinelli.

Jamie Ward said, "They want you for a press conference in an hour in the Tallyho Room."

"They?"

"Combined WNUSA and LBO press interviews. You, Larry Watkins, Selma Matterson, Chass Starkweather."

"Nope." He pushed back his damp disordered hair. "Not a chance."

"Hey," Jamie reacted in panic as people came up to shake Mike's hand saying, "Great stuff . . . that's telling it like it is . . . you're our boy."

Jamie persisted. "Hey, Mike, this is the big press associations—*Washington Post*, the *Times* . . . the network bigshots."

Davey sat back and shook his head. "Mike's right. Why dilute his glory tonight with all those other yea sayers? Martin baby, you call a press conference for tomorrow morning in Mike's suite . . . eight sharp . . . exclusive and Mike *alone*." He turned to Mike. "What do you say to that, sergeant?"

Mike nodded, waved, and shook a few more hands offered. "Makes sense." He seemed drained and still starry-eyed from the efforts of his speech. "I want to call home. Some of you mugs make an end run through the folks for me."

An hour later Mike was showered, lying naked on a double bed. The lights were out, the room just lit by reflections from the street. Martin had gone off with Davey after insisting Mike take it easy. Davey kept nodding, "And remain exclusive. That's the ticket. Don't answer the door or phone."

Mike lay feeling his body relax—like a boneless jelly fish. The six-minute phone talk with Terry had been a bit anticlimactic. She had asked how it had gone. Yes, Paul was sleeping; his temperature was still down, but the ear was red inside the doctor said, after another painful examination. Paul had cried during the last probing and asked for his Pop. Terry said she herself . . . yes, she was fine, oh just fine. And in her voice was a bit of resentment. She did say she'd had a drink to the success of his speech. He had, with heavy-handed humor told her it was, "a one drink speech and not a shaker of Gibsons." She had answered something like, oh yes, and added in her sardonic voice, "Yes sir, massa."

The hell with that—all dames are balls busters. Nothing could spoil his night. He was still groggy—but he knew he'd been good. His shoulder muscles, his gut were still a bit uptight. He'd get a masseur up in the morning before the press conference and get the kinks worked out. How did he feel? He couldn't yet feel everything. He could sense it, however. This was something solid and important. He had piled it on a bit there at the end. Hit them with everything he had—no Churchillian language, no FDR charm . . . just the kind of stuff the old man liked to hear on the radio from Al Smith.

Mike smiled, turned over the pillow to get a cooler surface. Look who I'm comparing myself against—those bigshots. Well, so what? Maybe I'm a bit scared, but not much. I can take on the press conference. Smart of Davey not to let me go on with labor's trained seals spouting the same old corn about the workers in a great country.

Hell yes, it *was* a great country. How else could a poor, uneducated slob of a Polak mill town kid, one of Mom's beaten down old American lines . . . get up here on his way to making it—and making it for the good of everybody—everybody who saw things his way.

A good speech because he had meant it. It was maybe not something to carve on stone but it was stuff that came up from deep inside . . . had just poured out, just the right words fell into place, and he got them out right and strong. Maybe Moz's original text was more solidly constructive and deep. But what he felt was Mike Brant all the way . . . explosive, socking it to them.

The tension was leaking away; he felt his limbs relax, his head loosen the pressure on his temples; his throat muscles unknot. He didn't need whiskey, didn't need a woman—not just now. He was his own booze, his own charge of body pleasure.

After awhile, as he felt good, he smiled. He didn't get upset at the knocking on the door of the suite, didn't hear the muddled tones of the phone ringing, which Martin had buried in sofa cushions.

Near morning Mike dreamed he was floating easy as a cloud over the morning factory whistles of his boyhood; he hovered over the factories below him. He moved, arms extended, floating like a great bird, not moving his arms, just using them for balance. Now he was over the muddy river and its barges and wharves, the whistles of the factories still calling to the workers to emerge with their tin lunch boxes or their brown paper bags—the tools of the machinists seeking jobs rolled up in their overalls, carried under an arm. Sleepy, stubbled faces not noticing him just over their heads—eyes half-closed, a cigarette dangling fron a coughing mouth. He swooped down, yelling. "The end of the world is at hand—at hand—at hand," and he awoke with the shock of strong sunlight in his eyes. Martin was drawing back the heavy drapes.

"What the hell. . . ." For a moment Mike didn't know where he was; was last night a dream? Then he let it all rush back; it was true, and he was he, and his bladder needed draining.

The Chicago meeting put Mike in closer personal contact for the first time with the men who were the power in the DWU: Harry Harper, ex-Rams halfback of the Northwest, Sam Winnick of the Southwest, Battista "Batsy" Cosimo who was in control of a great deal of the Eastern Shore dock areas.

Mike's most interesting contact was with Joseph Du-Bois, better known as "Kingbird" because of his beak of a nose. Kingbird was the man who kept Dick Seabrook in power, controlled the Gulf States, their locals, and their powerful consolidated vote that usually swung conventions.

It was a small gathering of the five most powerful men in the DWU in a South Side pasta palace, Kingbird having expressed a liking for "that wop food—you can't do better than veal the way they make it." Later in a taxi driving to the Palmer House—just the two of them—Kingbird had been frank.

"Want this little chitchat with yo. Ah know yo have yo eye focused high up, and that in a young fellow is fine. But good ol' boy Dickie stays as head man of the DWU as long as he wants. Fair warnin', Mikey?"

"Fair warning, Kingbird. Why is the ol' boy not here speaking for himself?"

"Oh hell, he's been sent by the cookie pushers in the State Department to visit with the Soviet Union, one of them good will missions to the Russkis."

"And you're minding the store?"

"Now, Mikey, bide yo time. Easy does it, as the ticklish bride said on her honeymoon."

Mike saw sense in not riling this needle-nosed Cajun bastard. They talked of Washington scandals all the way to the hotel. Mike put Joseph "Kingbird" DuBois down as the most serious obstacle to his plans for taking over the DWU. He had learned that southern politicians, seeming so pickled in mint juleps and love of *Gone with the Wind*, were formidable, skillful manipulators of power.

CHAPTER 26

Mike did not leave Chicago with the Kansas City contingent. He had been invited to attend a small get-together arranged by the Kordon Foundation, celebrating the departure of a research team, medical unit for the study of tropical diseases in Brazil: the Kordon Foundation put up a two-hundred-thousand-dollar grant to the project.

Mike at first had decided not to attend. "Another goddam cocktail party, wanting to show off a labor leader."

Martin seemed interested:

"Don't bite the hand of the Kordon Corporations. They employ at least a hundred thousand workers around the world."

"The DWU?"

"No. Mostly they're LBO."

"Then the hell with them. I've got to get back to Paul and Terry."

Martin looked at the typed invitation on very fine linen paper, the signature in a bold hand in very blue ink: *Julia Brooks, Humanities Projects Section.*

"It could be, Mike, they want to maybe break up the hold of the other unions in Kordon industries. Or just want to feed a real wild union leader with all his teeth."

"I thought foundations only put up the big jackpot . . . the donor isn't consulted."

"Right, and written into the foundation charter rules. But that doesn't, well, mean they don't hold hands. Anyway, you should go. Just to get used to seeing how endowed loafers work . . . and how they talk."

"You come with me. And what the devil is the Kordon Foundation anyway? . . . Let me try to phone Terry first."

In the taxi to the Lake Drive address Martin explained not only the huge foundation but the man originally behind it: "Old Eli Kordon was a mean, cranky old bastard and a genius. Bigoted, ingrown, came from some patched pants logging family in upper Michigan. He was good with tools and able to help himself to other people's ideas and inventions. He saw the primitive machines, the old-fashioned water and steam driven items were wasteful, slow—not practical. By the turn of the century Eli Kordon was making machines in mass production—engines, tools, gadgets, so simple any simple man could run and afford them . . . repair them with bailing wire. The Great War—1914–1918, remember?—gave Eli more growth, and by the time he was dying, Kordon products were around the world, with factories every place—nonunion."

"I remember that trademark; like somebody who wrote badly."

"Old Eli's signature. He never got past the fourth grade. Also he never trusted banks or Wall Street. Owned all the stock, but for a few early backers who sold out for millions. So old Eli died; God, he found out, has no respect for money. So the will set up the Kordon Foundation.

Two billion dollars in Kordon stock. Tax evasion, of course. Old Eli wasn't going to have his heirs pay away huge fortunes to the government in inheritance taxes."

"I remember now, it almost wrecked the Kordon Corporations, that foundation setup. Maybe the old bastard wanted that."

"There were, however, two nephews: real manipulators—Matthew and Eli III—who modernized, got great modern designers, and went public selling stock. Kordon Corporations is now among the first ten biggest businesses in the world. It's now unionized."

Mike peered out at the lake front apartment houses. People were beginning to move about tending their late afternoon duties.

"And DWU hasn't got a slice of that cake?"

The huge apricot-colored apartment house that the taxi drew up to had been built, Martin thought, in the 1920's judging by the style of it. No gleam of chrome or plastic, not a structural simplification into cubism or abstraction. It was ornate—carved icing in limestone—but neat; it suggested wealth with some ostentation, but not bad taste or show.

There was a doorman, aloof but polite, who phoned up and nodded. There was a lobby man, like a bank manager, who nodded but didn't speak. There were bronze elevators, and Mike and Martin were ushered into one serviced by a large black man who took his duties very seriously. On the tenth floor the heavy doors hissed open, and Mike and Martin were in a private area—a foyer; beyond it, two sets of frosted glass doors set in gilt silver; underfoot Mike saw Persian rugs.

"Class," said Mike, in some sort of mocking frustration, "class. . . ."

Martin said nothing. He knew Mike was impressed. Behind the frosted-glass doors were shapes of people, the buzz of talk, the click of glasses. Martin pushed a door open, and they walked in.

There were about two dozen people present; six servants of both sexes. Mike's eyes gave the setting a quick reading: There were large windows overlooking the lake, lead-colored clouds on the horizon . . . light walls of grain-waxed wood showed some few paintings; the frames suggested masterpieces to Mike—the art nothing; lopsided clowns outlined in too much black, pictures of tabletops too flat to be real with muddy-colored sections of fruit and wine bottles and what looked like real newspapers pasted down over some sections; a big painting of some people bathing among slanting trees—the people all out of shape and badly drawn compared to the human bodies in magazine illustrations.

Now to face this collection of fancy people . . . no one seemed to be paying any attention to Mike and Martin. There were several little groups engaged in low but animated conversation. Mike thought someone was speaking French. Servants went around with trays of tidbits: oyster gizzards, sea spawn; fish eggs maybe, and glasses of yellow wine.

Mike stopped one of the tray bearers. "Where can I find a phone?"

"In the library, sir." He pointed toward two teak doors hung with African ritual masks.

Mike spoke to Martin who was sipping the wine and looking amused at the gathering from which came the continuing sound of polite talk, the scent of perfumes, odors of well-fed, well-washed bodies. "Hold the fort, Moz, I want to try and get through to home."

"Take your time . . . ever been in this kind of splendid beehive before?"

"Yeah . . . I think a whorehouse in Frisco."

The library had walls of finely bound books in red and green leather behind clear glass panels. Solid stuff, no *Book-of-the-Month* selections by the looks of them.

The phone was just a black phone; somehow Mike had expected gold plate or one of those French jobs. He dialed and got the house. Charlie answered.

"Brant residence."

"Charlie, I tried to get the house half an hour ago. What's all the uproar?"

"Oh somebody just knocked a phone off the hook, and I just found it."

"How's Paulie?"

"He's doing fine, Mr. Bran' . . . he's sleeping . . . and he's regular again."

"Regular?"

"Had two movements today. Two."

"Movements?"

"On the toitee . . . just . . ."

"Never mind the privy news . . . put Mrs. Brant on."

A pause. "She's sleeping . . . knocked out·by all the working around she had to do today."

"Wake her."

"No sir, Mr. Bran' . . . she'll have my haid . . . she said, 'don't you wake me, Charlie, not even if it's Judgment Day.' Yes sir, she meant that and . . ."

There was a brisk tap on the teak doors. Mike looked up and said, "Dammit, Charlie, tell her I called and I'll be a day late. I'll call in the morning. She been on the strong stuff?"

"She . . ."

A door opened and a young woman came into the library, smiling—a very elegant woman in blue silk, cleverly cut, very black hair brushed back and tied off behind one ear.

Mike said into the phone, "Never mind. I'll call in the morning."

The young woman peered at him; he suspected contact lenses. She held out a graceful hand on which shone a large moonstone. "I'm Julia Brooks. Sorry I didn't greet you. Had to send a telegram. How are you, Mr. Brant?"

"I'm pretty good, Miss Brooks." He shook the hand, dry yet yielding, looked down on well-kept nails with a clear polish—one chewed up (the doll was human)—looked up at a very beautiful face . . . not much make-up, but it was used with great skill: crystal, shiny, large blue-green eyes, a long neck. Class he thought—not in mockery now—the *real* class.

"Good of you to come on such short notice."

"Kind of you to ask, Miss Brooks."

"The foundation asked that you be invited, wants you to know our interest in working people. Just a small gathering. My, you are a big man." She was measuring off his shoulder span between two hands.

"My," Mike smiled, turning on the old charm. "My you are a beautiful lady." He almost outlined her tits and hips with a gesture. He didn't score with the charm bit. She just gave a small smile and motioned to the big room. "I'd like you to meet some people."

"This your place?"

"Yes. I want you to meet John Wilderbrand, Mrs. Mosby Ames of the Humanities section . . . some of the others . . . and the Commission."

He followed a splendid back, a marvelous set of buttocks, slim yet ample. He kept thinking it isn't real; it's like the dream girl I used to think about. There are only trick photographs of women like this in *Vogue*. Only not as womanly as this Julia Brooks.

She was polite but not, he felt, much impressed by him. Just a set of shoulders. He didn't know if he should play the roughneck stud or the farm boy awed by his betters and wanting to be put at ease and liked . . . *well* liked. No, he wasn't going to play Willie Loman with this snooty broad. It can't ever be as good as it looks—remember the chewed fingernail.

Mike shook a tremulous hand, a fat one with a wrist of diamonds. Mike said, "Oh yes" to a broad face bracketed in a brown moustache. He stood with a drink in his hand getting a bit of anger up. It was a mellow brandy, and he took small sips. He refused a tray of small crackers with colored inserts and bits of overpink salmon.

Julie Brooks was back leading a short, middle-aged man with a big brow, brownish teeth: "This is Eli Kordon, III. Eli, Mr. Brant is the new type of labor leader."

"The hell you say." Eli Kordon III gave a short *ha-ha-ha* laugh. His hand grasp was solid; lots of handball, Mike suspected. "We have trouble with the old kind of labor leaders, and now we have the new kind."

"Not yet," said Mike, "but we'll try moving in on you."

"Well, why not. The government is up our back . . . good to meet you, Brant."

"This is my brother, Martin Brant."

"Ah, has the legal look . . . I can always tell a lawyer; there's the hunting hawk's look. Right? Right."

"Right," said Martin. "Any carrion today . . . ?"

Eli Kordon slapped Martin's shoulders. "You're all right," and moved off.

Julia was leading Mike toward a plump man with an expansive stomach, a round face under a flax-colored beard, and a waistcoat of red velvet (with food crumbs on it).

"Want you to meet Sir Arthur of the London School of Economics. He's doing a book on the early American labor movement."

Mike shook his head, took Julia's arm. "Whoa, Nellie, look I've met enough people. I want a few more drinks and a little personal information. For instance, like what do you do for the foundation?"

She looked at him, mildly questioning; damn, she was class just the calm, bitchy way she looked at him, as if he were something she had stepped on in tall grass and wondered what it was. She pursed her lips and seemed to think: Should she answer seriously or not? It was clear he was a new type to her.

"Mr. Brant, I direct some of the humanities studies for the foundation. My section is the condition of semi-primitive people, some of their taboos, fetishes, their emotional problems."

"I'm impressed . . . but that's what I do, too." He took her arm, led her to a window seat, and motioned for her to sit down.

"I don't have a foundation, and I don't use terms like humanities, but we're in the same racket. Want to hear about union taboos and fetishes? I'm up to my ass in them."

She laughed, but it wasn't insulting, and it wasn't related to any kind of attitude he'd found in a woman before. He had hoped she'd be a bit insulted at the ass line. She wasn't.

"Mr. Brant, I wish we could use your methods to get results."

"You mean my crude methods? The crunch, the shove in the gut, the brutalization you think of as unionization?"

"Arm breaking, fire bombings, assaults?"

Her nostrils seemed to flare as she spoke. Mike took her hand, felt her pulse. Calm. But she was excited by what she thought of him.

"You say all that as if it gives you kicks, Miss Brooks."

"Don't jump to conclusions." She withdrew her hand, looked at him calmly, and reached for a cigarette on a tray. She held it toward him. He glanced at the lighter— gold plated, shook his head.

"I'll give you a light if you'll have lunch with me tomorrow."

She didn't react—flare up the way he expected (get them riled and used to his method, and you're halfway home). He wanted suddenly to humiliate her, break her down. He was uncomfortable. She was too unreal—maybe class was unreal; maybe class didn't exist; you just built an idea up of real class appearance from the way they stand and talk. She pees, she sits on the crapper, her arm pits sweat.

"Mr. Brant, you are delightful." She reached for the lighter and lit her own cigarette. When she exhaled two plumes of smoke from those marvelous nostrils, he knew he had not fazed her. He was shit to her.

"No dice?" he said, rising from the window seat.

"Whatever that means, no dice. . . ."

She walked away on those long legs that seemed to start at her shoulder blades. He felt suddenly on the scent—fine; it was like the old hunting days when all he had on his mind was quiff, when he and Davey would go roistering around Tokyo, Honolulu. He smiled. Who would have thought it—and here.

He motioned to Martin, who didn't see him. Mike walked over to him. Martin was explaining some legal point to Lord Arthur, who kept wrinkling a large nose and gasping words out from somewhat of a congealed vocal box. "But I say, really, really, now I say, it's oddly done . . ."

"Let's blow."

"Had enough," asked Martin, turning. "Okay, good luck with your book, Sir Arthur."

"Very odd, your point there . . . yes. . . ."

In the elevator Mike asked, "What was that all about with Colonel Blimp?"

"Sir Arthur is a well-known Marxist economist. I was explaining the party's flaws here."

"Him a commie? They're all a cockeyed crew."

Martin inspected the black elevator operator, and asked him, "You organized?"

"Sir?"

"Is there a maintenance workers' union?"

"Union, sir?"

"You a member?"

"Your floor, sir. Watch your step, sir."

In the lobby Martin said, "Nothing like a servant who's a snob. How'd you like the gathering? Taste that brandy?"

"Close up they're just like the rest of us . . . just different packaging. Smell better, talk through their noses a bit—caused by too much education. But you know, Moz, it came to me—we're just as smart, just as able, once we get over our idea they're something so high up we have to get ladders to reach them."

"Cold tittie, I'd guess that Miss Brooks."

Mike walked out onto Lake Drive where the doorman stood; he inhaled deeply, enjoyed the blue-purple color of the twilight. "I'm going to fuck her."

The doorman didn't even blink as he motioned an approaching cab.

CHAPTER 27

Mike Brant had the knack, Jamie Ward insisted, the skill of being able to put aside a pressing problem, a mood, when he had to face a more serious situation that needed all his undivided attention. So Mike's resolve to see more of Julia Brooks, whatever emotions or attractions he was developing in that direction, faded out for the time being when he returned to Kansas City from Chicago.

Martin parted from him to go to the DWU offices; certain legal matters were about to come to a head.

Mike took a cab to his home, in his mind an active sorting out process taking place—attitudes toward Paul and Terry moved quickly to plans of expanding the DWU through other states—feel out dissatisfied leaders, organizers, to determine what locals, what new branches could be set up. Should he begin the drive to take over as president of the union so early or bide his time? What opposition would the Puskin put up? Token or tough

. . . would he see Mike's merits or fear him as a rival inside the umbrella of the WNUSA . . . damn, he'd forgotten to buy a toy dog for his son.

Mike came back to union problems, then solid reality.
The hovering directions of his thoughts focused as the
cab drew up before his house. It looked about the same,
even if the grass needed cutting and there were three
newspapers by the front door which had not been taken
in.

As he inserted his key into the brass lock (in need of
polishing), there came to his mind a little verse his father
used to sing to him as a boy. Mike used to think his old
man would someday explain it, but he never did.

> On the banks of the fatal Nile
> Weeps the deceitful crocodile . . .

Mike smiled in memory of those times when the home
life was quite different from his today. Moz insisted it
was not he who had wet the bed. Older and younger
brothers and sisters (I'm a negligent brother) and the old
man cutting the huge loaf of rye-corn bread—the round
loaf held against his breast, tugging the huge knife toward him, singing: "On the banks of the fatal Nile. . . ."
They lived on bread and milk, corn-meal mush when
times were bad; Mom putting on her blue nurse's cape
with the worn red lining to go out on a call . . . "Weeps
the deceitful crocodile. . . ." Why did the old-times
seem so much more a domestic good than now, when
poverty no longer threatened?

Mike pocketed his key ring and went down the hall to
the living room; the drapes were drawn, the smell of
burnt cooking and baby odor filled the place so that he
couldn't really identify its content. A quick look in the
kitchen and Mike saw piled-up, soiled plates; pots in
need of scraping, a brown paper bag from which protrud-

ed banana skins and a crushed cornflakes box. Back in the hall he called out: "Terry, Terry . . ."

There was no answer. Somewhere water sounded in a pipe.

"Charlie!"

Mike moved up the stairs, trying to go slowly. He opened the door to the boy's room. It was in half-darkness, the special shades down. Paulie was asleep on his little bed; a slight sucking sound came from the wet thumb in his mouth. Charlie was stretched out on the couch, also asleep, a look of exhaustion on her dark, shiny face; all the signs pointed to her having fallen into this deep sleep because she was tired, very tired.

Mike frowned; here it was eleven in the morning. He closed the door and walked across the hall to the bedroom. The door was locked. He tried to shove it open with a shoulder. He called again, "Terry," but not loudly. Someplace in the house a clock donged the hour, and he banged harder, not feeling the pain. The door was held by a flimsy bolt on the other side; it gave with a destructive sound as wood splintered and screws were forced out.

He almost fell into the room, stumbled against something underfoot that seemed to run away from him; he realized it was a bottle. He shot back the heavy dark window shades, and the room seemed to print itself in focus, the way he had once seen Moz as a boy develop a picture, the image becoming clear and sharp in the developing bath. At first, nothing was visible—then it became clearer and clearer, the scene sharpening.

He saw a disheveled bed, Terry lying on it as if flung there; an open dressing gown revealing much of her naked body, her hair in disorder, mouth open as if to caricature a snore—only an almost indecent sound emerged from her. There were several other bottles scattered about, all empty; a half-filled fifth of gin stood on the night table where a fresh scar from a burnt-out cigarette had spoiled the rosewood top.

A smell hit him: spilled alcohol, unwashed body, bad breath, unmade bed.

"Christ," he said softly. "Christ," he repeated loudly. "Christ," he uttered a third time as he swept the linen off the bed. He seized the sprawled Terry by the shoulders and sat her erect, her head wobbly, as if attached by a thread to a rubbery body, a nasty dribble sliding from her open mouth.

He slapped her on one cheek, then the other; the eyes remained closed, then the head seemed to draw away from his punishment. The eyes opened and the unseeing stare was blank.

"Wake up, wake up!" he shouted, still holding her firmly by the shoulders. "What the hell is this? What's going on?"

She seemed to see him now. Her head shook with a kind of a slow motion tremor, her voice sounding thick through some muffled barrier in her throat, groaned, "Huh, *huh* . . . oh, it's you."

"You're goddam right it's me, you damn lush . . . you. . . ."

What was the use he felt. She wasn't responding to him or his anger. She just stared at him, bent her eyebrows, licked her lips. She said, "Gimme, gimme a drink."

He was wise enough to know you do need some kind of bracer coming out of a big drunk. He poured a slurp of gin into a tacky glass and held it to her puffy lips as she swallowed. She sighed, and as Mike brushed back her hair she said, "I'm ashamed."

"Well, be ashamed, damn it. You really tied one on just when Paulie needed you, and I depended on you, to keep things rolling."

She said listlessly, "Duty's child has failed again."

"Never mind the smark aleck talk. Jesus, you stink like rotting clams. I'm going to get a bath going, get you in it, and sober you up."

"Oh sure."

* * *

He stripped her of the dressing gown; he didn't want to admit the kind of revolt he felt at the sight of this body, not young, not old either—solid enough. Into his mind flashed for a moment the image of another woman: Julia Brooks . . . how would she look stripped, naked to the touch? He felt annoyed that his mind was thinking these things. He filled the bathtub with cold water, then half-led, half-carried Terry to the tub, plopped her into the cold water which hit her like an electric shock, and submerged her.

She cried, *"Ahhhhh!"*

He pushed her back down and held her as she continued to protest, her teeth chattering.

"That's how we did it in the war, sobering up after leave. Now, just let it work on you. You'll wake up all over. Stay put, and I'll get you a couple of aspirins for that hangover."

It was ten minutes before Terry came out of the cold bath and stood while he rubbed her down with a big towel. All the time she made a moaning sound, her eyes closed, her hair still a tangle.

"A hell of a note. I come home and the wife is boozed to the gills, the kid and the housekeeper look like they've been through a hurricane. And Christ, look at you . . . where the devil is your goddam pride? Terry, the world-beater, the organizer, the intellectual. Did Lenin booze, did Eleanor Roosevelt go on a bat when FDR was off at Yalta? You always said you had principles I'd never understand."

She looked directly at him, eyes bloodshot, hands shaking as she tried to draw herself together.

"Go piss up a rope, mister."

"That's my girl, snippy and big-mouthed."

He slapped her behind. It sounded like a pistol shot. "Get dressed. I'm going down to make a pot of black coffee. When did you eat last? Don't go near Paulie; he and Charlie look knocked out. You must have given them a beaut of a time."

He kissed her cheek and went out, leaving her to look at herself in the full-length mirror. He would always love her, he thought—in his own way, he admitted. He was, about her, a sentimentalist. Terry had meant a great deal to him for a long time; he was aware that he was thinking of their relationship in the past tense. And that was bad; he was unfair. He felt a loyalty to her; he would always take care of her, not hurt her, no matter what turns and changes his life took. Mike's anger and shock had mostly evaporated. He could see and understand what had happened to his wife; time, turmoil, and the inevitable reordering of life patterns had taken their toll. Human existence was what it was . . . and always had been if the way Martin explained it was true. One had to accept everything that came along, face it, try not to go down before it, turn to drink, some daffy godhead, move to skid row.

He put on the coffee, found some marmalade and a half-dozen English muffins; he popped two into the toaster.

Mike was amazed to find he was still wearing his topcoat and hat. He threw them off and took off his jacket, pulling off his necktie without unknotting it. For a moment he thought of asking Mom to come out to see Terry through this thing. He shook his head . . . no, he always tried to present only the shiny side of his life to Mom. The coffee perked in anger, the muffins popped up golden brown.

Terry, her hair combed back, her feet bare, wearing a slip and a fresh robe, had had two cups of scalding coffee; she had managed to eat a half of a muffin with the marmalade on it. She wiped her mouth with a paper napkin, blew her nose. She looked at Mike sipping coffee with a dollop of cream in it from the Big Daddy cup.

He eyed her, his face expressionless, set down the cup. "Everything is going to be okay. You want a shrink or do you think Doc Zimmerman can give you something to help you?"

"I don't need a psychologist. I know what's the matter with me—*you . . . us . . .* I know."

"Us?"

"I've lost you to another love."

"Come off that malarkey . . . you know better."

"I don't mean a woman. I wouldn't give a damn about that. It's the union . . . the DWU. You only exist for three letters: D-W-U. They're your heart and soul."

"I never heard such cockeyed crap. You, Paulie, our life together . . . why you kook, it's what I depend on."

"We're just a setting for you—just background. You even fool yourself, you think you love us better than anything else. But . . . ," she shook her head. "Oh hell, nothing ever comes of these talks. Look, Mike, I promise you're not going to have any problem with me at home plate. This was just . . . just . . . , I felt trapped, brushed aside. Maybe I expected too much of the Chicago trip. I saw it as an escape hatch. Anyway, I felt I had failed my life. I knew we'd changed. Jesus, we'd changed. You were fine. Once we had such wide-eyed ideas, hoped so hard for what we believed in."

"We still do. I'm just getting where I can put over all we hoped for. Why don't you see that?"

She looked at him closely, fingered a fragment of muffin. "You don't see how it's different. All the gilt is off of it. It's all brass . . . pot metal, that's it. The whole goddam union movement dominated by men seeking power—grabbing it by any means."

"Let's not open that can of worms. The unions are being as practical as the big business combines we have to deal with. The methods are forced on us to survive. Remember Wallie Smith, the old IWW lug, saying: 'Survival is all.' "

He grabbed one of her arms and pressed. "Tonight, if you feel like it we'll go on the town."

She waved off a fresh cup of coffee he offered her. The phone rang. Mike picked the receiver off the kitchen wallphone. It was Martin.

"Mike, you better get down here. We got problems."

When in a half-hour Mike left the house, showered but unshaved, with only a hasty greeting for Paulie, he said to Terry: "I'll call you about tonight. Some kind of a hassle downtown. No drinkee?"

"No drinkee," she said. "Scout's honor."

He hoped so as the Starker held open the car door. He certainly hoped so; he had other problems on his hands.

Mike Brant had returned from Chicago with two resolves: to proceed with his set purpose of becoming president of the DWU . . . let the Puskin rave over tossing the DWU out of the WNUSA . . . Mike was determined to take over. The other thing he desired was Julia Brooks . . . a mad idea he admitted, clutching at something beyond his reach. She was out of his orbit . . . a lady, the kind he'd heard of but had never been really close to or felt about as he did her.

He wired her a huge collection of flowers with a text: *"To the lady of the foundation from a mug who admires her very much . . . M.B."*

He wondered if she had any reaction to that, but of course there was no reply. Ladies didn't answer for flowers sent them.

Three months later when he was in Chicago to meet some union officials to begin planning how to dump the old fart, Dick Seabrook, who was president of the DWU, he phoned her (having managed to get her private number from the foundation with a bit of fancy doubletalk). The phone rang, he heard it—but there was no answer. He called again that night but still no answer.

He would have called again the next morning, but the union meeting in his room at the Palmer House that night ran long after two in the morning. It was a brass tacks gathering of six old sweats and some young radicals—the hotheads of the DWU.

He said, "We're not going fast enough and we aren't ourselves being fully appreciated. Agreed? Agreed."

Harry Harper, on whom Mike depended to deliver delegates from the northwestern locals, pulled on his flat long nose. "Now, Mikey, this is just a talking over of prospects, understand—nothing definite promised."

"I know it, Harry. I just want to be sure as somebody said, 'who isn't with me is against me.' I figure maybe a year, a year and a half, and we'll be ready with a good slate. We all want a stronger union, free of the Washington big shots in their fancy building, jiving, living fat off us."

Ronald Wheaton was a black man, said to be lippy and sassy—but he was smart and able. He grinned at Mike. "And we all want some rewards for all the hard work we've done. Simple question here: Can you put over a nigger vice president?"

"Not alone, Ronnie. Mass effort is called for. Now, Dick Seabrook has been president a long time. He's a habit, not a real person. And he's done it—stayed in because a lot of slack locals of DWU vote for him because he comes out and pours the booze and talks of how it was for their old man in the bad old days. We can topple Seabrook if the new locals we form are run by our side."

Ronald Wheaton pursed his heavy lips, showed a corner of a tooth outlined in gold. "If we can keep signing up southern locals with lots of members, there's a chance. We need somebody to handle the peckerwoods that keep us out of the unions. But that Kingbird is smart, and he's for Seabrook."

"No, no," said Sam Winneck. "No color line in the DWU. Every man has a vote, every man votes as a working man. But, Mikey, it's not going to be easy . . . how you going about it?"

"First, we're going over the DWU books. We cook

them a bit, I know. But I'm going to have a deep, deep look into Dick Seabrook's investments, holdings. Hell, he owns a golf course, six apartment houses, a highway building corporation."

"But in his wife and son's names," said someone, relighting a cold, wet cigar. "No moss growing on ol' Dickie."

Mike tapped a thumb on his bottom lip. "Good. Who put up the down payments . . . what banks did him favors . . . how come he gets so many highway contracts? Now, this is not dirty pool. Maybe the next election will be based on real merit, and maybe we'll skip some goddam Federal investigation where we always bunch up to protect something we shouldn't."

The men were wary of Mike, but they also wanted change—to better their own positions, and also, as Mike well knew, these were soreheads, always complaining against those who held higher rank and clout. It was human nature as he knew it, and he was going to use it.

Mike spoke for an hour more, in sickening cigar smoke; he hoped he had made a few converts and some points.

Next morning he had to go to Cleveland to untangle a wildcat strike; this one against the position he had taken on Cleveland labor conditions. He saw he would have to find some way, when he was president, of controlling local action—not remove its autonomy, but figure out a way to be sure of events always moving in his direction. He was on the train reading some reports Jamie Ward had given him for his battered briefcase when he remembered Julia Brooks, the call he had planned to make.

He spent some of the rest of the journey thinking of her, recalling her image, the way her body moved, even his rash promise—the one he had made about her.

The Cleveland matter took two bad days, then he came back to Kansas City. Terry seemed in better spirits, Paul

lively: Terry not bouncing with joy. But whatever both-
ered her and annoyed him, still he felt loyal to her. He
didn't dare permit his thoughts to compare her to Julia
Brooks.

In the next one and a half years he did speak to Julia
once . . . from Pittsburgh, where somehow he got com-
mitted to see the opening of an art exhibit sponsored by
some charity providing free breakfasts for poor school
kids. The best families had loaned some of their personal
treasures. A huge painting caught Mike's eye: it was of an
amazingly graceful, animated woman dressed for riding
in a shiny top hat, a small whip in one gloved hand, in the
other she held up a length of riding skirt, revealing splendid, shiny boots. It was her stare—the tilt of her head, the
green-blue eyes that held Mike's attention—so sure of
her place, he felt, in the society that could commission
such a picture. The image seemed to be able to leap from
the painting. It was full length in a deep, gold frame. He
said to one of the sponsors of the show:

"That's one hell of a painting."

"Yes indeed, a Sargent."

"A what?"

"It's by John Singer Sargent. Marvelous brush work, as
good as a Hals."

"Oh sure. Who is it of?"

"Hm . . . one of the Brinkenhoff daughters . . . Alice, I think. Yes, Alice."

"Married?"

"Oh yes, to one of the Southerby's of Virginia."

"I'd like to meet her."

The man look amused. "Well, not too easy, Mr. Brant.
Alice Southerby died in 1916; she was then about seventy-two. That was painted early in Sargent's career."

That night Mike called Julia Brooks' Chicago number,
and she answered the phone. As simple as that.

"I bet you don't remember Mike Brant."

"How are you, Mr. Brant?"

"Up and around. I'll be in Chicago in a couple of weeks. We could have lunch or dinner, and you could explain the good work of the foundation to me."

"We really could mail you some of our booklets. They would explain better than I can."

"Oh. How about the lunch anyway?"

"I'm afraid, Mr. Brant, I'm going to Europe, to live. Work out of our Paris office."

That was that . . . a perfect brush. Not mean or fancy. But the way a lady would do it—a cool, easy letdown.

There was a stubborn streak in Mike—inherited from Mom perhaps—that hardened as he felt his power. If anyone had suggested it was tinged with some unreasonable romantic notions he would have been puzzled, for he saw himself as realistic, logical, and a determined observer of events. The stubborn streak, no matter how motivated, made him do some probing (he did this more as an exercise than because he entertained false hope) into the past of Julia Brooks. There were many ways of doing this. The DWU used certain channels to ferret out information; Mike used one of these sources, under the guise of seeking details of the Kordon Foundation and its humanities grants.

Julia Brooks was two years younger than himself (good) and had been born on the Hudson River in sight of Hyde Park, on the estate of a branch of the Brooks family, who were related to the early Adams'. But the family was neither as politically aggressive or as related to history. She won pony races at the age of eight, attended Miss Montley's school in Riverside, and the LaBlanc School in Switzerland, played ice hockey, tennis, won some. She enrolled at Smith but was not an overeager student. An English major, she wrote a few papers on Virginia Woolf and the Brontës; later she worked for a year on *Town & Country* covering horse and dog shows. At twenty she married John Hammond Whitham (what a name), who seemed to spend most of his time at the Harvard Club, attending commissions on the state of historic houses, and a little time in the offices of Starkweather & Company, Wall Street, a firm in which his family held certain shares.

The Whithams were divorced after two-and-a-half years of marriage (that's more like it). She worked for some time on *Newsday* in Long Island and married a sports writer on the staff, Daniel DeLong (another dud). There was some mystery about his death—hints of a drunken spree at sea, a yachting accident during the American Cup races off Newport (goodbye, Dan). By that time Julia Brooks was with the Kordon Foundation, having worked on grant proposals in Kenya, India, and Java. . . .

He put the information away in his files and admitted you can't win them all. She would most likely have been a lousy lay anyway.

BOOK FIVE

THE PINNACLE

CHAPTER 28

(From Martin's Journals)

Those who became aware early of the changes in Mike Brant did not understand his perception of the changing scene in industrial relations and labor legislation, see that he saw automation changing the structures of the economy that affected union's position. Unions, too, were assuming the prerogatives of management, buying and building; the change in their attitudes was brought about by the increasing inaccessibility of traditional channels of authority.

Mike expresses himself bluntly, describing past methods as the work of "cookie pushers, with minds like filing cabinets stuffed full of papers in triplicate. Hell, we can't waste time anymore in lengthy speculations, or in long hours of half-assed debating over the daily rolls of toilet paper a factory should furnish the workers."

Mike studies industrial methods; he reads (not easy for him) and keeps up with the *Wall Street Journal, Forbes,*

Business Week, Fortune and other publications, even if they usually do ignore the deep underlying problems in union procedures, masking them with a favorable viewpoint. He is developing a sense of abstraction, a sense he doesn't fully trust; he plagues me to clarify ambiguous questions. This shows in his behavior; he rages at times, when he feels frustrated by the limits on direct, quick action for positive decisions because some member of his council hesitates.

He does not want to boot out these dissenters; yet he desires quick responses to problems that actually call for considered study he would rather not wait for.

His querulous mood during this period of crisis caused him to gain weight; he ate all that was put before him without being aware of it. He kept up a facade of inexhaustible energy, tried to show no frailties. Also the charmer in Mike came forward more as he grew older, more sure of his goals. His ability to charm at will showed itself in his extraordinary effects on female company. ("Jesus Christ, they think he's the DWU Clark Gable," Jamie Ward would say.) Few suspected the nervous union of energy combined with a talent for subterfuge and deceit that Mike dramatized in collective bargaining when faced with questionable financial affairs. Martin put it down to bravado; as he told Davey, "Mike, he really doesn't understand high finance. He's dealing in millions of dollars—a man who used to look over menus to see if the bread and butter was charged—account statements are play money to him, and he's tossing it around in a wildly competitive environment, in what he thinks is democratic unionism. I say it's also to keep all those sharks and jackals he has to work with in line for him to stay up there. Mob alliances, he sees as something to use, but who the hell is holding whose head under water?"

Davey Wasserman shrugged off Martin's ideas.

"Now, Marty, don't get a wild hair up your prat. It's just he knows what he wants. Mike, he's ventilating his frustrations . . . what some shrink would think of as grandiose illusion is Mike's way of worrying. Otherwise, why would he have a drop-dead list and a shit list?"

Martin saw deeper, as he wrote in his notes:

> The ideal of union benefits and the operational differences between this hope and its results is a philosophical torment to Mike. His vociferous, vivid profanity is a smoke screen for doubt. In a jurisdictional fight he never can eliminate personal strife between the various men he gives power to. As he has come to dominate more and more in the central and southern states, he has begun to think in terms of state-wide organizations, not his old, pet idea of local autonomy. His whole philosophy of direct power to the workers has had to be tossed overboard because of the need to cut the power of negotiating chairmen to prevent, he claims, internecine, interunion squabbles. The closer he comes to his vision of national president of the DWU, the more he has used muscle against rivals, expelled troublemakers, limited policy discussions, even among loyal lieutenants.

Mike greatly admired industrial organization. He fought it for some time, but to continue to get impressive results Mike began to work in collusion with management. He explained it to Davey. "You see, you insert yourself where there's intense commercial competition. Centralize your area-wide bargaining, change, if you have to, the heads of dissident unions. Talk to management like a Dutch uncle. Tough, but seeing *their* side—yes, get them to feel you see their problems too."

The success the DWU had with Mike's dictatorial methods were visible in unified wage hours, better working conditions; the rank and file rarely thought beyond these benefits. Mike's method, perfected year by year, was to start with pressure on small scale entrepreneurs, and if he had to, somehow to get around restraining government regulations. That was Martin's job. He'd use, if he had to, well-coordinated violence from Spinelli's boys.

"Organize by coercion, ignore traditional boundaries," he told his labor councils. "Hell, to the union man it's his bigger paycheck, his fringe rights that count. Force closed shops to see the light. Begin to work an area by putting pressure on firms with less than two-hundred-thousand gross revenue a year. I'll furnish you lists. Their low profits are our advantage. Just remember, labor costs are sixty percent of gross revenue."

Davey smiled, reading a list of income reports. "You do your homework, sergeant."

"Damn right . . . I use leverage to extend unionization, to expand control. Always start with the softest ass to kick—then move up to the next higher group, till we hit the biggies. Play ball. Sure, have good relationships with employers once they come over. Take golf lessons, smoke their cigars, screw their broads. But don't press too hard. Helpful interreactions with them extends union influence."

"But the locals don't like this palsy-walsy conduct."

"Fuck the locals if it's for the good of the DWU."

CHAPTER 29

Mike leaned heavily on his brother. Martin had set himself up in a bachelor's pad, a small house near the Kansas State College, with John Fiora, born a Finsillo, a nephew of George Spinelli (a slimmer image of his uncle). John was also a lawyer, a young man on his way up to some sort of importance in the web of enterprises and projects of the Spinelli family and their satellites. He handled the public relations of the Central States DWU. He and Martin maintained a neat bachelor establishment with a Japanese houseman, subdued, not at all notorious or loud. But the place was the setting for parties, not for serious seductions. It was all on weekends—perhaps a swing trio for dancing and a half-dozen couples from the town's colleges—young people from advertising, radio and TV, and some whose backgrounds were unknown.

Martin, as chief legal head of the Kansas City and adjoining state locals, formed a partnership with a newly created firm: Krasner, Murray, and Brant. Young, aggressive lawyers, expert in all matters pertaining to the union: injunctions, defense of arrested pickets, accusations of sabotage, also matters of Federal restrictions, state codes, welfare. In court matters Martin, indeed, often found "the law is a great ass."

As he wrote in his journal, the very private journal he kept:

> I form no high opinion of lawyers; there is little justice for the middle class; fees are dishonorably high, conditions are generally weighted in favor of corporations and insurance companies so that the ordinary citizen is screwed, skinned, either when he goes to the law, or when the law attacks him. Many judges are venal or weak and they seem to favor the powerful or those who can reward them in some easy way from flattery to anything for their benefit. As for judges who have to be elected, most can be softened by support with funds—they will someday return the favor.

Martin knew he was being harsh in his judgments, but he lived in a world where things were done by influence, often by bribery, and sometimes by physical violence on both sides.

> Like Mike, (he wrote) I have come around to seeing no real division between industry and the workers. They are Siamese twins, Mike insists, grown together, and each half is fighting for power, material gains, a richer way of life. The same life blood—the demand for products, services—flows through the two of them, the rich, thick life blood. Withdraw or keep that flow from one, and they both sicken.
>
> If the relationship—the chemistry is not returned to balance, they can die as the Romans, the feudal lords—as the Russian tzars did.
>
> The items that make up these two united bodies—industry and muscle—are called vice presidents, personnel directors, chairmen, councils, directors, organizers.

No matter what title or what temporary power keeps them alive (either twin), they are human elements under such pressures that they die off like flies. Coronaries are an occupational commonplace . . . ulcers grow like roses . . . high blood pressure is a battle wound, and rewards are Eames suites, expense accounts, a push-button supply of women, whiskey, the gold key to the executive shithouse. There is the sense of power directed from a glass topped desk with a battery of phones that can reach further than any despot that ever ruled the Roman Empire. As for the pecking order of power in *both* twins, it was best expressed I think by Mike after a bad session with a strike problem. He got a bit high with me and John this one night: "In any organization it's finding your proper guy to screw and taking it from the guy who's screwing you. That's a well-run organization . . . in being fucked, it's permitted to fart in bed, but not to wipe your cock on the drapes."

If it were not for his domestic problem, I think Mike would not rush so toward taking over the presidency of the DWU. It would come to him naturally in time, without the harsh methods he is now proceeding with.

Martin admired Terry, found her, in her best moments—and there were many—good company, amusing, even witty. But the starch had gone out of her (as Mom would have put it). Martin tried to take her to lunch at some good place at least once a week. She was very good about it. A bit too much make-up, perhaps—and very sternly shaking her head when the waiter asked if they wanted to order cocktails. She would sip a little wine and laugh at some joke Martin told her was going the rounds of the lawyer's world.

As the lunch progressed one Thursday, she did become more animated. "I remember when Mike and me first met. We were so damn crazy about union organization, and we could not have afforded a meal like this."

"Everything, Terry, looks better in the past."

"Maybe it was, maybe, maybe . . . oh don't think I'm

knocking the way things worked out. But for my lousy nerves giving out. It must have come from those hard times on the docks and the year we tried to organize United Farm and Field. I had an aunt who had palsy and a grandfather who talked to birds."

"So did St. Francis."

"I don't blame Mike being away so much."

"You should. We all should, for his own good. He's spinning like a top and cutting through people's lives with a buzz saw. And . . ."

"You think, Marty, he neglects me? He tries to make it up to me, really he does." She rubbed a lean wrist. "If he plays around, I don't really care. I don't think he really gets much of a charge out of sex anymore. Maybe five or ten minutes in some hotel room, or putting a twenty dollar bill up some stripper's snatch."

She took a sip of wine, banged down the glass. "I'm sorry, Marty. Mustn't get bitter, upset; bad for me."

"Next week I know a little place great for fish soup. Okay?"

She took Martin's hand and pressed. "As we used to say when I was a kid in pigtails, 'you're a peach,' Marty."

"As we used to say in Milltown, 'you're some tomato,' Terry."

It took two full years to face Dick Seabrook for the presidency of the DWU. Seabrook had powerful friends in the union headquarters in Washington. Ol' Dickie was a wily old coot who had protected himself during his long and rather casual years as a union leader. He was still an impressive white-haired, old gent with good teeth—his own—and a genial way of displeasing no one on any side. His verbal art was a bit on the ornate side. Mike said: "Ol' Dick makes eagles scream at every event and uses the flag more than George M. Cohan did."

The climax to Mike's effort came in the big convention held in New Orleans at the end of the 1950's. All of his staff were there but for Jamie Ward, who was in the hospital with a flaming ulcer.

In November that sultry, humid city on the delta was filling with various delegates; hotels and rooming houses, seasonally available flats, all were filled with determined men—some roughhewed, some in the jeans and beards of the new youth movement—out for fun and politics. They had once worked a lathe, driven a tractor, set a cord line, pointed a row of fresh laid bricks; their talk was full of the jargon of their trades, bar comradeship given to jolly obscenity. Wearing gaudy sports shirts, they moved to the bars on Bourbon Street, ate in the Commander Place, Brennins. The women sat in the court of the Three Sisters; the men drank and ate with relish with their wives, or with hospitable girls of the French Quarter. The delegates did the expected tourist things, visited the lake, took the ferry to Algiers across the Mississippi. Some got drunk, got rolled, got laid, arrested, bailed out, and patched up. Led by Martin, some went to see the ramparts where Andrew Jackson defeated the British ("old Hickory not knowing the war had been over for two weeks").

John Fiora (born Giovanni Finsillo) discovered some of the real Dixieland jazz as they had played it in the days of Buddy Boldon and early Storyville; found it in a café on Royal Street on a platform across the back of a place where three very old blacks played, two with welfare teeth to take the riffs on their horns: "Lonely Train Blues," did "Livery Stable Stomp" while Martin and his guests paid a dollar each for a bottle of beer and listened.

One night when John and Martin were escorting two well-stacked senior coeds from a local college, the old jazzmen played and sang for the ten dollars handed up to them, "The Peehole Blues."

But under all this jolly tourism and mild, hedonistic, fringe sinning, the serious business of the convention went on in the Robert E. Lee Convention Hall in the tepid breeze from many fans and the stop-and-go air conditioning. Mike made an opening night speech outlining changes he expected this convention to make in the bylaws, as well as certain other demands the bylaws committee suggested be made about keeping hands off DWU matters.

Mike was popular with the crowd, but it was clear the delegates were ready to endorse their good ol' boy Dickie Seabrook once again.

The Seabrook floorman was Joseph DuBois, better known as Kingbird DuBois because of his beak of a nose. His grandfather had helped Huey Long to power, and his father, in New Deal days, had organized bayou workers, oil field roustabouts, and the shrimp boaters of the delta and Gulf. He was a cheerful, extroverted Cajun who was the inventor and promoter of the medicinal virility drink, *Bongolo* (which had a dime's worth of vitamins and a double martini in every three-dollar bottle of the bitter mixture, according to *Consumer's Research*).

While Dick Seabrook shook hands, and retold the joke about the man who was wearing a girdle on the golf course, Mike was getting organized. "When they asked how long he had been wearing a girdle, wait till you hear his answer, boys . . . the feller said, 'Ever since my wife found it in the back of the car last week! heh-heh-ha. . . .'"

Mike had set up an office in his suite at the Louis Royale. He entertained at the St. Charles, enjoyed the local jazz.

They roared on, shouted, applauded, and voted resolutions in the odor of peanut shells, sweat, and whiskey.

Two days before the final nomination for president, while the last of the union business ground on, Martin invited Kingbird DuBois to Mike's suite. Mike had visited, talked, made promises with the delegates in their steamy condition in the hall; he had looked over the legs of the women delegates, compared them (for a moment) with Julia Brooks, his lost dream woman.

He went back to his suite, showered, changed to a white linen suit, white kid shoes, tan silk shirt, pale yellow tie, added a tie clip with a tiny ruby set in it.

Moving away from the fireplace mirror, he said to John Fiora, "Turn the air conditioning down ten degrees. I want a little sweat from the Kingbird. And set out the bourbon within reach. He's been known to lap it up. Now, Martin, just put the briefcase in easy reach. Set the chairs so he faces the windows. Anything else?"

Martin said, "John Ford to direct the scene?"

Mike waved off that mockery with a smile. He knew he looked confident, but inside, it was touch and go with his gut. Two Digels, well-chewed, soon got that set of organs to lie doggo.

Kingbird DuBois came into the suite followed by a short man with weight in the wrong places, mostly in a protruding belly made, Mike thought, for a larger man. There were renewed greetings, handshakes. "This here is Max Kolinski, best friend ah ever had, a real white Jew, one of the best."

Max nodded and they sat down and chatted about union bylaws passed, the splendid progress the convention was making, and the doughnuts at the French market not being what they had once been. Kingbird DuBois didn't smoke but he accepted "bourbon with branch water, thank yo."

Mike jiggled the ice cubes in his glass. "Now, DuBois, I haven't made any secret, have I, that I want the presidency."

"Yo ain't been pawing the ground for nothin' all these months. Now just hear me out: Brant, I like yo fine—yo have done a bangup job of bringing back the balls and gisum to the DWU. Ain't I said that often, Max?"

"You have."

"But now let reason be reason—as I once told yo, but we don't dump a good ol' boy like Dickie. In five years he'll retire, and we'll be for yo like a nigrah for a watermelon."

"Nope," said Mike. "It's now."

"I promised ol' Dickie, a solemn oath, didn't I, Max?"

"You did."

"That's the way she falls, Brant, this time 'round."

Mike leaned forward, smiled, saw the sun in the Kingbird's eye, a bit of moisture forming on his large nose.

"You're one of the smartest men in the South, DuBois. And your drink Bangolo is your life's work."

"*Bongo*lo, suh . . ."

"Bongolo is going great guns; every man a sultan, every woman Catherine the Great. You're putting everything into an invasion of the North. So it's clear you've been careful of your capital . . . you owe the Federal Revenue department one million nine hundred thousand on unpaid alcohol taxes."

The Kingbird smiled, waved a wide, fat hand. "Of record, yes, but ah got connections, and they will wait until next inventory for payment."

"I have friends also in Washington, Kingbird. A legal action against you for nonpayment of past due taxes could break in tomorrow's *New Orleans Item*."

"I just admitted an honest business debt."

The Kingbird was a good poker player. He seemed amused at Mike's hand.

John Fiora said, "Think over the results of such a story."

"I'm not running for president . . . this can't hurt ol' Dickie."

"Maybe not. Now, you control enough delegates for a final vote to make a winner."

"Do I, Max, ever pressure a delegate?"

"You never do."

"So," said Martin breaking in, "in this final vote, Mike

wants you to instruct your people to move over to the Brant side."

"Why this here is a democratic organization. Ah can't go against that."

"Bullshit," said Martin, opening the briefcase and taking out a *Wall Street Journal*.

"There is a story on page six. Let me read some of it: 'Philadelphia-Delaware Monox Company, producers of popular Monox MeDo—mass-market health items, are in the process of negotiating to buy the DuBois-Bayou Health Corporation, makers of Bongolo, Daddy-Ease headache tablets, popular local products in the Gulf Coast states.' "

Martin looked up, then went back to reading:

" 'Philadelphia-Delaware Monox is a large holder of DuBois-Bayou stocks, and now is seeking to acquire the DuBois family holdings.' "

"It could be," said the Kingbird. "Nothing settled yet."

Mike took the paper from Martin's hand and threw it aside. "Now *if* there is a suit filed your stock will fall like overripe apples from an old tree. Monox will be stuck with a bag full of losses and a bad smell from Washington up their noses."

The Kingbird sat expressionless. "Yo got more by the look of yo."

"Five hundred thousand dollars worth of trucks, and there are certain loans against that fleet, amounting to over three hundred thousand dollars—loans from a certain private organization out of Vegas."

"Just banking, proper banking."

Max, without coaching, said, "Very proper."

John Fiora said, "Bealasi brothers made that loan."

"Now," said Mike, "I don't have anything against Joe and Tony Bealasi, but the Philadelphia-Monox crowd may not like the mob in your caw, and we have found out your books don't even show the loan against the fleet. Kingbird, you once sold a company full of watered stock, and when it didn't turn out as one set of books showed, you told them, the buyers, 'you buy a cow and it don't give milk yo can't bring that cow back.'"

The Kingbird laughed. "Yo do a pretty good country boy imitation of me, Mike, yo do." He slapped a thigh. "Why don't we lay our asses on the table. Maybe yo get nominated, ol' Dickie gets nominated, and some commie pricks they trot up Dodo Kelly, but he don't count. When do the delegates come over to you?"

"When it gives me the majority."

"How do we git ol' Dickie not to holler frame-up?"

Martin took out a batch of papers from the briefcase. "These are legal documents preparing to seek indictment of Richard Seabrook on charges of fraud, collusion, misuse of union funds, illegal loans from our welfare and health funds."

The Kingbird laughed. "Why ol' Dickie, yo naughty boy . . ."

Martin folded back a few pages . . . "Item: he did in June of 1952 form a corporation in his son Roger's name, with union funds as collateral, to buy eight hundred seventy-three thousand dollars worth of road making machinery from Wilbur J. Seldes, the brother of the highway commissioner for the state . . . true value appraised, when the firm filed for bankruptcy in 1954, at four hundred eighty thousand. The loan was illegally made; loss to the union of the major amount. Item: . . . Sarah B. Seabrook made a major stockholder of Rosemoor Land Company in 1957, and among assets, two office buildings in Central City, Ohio. One office building is rented on leases to the DWU of the state at rentals running twenty years. Rentals are four hundred thirty percent higher than rentals in other office buildings in the same neighborhood."

Martin rattled the sheets. Mike said, "Homer K. Melmar, CPA, now serving two years at Leavenworth for filing false income tax returns, has furnished us with notarized papers that he was the go-between who kicked back to Richard Seabrook in person twenty percent of these rentals through deposits in a personal account in a bank in Bermuda."

"Ol' Dickie did *all* that?"

Mike said, "Why go on. Kingbird, you can take these papers to ol' Dickie and you show them to him. He can burn them, we have the originals. So why don't we just have drinks together in the Mardi Gras Bar to pledge each other a good clean fight on the convention floor."

Kingbird DuBois stood up and shook Mike's hand, smiling. "Yo are one sonofabitch, Mike Brant, but I alus admired a sixteen-jewel Swiss movement sonofabitch, don't I, Max?"

When the two men were gone, Martin snapped shut the briefcase. "Will he doublecross us?"

Mike shook his head. "Hell, no. The Kingbird, he wants to be on our team. He smells power for himself. He'll take ol' boy Dickie's place as main dog on the Gulf. And he wants to take those Philadelphia-Monox jaspers with his Bangolo setup."

"*Bongolo*," corrected John Fiora.

It was as cheerful and pleasant a meeting in the Mardi Gras bar as was ever seen, (Martin wrote in his journal). Like some fat cats that had just eaten their prey and had enjoyed it. Ol' Dickie was at his best, told some grand darky stories. The Kingbird kept up with the bourbon and branch water. Everyone left early for dinner appointments, shaking hands and being photographed in the lobby by a news cameraman. Next day the pictures were in the *Item*, headlined:

TWO LABOR LIONS MEET BEFORE FINAL FRAY

The rest is labor history and not really very interesting. I saw that the opening nominations went as expected. Dodo Kelly's followers were few and had to be escorted from the hall until they cooled off . . . they having insisted without evidence that the convention was framed to continue a sell-out of labor.

On the first ballot Dick Seabrook led by ten votes, nowhere near the two-thirds needed to elect. On the second ballot Mike was ahead, but still not enough of a majority to elect. Just before the third balloting, I saw a scurrying among certain delegates (and rumors later of rolls of bills being passed—certainly an invention—all the deals had been made the night before). On the third round Mike won easily.

In came a blaring jazz band, banners, streamers, and later, it turned out, several pickpocket gangs. The din lasted for twenty minutes by my watch. The jazzmen played *"When the Saints Come Marchin' In"*, and Dick Seabrook himself introduced Mike from the platform: "If it had to be, I'm pleased it went to a young giant among us, to a man—a standard bearer of staunch purpose—who sees the destiny of labor, of the DWU, as the exalted pattern for what we have all hoped for; the rightful place of the American worker in the forefront of the national scenes . . . now, Michael Brant, our president."

Mike looked good up there, changed to a freshly pressed gray suit, pale pink necktie, standing there, waiting with serious patience for the second round of carryings-on to stop. He held up both hands, then stepped to the mike, and into the TV lights. He looked around the hall, to the right, to the left; he knew the drama of that few moments of silence—just before beginning to speak.

"I am not a humble man, and this is not a humble union. We together are going to tractor-out all that stands in the way of the progress of the American worker, and we—you men—will raise up from the rubble an organization whose aims will . . ."

It can all be found in the press. Copies of the speech were mailed to all members, a report bound and lettered in blue, titled, *You Speak Through Your New President.* It was a good speech, well delivered. Mike had learned how to sway an audience, how to change the pace and tone of his delivery; now speaking low and solemn, now adding a burst of earthy humor, then the statesmanlike stare, the direct delivery like the Lord handing the tablets down to a collection of Moseses.

Basically it's a rewrite of many of the speeches I had written for Mike . . . generalizing, emotional. Once away from the lights, the emotions of the scene and time, it is rather overdramatic and banal.

The next day, as we flew back in a chartered plane to Kansas City, Mike seemed hunched, deep in some private thoughts. He looked out at the scudding clouds.

"Moz, I'm moving . . . setting up in Chicago, also in Washington. And have Jamie Ward, when he gets out of the hospital, arrange for us to buy an organization jet."

Martin, according to his journal, wanted to respond, "Caesar has spoken." But didn't.

CHAPTER 30

In the spring of 1962, as the president of the Drovers &
Wheelmens, Mike was invited to address the convention
of World Trade Unionists (with no workers' representatives from the Eastern Bloc) at Congress Hall of the Trade
Union Congress in London. He flew overseas with an en-
tourage worthy of a man rising in the international labor
scene . . . Jamie Ward as door guardian; John Fiora,
nephew of George Spinelli, in charge of press publicity;
Maggie Kline, a middle-aged, able personal secretary—a
former Wac, with military shoulders and voice, a degree
in literature from Berkeley. She also served as an editor of
Mike's outgoing letters, which she amended, taking out a
certain crudeness and the vulgarisms; in most cases she
knew when to let Mike's language go through to do its
worst.

There was a Brant suite at Grosvenor House, and the
first press conference with the British press went off well.
John Fiora was a graduate of the Harvard Law School. Ja-

mie Ward had shaken his head at his appointment: "The
unions are getting so filled with fancy college graduates
and Ph.D.'s, the workers gotta wonder if they shouldn't
be at Yale, not General Electric."

John Fiora kept the assembled English labor press in a
good mood with sandwiches, roast beef, grouse, and caviar set out with Vat 69 and Johnny Walker. Miss Kline had
typed up notes for Mike of what an American union leader should express to a group of nations some who had na-
tionalized their industry and some who had accepted
very radical unions in major factories.

"I have no answers for all world workers and production problems. We have in the United States workers
problems back in what some English may still call 'the
colonies.' We observe with interest your experiments.
Americans, however, are still in many ways frontier folk
with a lot of hoot and holler, and a sense of feeling. On a
national scale, if they had to wear a dog collar, they'd
complain and beef. We may not have the Magna Carta,
but at home labor is stuck with the Taft-Hartley Act."
And so on for half an hour.

The reporter from the *Daily Event*, drink in hand,
asked, "Mr. Brant, do you approve of certain actions
American unions, particularly your own, which uses violence and sabotage?"

Mike looked as if all this was news to him. "Violence?
Self-defense would be a better word. Our locals have to
face a great deal of reaction from those misguided indus-
trialists who bring in outside terrorists. But let's be fair,
the DWU's relationship with most of our great corporations is smooth, efficient, and productive for the economy."

"But the wrecking of those presses in that southern
printing plant when there was what—oh, yes—a lockout?"

"The American media is antilabor. The report was

wrong. Birdward Printers has maintained an open shop for fifty years and locked out the men who tried to form a union."

"Your union was fined two million dollars for those presses."

John Fiora stepped forward, glass in hand. "If I may insert some facts: We have evidence that Birdward Printers sabotaged certain of their old presses to bring a charge against the DWU before the Labor Relations Board."

Mike added, "We'll not pay a penny of that two million."

The *Daily Star* girl looked up from her notes. "Drovers and Wheelmen, just what are they and are there any such people in your union, Mr. Brent?"

"Brant, Miss Kelton. DWU was organized in 1894, during desperate strikes against Pullman, Great Plains Harvester, and the International Freight Movers. Drovers were cattle workers; wheelmen were dray drivers, cask and timber haulers, workers in the big lumber forests of Michigan."

The middle-aged journalist with the silver-rimmed eyeglasses (*The Liverpool Gazette*) spoke up: "From this handout we were furnished by one of your people, it seems the DWU hardly represents such obsolete workers. I see plastic suppliers listed, machinists in various modern crafts, film and stage crews, deep sea divers, and yes, oh yes," he peered at the list, "bakers and highwire riggers. Highwire riggers?"

"Circus work specialists."

Jamie Ward had a copy of the brochure in his hand. "We don't claim to represent *all* workers in all those crafts. Each section of the country's locals, under shop stewards, organize in their own way, often under the umbrella of the DWU. There are still wheelmen in the logging sections, but now they drive cats."

"Cats—I say . . . ?"

"All tractor gear is known as a cat."

"Lumberjacks drive them?"

Mike said, "Never call a logger a lumberjack. That's a term never really used by timber workers. Now, excuse me, I must get going. I hope you'll be at Congress House Friday night."

Had the press conference gone well? Even if not Mike felt expansive, and he looked down on the green of the park and away to the passing by of the Royal Horse Guards in their lobster-colored uniforms, silver helmets and plumes, passing to the *clop-clop* of their horses' hoofs, a good satisfying sound.

Jamie said, "Too bad Terry and Paul couldn't make it."

"Yes," said Mike, "some sister of hers, very ill. Damn family always gets in the way at times."

Actually Terry was in a sanitarium outside Green River, Ohio. A good private place Dr. Zimmerman had said, that took care of "tattered nerves." Mostly brought on by alcohol. It had seemed best after a not too bad drinking bout for Terry to "rest." One had to expect a bat once every six or eight months from her. Otherwise she seemed normal enough—perhaps a bit withdrawn. If Terry's condition was worsening, it was doing so very slowly; and so, for a period of two, three weeks, Charlie took care of Paul. It was accepted by some that Terry was at a reducing farm, taking off extra pounds. She did return home thinner.

In London, for all the interviews, visits to some historic places, Mike was lonely. There was a night of drinking with some of the labor leaders above a pub, the Bunch of Grapes; there was a tour of the city—Inns of Chancery, Guild Hall—in a borrowed Rolls. Mike was bored in Westminster Abbey, thought the Elgin marbles were a broken discolored mess. He told a journalist the ancient Greek horses were too light and small to make much of a race at Hollywood Park or in the Belmont Stakes. He did have a suit tailored by Henry Poole in Savile Row.

* * *

Mostly he missed Martin to bounce ideas off of—to listen to his advice. But that couldn't be helped. There were the usual half-dozen urgent union problems to be faced: injunctions from Federal judges; harassment of the union's Board by discontents in some local, making false charges of misuse of power that had to be answered. Also fines for illegal striking or picketing to be knocked down by the friendly action of some favorite judge.

Miss Kline asked Mike if he'd like to see Lawrence Olivier at the Old Vic.

"No, but I could use some easy walking shoes."

"There are fine shoemakers—Maxwell's, Lobbs, and others . . ."

"Hell no, I've seen those heavy shoes, made of petrified orange peel; they weigh at least three pounds each."

"There's a Bally on New Bond Street. They make a light shoe."

"Good. Get them to send up half a dozen . . . size ten and a half . . . C width."

Miss Kline said that wouldn't do and badgered him into going to the shop in person. It was near noon as he walked down Old Bond Street. He was speaking in two days, and the damn speech seemed dull. Was he chicken and unsure of himself because he didn't know how to speak to an international labor gathering without the use of his usual hard-hitting ways? He had been drinking at the Green Man, the Salisbury, a bit too much. But it had no bite, and he was off his feed. The food at Rules didn't impress him, even if he sat under the caricatures of H. G. Wells and J. M. Barrie. And the waiter at Cunningham's seemed very snotty to a visiting American laying out ten pounds for a meal.

Mike entered Bally's, revived by the smell of fine leather, saddle soap. He looked around as a sales person advanced with that pleased smirk of an irked Uriah Heep (Miss Kline's view). Just then a woman swung into view.

She was trying on a dainty pair of dark brown pumps, had the most wonderful ankles Mike had ever seen. His glance followed the leg up to the calf and the stylish dark green skirt, and there he was, staring at Julia Brooks in a mannish hat set well to one side on her dark hair, olive and yellow scarf knotted loosely around her long neck.

Mike waved off the salesman. "Jesus H. Christ, somebody someplace has heard my prayers. Good morning, Miss Brooks."

The woman pivoted, looked around, surprised, but calm, and lifted her eyebrows as if spurring her memory. Then came the smile of good breeding, no matter under what condition.

"Who would curse his Redeemer on such a fine morning? Who but Mike Brant?"

He moved closer. "There's a lousy expression, 'a sight for sore eyes?' Take it for what it's worth."

She inspected him, still smiling: "You in London, and I'll be damned." She laughed. "Even the furled brolly."

"Brolly?"

"Umbrella. But no bowler."

The salesman was at his elbow. "Could I be of service, sir?"

"Not just now. Thanks anyway." He took Julia Brooks' arm. "Look, I bet you know this town?"

"This city, yes, I suppose I do."

"How about showing me where to have some food that isn't famous because some king gobbled it or full of wine sauces. And I don't want fish and chips either."

Julia Brooks looked him up and down, stepped out of the new shoe. "A bit more solid, a lot surer of yourself. You'll do, Brant."

"Don't ask me what I think of you, even if you kept giving me the brush."

She stepped into her old shoe. "I'm sorry." She didn't seem contrite. "All right. I'm hungry. Been to Locket's

. . . no? Good, well we'll eat there, and I'll introduce you to some of the Lords and members of Parliament who gather there."

"Only if you *don't* introduce me . . . you're buying shoes?"

"Three pair. I always do things by three."

She addressed a young woman behind a showcase. "Send them, please, to Lady Minton-Grams where I'm staying." She handed over a small card. "And put it on my account."

Mike had a glimpse of the two of them in a mirror as they walked toward the street: a big impressive man with solid features—you could call him handsome, in a hard-faced way, and his companion—a very elegant woman, slim, but not too slim, walking with well-bred grace. Mike felt: You lucky sonofabitch . . . if this isn't real, hold on anyway.

"Mind if I take your arm," she said.

He cocked an elbow. "There's no escape, Julia Brooks. So don't try."

He waved his brolly at a cab as he had seen other Londoners do. It seemed suddenly the most natural thing in the world to be here, with this beauty, this very desirable woman, and her holding on to his arm as she said: "Let the first two cabs go by. I really like to do things in three's."

Two hours later they were in Lady Minton-Grams' bed (she was fortunately away on a tour of the Greek Islands) making deeply felt love, naked body to naked body on the great Regency spread; they absorbed each other's action—passionate and vigorous. A Watteau sketch, a Rowlandson engraving of a country fair, and a painting of Malta, where the later Lord Henry Minton-Grams had commanded a naval flotilla in an early war, looked down upon them.

Preceding all this, the lunch had been mostly a confession by Mike of his long-held desire for her, gripping her hand, glove removed. He put it to her earnestly that he was a man who could love deeply, and that he had loved her since he had first seen her on that afternoon at the foundation meeting. He had fought it, he confessed; he had tried to ignore it. But he had called her place, the foundation, sent flowers. Now, he asked simply, what was going to happen to them?

He put it to her over the Dover sole; what now? Forget, he said, their situation, the impossibility of it, other problems to face. What's now?

She had put down her fish fork and knife and said there could only be two ways for this improbable situation to go. She could thank him for the lunch and be flattered by his avowal (he liked that word *avowal*), avowal of his so personal interest in her. She knew, she added, it was no casual adventure he sought, and she was no sexual adventuress. Whatever had been, her marriages and some intense friendships since, she knew a serious emotional crisis when faced by it. The maitre d' came up and asked if the sauterne had been all right; Mike nodded, waved him off. They had sat there, looking closely at each other, hands held across the table over the melba toast.

He had said there was nothing for it but to go to bed. She sat for a few moments not saying anything, and for Mike, the darkest moment of his soldier life in Korea returned. Then she spoke simply, in a controlled tone of voice as he asked for the bill. "I think we've had enough."

He followed her out to a cab, then they rode to a fine house on the eastern side of Berkeley Square, went up a grand staircase. On the upper landing he had seized her and felt her body arch against him. Her buttocks stiffened, her mouth opened. They kissed and sent each other's hands to search about. Then she said, breathing a bit hard, a moisture on her brow, "We had better go to bed right away, my darling," and he agreed.

* * *

She was even more amazing to him naked than in the clothes she wore with such grace. So they lay together and engaged in a sexual coming together, fierce but understanding. She was so marvelous in his grip . . . spread-eagled, so active under him, so relating to his every move and thrust that he sensed he had arrived at something in his life from which he must not part. Her orgasm was prolonged into a series of little gasping deaths and recoveries . . . her wide open blue-green eyes kept their focus on his face; she never swooned away into a state of closed-eye ecstasy. He had felt the gradual amazement of a greater fury of passion, something that he felt he'd lost years ago, that innocent, egotistical delight at the power of glands to rule one's body and mind with such intensity.

Afterward they lay for some time recovering breath, pulses slowing, arms around each other. She began to rub her head against his chest, began to produce from that marvelous torso and throat a purring sound. She returned to that calmness of expression that she normally wore, but her fine limbs began a kind of ballet movement against his body, and with a delicate, yet bold, butterfly flutter her long fingers shamelessly explored his body. This was no dominated female love-object subservient to a dominating male. Such boldness!

They made love again and prolonged it, and now her body, lightly covered in sweat, seemed tired, but still ardent. They lay side by side in Lady Minton-Grams' bed; the traffic outside in the square seemed unreal, like a recording. A faint breeze stirred the drapes, coming from the six inches of raised window.

After some time she suggested a drink of brandy, and he, naked, found in a paneled room a rack of cut-glass decanters and poured two inches of amber brandy into two snifters, took them back to the bedroom. She lay, he thought, like some pearl in a giant oyster, and there his imagination failed him. For beyond that image he had no verbal resources to make images—only the conviction he must never lose her . . . but how?

He looked down at her body spread upon that bed, a satin pillow behind the dark disorder of her hair that smelled of her—that of a woman, not a bottled dew . . . the fine tits, taut (he was never able to think of the word *breasts* as satisfactory), her pubic area hardly hairy at all—just some dark fuzz. He handed her a glass, and he stood looking down at her as they warmed the glasses with the palms of their hands and sipped and looked at each other with satisfaction.

Yes, he knew he had satisfied her, perhaps even carried her beyond some boundary she had not passed before. He was sure she had flung aside whatever restraints had held her from responding to his first efforts to reach her. He was aware that she loved him as much as he loved her. If so, it could be there was another self—not a bastard called Mike Brant of the DWU. But that didn't matter now. This could be the jackpot of his life, his private life.

He leaned over and poured some of the brandy over her pubic area. Maybe it was a shock; she did twitch, but her eyes followed his action as he lowered his head, nuzzled her between her damp thighs and put his tongue into her.

After awhile she said, "Enough of that . . . my darling, come up here and make it three."

Neither suspected the years ahead and how long this implacable, impossible love affair would last.

CHAPTER 31

The Uroan Bati Congressional Commission in 1972 was focusing its attention on certain union activities in politics, and calling witnesses the unions favored, or those people that could be used in strengthening union power.

Mike Brant of the DWU was one of these called to testify before Senator Bati's committee. Mike had been living for some years in Washington, in a large Regency house on H Street, the house and its furnishings a gift collected by contributions to the union, on his success in enlarging the DWU's power. He was living with a very beautiful woman, had been for some years. Gossip columnists made items: "Big Eyes" on the *Washington Observer* identified her "as good and dear friend, Julia Brooks;" "City Wise," of the *Washington Banner* mentioned them as often attending an embassy party or the preview of some show, hopefully, bound for Broadway: "One of the most powerful union figures in the nation,

Michael Brant, and his constant companion for many years, Julia Brooks (one of the ten best dressed women in the Capitol) sat through the first act of 'Rough and Ready' on opening night and decided it might have been rough but was certainly not ready ... "

Beyond such items, no one really pried; it was a respectable menage, and only a sensational magazine, *Secret Scenes*, which didn't survive long, compared them to the Tracy-Hepburn long-standing romance under the title "The Roughnecks and the Ladies."

The new DWU building was rising in Washington, fifteen stories of solid stone (union cut) and bronze, standing on stilts, a tropical rain forest at its base, with a Henry Moore styled modern sculpture, an abstract figure of a man and a woman worker, hands clasped over their heads. Mike had wanted Julia to dedicate the building on its completion, aided by Bishop Waldmer and Rabbi Ellenbogen, but she had shaken her head as they sat discussing it in dressing robes, having breakfast in the sunroom overlooking the flowering garden Julia took so much pride in.

"Just remember, darling, even that event—our relationship—can be brought up at the Bati hearing."

"He's running around with a chippie stripper himself."

Julia had matured without growing plumper; there was still the fine delicate skin, the same blue-green eyes (behind the contact lenses she wore more often). She had cured herself of nail-biting, but had to watch out to keep from pulling on her fingers at times. Mike, she had to admit, had gone a bit gross but was still massively handsome in certain lights. His jowls were now more noticeable, his front teeth had been skillfully capped; and while his hair had thinned, combed in a certain way, it still would, as Julia said, serve.

They had remained very much in love with each other: wisely understood the tolerances one had to give and make while living with someone. Julia was given to long periods of vocal, not loud, brooding, but she usually lived on a placid level, was always ready—if not eager—to make love, to accompany him on some irksome journey. She could travel with only a shoulder bag and one suitcase if she had to and still appear beautiful, well-dressed, and with a sense of grace. She was able to make herself interesting to an Arab degenerate rich in oil, a steward of a grease-rendering factory unit (oy!), or the weatherbeaten wife of a crop picker (the DWU had not yet been able to establish a solid field workers and farm hands union). At times she suffered from migraines and read her daily horoscope in the paper.

Mike had grown harder, less resilient, more opinionated, but he could still charm, relate well to problems and solve them. He had not become cynical, but there was a touch of tired irony, a far off stare in his eyes (he now used eyeglasses in private) as if searching for some valid clue to something he never discussed, even with his brother.

Martin had filled out a bit but was still slim—had the face of a wise, young priest. He headed a legal force of twenty-six lawyers who kept the DWU swimming safely in the sea of problems, assaults, and infighting which made the law and the law courts the testing ground of Mike's domain. And as Martin admitted, the covering up of much of certain DWU activities was a problem.

Mike was working in collusion with industrial management. By passing some state councils he was centralizing area-wide bargaining to get uniform wages, hours. He did not permit discontent when he felt it to be unfair in some locals. Martin had to plead nolo contendere on a Federal charge of conspiracy to force out certain rival unions. It was no secret that he used mob alliance to perpetuate power. Some said Mike had a talent for subterfuge and deceit . . . others that he was a genius at collective bargaining and the handling of financial affairs, the welfare funds channeled through David L. Wasserman—known as "The Money Tree."

Martin saw to it that the DWU certified bargaining rights were binding in their claims, controlled the bargaining representatives for all locals dominated. Local autonomy existed on paper, with certain added clauses that hamstrung them. The DWU was known to be aggressive and challenging; its General Executive Board approved expanding beyond the normal DWU boundaries. It set up coordinating bargaining units with satellite unions in far-flung industries; enjoyed collaboration, expansion, interrelationships close to illegal restraints, such as banned secondary pressures of boycotts.

It was the year that the Puskin executive council voted the full expulsion of the DWU from the WNUSA. Of this long-threatened, long-expected action that lost the WNUSA a third of its membership, Mike said, "About time." His reaction was indifference. He sat in his splendid tenth-floor suite of offices in the new DWU building; a suite not yet fully finished: wall paneling, some lighting fixtures were still to be placed.

"We've been the tail wagging the goddam WNUSA dog long enough. So they don't like our progress or how we do. But we're practical—pay is bigger, benefits stronger, and the health and welfare pension funds the largest of any union . . . and growing."

Martin and Davey Wasserman, sitting across from Mike in deep blue leather chairs, could only agree. Martin saw it as, "A time that had to come. We were always an outlaw union to the Puskin boys. But those boys copy our methods as much as they can, controlling all potential sources of power by wide organizing, and they're not above using hard pressures."

Mike waved off any more talk on the subject. "What about the Tri-State damage suits against us?"

"We're going to lose that one . . . damages for allegedly destroying their merchandizing system by terror and sabotage."

Davey said, "We don't lose many, Mike. Few suits against the DWU are successful. Mike has this wacky idea, Martin: We get firms we are cozy with to buy out the suing companies, then set up costly legal obstacles to collect damage awards."

Martin smiled. "And how are these sweetheart companies going to buy out the firms suing us?"

Mike sat back in his chair and picked up a tan, flame-grained pipe bought in Paris that spring.

"I've talked this over with Davey. Our health and welfare funds loan them the money. Any such firms that lack the financial resources, we help them."

Martin sat very still; when he spoke his voice was low. "It's just legal, but, Mike, it's *very* dangerous."

Martin saw Mike as a general—win battles, sacrifice soldiers to do it.

"If any local gets obstreperous, Martin, you get court orders against them for us to take over office funds, properties . . . the DWU board to be declared certified bargaining agent for all disloyal locals. Make it damn clear our best interest requires only *one* bargaining representative for all area units that give us trouble. And be sure the right man is picked."

Council control of the union was so firm, so soon in Mike's hand, and in the hands of his well-picked assistants, that resolutions he thought bad, or going against his own position were never reported out of committee. At conventions any rival or doubter was defeated by Jamie Ward or Spinelli, each with pockets full of proxie votes. To get votes Mike didn't mind alignment with radical unions—the Marxist tainted Mutual Mill Workers of the Southwest, the hard hat Bircher-salted Mechanics and Welders Association of the northwestern border states.

In the Senate hearing chamber Senator Uroan Bati

fingered some sheets of paper folded twice. "I have here, Mr. Brant, an official petition given me in St. Louis by the *New Force United DWU Committee*."

Mike shrugged. "They're some leftist bastards . . . troublemakers. No official standing in the unions . . . their charter revoked."

"Tell me if the figures I'm going to read are correct."

Martin objected. "These are not certified figures."

"Go ahead, Senator, let's hear what those commies have sent you."

"They claim it can all be proved. I quote:

"'The rank and file each pay three-hundred twenty dollars to four-hundred dollars a year in dues. The leadership enjoys benefits unmatched in any other union and in few corporations today.

"'The top DWU appear as executives with six-figure salaries, including free vacations, French chefs at headquarters in Washington. Besides the big executive jet, there are three jets and turboprops. The air force of the DWU is one of the largest private fleets in the country. Last year ten officials received two hundred thousand dollars a year, with some getting more than two hundred fifty thousand dollars.' Unquote."

"All proper, Senator."

"You, Brant, get three hundred twenty-five thousand dollars, plus expenses. Multiple salaries in the DWU are common. James Ward holds ten posts, including 'general organizer,' a title you give out at will. It brings few duties and carries a one hundred forty thousand dollar salary."

"And he earns it."

"You earn your three hundred twenty-five thousand dollars a year . . . plus?"

"I do . . . as do Henry Ford II, David Rockefeller . . . the NBC, the CBS, the ITT brass. It's what's being paid for good men. And goddammit . . . pardon me, Senator, I'm good!"

"Good enough so Local 188 in Ohio gave one hundred

seventy-two thousand dollars in bonuses to three of your officials, including the president and his son, and the secretary-treasurer. And deals on cars—nine DWU officials each bought surplus late model autos from the union for a total of twelve hundred dollars. Top officials got fully paid vacations with expenses for wives, secretaries, aides, and dogs?"

Martin said, "Senator, this is not on any record."

"Which doesn't prove it didn't happen. The DWU, unlike colleagues in the WNUSA and LBO unions who prohibit salaried officials from being paid for running pension funds, have set up these funds as another source of bounty. For managing the fund David Wasserman got nearly one hundred twenty thousand dollars over and above his regular salary of one hundred forty-six thousand dollars, and the one hundred thirty thousand eight hundred ninety dollars he got as a general insurance organizer."

"He is a most able man."

"Non-DWU people share the pension riches. The administrators of the insurance units, Leonard and Morris Katenstein, were paid eight hundred seventy-eight thousand nine hundred dollars from insurance assets. That's for last year."

"Our audits, Senator, show a healthy condition."

"I have official figures on losses you've had to take on land speculation—three hundred ten million dollars on a loan to enterprises by the DWU health and pension fund, brokered by George Spinelli and and Giovanni Finsillo, also known as John Fiora, who have been listed as national crime figures."

Martin rose, spoke calmly: "Gentlemen of this committee, and Senator Bati, I must advise the witness to withdraw from this hearing if it continues to fling about unproved charges and gossip. Neither Mr. Spinelli nor Mr. Fiora has been indicted, tried, or convicted as major crime figures. What of hundreds of others who are helped by the DWU . . . while the reckless press and a publicity-seeking minority in the Justice Department make unproved charges. This is not right or proper."

"We are concerned here, in questioning Michael Brant, whether huge sums of money are flowing from the coffers of the DWU."

Mike stood up. "Any money flowing is from our banks, not coffers, and is properly invested for income with American business. We make loans, invest in corporations, not in individuals. Individuals, of course, form corporations; these are properly and legally formed companies. I'm tired of having the DWU smeared every time some crackpot editor wants a story. I'm leaving this hearing."

"You are leaving yourself open for a charge of contempt of the Senate."

Martin put a hand on Mike's arm. "When this hearing of respectful members of the Senate will bring facts, not hearsay, on the use of union funds before us, Mr. Brant stands willing to answer all questions."

The hearings ended in a week with promises of future investigations.

Mike put it to Martin as they read a report of the hearings. "Does it have to be as that English dude you're always quoting has it—that all power corrupts?"

"It doesn't have to be, but to get results it usually works out that way. No matter what government or organization you dream up, no matter how high its ideals, there is corruption, which doesn't mean a tainted government or organization doesn't do some good."

Mike grinned. "You trying to soft-soap me? Hell, Moz, I know I've been corrupted . . . am as corrupt as some of the Senators sitting on their prostrates . . . they judging me? But the whole magillah, it all added up, even if some of the figures were phony. I hadn't figured things were *that* bad. The boys have been really feathering their nests. To you, I admit it's my fault they're stealing the union blind."

"You going to clean house?"

"Ha, I'm up to my neck in it. You know damn well the biggest boddle-grabbers are my best people. They get things done. Besides, they would no more let go without making a big stink than I can be a choirboy again. Or you, Moz."

"I'm just the towel boy. But you better start warning the boys to trim the fat—ease off—and not be so greedy."

Mike tapped his lower lip with a fist. "I'm like the guy who fell head first into the outdoor privy, and while sinking, yelled, 'fire!' When they dragged him out they asked, why did you yell fire? He said, 'Would you have come if I yelled shit?!' . . . I've got to keep yelling fire for the survival of the union, and me . . ., but I'm beginning to smell the crap."

DWU LABOR LEADER WARNS ON
"DISRUPTION" BY DISSIDENTS

Chicago—Union President Michael Brant said at an appearance here that the only possibility of a nationwide strike by the DWU would be if the union was provoked by dissident members.

Brant made the statement in response to a question at the annual Conference of Workers' Welfare Ball. The issue is of concern since the 2-million-member union is under investigation.

His statement appeared to be in response to a meeting of dissidents earlier this week in Memphis, at which about 350 DWU'ers vowed to unseat Brant on grounds of corruption.

Although the powerful union president first pledged an "expose of radicals," he then referred to reform movements in other unions and tied it into the DWU. Questions from the press were not permitted, and it was not clear what Brant meant. He discussed "Marxist dominated fanatics—forces which still proclaim socialist programming."

He said, "They've thrown charges against me and every time that they have a meeting with six or seven people, the media is there . . . television . . ., and as far as the actual fact is concerned, it's all twisted to fit cheap hits . . . press sensations. The Drovers and Wheelmens Union is the workers' trusted friend—except for a few (obscenity deleted) lamebrained halfwits."

CHAPTER 32

If some rivals developed an ill-conceived ambition to begin a remove Brant movement, they were exposed as embezzlers, freeloaders who fed off union funds. At times there were beating and bombings. However, there was never any proof that the death of a rival—Kivis Ames, Los Angeles business agent for DWU—in a fire-bombed ranch in Nevada, or the thirty-story fall of Mason Chararoff, a union leader under indictment to produce health welfare records, was the result of Mike's complaints to Spinelli. Dissenting officials soon found they had no appeal but to Mike, but it was doubted by Martin that any deaths had originated with his brother.

Mike's best ploy to get rid of rivals was to accuse them of undermining the progress and the DWU standards. Mike had extreme tenacity, and by this time, it was clear the national president, with his aggressive and challenging drives had won bigger benefits, inflated guarantees, additional holidays for the members, and he alone decid-

ed which were the better contracts. He also was beginning to drop his old lieutenants when they seemed to fail
to grow or understand that their positions rested on the
emphasis of a personal and supreme loyalty.

Martin fought bitterly over the retiring of Jamie Ward.
He and Mike, in a Miami hotel suite for a national convention, were going over the secret funds which were
passed on to certain key congressmen and senators up for
re-election in heavy industrial regions.

"Why dump him? Jamie has been good at this slush
funding, Mike."

"Jamie is going on pension as of next month."

"Christ, Mike, he helped you up, taught you a hell of a
lot, and he'd cut his arm off for you up to here."

"I've got a one-armed man already." Mike reached for a
pipe from the rack. "He'll be taken care of. He's a sick
man . . . those ulcers."

"He's always had them, Mike. You're kicking him out.
He's said something that riled you, hasn't he? How you
delegate less and less authority . . ."

"Jamie is a good joe, and I like him. But he's also an old
fart, still a romantic socialist about the noble workers.
Like it's painted on the wall in murals. Workers are
mean, tough, real, like the rest of us. Jamie, he doesn't
trust a computer, or brain-storing, or surveys. 'Touch the
flesh,' he says. He's got to shake horny hands and ask
how many cavities the worker's kid has. Nice, nice
touch, but . . ."

"You know that isn't why you're giving him the heave
ho. Like you did Donaldson and Kahn and Adamson.
They and Jamie wanted it explicitly spelled out as to the
rights of any union head to control and negotiate personally all contracts and policies."

Mike laughed—looked down on the Florida landscape,
"*You* added those constitutional changes as to the valid-
ity of my actions. Look, let's enjoy this convention."

"Mike, you know any challenge in the courts of our charter changes by amendments that the whole union didn't vote on, is shaky, and you can be in a jam. Let me talk to Jamie to soft pedal."

Mike stared at his brother, eyes unblinking. Martin heard the pipe stem break in Mike's fingers.

Jamie Ward retired to raise Big Boy tomatoes in Orange County, California after he tore up the photograph Mike had signed, "*To the one and only Jamie, who taught me all, Mike.*"

Jamie Ward was not the only member of the old group that was retired. Terry had some years before moved to Santa Barbara on the West Coast. She and Paul had acquired a villa on Pineknot Road, a small but well-built structure of gray stone with a red-tile roof. A wide slope of garden backed by Japanese pines led to a view down to the Bay; behind it, mountains, gray-violet in color, and hills where there were other houses, lined both sides. There was a blue Mercedes, a Spanish-speaking maid, Chita, who preferred to do her work barefooted, her cooking on charcoal.

Terry, in her forties, seemed to have acquired dignity and poise. She wore her gray hair cut short and was healthier. Her skin was tanned and weathered; she looked more alert than in the bad years in Kansas City. She was now an active member of the local branch of Alcoholics Anonymous, available at all hours for the call of help from a failing member. She herself would fall from the wagon perhaps once a year, go up to San Francisco to a small hotel with a half-dozen bottles of Old Forester, and return in a week or so, soberly under control.

Chita knew better than to talk back for a few days; then the routine of the red-roofed villa went back to its regular, rather casual, but pleasant way of life. There was shopping, planning meals, watching television, reading, handball on a small court behind the garage; Terry, Chita, and Paul (growing tall) banging out a wild but rather strenuous game.

Twice a week Terry and Paul went for tennis at the Bayside Club. One night a week, usually a Tuesday, she went to Montecito to visit a young, bearded guru, Sri Kelly. Here, after a few bits of meditating and some going through the simpler lotus positions, they would rub their naked bodies with scented cocoa butter and make love in the styles of Shiva.

Life was satisfactory, and Terry's relationship with Mike was long-distance and coolly friendly. There had never been any talk of a divorce after Mike had made it clear he was setting up permanently with Julia Brooks and didn't want to hide it from Terry. He gave no detailed reason for the change in their life pattern. None was needed, he felt, beyond the fact that he was infatuated with the woman. Terry referred to Julia as "that high-assed society cunt," and without making a fuss, had agreed to a parting. Mike had some time before seen that Terry became the major owner of a series of industrial laundry and maintenance services. This was arranged for Mike by George Spinelli, whose family was involved in many such projects—in cross-country auto hauling from distant factories and handling and processing factory wastes.

Terry's holdings brought her in a good income, and she had little to do with their management but to sign, twice a year, certain papers and deposit the checks that Davey Wasserman's accounting office sent her.

She was not a forgiving soul, and no matter how Sri Kelly had her meditate on the worthlessness of worldly desires and physical manifestations, she could never fully forgive or accept Mike's position, or see Julia Brooks as anything but a conniving bitch who had knocked off Mike, seduced him with her society airs and her fancy

jet-set background—these appealing to Mike's snob-
bery—a Polak's idea of class. Terry could not imagine
how Mike could ever love anyone as he had loved her.

Paul, as he grew older, went back East, usually in July
to visit two weeks with his father and Aunt Julia. He accepted a dad in the East and a mom in the West. Paul was
a polite boy, given to observing and enjoying his visits; he
had a secret liking for Aunt Julia. She favored sailing and
fed him things he liked that Ma called bad for him.

Mike, on his visits to the West Coast would sometimes
come out to the Santa Barbara villa for lunch. Chita
would serve chili-seasoned sea bass or Spanish chicken
and rice; the three of them eating on the sun-flooded terrace in good weather.

"A very nice view," Mike observed.

"Dad, you'll stay for the sailboat races tomorrow . . ."

"Your father is a busy man."

"I have to be in San Diego tomorrow, son, but if I come
back next year, for sure."

"I'll be old enough for the junior races, huh?"

"We'll wait a few years, thank you, if you don't mind.
Paul, it's time to walk Tiger."

The boy was aware it was time to leave his parents
alone, and he went to find the fat Victorian pug that preferred to stay in the house and sleep on his cushion rather
than enjoy the open country.

"How you making out, Terry?"

"I'm making out . . ."

"Paul looks fine. How's his school work?"

"Passable. He's more interested in machinery, short-
wave radio . . . taking the Waring mixer apart."

"He's a good kid . . . anything he needs, you need?"

Terry set down her coffee cup with a bang. "Jesus,
Mike, stop playing the guilty husband making small talk
he doesn't give a shit about."

"You're getting paranoid, you know that, Terry?"

"You're getting the best of everything: that society

pussy *and* a little look-see at your dear little family." She shook her head. "I'm sorry, Mike; the old scar tissue still aches. I wish you well; climb as high as you can on the bitch goddess success. It's really the true you . . . the climber . . . the rest of us—with you, without you—don't really count."

Mike stood up, leaned over and kissed Terry on the brow. "On that good-sounding note I'm going to pull tracks. I'll see Paul down the path."

"Wait till your tootsie Julia catches on to you."

She waved her hand in a farewell gesture, and somehow nothing mattered. She didn't need a drink and soon, thank God, they would all be dead a hundred years.

CHAPTER 33

Mike's visits West were eventually neither pleasant for Mike or Terry. In the next few years Mike worked in the DWU to remove fully what he had so long fought to establish, the jealously-held local autonomy. He broke these rights by amendments to the DWU constitution, even secretly supporting corporations to stand against union demands and then moving in to settle matters properly, for what he called "group welfare against individual issues."

Davey Wasserman had shown how money was the source of power, particularly of union power. He forged the use of a chain of recipient banks as deposits for DWU funds, spending millions in friendly banks and certain insurance companies for whom cousins of his were the agents.

"The power of the purse, Mike . . . it's better than being a purveyor of violence. Money . . . funds, investments are what give us the muscle."

* * *

Mike was eating lunch with Davey at the Burning Tree Club in Washington, D.C. and agreed: "We may even do better to bypass the banks . . . someday lend directly to the proper people, Davey—those we can trust: lawyers, accountants, consultants, politicians. Our kind of supporters."

"You mean lend bigger?"

"Lend for sanitariums, sports resorts, nursing homes, shopping centers. So people can see we are helping needed things that workers also can enjoy. The country is getting crowded. Land developing should be a very big thing."

"The Spinellis and the Fioras are really going into that. On our funds."

Mike forked at his boned blue trout. He was becoming less interested in food, in the theatre; most of his needs seemed to be satisfied by running the DWU. Julia was a good sport (his version was she didn't seem to mind). Over the coffee, which Mike liked very strong and to which he added a great deal of cream and two spoons of sugar, he asked: "What's with Montross-Cane, that goddam department store chain?"

Davey looked at two girls in scanty sports attire.

"We're getting no place with certain demands for collective bargaining. You'd think with outside financial people trying to take over the present board, they would play ball with us. Not run the risk of unionized help walkouts."

Mike sipped the coffee slowly, its thick sugary flavor reminded him of Mom's coffee when he was a teenager home with a sore throat; Mom used to make him sweet coffee even better than this.

"Who's behind the takeover of Montross-Cane?"

"The Andersons—Colorado yokels with a lot of oil dinaro."

"Buy, Davey, two million dollars worth of Montross-

Cane stock. We'll maybe hint we'll support the Andersons, the outsiders to win a proxie battle to take over."

"Will that be enough?" asked Davey Wasserman.

"If not, buy two million more. Check with Martin how to do this legally for the union. Who's the big shot at MC who hates our guts?"

"General Harden—Elmer 'Three Star' Harden—very hard-nosed old bastard."

"Hell, he'll be kissing our ass in full uniform in a week not to support a takeover by outsiders."

The general, however, didn't try to make contact with the new owners of so much MC stock. But a certain Chicago law firm noted for its high fees, dishonesty to certain of its clients, did ask Martin and Mike to have lunch at the Sky Harbor Athletic Club with a vice president of the department store chain.

General Harden retired to grow roses in LaJolla.

Not only did the union funds make a good profit when the stock went up on the news that new directors had successfully fought off a raid by outsiders, but that the Drovers Wheelmens Union had been invited in by management to set up collective bargaining, compulsory union membership—thus avoiding damaging profit losses by a strike.

It was a new development in union methods to bend huge companies to their will, and Mike was to use it several times against some industries that stubbornly refused to deal properly. Not until Federal injunctions began to limit the buying of stocks in corporations for certain reasons not related to mere investment of funds did Mike change his viewpoint.

Serious warfare developed between the DWU and the WNUSA. There were savage street battles to break rival picket lines. Then in a fight among the canneries and food packers all along the West Coast where the WNUSA locals were fighting hard to organize fully, the DWU began to make sweetheart agreements with canners and processors, offering union guards to keep the WNUSA organizers from approaching the fields and canneries—beating up organizers (WNUSA men), when they appeared.

The sheriffs and local police seemed always to stand by until the organizers were well-bloodied before making arrests, usually of the WNUSA people. However, Mike could not keep the National Labor Relations Board from demanding new supervised elections with secret ballots.

Mike, at this news, gave orders: "Beef up our organizers, field foremen and get a legal brief filed that we consider this election illegal, they're voting wetbacks and other cruds against us."

Turmoil in the canneries and fields continued. The elections were confused—often invalidated—neither side seemed to have a victory. Mike put aside the taking over into the DWU of the cannery and farm workers for the time being. He hated to lose, but he also, as yet, knew when to let the dust settle and prepare for a new attack.

Mike had delayed appearing before the renewed Bati Committee, but he could no longer avoid that scene. Martin had prepared a series of papers indicating which subjects Mike could testify on and which he was to avoid getting entangled with. "Bati wants a shot at the White House—so watch out."

The day he was to appear Mike awoke as usual at six o'clock, heard the birds in the garden start their chirping, the newsboy's car as he dropped the *New York Times, Washington Post* and *Star* in the driveway. He and Julia had since their first days together slept in a huge double bed. He sat up, inhaled deeply and exhaled a few times . . . got out of the bed carefully. Julia slept on her side, turned away from him. She was a good, untroubled sleeper, and in her transparent nightgown she looked

beautiful, desirable. After all these years he still had this
yen for her.

For a moment he was undecided; he was on the verge
of a hard-on; could knock off a wonderful quickie with a
drowsy, responsive Julia becoming more and more
awake, until suddenly, he turned her on her back for a direct attack.

He decided against it. In his mid-forties Mike still
could perform, he was sure, when in the mood, like any
of the young studs. But he had some thinking over to do
about his appearance in the Senate hearing chamber. He
shed his sleeping pants, no tops ever, went into the black,
glass and silver bathroom. He performed his morning duties, shaved closely. On the john he figured out his opening statement to the press boys before entering the hearing chamber. He dressed in a pale blue shirt, a neat dark
brown suit. Downstairs, Wagner, the German butler-
valet, was stirring about, seeing to the breakfast setting
in the sunroom. Hilda, his wife, was in the kitchen brewing strong coffee and preparing Mike's breakfast.

Wagner was stiff—had short, bristling straw hair, and
was as formal as a Nazi *Gauleiter* (maybe he had been,
Mike would sometimes think with a smile).

Wagner set down and flattened with a heavy hand, the
three newspapers on Mike's right.

"It looks ein fine day, sir."

"Sunny, anyway."

"There was talk, sir, on the *rood*io of this morning's in-
quist."

"Dammit, Wagner, this isn't Nazi Germany, it's just a
hearing. Now get me the eggs and bacon."

While he ate, Mike saw he had made the front pages of
all three newspapers. He consumed the eggs and bacon,
three hot biscuits with butter, and had his organic juice
afterward, as was his habit. He ate some bran and four
stewed prunes, two stewed figs. Tensions having to do
with Federal matters always made him irregular. He

went into the garden after glancing over the front pages of the papers. He wasn't in the mood to dig out the gossipy items he and Julia enjoyed and were amused by. Wagner had turned out the two house dogs, Balzac, Julia's gray poodle, and Sam, Mike's who-knows-what—a mutt he had picked up as a discarded puppy on the New Jersey Turnpike—it being in danger, as it whimpered, of being flattened by the traffic.

Sam came over frisking and lapping, gave his short bark, whip tail swinging. Balzac came over with a wary cock of his tailored, well-cut head of pearly colored hair. Mike had been known to kick him in moments of exasperation.

The garden looked well; a bit too formal. Wagner dominated the old black gardener who came twice a week to water and take care of the flower beds. Mike would have preferred a wilder garden, something somewhat more natural, untamed. But he had no time to argue it out with the damn Nazi. If Wagner and Hilda didn't do such a great job of taking care of them and the house, he'd have had a jolly old-fashioned darky couple toting for them, with the fake shuffle and all.

When Mike came into the house with the dogs he was surprised to find Julia up, wearing a floating pale rose gown. She usually slept till ten, had her bath, attended to her cosmetic needs; she rubbed most of her body with ice cubes for ten minutes every day—examined herself for moles (there were very few), saw she was still smoothly hairless as to legs and face—the breasts with just a bit of a sagging.

In her forties, Julia had retained much of her beauty, her grace, but she imagined she felt a tightness in certain joints. Her hair was still its dark night coils but now a bit of chemical aid was called for. She did not desperately fight aging, but she resented it. Certain little lines around the eyes, a little slackness in the chin line, if she got careless when she moved and talked. She did not fear Mike would lose interest in her. He satisfied her need of "a violent barbarian," as she thought of him—a brute with great affection. Her two husbands, the love affairs before meeting Mike, had never been rough enough to be satisfactory. Mike, on the other hand, in his direct assault—his fierce lovemaking—had fully delighted her. She never admitted to him that she no longer was carried away by sexual ecstasy; she continued serving his needs with no resentment—took comfort in knowing he took such violent pleasure in her.

She was happy in the solid companionship, in the vividness of their lives in Washington society. She did not try to appraise his union activities. She avoided thinking what he did could be wrong, often debased. He was her lover, her reason for being. She now said, as she surveyed the breakfast table, "It's a special day and I want to send my warrior off properly."

"Oh hell, I've been before these cockamamie committees before. Goddam showoffs for the television bastards."

She saw him to the side door where the big Caddy waited (he would have preferred a Rolls but that was not made by American union men) with Wagner opening the door . . . Solly Bianca at the wheel. Solly was one of Spinelli's best drivers, rumored to be an old hit man, retired because of a shotup leg.

Julia kissed Mike, and he got in. He'd pick up Martin on the way. He waved to Julia and the dogs.

He breezed through the hearings with ease. Senator Bati was now aware of the huge army of voters the DWU could send to the polls, and he did have his eye and hopes on the White House.

CHAPTER 34

In 1974 it was clear to Mike that he would have to fight to continue his hold on the DWU leadership. Besides a rising tide of opposition from men surrounding Kingbird DuBois, who was feeling his power in an expanding, industrial South and beginning to encroach on certain rights which Mike felt belonged to the national organization, other Justice Department hearings continued— were issuing reports damaging to some of the men around Mike.

George Spinelli was named as one of the five ruling dons in the Chicago area; the Department of Justice identified him as *capo de capo*, boss of the bosses. George had turned most of his union activities over to his nephew John Fiora and had built for himself, at Elmwood, in the suburbs of the city, a half-million-dollar estate with a marble-lined swimming pool, a lily garden, three tennis courts (one grass), and a half-mile, private racetrack to watch his trotters and pacers work out. He had become mad for harness racing—breeding the pacer, Pale Fire. In rose-colored stone, imported from Sicily, he had erected a shrine to Saint Concetta Calogero of Palermo— *Sempre sorda*—in memory of his mother.

Although there was a danger of their phones being tapped, Mike called Spinelli: "A hell of a note, George, a hell of a note that Department of Justice hanging that capo tag on you."

"Well, Mikey, they're always trying. Think nothing of it. How's our friend Davey?"

"Fine. He got married, you know. Nice Jewish girl; family in iron and steel, tearing up old railroad tracks— cutting up Vietnam war surplus ships."

"Tell him his collection of old Chinese pots is going at a good price. Lots of talk. He ought to sell."

"I'll pass it along, George. Keep your pecker up."

Chinese pots was a code word for loans the union's Health, Welfare, and Pension funds were lending to special friends of the union. Such friends were okayed by confidants of Spinelli for union loans which were okayed by Davey Wasserman. As George Spinelli put it, "When Johnny Fiora speaks for a loan to someone, he speaks for me." Most of these loans were listed under strange categories—to a front or dummy organization.

Davey struggled to keep ahead of being submerged in the confusion of records. He had two nephews, Lennie, an insurance broker, and Morris, a CPA. They handled the union's insurance and compensation policies as agents for two major insurance companies that were willing to overlook certain extra fees and commissions to shadowy secondary agents, as well as the fees and costs paid to Lennie and Morrie Katenstein as "discovery brokers."

The Justice Department was insisting that a check be made on all funds borrowed from the unions. Mike, to better control these checks, began to create a pool incorporating twenty-eight of the states' funds into *one* big fund. This was headquartered in Kansas City as the Inter-State Areas Health and Welfare Pension Fund. Mike had it administered by six people, including Davey Wasserman and John Fiora. Federal investigators soon reported they suspected the fund was one of the major bankers to "wash" mob crime money in America.

It was a huge fund; the various branches of the DWU delivered into the fund a million three hundred thousand dollars a day.

Martin, weekending at Saratoga with Mike, shook his head at these figures: "You can hide what you're doing with say half a million in loans; you can cover what's being done with a million or so in loans. But, Mike, in the last fiscal year—listen to me—there are total assets of over two billion dollars in the fund. Davey doesn't really know where this is all being invested or loaned."

They were in a box at the Saratoga Track Club. Mike didn't seem impressed. "Over half, Moz, nearly nine hundred million is real estate loans. That's above board."

Martin had folded into his racing program the yearly union report—a private one for only six people. "The union owns three hundred million in real estate because of defaulted loans. The Justice Department and IRS are going to question *that* with lifted eyebrows. We know who's got those loans and who walked off with them to Swiss numbered accounts, leaving the WDU fund holding the bag."

"Moz, that's a legit business risk . . . at worst, bad judgment. Hell, look at the Edsel car, the movie *Cleopatra*; someone made wrong guesses there, too . . . who do you like in the third race?"

"Mike, we have made some really crazy loans. Just a dozen people in Chicago, Vegas, and L.A.—the Fioras, the Brutzos—seem to be getting a lot more in loans than most anybody else."

"Let me watch the goddam races."

Mike beat the ends of his fingers together. He looked tense, and there was a rising anger as shown by the quiver of his jowl muscles.

"Dammit—don't I have enough with Kingbird boring from within and the Feds making *turiz* . . . do I have to listen to you croaking on about how things are? I need these capa people or we would be out in the cold on the balls of our ass. The workers are loyal to me, you saw that when I got in Seattle, in Denver. . . . The horses are parading . . . I got a G on Run Steady. . . . "

"Why shouldn't rank and file love you . . . you've given them high pay, big fringe benefits, health insurance. But that's not what the problem is, Mike . . . I think over a billion dollars of fund money has gone down some rat hole. Somebody will go to jail for it."

"Don't be a gloomy gus . . . it would take years to untangle the books, and by that time we'll have maybe four, five billion on tap. Haven't we hired an old FBI guy, Maxwell Case, like the Feds wanted, keeping his eyes on things for us?"

Martin laughed, and not because he was amused. "Mike, Mike, we're paying this soft-shoe creeper a hundred grand a year, mostly to wear blinkers you wouldn't dare put on one of those race horses. So he reports what he knows Washington wants to hear . . . keeps us happy at the same time."

"Davey is there to keep things in order. . . . Post time . . . "

"Hell, you know Davey has no real authority over loans of the Interstate Funds. Lots of times he hasn't any access to loan information as to who is who, and who's getting it. He's becoming more and more an office manager with a large staff to manage and a hundred twenty-three million dollar stock portfolio."

"*They're off!* Come on, Run Steady! . . . Don't worry over Davey. What they call kickbacks he gets on certain loans he okays are just commissions as if he were an agent . . . come on, Run Steady . . . he's up there."

The brothers watched the race. Run Steady won easily, but at low odds. Mike shook his head. "Too many people had feed box information."

"Mike, Davey may end up in jail. He's just your surrogate, and you and Spinelli, Fiora have the big leverage in the fund's decision making."

"Enjoy the races, Moz. You're acting like Jamie Ward used to. How is old Jamie?"

"Growing prize tomatoes among the Birchers in southern California. Saw him last trip out. Joined some jerked-to-Jesus group . . . really thinks you are in the power of the Devil."

"You know what Mom always said, 'To eat supper with the Devil always use a long spoon' . . . who do you like in the next race?"

Martin shrugged and didn't mention his own personal worries. The sun was high, the sky robin blue . . . enjoy it. He was getting a retainer fund of three hundred thousand a year in legal fees from the union, and Davey Wasserman's nephews were getting a hundred twenty-five thousand each; Lennie and Morrie were also deep into loans from the fund: sixty million deep—they were building a hotel and gambling casino in the Lake Tahoe district of Nevada, a building called "The Great Babylon." And were seeking a commitment for forty million more; for there was a movement growing in New Jersey to open Atlantic City to legal gambling à la Las Vegas.

It was in May of 1975, after midnight, that Mike awoke to hear his private phone ringing in the top drawer of the night table. He came awake for a moment with the fears of a child of eight hearing the whistles of the factories announcing the end of the world. He shivered, the skin on his back quivering like a nervous horse's hide. He got the phone and rubbed his face to become fully awake.

"Hello, what the hell . . ."

"It's Martin. Davey, his nephews Lennie and Morris Katenstein, John Fiora, are being indicted for cheating the Health, Welfare and Pension Fund."

"In the middle of the night?"

"I've got somebody inside who just called me. Trial opens in three weeks in the U.S. Courthouse in St. Louis."

"Well, defend them . . . postpone, stall . . . make up a team of legal eagles."

"You and Julia better take that trip to Japan . . . get away."

"Why . . . they can't touch me."

"Want to get called on the stand and help send Davey to the Federal slammer? This is a serious, well-documented effort by Justice."

Julia had awakened. Her sleeping pill kept her halfway under. "What, *what* . . ."

Mike replaced the phone on its cradle. "Honey, go back to sleep. Pack in the morning. We're flying to Japan. I'm accepting that invitation to address the Tokyo World's Fair Association."

The trial of the four men—two of them Davey and Fiora (fund trustees) lasted four months. . . . Martin and two very costly lawyers from Washington, D.C. defended them. J. Hasting Ott, a round, pink-faced, dignified Washington man about town, presented himself as a white-haired, old-style gentleman who talked like a character in a Henry James novel. He could appear confused, always objecting politely in a case, then declaiming on human rights, Roman law, and certain quotes from Voltaire, Samuel Johnson, Cardoza, Frankfurter, while managing to assume the mantle of an older, firmer philosopher in the realm of justice than the judge.

Wilbur William Scudder was a fashion plate, solid gold locks on his dispatch case, the firm-jawed face of a western film actor who radiated fine virtues, the code of the men who settled a nation. Both were actually deadly skillful legal foxes of tremendous slickness in outwitting inferior, or inexperienced government lawyers.

The evidence of the handling of loans, of the type of loans made, the kickbacks, special fees, commissions, made it crystal clear that Davey and the three other accused men were in deep trouble. So much evidence existed that special golf carts appeared in the St. Louis Courthouse, on the tenth floor, to carry about the several hundred pounds of documents the United States attornies presented.

In four months much disputed evidence was presented. Charts were shown, land and real estate records presented. Martin, Ott, and Scudder handled the defense with vigorous rebuttals but their own evidence was very weak. Ott admitted the weaknesses over a two-pound lobster at the L'Emitage. "Very weak indeed. We're bailing a leaking ship, Martin. If only we could plea bargain."

Scudder, impressive in a neat English check jacket, a thin gold bar on the collar of his London shirt, shook his head and began to open the first of the three hard-boiled eggs he ate every day for lunch—nothing else but two glasses of club soda.

"Not a chance. The U.S. Attorney thinks they have a case as tight as a bear trap. Of course it must all be sworn and testified to by their witnesses."

Martin cut slowly into his rare sirloin. "That bad? We have a staff of twelve lawyers here."

"One never knows. But they have two dangerous witnesses. We'll see if we can cut them down on the stand."

Later, as Martin signed for all the meals—as he did for four months—with a DWU credit card, he decided lawyers eat well when on a case (unless on an egg diet), charging the clients for gourmet food and much drink.

Martin, in his journal, wrote: "The way our over a dozen lawyers eat at our expense on the flesh of their clients, it's almost cannibalism. You dream they are devouring, eating the victims they should be defending, and using the clients' bones as jewelry."

Mike called one night from Japan. "How's it going, Moz?"

"We have hopes . . . nothing beyond that. How is it with you and Julia?"

"She's buying obis—some kind of silk sashes, and looks great in these kimonos. I've seen ten miles of temples and museums, drunk cat piss called saki—the beef is great, the Japanese food lousy . . . seaweed and rotting pickles, herring scales soup. The Ginza is Coney Island . . . how long do I keep this up?"

"A couple more months, I'd say, Mike. Go to France, London."

"Christ, I'm up to my navel in culture. You tell Davey I'm rooting for him. Ott and Scudder have pinned back the ears of the Department of Justice before. Julia sends regards. She asks you to send someone to see if the dogs are okay."

Of the two government witnesses, one—Raymond K. Pepper—twenty-eight-years-old, a labor insurance manager for the National Eagle Insurance Company living in Clearwater, North Carolina, was having breakfast with his wife and his two small daughters when two strangers invaded the breakfast nook. They blasted Pepper into nearly bloody rags with two sawed-off 12-gauge shotguns. They left without saying a word and were never apprehended or identified.

The second witness, Charles Delsey, was the former general office manager of Lennie and Morris Katenstein's projects. He, in court, gave direct evidence of the setting up of the Katenstein holdings when the loans—huge union funds—were being poured into them and illegally used. The murdered man Raymond K. Pepper could have backed up much of this testimony. But he was already buried, with military honors, having served in the Korean War.

Ott and Scudder took turns battering Delsey, the surviving witness. He seemed to stand firmly by his testimony.

"The whole trial now rests," Ott remarked to Martin, "on the jury believing a sole witness with *no* corroborating testimony."

With the jury sent out by the judge to find a verdict, the defense lawyers sat in the lobby of the Hilton. Ott seemed placidly set in dour doubt, winding the heavy gold watch he wore on a thick butter-gold chain in a tattersall waistcoat. From the chain, Martin observed, hung the insignia of Yale's Skull and Bones. "I don't know, Martin. We didn't make much of a dent in Delsey."

Martin shook his head. "Juries don't think like lawyers."

Scudder smiled. "Perhaps that's just as well."

That night Mike called from the George V in Paris. "Mike, it looks very cold and dark."

"Can we get Davey out of the country . . . like that bastard who got to some West Indies island with his loot?"

"Don't dream, Mike. That would cause such stink in union circles it would blow you right out of the president's seat."

"Can we get them sentenced to one of the plush country clubs—one of the no walls prisons Justice has—all tennis courts, swimming pools, color TV. I mean you know where they send some of the Watergate bad boys to get their wrists slapped."

"Calm down, Mike, and don't bake a cake with a file in it yet."

It took the jury two full days to reach the verdict. *Not guilty.* Davey and the accused sat smiling.

The jury had stood ten to two for conviction on most counts, Martin discovered from interviews with a juror. But the two who had asked *why* other trustees also were not on trial managed to sway the jury at the end of two days of hassle.

J. Hasting Ott, as the verdict was read, motioned to his assistants to pick up the heavy briefcases lettered J.H.O. "I'll have fee accounts and our staff expenses in your people's hands in a week." Wilbur William Scudder, retaining his dry expression of rueful rancor, shook Martin's hand firmly. "A jury has done its duty. If I can ever be of service. . . ."

Mike was in London at Inn-On-The-Park when Martin called him with the verdict. Mike was delighted. "Those sonofabitches Ott and Scudder could get Judas Iscariot off and have Christ's estate pay the court costs."

"Mike, it was two shotguns saved their bacon. Not the lawyers."

"Well, this clears up any government hoopla against the union. Julia bought a Turner at Christie's . . . know what a Turner is?"

"I know, Mike. . . . The Justice Department is boiling mad at losing this big one. They're going into the financing of the Fiora Golden Sunrise slot machine company and those businesses you had set up with Spinelli for Terry."

"Terry's companies? They're as honest as God."

"There are a lot of Gods, Mike . . . I hope this is the right one."

CHAPTER 35

Mike returned, ready, and in a perverse way, almost eager for battle. He was at his most skillful when defending himself; he seemed to gather strength when faced with problems, and in the years since his rise to the full control of the DWU he had early been tested, and savaged, had always managed to come out the victor in major battles.

Now it was to be, (as Martin wrote in his journal) perhaps not in the Churchillian sense, but Mike's finest hour. He retains, as always, the loyalty, one could almost say the adoration of the rank and file. He has greatly benefitted their incomes, their way of life, even at the cost of huge assessments—the highest rate of dues in any union. This is his backup, the membership; he is like a gunfighter sure of the wall behind him. And the trouble is mounting: the southern and eastern locals are in revolt, their leaders anyway, under Kingbird, and the fund is under continual attack. Ott's and Schudder's staffs are scur-

rying under Mike's orders all over the country trying to
fathom the legal obligations in force and the faults com-
mitted in the past. Oddly enough, the minor matter of
Terry's service companies, industrial laundries, are
among the most dangerous items open to government
investigation. There is a kind of rough, ironic justice in
this, and if I were still a choirboy and in a state of grace,
I'd say perhaps some divine but mocking pattern of justice
may be in the works; in helping Terry, Mike pricked his
own balloon?

Mike himself sensed a time of battles ahead. He felt
confident, alert; charged around the country in the DWU
executive jet, shaking hands, making threats, consulting
with Martin and the other lawyers. Late in the night in
hotel rooms in Dallas or Boston, he read legal papers that
came to him by the pound. It was clear that between the
attacks on his leadership led by Kingbird DuBois and at
least four other union bosses he had once depended on,
and the Department of Justice effort to pile up and prove
criminal actions against him, only the boldest actions
could insure he remain on top

Davey Wasserman was his first problem. They met in
Davey's big *gemütlich* duplex apartment high over Chicago, almost adrift in space. There was a *gemütlich* dinner, too much dinner, and Davey's wife seemed a bit
frightened of Mike, with her dark, worried eyes wide, her
pale brown hair in order; the proper Jewish princess.

Davey, a family man, beamed as the two sat after dinner in a paneled room with shelves that held too few
books and many Meissen figures. Davey had worn well
over the years: the empty sleeve from his missing arm, as
always, stuffed into his jacket pocket. The amused hawk-
like look had mellowed, but the humor in the eyes and
mouth was a bit less now that he sensed the problems he
had to face.

"A great girl, my Florence. Should have been married

again earlier, but like you I had it right second time around."

"Julia and I aren't married." Mike had lit a pipe and was relaxing in a deep chair after too much roast chicken, a potato pudding, a well-seasoned California type salad, the apple pie and cheese he could never resist . . . topped by strong coffee—two cups with cream and sugar. "I've thought about it. Marriage, Davey. But Julia doesn't give a damn about appearances, and there's Terry, still legally my wife. She can be mean. So we let it lay."

Davey had a lit cigar, one of the good Havanas he managed to get from the Canadian DWU office in Toronto.

"You never really let me know too much, Mike. Oh, I'm not blaming you, things moved fast in the DWU, and things had to be done. But now with those schmucks Leonard and Morris buggering things up, we're going to· have to produce a lot of records."

Mike belched silently. "Records get lost, Davey, get shredded. You know the shredding machine has done more for secret diplomacy and industrial problem solving than Eli Whitney and Thomas Edison." He puffed on his pipe and thought: the meal sat heavy, and he wondered if he could ask for some Di-Gel. "You ever think, Davey, when we were getting our G.I. asses shot off in Korea and banging the wog broads in Inchon that, first of all, we'd survive Mac's crazy John Wayne war, or that we'd even amount to much? I mean we have everything we could ever have wished for, and sometimes I think maybe I'd have been better off as a twenty year top sarge, drilling redneck kids and burrheads at Fort Ord."

"Nostalgia *dreak*, Mike. These are the good old days. Even if there are a few storm clouds on the horizon."

"You know the old army slogan; PYA. Protect your ass."

"Even if a lot of your buddies get the deep six?"

Mike found Davey glance, searching for his answer, Davey's big handsome eyes wide.

Mike took the pipe from his mouth. "It's not every man to his own escape hatch for survival. But it's like dying too—nobody can do it for you. Don't worry, you're too much a part of me to have me let you down. But those cocksuckers, Spinelli, Fiora, they'd as soon deep six me as I would them, if it didn't mean we go down if they do."

"That's where we're in trouble with those damn industrial laundries and maintenance companies set in the same holding companies with the Fiora slot machines and gambling equipment outfits."

"Davey, I had a choice; have them in or no DWU as big as it is now."

"Government has proved the ties of these companies with organized crime figures, some of them big stockholders. Who would have figured it would have come to . . ."

"Never mind that. What has the government got on the Fiora family?"

"They are into the union funds for thirty million dollars, and this year they finagled fifteen million more at six percent. You follow me?"

"The prime interest rate all banks are charging is around ten percent."

"That's our hole in the dike. For Congress has also passed that new law, the Employment Retirement Security Act; the strongest section is there to make union welfare and pension funds like ours accountable to the Federal government. The Labor Department now has the right to audit, with their own men, the books of any union, and they can demand full reports on all dealings."

"How far back can they go in their audits?"

"We don't know, Mike, until they test it in court."

Mike frowned and closed his eyes. "Okay, from now on we change our way of making loans. We no longer loan directly to some person or firm that might not smell

kosher to the law. We just deposit the money in a bank
we deal with as a certificate of deposit. Get it? Then the
bank makes the loan, *not* the union."

"I get it," said Davey, gleefully puffing his cigar to its
glowing end, "the welfare pension fund doesn't show to
whom the loan is really made; it just shows up as another
bank deposit. And we look good in the financial statements with money on deposit for the fund. Mike, if I
were wearing a hat, I'd tip it to you."

"I've been thinking this out for a long time with Martin. It's like war, Davey. You make a better tank-gun,
they make a better tank, so you have to be always changing the ways of things being done. Now we also have to
change the insurance setup. The employers and workers
are now set for not too many wage raises, but more welfare benefits, health insurance, dental, medical care. Employers are paying a big fat share of all this. Insurance premiums are bigger and bigger. We've been working with a
few friendly insurance companies. Know what I mean?
You rub me, I'll tickle you."

Davey nodded and showed the palm of his hand as a
gesture of yes, of course.

"Now, Davey, let's set up complete coverage insurance
agencies and companies of our own to write the actual
policies on the millions coming in, compliments of the
employers. We'll have to let Spinelli in; we need his good
will."

Davey thought, bit on a thumb: "Say a seven percent
commission to him and Fiora? He'll ask for ten of course,
but I think he'll give up three points to where we have to
use it."

The door opened and Florence Wasserman put just her
head in. "If there's anything else the servants can get you,
Mr. Brant, or you, Dave, why. . . ." She stood as if waiting for a command. Mike shook his head. "No, no,
Florence. It was all fine, swell meal. And I'm going now.

Thanks for everything. Getting late and I have to be in Detroit in the morning."

Mike parted from Davey with a manly hug; with a feeling there is nothing like a comradeship based on once being soldiers together.

Six months later David Wasserman was indicted on evidence to a Grand Jury that he had met with known crime figures to set up a union insurance scheme in which the crime figures would participate. During the trial, no matter how Ott and Scudder fought to keep out legal wiretap evidence, it was permitted. The voices of Davey, Spinelli, and Fiora were identified, and the taps showed that mention was made of kickbacks to be paid out from insurance policies to companies controlled by the mob through employees of the union welfare pension funds.

Martin did succeed, in the cases against Spinelli and Fiora, in getting the wiretaps not admitted as evidence in their trials, as by then the Attorney General and his assistant refused to continue their early permission for taps in the former matter. It was a strange decision but it stood, and the jury was influenced, finding the two defendants not guilty. David Wasserman, however, was found guilty on three counts of misuse of union funds and sentenced to four years in the Atlanta Federal Prison. No soft Federal country club for him.

Out on bail for an appeal, Mike invited him to lunch in his private suite in the DWU building in Washington. Davey bore his punishment with a kind of sad dignity . . . with some sort of remains of Talmudic grace; he even, at times, felt the justice of it all.

Over the coffee he reached for his cigar case and didn't find it. "Well, it's just as well I give up the Havanas. I'll be smoking one-handed-rolls in Atlanta."

Mike shook his head. "We'll keep trying to get you to

the Federal farm in Alabama. And Christ, we'll keep seeking appeals."

"No good. I hear the Supreme Court is loaded now by you know who with antilabor."

"What a hell of a way to end," said Mike. "But you'll have your pension—it's hefty—and you have something put away. I'll see to Florence . . . don't worry."

"She's pregnant. It's a hell of a load on me, Florence. I shouldn't have married."

They sat silently while the waiter and a busboy cleared the table, set down the brandy decanter and glasses. After two brandies, toasts to dead comrades of the second Airborne, they just sat in that nonverbal communication of old friends who have said everything, understanding each other without added words. It was dusk when Davey went to catch a plane for Chicago, well aware of the FBI man tailing him.

That night Mike and Julia went to a festive dinner at the British Embassy, a fete for several important figures in the Common Market on their visit to America "to study methods and procedures." Mike joked with Bertie Wombeely, head of the British Mechanics Union ("still loafing on slowed up assembly lines?"). He made a short speech about the new kind of cooperation between nations on vegetables, which he hoped would extend to those who grew, processed, and packed the products of the Common Market.

Later, sipping champagne with Julia in one of the smaller rooms away from the people listening to a quartet playing Purcell, he spoke to Julia: "This may be the last time we'll be dolled up for such a fracus."

She took his hand—she looking very regal in blue water silk, her hair piled up high in a new mode—ears and wrists ornamented by blue stones set in diamonds. "Come on, my darling, Davey is weighing on your mind. You did your damn best."

"I also shoved him into the firing line, and I've got this gut feeling they're out for bigger game . . . me."

"Well, we'll face it—we've faced a lot, mister, they've dished up. . . . Will you dance? They've changed bands."

"Hell, why not."

They circled the floor at a brisk Irving Berlin pace, he holding her close, taking in the scent of her, feeling Julia still so limber, so well muscled; Christ, so much woman in his arms. Was it all real . . . all the damn snooty limeys and their duked up, posh guests. And this woman . . . he had slept with her thousands of times, been intimate in many ways under so many conditions in so many places. But wasn't he still that Polak kid with the soiled shirttail, eating corn meal mush—and his old man coughing, cursing working conditions, and Mom putting on her blue nurse's cape with the faded, red lining, going out to watch some rich old swat go into his death rattle; he and Moz stealing lumps of coal, and the cold sky, the color of fat congealed on a soiled plate.

No, Mike shook off pictures that seemed to be recurring more and more in his memory. This was the very tony British Embassy, its walls lined with genuine oil paintings of the queen and the Royal family, not looking too bright but very well dressed; and all this crowd respecting them, in a setting of gold and scarlet, rare rugs and upholstery . . . the women all looking like ready lays, the men, even the faggots, having class. You could see that. Class. Mike had always felt in some awe of class. And here he was, class himself (maybe like it was in the main salon of the *Titanic*, but class at least on the surface). Hundred-and-ten-dollar shoes, evening clothes tailored with the care of Cinderella outfitted for a ball.

He reassured himself as to appearance: cufflinks made from T'ang dynasty buttons which Julia had gotten for him in Peking just three months before; on his wrist, two thousand dollars worth of Swiss watchmaking; even his

damn underwear held the letters MB near his crotch; and
in his gut the finest of fine champagnes, plovers eggs,
caviar, fish with slices of truffles, rare roast beef—
already, he thought, breaking down into their chemical
parts. I *am*, Julia *is*, all these shuffling freeloaders, pho-
nies, posers, cookie pushers in power, are all breaking
down into chemical elements—all becoming no better
than anybody else. No matter who your grandfather laid
in the garden house, or the shape of grandma's nose. All a
person was is ninety-eight cents worth of chemicals. But
with inflation he figured, multiply by four. This idea left
him feeling in a very good mood; just why he didn't
know. He danced three more dances with Julia, had a lot
more brandies and hoped to make very ardent love to her
when they got home. However, he fell asleep in the car
and had to be awakened, and he sang his old man's song
of how on the Nile lived that crocodile—sang all the way
up the stairs, leaning against Julia.

There was no great surprise when Michael Brant, President of the Drovers & Wheelmens Union, was indicted
and ordered to stand trial on seven counts of defrauding
the Health, Welfare and Pension Fund . . . through in-
trigue and dealing with crime families in several cities;
for approving loans at a very low rate of interest to questionable firms or dummy corporations; for permitting,
and even ordering, certain so-called legal fees and expenses for services to him personally, not the union; for
instigating the bank deposit scheme in which the union
actually gave risky loans and covered the identity of the
takers by having certain banks (now under investigation)
cover the loans in their own name; also for personally
borrowing without the full approval of the trustees of the
DWU, sums of up to one million four-hundred-eighty-
thousand dollars for projects of his own, including dealings in soya bean futures; for playing the commodities
markets in hog belly futures; also for not reporting cer-

tain overseas investments, and for setting up, through
members of crime syndicates, certain industrial service
businesses in the name of his wife, Mrs. Michael (Terry)
Brant. These were the major crimes Mike was charged
with. Some of the others were, Martin felt, added to increase the size of the general indictment.

Mike took it quite naturally; he'd been expecting it. He
sat at breakfast with Julia and Martin, the dogs at his feet.
Wagner served them and withdrew.

"Well," said Mike stirring the two lumps of sugar into
his coffee. "Here we sit, about all that's left of the original group . . . all that matters . . . Davey in the Federal   slammer . . . Jamie   retired,   growing   his   gar-
bage . . . *all* the rest," he made a gesture of dismissal.
"We'll give the courts a good fight, and we'll beat them!"
He took a sip of the coffee. "What brand is this? Coffee
tastes like they've been bathing the damn dogs in it."

Julia said, "I'll have Hilda make a fresh pot."

"This *is* a fresh pot. Well, Moz, how long can you delay
and delay?"

"Three, four months. Ott and Scudder are mounting a
huge defense setup."

"And a huge set of fees, I bet."

Martin picked up a briefcase from where it had been
resting on the sunroom rug. "A million, maybe a million
and a half in legal costs, if it gets complicated. We lawyers, Mike, are nature's revenge for setting up a cockeyed
civilization. In ancient Athens no lawyers were permitted; a judge called people in off the street to decide a case.
A great idea."

"We're a culture," said Julia. "I never thought we had a
civilization. Now, Mike, let Martin run things. You'll
only offend the judges. Ott and Scudder are experts on
judges."

"That'll be the day I trust any shyster. Moz is a relative
and trustworthy, but every other law school creep would
shoot his mother and bet you which way she'd fall."

It was an old jest of Mike's, and Martin decided Mike would face the months in his usual style: too talkative, too angry—but solidly aggressive.

"Draw me up, Moz, a list of people we can really depend on inside the union."

It turned out to be a very short list. But for the members of the union's rank and file—"the working joes," who had benefitted greatly by Mike's way of negotiating, and a few local heads, old-timers who had known him for many years, there was no one else he could depend on for full loyalty.

Certainly the leaders of other unions were delighted in Mike getting his comeuppance, as the Puskin put it on his appearance on the television show, *Meet the Press*: "In 1972 I expelled Mike Brant's union from WNUSA, the DWU, kit and kaboodle. He runs it like a South American dictator; I expelled them all and a good thing, too. They can come back to the Workers National Union when they have cleansed themselves of their tainted leadership . . . and not before."

John Atkins, *Los Angeles Record*: "Would you still feel this way if Mr. Brant is found not guilty of the present charges against him?"

The Puskin chewed his gum slowly: "People who are not morally good to start with do not become good suddenly. As to a final judgment of guilt or innocence, I leave that to an American jury of twelve good and true men. I have great and unbounding faith in the American system of justice."

Soren Verner, President of the LBO—the Labor Brotherhood Organization—did not speak out as strongly when appearing on *Face the Nation*: He said, in his quiet way, hardly moving his lips, "I haven't read all the charges with any great care. We must remember that legal charges are not a verdict of guilt. Mike Brant, one must admit, has done a great deal for the American worker. He is responsible for much labor welfare benefits, written into today's union contracts. For wage rises, health and welfare protection. But what must be condemned, if these charges are true, is the method, the intent to supercede the law of the land—and not the American unions."

Manson Ramon, *Science of the Mind News:* "Mr. Verner, how does one separate moral values from a philosophy of the end justifying the means?"

Soren Verner, a wry Swede, gave the question some thought: "I'm afraid that's a question that people have been trying to answer for centuries. There is no clear satisfying answer that I can recall."

Mike himself, on the advice of Martin, refused to appear on any television program on the grounds that he did not want to confuse the real issues with any statements that might be made outside of a courtroom. He did give one interview for the *Amalgamated Press'* Nelson Crandell, over a lunch of soft shell crabs and terripan stew at the Potomac River Club:

"The whole cockeyed hullaballoo, Nelson, is really the attempt of the Justice Department to try to nail something called the Mafia families, using the DWU as a cat's paw to pull their chestnuts out of the fire."

"Aren't there, Mike, crime family members involved with your union? And holding positions in the various branches, like the Health, Welfare & Pension Fund . . . the insurance sections?"

"Are there Marxists, Birchers, hardhat Nazis, vegetarians, fags, holy rollers, and people who swear the earth is flat among our membership? I'd have to answer, most likely. So, as for what is called the Mafia, well, the locals have the right to elect members, elect officers with Italian names; and if they have gang connections, let the law grab them. In a democratic organization we don't ask if they ever stole a hubcap, or shook down a chow mein parlor. My answer is yes, we have people the Justice Department lists with criminal connections. But if so, *why* are they free, walking around? Why aren't they in prison?"

"Maybe they will be, Mike, *if* this probe continues."

"Nelson, *if* my grandmother had balls, she'd have been my grandfather. How about another tray of crabs?"

And yet, Martin was aware that Mike was more worried about the crime family connections inside the DWU than he indicated over a lunch of soft shell crabs.

BOOK SIX

THE PRICE

CHAPTER 36

From Martin Brant's private journal:

The basic complaint about Mike's handling of the DWU was, and is, his close connection with the Mafia crime families, permitting their often powerful influence in certain locals, forcing their way into loans from the Health, Welfare and Pension Fund. Mike has never tried to defend himself in any great detail about all this, but at times he has spoken out to me, so I can set down certain of his views.

"There came a time, Moz, when I saw just who the union was fighting and where it could lead—to nothing. That's when I began to study industry's methods—adapt them to our own use. Hell, anybody can tell you that over a billion dollars a year is paid out in bribes all over the world by the big airplane producers, the huge oil combines, the carmakers, the chemical and metal corporations. They have spies planted among their rivals; pirates steal computer information, swipe patents. The bastards

383

have no more Christian morals than a Chinese goat. All right. We had to have clout or unions would end up as they did when Federal troops busted the Pullman strikes, when the Rockefeller goons shot down men, women, and children in the Colorado mines . . . when cops murdered strikers on a Memorial Day picnic in 1937. Me, I saw we had to be as hardnutted as industry. All I could get was the mob. They were already in big business in Vegas, in control of waterfronts, trucking. Damm it, if they are so illegal, why are they still running things? Anyway, I had no choice. It was them, Moz, or a union scarecrow made of horseshit, begging favors, crumbs.

"From who, Moz? From an outlaw materialistic society that pays lip service to morality but buys elections, like Joe Kennedy did—owns most of Congress. We, too, had to pony up. Didn't we dump a million dollars, secretly, to Nixon and his pals. Didn't industry sneak in a hundred million dollars themselves—even 'washing' money in Mexico?"

This kind of talk is a song and dance with Mike when anyone brings up union wrongdoing. It's all very well for Mike to point out the faults, the "diseases" as he calls them of industry. But he avoids the really basic crimes done in the DWU . . . brushing off news of the attempt to bribe a congressional investigator: "Look at the financial malpractice common on Wall Street and among stock dealers, or the over-and-under-the-table negotiations big business uses. A union should be able to deal realistically with the use of force, even the Cosa Nostra, without admitting them to power."

But I have defended over one hundred DWU officials and associates and seen most of them convicted of various crimes. I could write a chronology of corruption under Mike (but never will). There are now, for instance, over fifty indictments from the Justice Department against various DWU officials.

How does Mike balance all this against what he calls "benefits to the rank and file." He's a great one, as he points to gains while he sits in the modern twenty-million-dollar DWU building in Washington, sits at ease at the sixty-foot teak table at a board meeting of eighteen trustees: lawyers, appraisers, investment counselors, public relations people. "It could be, Moz, a board meeting of General Motors, ITT, or Chase Manhattan Bank." Another time there may be a half dozen of the fifteen vice presidents present and the secretary-treasurer discussing investment banking, a documentary feature film, land developing.

Mike, in his tenth floor executive suite with a private elevator waiting, sits like the Queen Bee in a splendid hive. There is a four-thousand-volume law library, a French chef for gourmet meals to certain persons, a live lobster tank, a sauna, gymnasium (with masseurs), and calisthenic sessions for female employees. The newest movies come air mail (gratis) four times a week from Hollywood studios to keep the labor peace, and Mike sits in control of an intercom system with a hundred outlets.

"Sure, a lot of it, it's all front. You have to look good here in Washington and act like you expect to be treated with respect. Figure out what big business lays out here for lobbies, nookie on the cuff, booze, meals, junkets to kill wild ducks, and gifts all along the line in this town, and you can see we're in style. Small, compared to some airplane maker laying out fifty million to a greasy Arab con man to buy jet toys—or the Korean CIA dropping ten-thousand-dollar bundles like Easter eggs on the White House lawn for senators with their hands out, palms up. Don't let any sonofabitch talk about corruption in the DWU unless he's also willing to turn over the rocks and show the big chemical, drug, and metal shapers with their pants down jerking off."

Mike would mix his metaphors, but he did bolster many of his personal doubts—if he had any—by pointing to the bad deeds of others. As a lawyer, if I had been a saint, I would have reacted with horror, but I was born an ironic pessimist and held by a fascination of how things are done wrong by legal means to bypass true justice. Industry keeps thousands of high-priced law firms on huge retainers; their major work is defeating, or bypassing, legislation unkind to their clients' way of life. It's fascinating to Mike how corporations get their way. And so I practiced, aided by Ott and Scudder, for the benefit of the DWU.

Also there is a loyalty to Mike, more than blood and background: It's the fascination of watching a man climb, watching him hang on, and wondering will he fall, and if so, *how*?

He himself has no doubts of victory—at least in conversation—is dedicated to see things through. "They can try to knock me down off my perch. If they do, I'll take a lot of fancy schmucks and not so fancy bastards with me. But hell, unions are now part of the establishment. The Siamese twins of *us* and *them* locked together tight as a bull's ass in flytime. Not only the same blood stream . . . I think the two brains are merged into one . . . see the same picture, work toward the same ends . . . keep things humming and moving. The name of the game is Produce. The slogan? *'Fat City for Everybody.'*"

Mike, so very early in the day, was expecting a visitor. It was six in the morning, and he was sitting in the open-sided garden house looking over various cactus plants in pots, a collection that had been Julia's interest two years before. There were dozens of the spur surfaced, waxy plants: twisted, tormented, desert shapes. Some had flowered into unreal, strange blooms. The glass roof overhead was clouded by pigeon life. Mike had slept deeply when he slept, but had awakened several times during the night in a sweat.

From the house there was little sound—the dogs were still upstairs. Hilda was moving about in the kitchen, busy with some early baking. Wagner would be in their room, shaving, admiring his wooden Teutonic features in the mirror, ready to appear at the breakfast table in his white morning jacket, black tie knotted just so.

Mike heard a car stop out front. He looked at his wristwatch: 6:17. The face was set with small gems, a presentation from the Shipbuilding Mechanics and Valve Placers, after a good victory in a now forgotten walkout. The hollyhocks were out, but the beds of tulips—five bucks a bulb—had been dug up. Mom used to plant morning glory seeds, gathered, saved from the year before, and he and Moz and Mom would save string to use as strands for the morning glories in pinks and pale blues to send up their vines of trumpet shaped flowers. "The orchids of the poor," Mom had called morning glories. They had covered the back porch, the house's unpainted wooden walls, even crawled over the packing box bin which held their meager supply of winter coal. . . . Hell, you don't see morning glories anymore; out of fashion, like Airedales.

The man who came out into the garden, Hilda having let him in (or was Wagner down early?) was not the visitor Mike had been expecting. John Fiora, in a fingertip-length, pale, topcoat, a Rex Harrison tweed hat, came toward the plant house and extended his hand. Mike didn't take the hand.

"George . . . where's George? Goddam it, I made it clear I want to speak to George."

"My uncle isn't too well, Mike. He's had a oh . . . small, not serious, heart attack. Yes, small, we hope. He's not permitted to leave Chicago."

"He looked fine when we met three weeks ago in Detroit. Nice tan, laughing all the time."

Fiora sat down on a white, cast-iron garden bench.

"Uncle George has full confidence in me. Anything we talk over is like you talking to him."

"The hell with that. I'll talk—get him on the phone."

Fiora shook his head. He wasn't the young dude anymore—the young dago who had been so respectful back in Kansas City. He was big now—look at him—with the importance of the Spinelli and Fiora families that had pretty much driven out or destroyed the other crime *capos*.

"My uncle is not allowed to answer the phone . . . maybe even use it, for a couple of weeks. A small coronary, God willing, but the specialists are taking no chances. No contacts on any matters for any reasons. You know how excitable he is."

Mike took out a pipe from a pocket, thoughtfully rubbed the bowl against one side of his nose. "They haven't sent for the priest yet, have they, Johnny? Maybe the Bishop?"

Fiora ignored the sarcasm in Mike's tone.

"Nothing that serious, God willing."

"Okay, Johnny, what I wanted to say to George Spinelli face-to-face is that no matter what comes out of my court appearances, we'd be horses' asses to bury ourselves deeper by he *or* me talking of any connection any don or his family had with the union . . . *capisce?*"

"Uncle George never felt either of you would do otherwise. He wouldn't cooperate with Justice. Never."

"They'll have plenty of crap they've gathered on the mob and the union . . . old records haven't been shredded, damm it, and that bank deposit gimmick we used to give the dons loans. But for the courts to put it all together will be like weaving with water. Christ, George and me, we worked together from Kansas City on, over twenty years ago, when you were still beating your meat, Johnny, in some prep school. Relationships, the kind your uncle and me had, they don't grow on trees. Your generation believe in loyalties?"

"Mike, we're no different breed, just dressed different, see . . . in a world run by computers and communications, seconds to contact any part of the world."

"We Polaks, hunkies, ginnies, have done a hell of a lot of space travel in a very short time, eh? Your great grandfather was a Moustache Pete with the Black Hand on

Mulberry Street. Your grandfather really made Midwest bootlegging a big thing across the Canadian border. He kept out of Capone's way, sent his kids to good schools, and gave the church a nunnery, learned to eat more than pasta. A great guy, a Knight of St. John. I liked him. And George, now, a real gentleman, moving the family's share into the solid, legitimate world, besides holding on as a real don. Never had to hit the mattress."

Mike blew through the stem of the empty pipe. "I suppose, yeah, that is progress."

Fiora sat poker-faced. "Is there anything else to tell my uncle, when I'm permitted to talk of business affairs to him?"

Mike clenched his jaw line. "Yes, when he's able to hear what I've just assured him on my side, you just pass it along."

Fiora didn't extend his hand again. "Everything is going to be all right, Mike. I represent the family."

"Get it around, what I said. So the Soroldi brothers in New York know it, and the Consodullios in Boston, and Tony Banchinni in New Orleans. And who the hell is the bubblehead in L.A.?"

"My cousin, Calogero."

"Yes, of course. He's out of Leavenworth. I remember."

Mike offered his hand this time. Fiora shook it, and for a moment Mike wondered if he was going to get a Sicilian hug, "the touching of cheeks." But no, that sign of brotherhood that sometimes preceded a farewell for good was omitted.

Mike watched Fiora move through the garden and into the house. Then Mike waited for the sound of a car motor to start and move off. He slowly filled his pipe, lit it from a gold lighter that threw a thin intense blue-tipped flame into the bowl. When the pipe was drawing well, he moved toward the house.

Wagner was up and about shouting orders to Hilda,

cursing out a dog in gutteral German oaths . . . Balzac
had peed on the stairs. (Balzac, when irked, scolded, or
just in a nervous moment, could not control his poodle
bladder).

Martin owned a small but solid colonial house, set in
half an acre of riverside on the Virginia side of the Potomac. He drove a Masarati sports car, owned a formal Lincoln he rarely used, was served by a middle-aged Dutch
housekeeper, Heidi Brunner. He never brought any of his
girls home; shared a flat in Alexandria with one of the
younger lawyers in his office. Latch keys for both of them
and a coded notebook were kept in the mail box to keep
track of who wanted the use of the place, when.

Martin had matured into a wise rather than a clever
lawyer, a serious student of legal history and its relationship to major social changes. His small library of rare volumes on early colonial law and his manuscript records of
17th century court hearings were the envy of the Library
of Congress. Martin played tennis for his health, drank
good wines, but drank little hard stuff in a martini and
Scotch dominated culture. He belonged to the Burning
Tree Club but rarely played golf. Martin attended opera
and the ballet, and like Mike, didn't care much for the
theatre. In art he was careful, well-informed. He disliked
the modern American school of dots and lines, found dull
works that displayed a goat with a worn tire around its
belly, crumpled auto fenders, and white on white on
white, or black on black on black. He favored Redon
prints, owned two original oils by Francis Bacon, and a
magnificent Lundeburg surrealist painting of a chair, a
dangling light bulb, and piece of fruit, all done in muted,
yet intense colors. It relaxed him, this picture, and he
would, when facing a difficult problem, study the painting for hours.

Martin had a four o'clock appointment for a private
chat with a certain person in an appeal case, but had

called it off when Mike called and said he would be driving out. It wasn't like Mike to come to him. Martin had long ago accepted the role of the younger brother who came when called. Mike needed a great deal of advice and took it most of the time. He leaned on Martin and respected his ideas of things. Martin was a man with a normal ego but not an overwhelming one. He was blandly philosophical, preferred the Greek idea to the Roman logic and accepted sadly Freud's statement: "Most of the human race is trash." He wondered if Freud had really meant that, and if the German's word for *trash* actually was that strong.

Mike arrived driving Julia's pale, umber Chrysler. From Martin's living room the Potomac could be seen through a bank of French windows, pale lemon drapes. There was a good pastel Persian rug; comfortable chairs, well-polished antique furniture ("some of it genuine").

Mike eyed the two Bacons on the wall. "Jesus, that's art? Scare the shit out of you, don't they?"

"It's a version of the world as good as Bosch's."

"Well, you know what you like. Moz, I have this cock-eyed problem with Spinelli. He's supposed to have this trouble with his ticker—some touch of a heart condition. Who the hell knows. If it's true, okay. But if he's playing coy, I want to know. Fly to Chicago. I've had the union jet made ready, and you talk turkey to George."

"You mean go today?"

"Right away, today. Give it to him straight; the crime families aren't going to hear any testimony from me about them in the courts. İt's not really that; I don't want their lawyers starting any actions against me or the union. Know what I mean?"

"The defense on their part as an attack . . . you figure they may turn on you? And offer Justice records, testimony, in some deal that can sink you?"

"You know those fuckoffs in Justice would love such a deal. They did it with the Mafia over Cuba through the

CIA. So will you get the hell to Chicago and see if you can talk face-to-face with George on this thing. Put it on the line. They don't have to fear me; I don't have to fear them. Imagine, sending me that young bastard, Johnny Fiora. I knew him when he still had pimples and screwed Rita Hayworth in his dreams."

"John never had pimples, Mike. He is his uncle's choice to take over as don some day. Okay, okay, I'll pack an overnight case. Where's the jet . . . Dulles?"

"No. Washington National Airport . . . now you phone me the minute you've seen George, no matter what the hour."

"Even if I don't see him, I'll phone."

"Discover if he's really sick. Call the specialists, whoever they are. Matt Shonefield out of the local there knows every secret grave in Chicago. He'll help you. If George is playing possum, then, Moz, they're planning to sell me out for a deal of some kind."

Martin assured his brother that his fear was far fetched, but personally, on his way to the airport to board the union's executive jet, he wasn't too sure. He wasn't sure of anything in the turn of events; the climax that had come to Mike's career . . . as he had feared for years . . . , yet it had come with force and a drive he hadn't expected. With anyone else but Mike an early deal might be made . . . some plea bargaining, *even* a few months at some Federal country club. Mike might be out of office for a while, if he had to resign as part of a deal. But Mike would be back on top—he had those thousands and thousands of union members to rally round him.

The trouble was Mike's stubbornness against a deal, plea bargaining.

The weather was fair as the big jet took off, a bit of a wet roughness over the midlands, but calming into a drizzle when nearing O'Hare. Martin was the only pas-

senger in the million dollar jet . . . the two pilots up
front were chattering, the sound of their voices very faint
on the intercom, about some ball scores and fishing for
marlin off Key West. The stewardess with the pale pink
hair and too thin legs had made Martin coffee and gone
back to reading a novel, *The Leopard*.

Martin had tried to get Mike to read the book, but
Mike had given up after a few pages. ("Hell, there's no
story, just an old geezer remembering when he ruled the
roost and laid all the classy broads in the neighborhood.")

The intercom went on. "We are beginning our descent
for O'Hare. Please fasten seatbelts. Weather misty, rain
expected, temperature 67 degrees."

Martin tightened the seat belt, looked around at the
luxurious interior of the plane: red and gold velvet walls,
deep club chairs which were attached to the floor but
swung in all directions . . . the dining area in char-
treuse yellow was ahead, and someplace behind were the
sleeping alcoves. Martin smiled; he remembered a trip
when a senator had laid a European actress over Houston
at thirty thousand feet, and his feet got so swollen he
couldn't get his shoes on again until they landed at Kennedy to dedicate some Federal boondoggling.

Martin felt the plane slow, heard the landing wheels
being lowered. The stewardess put a folded slip of paper
between some pages of the novel, near the end, to keep
her place, and closed the book. The plane descended
quickly, rain beating lightly against the windows, and all
that was visible was the mist. Martin wondered if the
stewardess had been reading the section from the last vision of Prince Don Fabrizio, when the dream woman had
come. Why she came to him in his semi-conscious state,
she, one so young, ready to yield to him. "She raised her
veil and there, modest, but ready to be possessed . . ."

It was at that moment in Martin Brant's thoughts that,
out of nowhere, a wandering, lost Cessna crashed with a

tearing impact into the left side of the control compartment of the jet, killing both pilot and co-pilot immediate-
ly.

It was not the phone call Mike was expecting. At 1:22
A.M., Ralston Ellis of the Washington Bureau of the *New
York Times* called.

"Hello, Mr. Brant, this is Ellis of the *Times* Washington office. Have you been informed of the crash of the
DWU executive jet outside of Chicago?"

"Have I been informed of what?!"

"Just thirty-two minutes ago the jet was rammed by a
lost, four-seated Cessna private plane. Both crashed, and
the jet burst into flames. Four bodies in the wreckage, but
identification is difficult, as you can imagine."

"Burst into flames, crashed . . . how could such a
damn thing happen?"

"Bad weather set in suddenly, blotted out visual contact. The private plane was violating all regulations. Can
you tell me who was on the plane? Any official of the union or . . . hello . . . Mr. Brant? *Mr. Brant?*"

Mike was vomiting into Julia's favorite wastebasket.

CHAPTER 37

Dear Mom,

You already know. Tried to phone but you must have been out on a case. The radio, the television has been having a great time with poor Moz's death. I can believe it; I know I have too. But he's alive and standing by my side. I can feel him. At night I talk to him. Mom, Mom, you and Julia and he were the closest things in my life.

It's the next day now, and I haven't been able to do more than sit and ache deep in my head. And all the things I have to do, must do are pressing in on me. Nothing, nothing has ever hit me as hard, so I can know, Mom, how you feel.

I shall be with you in two days. You see, there are things to be done right away, investigating the accident, getting the dental charts flown out for identification. They say it was all so sudden and complete a smack that he didn't suffer, and for that, thank God. I'm going out to Chicago and will bring Moz home so we can put him to rest by the side of Pop. The old man would have liked that . . . one of his boys who made it big in the fight for the rights the old man never got in all his working days is going to be with him forever.

Julia has been pretty wonderful. Without her, I don't know if I wouldn't have landed in some laughing farm. Only you know how daffy I can feel about certain things. But Julia, she's been true-blue, and she and you now are all I have close. There is Paul, of course, growing nicely, but I only see him a week or so a year. When I see him, we have to start all over again getting easy with each other, and when we've just begun to be casual with each other, then he's gone for another year. Terry, she called and said she remembered Moz, his kindness to her and the efforts he made for her when he first knew her. I have to admit back there in Kansas City I was too rushed and involved to be a good husband, and Moz, he used to take her out to dinner or to some show. She said all this to me, and that made it worse for me remembering all those times and how it was for us then. I suppose that was what broke me and Terry up. We couldn't relate those years I was a fire-cracker, building the union; she grew bitter and why not admit it, nasty, got hooked on the booze. I let her down.

But now one has to go on living. Like you used to say, people are dying who never died before. I thought you were too, too tough when Pop died, didn't cry or carry on, but I can see now you had your own leftover years to spend, and you couldn't spend them moping.

I am, as you know, in a kind of a bind with this government case coming up against me. Much as I miss Moz as a brother, I miss him as much as a lawyer. He sure knew how to handle the bastards who will defend me, and he had a mind better than theirs in seeing the intricate game of law. "Mike," he used to tell me, "there is no justice, no Mike, just two teams of lawyers tossing points of law . . . f——justice. The team who racks up the most points gets the winning signal, Mike, from the judge and the twelve halfwits and paranoids that the lawyers have picked to sit there and confuse."

Maybe so, and now I'll have to do my own watching and

ducking and weaving. I have very high hopes of beating the accusations against me. Sure, I did all those things—I wanted clout, and it was all for the workers. What I did I did to make the union exist. From their cockeyed angle I was crooked, dishonest, brought the crime boys into the picture. For me, I was, as that stale saying has it, fighting fire with fire.

Well, we'll talk more in a few days. I wish it were for a meeting on a more joyful occasion, but we take the things that happen to us as they come. As Moz used to say, quoting some guy he liked: "If you're good at what you do, everything that happens to you is your own fault."

Julia sends her love and regards. She's all busted up, too.

from your son,

MIKE

CHAPTER 38

Martin was buried on a slight, emerald-tinted slope dotted with buttercups, in Evergreen Cemetery. Mom had gotten a young minister to say a few words. Pop had no religion, and Mom liked them all. As he spoke his Adam's apple bobbed, his badly shaved red face looked raw. The state police kept out the cameramen and the journalists. Mike and Julia, on their return home, decided to hide out some place outside Washington—just the two of them and the dogs.

The national news services and the television networks were actively building up the coming trial of Mike Brant. One morning he found a reporter in the garden waylaying him for a statement; flashbulbs went off in Julia's face as she drove off for shopping or lunch with a friend.

Mike decided to move into Martin's waterfront house in Virginia; it was a half mile from the main highway, set among private estates—very well patroled; the local police keeping strangers away.

* * *

At first it was hard, living where Martin was still a presence. His well-brushed clothes in the closet; the shoes were, for Mike, the worst to look at; you could see them running down a courthouse hall or crossed on black silk hose in a club house chair—Martin, a wine glass in hand, talking of the problems due to justice betrayed.

Julia took care of all this, when Mike went to have a last interview with Wilbur Scudder. Razors, toothbrush, clothes, the collection of canes. She managed to get rid of all personal items, giving them to some welfare group.

Martin's will was very simple. He left most everything—stock, real estate—to Mike, but for a trust fund for Mom. His books and manuscripts were to go to the Library of Congress; the many volumes of his private journal were to go to the National Archives, with the proviso that they not be opened to the public for thirty years. There were also three women to be given twenty-thousand dollars each ("for cheerful and pleasant times") and certain items of his personal jewelry. The young widow of a Civil Service Grade G-4 and a gym teacher in Baltimore accepted their inheritance, but the third woman, a black girl, Linda Welsh Johnson, was reported to be in Zambia with the Peace Corps, and she never did claim her share. Mike tried to follow up a rumor that she had borne Martin a child, but nothing came of his search.

Wilbur Scudder sat at ease in his office of knotty pine; Mike observed several silver-framed pictures of family faces—people with dogs, horses, girls with braces, bald elders gathered in festive groups for a celebration or anniversary. It seemed unnatural somehow to Mike for a lawyer of a tough reputation—known for his many defenses of notorious cases—to have a normal, rather dull-looking home life of puppies, children with skinned knees, and a wife who looked as if she'd had a nose job.

"Now, Mike," said Scudder, interrupting Mike's study of the pictures—stabbing at his desk blotter with an ivory letter opener, "next Tuesday is our first day in court. We are going to drag this out longer than a tapeworm. Just don't get impatient. Ott is good at this slow cake-walk . . . the simple Jeffersonian, aristocratic defender of democracy."

"He gives me a pain in the ass."

"He gives the judge and jury the idea he belongs to another, better age, and they respect him for that. Now, we don't want any surprises dropped on us, as to the Mafia's attitude."

"There is no attitude. Spinelli really has had a coronary and is out of things. Johnny Fiora, he'll do whatever his uncle would. The families that you call the Mafia, hell, it isn't like that . . . it's a looser kind of thing. They are going to lie doggo."

"I don't plan to put you on the stand, so they can't ask you about the crime families' loans."

"Dammit, I want to go on the stand. It's like a goddam platform for me to stand up and say what I did for the union, what I stand for."

Scudder dug under a fingernail with the letter opener. "Dangerous, very dangerous, Mike. The government lawyers would be all over you in cross examination . . . like jackels on a lion they want to bring down."

Mike wished more than ever Martin was alive and present; this fucking poetry of jackels and lions was a hell of a way to see the ordeal ahead.

Mike and Julia lived very quietly in Martin's home. They had left Wagner and Hilda in the Washington place. Martin's Dutch housekeeper, Heidi Brunner, stayed on. Julia did some of the cooking, and but for a burnt finger, did fairly well with souffles and chops. Mike studied the briefs and files the lawyers sent over to the DWU building. Every day he drove in, in the Caddie, to pick them up and attend to union matters. Certain office files had been sealed by the Justice Department; some of the bookkeeping records had been photocopied by the Internal Revenue. Mike cursed, but tried to keep his activities along normal lines.

Most troublesome were the loans from the Health, Welfare and Pension Fund; a board of mediators was now in charge, half union, half government. They sat in judgment on all requests.

There was an outlay of at least a billion and a half dollars in what looked like losses to the fund. Money that had somehow disappeared . . . six hundred million in loans which would most likely never be repaid or recovered from land projects, sports centers, imitations of Disneyland, investments in gambling projects in Vegas, the West Indies. Many were nebulous when investigated, the loans drained off into crime families' hidden assets, into Swiss bank accounts, even into the international drug traffic. Hardest to explain were monies that had illegally been transferred to certain political figures running for high or low offices . . . secret millions to party chairmen or their organizations—even into the highest office in the land.

But as J. Hastings Ott explained, "Don't worry over what was slipped into the White House, or in a brown paper bag to some liberal candidate. One thing, the Senate insists on, Michael, is that the courts never go deep enough to expose the roots of the money trees—the greedy habits of the club . . . that's what Congress is; a big private club of the privileged; like doctors, the senators never expose the sins of fellow members.

"Now, I hear, Michael, the crime families, the Fioras, with the don sick, are moving away from the control of the Spinelli faction."

Said Mike, "I know them, we'll have no problems with them . . . look, leave them to me."

Ott fingered a college insignia hanging from his watch chain. "They only kill their own, eh?"

* * *

The day before the first appearance in court Mike and Julia spent secluded in Martin's house. The television was active with interviews with government lawyers. Ott was caught at the Whist Club. Certain union officials, like Kingbird DuBois, made meaningless statements.

"It's more like the preparations for a Roman circus," Julia said, "than a coming session of a court of law."

"Oh hell, honey, it's the free publicity . . . like Jimmy Durante used to say, 'Everybody wants to get into the act.' "

The news cameras caught several figures in full dress at a big church wedding. All the cameras got were cold stares and pictures of folded newspapers held in front of the face of Dom Pagnocci, and a hood knocked a legman for NBC News into the gutter in front of St. Thomas's. The crime families were not talking.

That morning while Mike and Julia sat in the sun on the lawn, they watched a Coast Guard vessel go past Mount Vernon, its flag being lowered and raised, the crew standing stiffly at attention.

"Do they always do that, Mike?"

"All government vessels do. Respect to George Washington."

"A splendid idea."

They walked the dogs, had lunch on the lawn—heavy glass ashtrays anchoring the tablecloth in the slight breeze. A mixed shrimp salad, a gumbo-okra soup, and the apple pie and cheese Mike liked . . . Mr. and Mrs. Everyman, Julia suggested, eating their noonday meal.

In the afternoon they went down to the dock and sat in the forty-foot sloop-rigged craft, *Seapot*, Martin sometimes sailed. They did not take it out, as neither was sure how to properly handle sails. They walked hand in hand along an old tow path wild with daisy borders and silver queen butterflies in the yew hedge, had tea at five, and in the gathering dusk saw the fireflies signaling to each other. Dinner was formal; on that, Julia had insisted: paté in aspic, Beef Wellington, a Vienna tort that she had ordered specially from the Beagamann Bakery in Alexandria.

Mike tried to do justice to all this effort and did fairly well, having a second helping of the tart. Afterward they opened champagne but decided to switch to brandy.

There was a fire of hickory chucks in the mottled marble fireplace with the Adams mantle, anyway Martin had assumed it was a genuine Adams mantlepiece. Over it hung the Lundeberg surrealist painting. They sipped their brandy and studied it as its late owner had done when faced by some dilemma or problem.

They went up to bed very late, fairly steady, leaning on each other, making small intimate talk, teasing each other with rather indecent love talk.

In a haze of brandies, aware of the weight of tomorrow, their personal itch for sensuality heightened. They made love . . . made it rather badly, Julia thought, and she clung to him, calling out, "my darling, my darling," until she, too, fell asleep.

No one heard the dogs get out of the lean-to by the kitchen, or chase the small wild animal in the night—life in the bone-white moonlight. A fish the color of silver leaped free in the river, the dogs lost track of their prey.

Mike had asked Julia not to see him off in the morning. Nonetheless she had come down to breakfast in one of her crayon-blue dressing gowns. From the crease on her brow between her eyes and the way she squinted, he knew she had one of her migraines.

"Now, honey, you hike right back to bed and take one of your yellow pills."

"It's nothing much. I wish you'd let me come with you."

"Not a chance. It's going to be a day of hassling, waiting, and jockeying for position. I've got to pick up some staff lawyers at the DWU. If only . . . ," he paused, and

Julia knew he was thinking, *if* only Martin were with him today.

"We'll have dinner here at home . . . cozy."

Mike nodded as he drank his second cup of coffee. "I'd like to take you to the Riverhouse for dinner, but the goddam reporters and cameramen would be all over us like a land rush."

They looked at each other with tense smiles, and neither said anything else. He kissed her on the cheek, on the mouth, pressed her hands with his, and went into the hall. He took his tan topcoat from the closet. It was his lucky topcoat . . . never failed him. He'd done good duty wearing it to certain meetings. He turned and said, "Bye."

"Bye," said Julia. They never wished each other good luck, feeling a kind of superstition about such farewells. He went through the Dutch door on the side of the kitchen and inhaled the good day; a warm but not punishing sun, and birds . . . he had never noticed the differences in the birds all over the place. The river was dimpling into little waves, like gold coins; he had given Paul a small collection of gold coins on his last birthday.

The morning sun glinted on the rather neglected rose garden, and his thoughts turned to the momentous day ahead of him. He'd been in court before on various motions in the past, for certain dismissals. But this was Mr. Big Day. They had him by the balls, and they were going to hold on and press. Changing the image in his head . . . they had the deck really stacked against him. The charges of his misdoing had been skillfully presented and properly documented—the grand jury had been pleased at the way everything against Mike Brant had been presented. William Scudder had also been impressed by the government lawyers' way of building their case. ("You have to hand it to them, Mike; beautifully done, beautifully . . . you feel that foreman is worthy of your steel.")

I wish, he thought, they put their steel up his asshole

and not mine . . . as he opened the garage door, a great wave of depression overcame him. *This was for real, Mikey boy . . .* you could be put away for years, the union presidency lost, all the good life you've enjoyed, talking to conventions, making out with union locals, the cheering to the rafters—all is going, slipping away like water down the drain after your morning bath.

Jesus! Christ! It just couldn't be. He walked to Martin's Masarati—his brother's other car had been sold. The car needed washing, waxing, the leather looked dried out. Mike ran a hand across the door, twirled off the dust in his fingers. Some day he'd take it out and open it up. Moz claimed it did a hundred and ten miles per hour.

Moz wouldn't have been so drag-ass when facing a court. After all, why do I feel bad? I have the two most fancy shysters in the country. They've licked the government time and time again. Gotten pardons, deals way high up, blasted evidence to bits by their cross-examining.

They had suggested he could help his case by doing a little talking, off the record, about the Mafia people entrenched inside the union, and how certain loans went to whom they did, and how the divvy was done. But he made a grimace of disgust. He didn't play ball that way: there was more than a good chance he'd beat this . . . the old Brant luck. Moz was right, you don't call it justice in those courtrooms with a dusty flag and usually a picture of Washington and Lincoln on the walls. No, it's not justice, but rather the skilled game of the lawyers making points, and Ott and Scudder were great point makers.

He got in the front seat of the Caddie, thinking: I've been neither good nor bad. I've done things you could call evil . . . who hasn't? I've done things that have made me a hero for lots of the people who sweat and work. I've been a shit, sure. I'd hate to get on the scales and be weighed, see which way I'd balance. Old Wallie Smith, the IWW survivor, put it right one cold windy day on the docks of San Francisco, our toes freezing, when we were hungry and waiting to be hired to carry picket signs. Wallie and his goddam knowledge picked up reading in the clink, reading, reading. "The way it is, sergeant, these Oriental people have this Buddha—their Jesus head man—and he saw life as a wheel, see? And those on the bottom will have their place on top as the wheel turns; and those on top, they'll be in the mud when their turn comes. But you see, as the wheel is always moving, everybody, unless he falls off, can get a ride on the top . . . for a little while."

Crazy little coot, that Wallie. Mike inserted the ignition key, checked to see that the shift lever was in P for Park, turned the key.

NPA *Special Wire to All Subscribers:*

Dateline Washington: October 12 . . . At 9:47 this morning near Alexandria, Virginia, a powerful bomb, consisting, police suspect, of several sticks of gelatin, went off as Michael "Mike" Brant, President of the powerful DWU (Drovers & Wheelmens Union) started his car. Brant who was on his way to appear in Federal Court for the first day of his trial, was accused of misuse of union funds and assisting various Mafia families who had infiltrated the DWU in looting the union's Health, Welfare and Pension Fund.

The explosion, which was heard for two miles, broke windows in the house on the Potomac where Brant was staying with his constant, long-time companion over the years, Julia Brooks. She told the state police who arrived on the scene ten minutes after the explosion, while the garage and wreckage were still smoldering, that she was in the upstairs bathroom taking a headache pill when the doors to the upper deck sun porch seemed to just shatter and fall in fragments about her. Unhurt, she ran out on the porch and saw the flames and smoke envelop Brant's torso.

The Cadillac was in fragments, with pieces of debris landing in an elm tree fifty feet away. The body of the union leader, severely altered by the powerful blast, was tentatively identified by Miss Brooks who recognized an expensive Swiss Paloka wristwatch and a Bally shoe he had been wearing.

It is the opinion of the Virginia police that the gelatin bomb was planned to go off when the ignition switch was turned on; that it was most likely the work of one of the crime families involved in Brant's difficulties who feared Brant might testify in detail as to their methods, and perhaps, identify persons who had funneled money into large numbered accounts which the crime figures are said to hold in Swiss banks.

James Ward, retired from the DWU for many years—when reached in Sunland, California—gave as his theory of the killing that it could have been engendered by rival union leaders who, seeing how popular Brant was with the average union member, removed him before he could again seek nomination as president.

Investigators, including the FBI, who have come into the case, are following several clues and have made no comment on either theory.

Brant is survived by his wife, Terry, of Santa Barbara, California, from whom he has been separated for many years; by a son, Paul; by his mother, three brothers and one sister. The only member of his family he had actually been close to was his brother Martin Brant who was killed in a macabre plane accident two months ago. Internment will be in Milltown, New Jersey, just outside of New Brunswick, where Brant was born.

(On the six o'clock Full Press News with Snow Williams)

"This cool, brisk morning three days after his death caused by explosives placed in his car, Michael . . . often called "Iron Mike" Brant was buried by the side of his brother Martin, the victim of a tragic plane accident earlier this year, and near his father, who was one of the early union organizers in the days before the relationship between labor and capital was established. Delegates from various unions attended a service at St. Peter's Church in New Brunswick. Then the body in its bronze casket was escorted to the small Evergreen Cemetery on the outskirts of the town where this giant of labor was born. At the final interment police and state troopers kept out all but a union delegation, led by Joseph DuBois, who will most likely succeed Brant. Present at graveside' were Brant's mother and his wife, who had flown out from the West Coast with their son Paul. Not present was Brant's companion of many years, Julia Brooks. Rumor was she had been asked not to attend; neither was a tribute of yellow tea roses, said to be from her, placed among other tributes around the grave."